CW01160147

Cloister

Cloister

a novel by
Will Fraser

Published by New Generation Publishing in 2024

Copyright © Will Fraser 2024

First Edition

The author asserts the moral right under the Copyright, Designs and Patents Act 1988 to be identified as the author of this work.

All Rights reserved. No part of this publication may be reproduced, stored in a retrieval system or transmitted, in any form or by any means without the prior consent of the author, nor be otherwise circulated in any form of binding or cover other than that which it is published and without a similar condition being imposed on the subsequent purchaser.

Paperback ISBN: 978-1-83563-526-1
Hardback ISBN: 978-1-83563-527-8

New Generation Publishing
www.newgeneration-publishing.com

IN MEMORY OF
JOHN FRASER (1928 – 2023) AND
CAROL HOORN FRASER (1930 – 1991)

(Not relatives of mine, but John was a friend and mentor;
his scholarship ranged from *Violence in the Arts* to *Nihilism,
Modernism and Value*; Carol was a wonderful and great artist.)
www.jottings.ca

THEMA

dum vixi tacui; mortua dulce cano

in life I was silent; in death I sweetly sing

I

Matthew Marcan had been looking forward to New Year's Day 1993, which he hoped to spend immersing himself in music with no interruptions. All the Christmas rehearsals and services were out of the way. He had no commitments, and Bamberg was unseasonably mild: he wouldn't have to struggle through the snow or brave the bone-chill of the Domkirche. Then his father phoned from England to say that Richard had died.

A call from the underworld that pulled him down. For hours he could do nothing. He hadn't been there for his mentor. He'd meant to phone Richard, but had put it off repeatedly. Richard was unmarried and his kindness never fully covered a shade of remoteness. Would he have wanted to speak to Matthew? Richard had made that final journey alone. After his heart attack he had been taken to hospital, where he had not regained consciousness. At what point had he slipped away, and to what degree had he been aware of dying? Memories of Richard's warm presence swirled through his head…

'This'll test you. Play just the soprano and alto parts. I'll take the tenor and bass.'

This memory of Richard was from a decade earlier, when

Matthew was still at school, learning the secrets of musical counterpoint with the ardency of his youth.

The seventeen-year-old Matthew pulled out a selection of stops and reached towards the keyboards of the organ of Bristol Cathedral.

Sitting next to him on the bench, Richard tapped his arm: 'Close your eyes. See if you can do it blind.'

As always, a test. Matthew shut his eyes. With his left hand he reached towards the third of the organ's four manuals. Feeling for the black keys as reference points he found his opening note, middle D. He played, and heard the alto theme emerge out of the darkness, singing out of the tin pipes around him into the resonance of the nave.

Like many Bach fugue subjects it was deceptively simple: progressing through the notes of two chords over four bars; tonic, dominant and back to tonic. With his right hand he brought in the soprano line, the same melody but at a different pitch on the uppermost keyboard. Richard's turn came. He introduced first the tenor line and then the bass on the two lower keyboards. In a comfortable closeness Matthew could feel the warmth of his teacher's arms extended just below his own. The piece written for one player was recast as a duet.

Matthew had chosen a different stop, or sound, for each of their four hands. The consequent clarity added to the geometry of the music, but made any mistake sound worse. He hit a wrong note that stood out painfully from the harmony.

'You're a fifth out. You should be starting on an A,' said Richard.

Despite his interminable practice, Matthew found himself faltering under pressure.

'Come on, you can do this,' said Richard.

Matthew felt sweat break out on his temple.

'Get ready for your next line.' Richard played faultlessly himself. 'Soprano, on A. One, and—'

Matthew brought it in.

'And keep the alto going. It's in quavers. You know it.'

With his surprisingly frail voice Richard sang the alto until Matthew was able to resume it. Then, towards the end of the fugue, where the inner parts interplayed with multiple suspensions, Matthew fully remembered Bach's lines again. Richard reacted to his new confidence. Teacher and pupil challenged each other with subtle accents and intricate off-balances. The musical lines caressed each other. After the final flourish the last chord ebbed into the darkness of the nave. Matthew opened his eyes. The organ loft and his teacher materialised around him. Blotches and creases skated across his vision as his eyes adjusted to the warm light of the organ loft.

'You don't know it yet.' Richard smiled. His laugh lines and silvering hair added benevolence to authority, his open-necked shirt and corduroy suit added warmth to formality. 'It's up to you to live up to your own aspirations. It's not magic. You have to put in the time.'

The memory of Richard's exhortation to work compelled Matthew to set aside his grief, and he made his way from the cathedral of his memory to the current cathedral of his work: the Domkirche in Bamberg. He climbed the spiral staircase to its post-war organ loft, cantilevered from the sheer north wall, and did an hour of practice far above the honey-coloured flagstones.

When he had finished, while putting on his coat and scarf, he looked down from the organ loft. Having played with his eyes closed, blotches still moved across his view. Among them two groups of tourists milled around thirty feet below, each following a guide who carried a fluorescent umbrella. Almost all dutifully examined the tombs and statues. One exception, motionless among the milling crowd, peered up at the organ through binoculars. Matthew saw his sensible clothes and mackintosh. The backpack probably held his sandwiches, and the brochure that protruded from its pocket was doubtless about the Domkirche's organ.

Well, *he* thinks I am one of the happy few. Matthew put away his music, snapping shut the flap of his dried-out leather satchel.

He set off for the office of his boss, Heinz-Günther, the Domkirche's director of music, but ran into him outside on the uneven cobbles. The two men walked among the leafless lime trees with benches built around their trunks. The hilltop cathedral presided over Bamberg's riverside *Altstadt*. They looked over the low wall on the townward side of the yard across the uneven roofs and steep gables.

No other large German town that Matthew had visited had escaped bombing. All the major cities had been reconstructed since the war. Their buildings and streets were new and straight, their paving stones perfectly laid, their souls incinerated, unless you could reimagine them. But here the walls and lanes had been organically planned and built long ago by hand. They undulated with unmachined beauty and led you into the past.

'Are you sure you want to go back?' asked Heinz-Günther.

'Andreas will play for the vespers that I'll miss. It's only a few days.'

'It's not your absence about which I worry. I was sorry to hear about Richard.'

Matthew looked down at the cobbles.

Heinz-Günther continued: 'I worry that you'll get yourself drawn in.'

Matthew glanced at his boss.

Heinz-Günther added: 'Do you want to succeed him?'

Matthew faced out over the city. That's my wish, he thought but didn't say, and this is my summons.

Heinz-Günther put on a received English accent: 'Will they want you to be their organist and master of the choristers? Is that what they call it?'

'Now they call it director of music.'

'Did Richard want you to be his successor?'

The questions were too big and too fresh, and speaking answers aloud would make his future seem too fragile.

'What if I wanted you to be my successor?' added

Heinz-Günther. 'You're one of us. You belong in Mittel-Europa. Your father must be glad you're here.'

'He's Czech, so he might not approve,' said Matthew, 'but spiritually I've always felt German. If you don't grow up where you're from, you don't know where the borders are.'

'Knowing where borders are. That's exactly my worry, Matthew.'

After they had said their goodbyes, Matthew walked the short distance to his furnished rooms. He entered one of the ancillary doorways in the old Bishop's Palace and climbed the four flights of backstairs to his eyrie.

Looking around, he knew the time had come to dismantle what had only ever been a campsite. He could get all his possessions, aside from his sheet music that lived in a special trunk, into two suitcases and an overnight bag. It was just the bag that he would need for his short trip to England. Everything else had either come with the rooms or could be decanted into the bins. He'd made no impression on the place at all. If you took away the walls and floor, he might as well be housed in mid-air.

II

Bristol. First there was a long tunnel. Its mouth opened into a cutting, then they crossed the river, then they were flanked by industrial buildings. Disused carriages decayed in sidings to left and right. Beyond, Victorian houses overlooked by blocks of flats where the Luftwaffe had redesigned the streetscape. Ahead, the neo-Gothic university tower commanded the ridges from which eighteenth-century terraces spread down, uniformity battling topography.

Matthew imagined the centre of the city he couldn't see, where Mediaevalism and Brutalism had fought to an uneasy truce around the harbour. In his mind's eye he saw his destination, the long cathedral with three towers that adjoined a triangular green from which ascended a hill lined with Georgian shops.

The sense of homecoming gave him butterflies: both exhilaration and trepidation. Over the last couple of days, before leaving Bamberg, he had thought through his position. He wanted to succeed Richard as the director of music of Bristol Cathedral. The rich years in Bamberg gave him special gravitas and plenty of experience. Yes, he was grieving, but it was time to plan for the future.

The imagined sights were curtailed by the canopy of Temple Meads Station. He put away his Walkman. He'd used the hours of the journey to feed on new music: this time, Messiaen's opera *Saint Francois*; he'd listened to its four hours twice. The train drew to a standstill. He reached through the open window for the handle and swung open the heavy door, emerging into the still air of the arched interior, whose cast-iron framework supported an enormous area of glass. A cathedral of the industrial era. An enthusiast in a mackintosh focused his binoculars before noting the numbers on the locomotive.

Outside, the day was bright, especially for January. Matthew hailed a taxi. In the past a taxi-driver's radio was tuned to soft rock from ten years before, but now Bristol was cool. Trip Hop was playing. The fence of a building site had Massive Attack written in graffiti. He liked the sampled beats and subversive lyrics with vintage instruments and sounds, but under this temporary surface it was the same old city: the Bristol Sound didn't touch the lives of most of its inhabitants. A serene and affordable existence in a Georgian terraced dosshouse was easier than straying too far into the world beyond.

In ages past the city had altered the history of the world with mercantilism and slavery. A Bristol sailor had even discovered Newfoundland. Its blithely charmed architecture and institutions still lived off the proceeds. It gave the impression it was happy to be no longer one of the most consequential cities in the world.

Traffic was light so there was no danger of missing the start of the funeral. Matthew was carried to College Green in just a few minutes. The taxi dropped him close to the east end of the cathedral. It was sited right in the centre of the city. Traffic on Park Street and Deanery Road droned by within yards of it.

Bristol Cathedral was an urbane building, not a bespired, statue-encumbered edifice like the cathedrals of Salisbury or Lincoln, and it wasn't sequestered in a Close which, however picturesque, presented a boundary between a cathedral and the real worlds of, say, Wells or Norwich. No, when an ambulance went up Park Street its siren echoed round the cathedral. You knew someone was in trouble. The cathedral was better for it;

part of the city. And the cathedral organist served the city by giving it music.

As Richard had done.

Standing there, facing the building that embodied a musical vocation, Matthew felt his emotions churn. He wanted to cry but he mustn't. He must make a good impression. He wasn't there just as a mourner. He had to keep a venerable tradition going. He must battle down his feelings and act maturely as Richard's rightful successor. He waded into the cathedral.

Inside, the cloud-softened sunlight was further diffused by the enormous windows and their acre of glass. Wavering candle flames stood out warmly on the altar and in glazed holders on the choir stalls. The nave, which was empty as Matthew passed through it, had been added by a Victorian architect, who had also contributed the understated stone rood screen that separated the nave from the mediaeval quire, and the multi-coloured marble floor which, as much as the carved stalls and the double-fronted organ, gave the quire such arresting richness.

Matthew passed under the screen, not expecting the ornate stall directly across from the organ – the seat he had favoured in his last years at school – to be free. But the whole row was available. He sat down, shocked. The quire was virtually empty. Where were all the mourners?

The organist was playing Bach's *Erbarm dich*. He didn't recognise the face he could see reflected in the angled mirror in the organ loft that allowed the player to watch the choir and conductor, but also be seen. The chorale passed through its various embellishments.

The head verger, still Mr Quantock of old, stood ready with an armful of Orders of Service. Hardly anyone was there to take them. Matthew couldn't see any of Richard's other former pupils or choristers. The few people were in their sixties or more, a decade older than Richard. The chief undertaker escorted in a family group: three couples in their fifties and sixties who were perhaps cousins accompanied by their spouses, and a single elegantly dressed lady in her sixties, who held herself with dignity though she was crying. Matthew guessed she must be Richard's sister. If only he could grieve publicly with them and be acknowledged as part of the family, the son Richard never had.

The congregation stood up as the choir in their black cassocks and white surplices filed in: two rows of children and, behind them, adult singers, mostly of student age. An influx of youth and vibrancy, even if the black-clad cherubs were to sing of death and eternity. Matthew didn't recognise the conductor who followed them: no doubt a temporary replacement.

A cleric appeared under the arch of the rood screen and raised his arms: 'I am the resurrection and the life, saith the Lord: he that believeth in me, though he were dead, yet shall he live.'

He declaimed this with an American accent. He must be the new dean whom Richard had mentioned.

Richard's coffin was carried in by the pallbearers. Matthew composed himself. Now he must honour Richard and push thoughts about his own future away. The organist led a favourite hymn by Purcell. After the Bible readings, the choir attempted a Bach motet – a bad choice since they didn't know the difficult music. Their leader conducted as if all was going well, however, his blithe and non-committal gestures offering little guidance to the singers.

An easier anthem by Purcell, Tallis or Byrd would have been more suitable. Many such were in the choir's repertoire and the singers would have remembered how Richard liked to perform them. It would have enabled the singers to do justice to Richard's ample and learnèd musicianship, and would have sublimated the sadness of the occasion.

After the motet, the dean gave a short address, concluding: 'Richard Galvin spent more than a quarter-century here, perfecting the sound of our choir in thousands of choral services. What you hear today is the result of his work. He will always be alive here.'

Matthew smiled: Richard's work would live on in his pupil.

The pallbearers bore Richard through the cloister to the garden of peace that nestled between the former monastic buildings and the alleyway that led down to the industrial waste-ground at Canon's Marsh. They set down his coffin and it sank an inch into the mossy turf. They waited for everyone to assemble. Past organists were buried to right and left of the fresh grave. The mourners gathered round. Matthew stood by a worn stone that marked the grave of Orlick Strange, chorister, aged twelve, 1714. 'He cometh up and is cut down like a flower.' A reverie came over him…

Twelve years earlier, Richard was playing Bach's *Erbarm dich* as Fiala Marcanova's coffin was carried out of the single-aisled flint church in the little village of Chettle. Matthew, aged fifteen, followed his mother as she was borne towards her grave. The vicar, Dr Weyman, waited until all the congregation was gathered. Matthew heard the organ music come to an end. His father Jiří stood to his right, hands joined over his girdle.

Dr Weyman started the funeral sentences: 'We brought nothing into this world, and it is certain that we can carry nothing out…'

His mother's coffin sank into her grave.

The memory ended there. For decades he had held on to the fragment. It had long since detached itself from the rest of that day, ultimately becoming film-like, with a fade-to-black at the end. Now he waited for another fade-to-black. When Richard's coffin was lowered into his grave there was a clunk, but no conclusion. Matthew blinked as the present went on and didn't end. The sun went on diffusing through the grey clouds. The hubbub of the city rumbled on. The crows still cawed. The mourners still stood around.

The dean said his final words, threw in a handful of ash, bowed his head and stepped back. The pallbearers let their webbing fall and sloped off. The family dropped sprigs of heather into the grave from a pewter dish. Others did the same. When it was Matthew's turn he looked down into the grave and felt a surge of grief. He knew some of it was the old pain for his mother. But he mustn't cry. Richard was there, not far out of reach, perhaps even in his old corduroy jacket. Matthew dropped in his heather.

He remained by the grave until everyone around him was leaving. The undertaker murmured that they were adjourning to a hotel close to the cathedral. He wanted to stay where he was, but dragged himself after them, back through the cathedral and around College Green to the five-storey Victorian hotel, where Richard's sister greeted the mourners in the foyer. She had been crying.

Matthew, an only child, was stabbed by the envy he had felt many times when glimpsing the shared intimacy of siblings. Death had not ended that mutual adventure.

'Thank you for coming,' she said to Matthew, as she had said to the people in front of him.

'Are you Richard's sister?'

'Yes. Agnes Westmoreland.'

'I'm Matthew Marcan.' His name produced no flicker of recognition. 'I was a pupil of Richard's.'

'How nice of you to come.'

Matthew stayed rooted to the spot. He wanted her to say important words to him that recognised his rôle as Richard's favoured pupil.

'Please help yourself at the buffet,' she added.

He didn't move.

'It's along there on the right.'

He propelled himself onwards. A section of the reception hall was cordoned off and staff waited near a table spread with canapés. Squadrons of glasses stood ready for a supply of Madeira, sparkling water and orange juice that the few guests would not be able to finish. Matthew accepted a glass of Madeira.

The dean stood nearby with no one to talk to. Matthew felt a stab of self-doubt in the face of this ultimate arbiter of the cathedral's decisions. Was he going to have to lobby for the job, persuading the dean that he had rightfully returned? Would the dean have any respect for his credentials and vision of the future? What if the American wanted someone else? He had to move in and impress this stranger, make him realise he was meeting the incoming director of music. He forced himself over and introduced himself.

'Nice to meet you,' the dean responded. 'I'm Bryce Volanté.'

They shook hands. Matthew was six inches taller, but Bryce's petite hand was strong. He was bald and shiny on top, neatly bearded, and possessed a quick smile and intelligent, darting eyes. His hands were hairy and a wisp of chest hair protruded above his dog-collar.

'I agreed with your sermon,' said Matthew. 'I hope Richard is still here, in us. Now he's dead we can see him in totality for the first time.'

Bryce's eyes flickered. 'Do you mean he's experiencing life after death?'

That wasn't what Matthew meant. 'What is life after death?'

'I wish I knew. If a priest tells you they know, don't believe them, because we won't know till we rise in faith. That's what faith is. The Bible tells us that God is a God of the living, not of the dead. Sometimes it's best to keep the emphasis on this world.'

'Well, Richard's alive to me. I feel he's in the next room.' That was what Matthew wanted to feel. He wanted to say something meaty for Bryce to respect. 'I feel we're in an enfilade of consciousness, life and death, and Richard has stepped from one room to the next.'

Bryce opened his mouth but another voice cut in.

'Does the enfilade have mirrors at each end, or perhaps a *trompe l'œil* painting?'

Matthew turned, surprised. He recognised the speaker: the conductor of the choir during the service. He appeared to be in his fifties, and buzzed with confidence. He popped a blini with lumpfish caviar into his mouth.

'Matthew,' said Bryce, 'meet Geraint Perryman.'

Geraint wiped his fingertips together and extended his hand. He had a firm handshake and handsome, military features. But he had let himself go. Close up, his chin and throat had lost their definition, and his skin was reddish, aside from pale patches under his eyes.

'I didn't mean to interrupt,' said Geraint, 'but I do love metaphysics.'

Matthew wanted to go on talking to the dean, but Geraint hovered as if demanding a riposte.

'You strike me as a man who might not be frightened of death,' said Matthew in as jocular a manner as he could muster.

'On the contrary,' said Geraint. 'If you lead a full life, what can be said in favour of extinction?'

Bryce laughed. 'You're both giving rather wayward interpretations of doctrine. I'm hoping Geraint will pay attention to my sermons. He's our acting director of music.'

A poleaxe fell on Matthew. They had already replaced Richard?

Bryce went on speaking: 'But Matthew, what's your connection to Richard?'

Matthew's throat had turned dry, but he answered as best he could: 'I was a pupil of his. I'm another organist.' He addressed Bryce as clearly as he could and hoped his voice wasn't shaking. 'I don't know how long Geraint can stand in for, but I can rearrange my work if you need any help running the music department.'

'I've committed full time,' Geraint cut in. 'Where do you work?'

'Bamberg, the Domkirche.' He hoped they would find this impressive. 'I'm the assistant director of music there.'

'You've come all the way from Bamberg?' Geraint's tone

implied this was too far to journey for a trivial funeral and job prospect.

'Yes. Of course. I…' He wanted to say 'loved'. Did he need to stifle that emotion in present company? 'Richard was more than a teacher. He was a mentor, an example.'

'We all have our sentiments.' Geraint raised his chin. 'In that case it's good you don't feel death is something to be afraid of. That is what you said? You're not frightened of death?'

Matthew tried to remember if that was what he had said. He couldn't tell if Geraint was being patronising. But it was a big question and Bryce was looking on.

'No, I'm not. And I don't think Richard would have been either. For at least a moment he knew what was happening to him. It's that moment I've always been curious about. In a way I'm looking forward to it.'

Silence. Then Geraint's eyes gleamed and he raised his long-stemmed glass of orange juice. 'That's why people like being blotto. It's like suicide, but you get to do it again and again.'

Bryce raised his chin. 'We've left theology far behind, but isn't what you're saying what we all feel every night when we fall asleep? And when was the last time you were aware of that? Even if we're awake, we might not notice our transformation. But I hope you have your moment.' He raised his glass. 'Here's to your death wish, but I hope you find life on the other side.' He took a priestly sip. 'I have to circulate now, though I don't think there'll be any other conversations quite as engaging.'

Bryce left. Geraint, an inch or two taller than Matthew, looked down at him.

'It was kind of you to offer to help, but the changeover's gone rather smoothly, especially considering how suddenly Richard died. Bryce phoned me last Tuesday, and I happened to be free.'

He said 'free' with enough irony to suggest he had been under-employed at the time.

Geraint continued: 'I never wanted to work in a cathedral again, but it's actually rather fun to be back. So I've asked Bryce about taking the job permanently.'

Matthew remained mute. What about what Richard had wished? If Bryce gave a sermon in which he praised Richard's legacy, should he not observe his wishes?

'Maybe you can help, though,' added Geraint. 'We've got some young things straight out of college who are auditioning for the assistant's job tomorrow. We need someone to accompany them when they conduct the choir. I could, but I'd prefer to listen.'

'The assistant's job is available too?'

'Yes, the present one's decided to leave. Both jobs are vacant. Well, the assistant's job is a little more vacant than the director's.'

Matthew felt powerless. He wanted to assert his claim to Richard's job, but he could sense how badly that would be received.

'Sure, I'll do it,' he said. 'What time?'

'About ten?'

Matthew agreed to be there, then said his goodbyes. Outside, dusk was falling and lights were coming on – a beautiful time, but Matthew didn't notice any of that beauty. So that was it. Richard's life was cleared away to allow change, and there was no room for the dreams Matthew had nurtured for years. Inexorable. His grief welled up and the lights blurred with his tears. He leant against a tree and finally wept.

III

It was fully dark. Matthew walked along Deanery Road, away from the centre. The outer core of the Georgian city rose to his right; car parks and decrepit industrial structures could be glimpsed through gaps in the buildings to his left. He was keeping the tears back. He tried to think clearly. If Geraint was given the position, how would he cope with his disappointment? He could already feel it growing. If it had been anywhere else he could have walked away. He already had an ideal musical rôle in a beautiful city in Germany, surrounded and appreciated by a culture he understood and loved. But that was not what he wanted now. He felt drawn back to the city he had adopted as his home. How could he convey that to Bryce without seeming both presumptuous and mad?

He reached Hotwell Road, and now the sweep of the harbour's outflow toward the ocean lay on his left, dotted with Victorian remnants such as the hulk of Brunel's iron steamship, *SS Great Britain*. He carried on, and the buildings changed from industrial-age housing to those of the once-gracious eighteenth-century spa, Hotwells, first a source of medicinal water, then eventually polluted by the very factories that sprang up to bottle and export it.

To his left, the lanes of a traffic system began to curve and rise above the locks where the harbour encountered the river

Avon, which then oozed toward the gorge and suspension bridge. These were invisible, but somehow were an overbearing presence. This area at river level had been superseded by what was uphill, Clifton. He walked on, past a concrete apartment building where a German bomb must have fallen, then Clare's House of Mercy, dated 1784. Ahead, the road began to climb, but to the right a gentle space opened up – Dowry Square, with idiosyncratically built terraces rising from ancient flagstones around a gracious central garden.

Matthew carried on for a few doors towards the top right corner and stopped before an early Georgian dwelling with three-storeys and an attic, its façade graced by subtly arched windows and delicate brickwork. Richard's house belonged to the cathedral – as did the entire square – and had been the residence of its director of music since 1881. Someone had left the hall light on. Warmth shone out through the fanlight above the front door. Matthew was flooded with the happy associations of his many visits there.

He looked around him. He could hear some exuberant merriment – perhaps teenage drinkers – from the communal gardens inside the square, but their antics were obscured from him by the trees, shrubs and shadows. As with many seventeenth-century houses, the basement kitchen windows opened into a moat-like subterranean courtyard in front of the house, bridged by the steps up to the front door. This area was dark and unwatched. A gate in the railings opened on to a precarious staircase. The stairs dropped steeply into the sunken area, in the direction of the scullery door. It had always been kept unlocked.

Matthew began to pick his way down the stairs. No one had been that way for a long time. They were slippery with moss. One was broken. He missed his footing and plunged. His bag tumbled away. The heavy octagonal brass handle of the scullery door swam before his eyes. He flailed out and grabbed the rusty railing, yanking himself to a halt. He righted himself, dizzy, shocked and chastened, as if he had done an unexpected cartwheel. His arm felt wrenched out of its socket, but as he caught his breath he realised he was fine. His limbs were certainly strained yet nothing was twisted or damaged.

It was a miracle he hadn't smashed his head on the door handle. He collected himself, picked up his bag from the damp darkness, and leant against the door until his breath returned to normal. Then he tried it. As expected it was unlocked, but it barely budged until he put his shoulder to it. After three shoves the door scudded open across a crescent-shaped abrasion on the old flagstones. He had to force away his nerves and push himself into recklessness. This was going to be his house, now, wasn't it? It was his to enter, and damn the people who said no.

He stepped into the house and passed through the little scullery into the kitchen. He was hit by the chill of the room and the smell of damp old masonry unleashed by the cold. In the past, to enter the kitchen was to be engulfed by warmth, but now the cast-iron range had long gone out. The satisfying meals Richard would prepare, and carry on a tray up the two flights of stairs to the sitting room, seemed a long way away.

Familiar objects emerged out of the gloom. A heavy oak table, Windsor chairs with comfortably worn cushions, a dresser displaying serving plates arranged on their edges. It was a family kitchen, even if Richard had never married and was now dead. But the room would come back to life as soon as the range was relit.

Matthew climbed the dogleg stairs, past the ground-floor dining room and the narrow front hall where the light had been left on, and up to the first-floor sitting room. The shutters were open and the square outside was detailed by the now-electrified street lanterns. He took off his overcoat and sat down on the box sofa. He wouldn't turn the lights on in case anyone who knew Richard passed. There was plenty of light from outside playing on the antique volumes on the shelves, the harpsichord, the prints, the low velvety chair Richard used to favour. This would be his base for the night. He wouldn't go up to the upper floors for fear of finding signs of Richard's final day yet to be cleared away. He didn't want to blur the memories of him in his prime.

Richard had worn a jacket and tie at home, and sat formally in his desk armchair. After their lessons he would pour white port or cherry brandy into delicate glasses and light Turkish cigarettes for the two of them with a lordly disdain for school rules. Matthew was introduced early to the pleasures of smoking: the fragrant smoke rippling through his throat and nostrils; tobacco's happy stimulation of creative thoughts; the warm aura of sophistication.

Matthew once asked about the Latin words written in mother-of-pearl above the keyboards of Richard's harpsichord.

'*Dum vixi tacui*: what does it mean?'

Richard chuckled as he arranged a score on the music stand. 'It means "In life I was silent; in death I sweetly sing." A possible mantra for you?'

Matthew felt it could be: giving yourself to the greater causes of music and posterity.

'It simply refers to the tree the harpsichord is made from,' Richard went on. 'It's not pointing to a great truth.'

Wasn't it? Your contribution to life should sing sweetly after your death, and in life you shouldn't make too much of a fuss while you practise your art. Your body of work, the extent of which would be revealed when you died, should speak for itself.

That wainscoted room with its worn but warming leather bindings and upholstery wasn't sham gentility in a world filled with poverty. It held the aura of the past world he loved most – that of Bach, Buxtehude, Weckmann and all the others – so he could bring them into the present through his playing and help keep their music alive for the future, help them sing sweetly for the city centred on its cathedral.

Matthew crossed the uneven floorboards to a warped half-moon table and opened its drawer. He took one of Richard's stash of

Turkish cigarettes from its soft pack then returned to the sofa and lit it. Why not? He was at home.

Downstairs, the front door opened, tired feet entered and scuffed themselves on the doormat. Matthew froze. The door swung closed. The footsteps shuffled across the hall and reached the stairs. Matthew's skin tingled as they began to ascend. What now? The footsteps rose towards him. They seemed feminine. It must be Agnes. She must be staying here. Why hadn't he considered that? They reached the landing. How would she react when she came into the sitting room and found him sitting in the dark? Matthew sat back further, as if a more comfortable posture would better explain his presence when she turned the light on.

But the footsteps continued upwards; he might yet escape detection. They reached the next floor. Then the bathroom door closed and locked. He stood slowly so as not to trigger the springs of the old sofa, picked up his bag and coat, and moved as swiftly and quietly as he could.

Anger rose in him. Because Richard was dead, their former bond was no longer recognised. The family and the cathedral could close ranks and exclude him. He grabbed a pack of cigarettes from the drawer. Then he drew and exhaled smoke. Didn't ghosts sometimes manifest themselves through smell? She would have to attribute the smoke to Richard's spirit. Then he left the sitting room. Downstairs, he unlatched the front door, overcame an urge to slam it, and sidled out into the street.

His momentum took him past the teenagers and out of the cobbled square. He stopped at the main road, the blankness of the water and the tangle of flyovers ahead of him. He felt beached. He finished his cigarette.

His destiny lay not on Richard's box sofa but in a modern chain hotel. He trudged back to the centre. He found a hotel close to Queen Square, a concrete edifice overlooking the calm ink of the harbour. It was expensive for what it was, but the others would probably be the same. He had enough money so he booked a room and checked in.

It was too early to turn in and despite his long walks he felt caged, so he stepped out for a drink. He followed the main road diagonally across Queen Square. A large and splendid Georgian formation with a park in the middle had been dissected by a dual carriageway, and in part this summed up Bristol.

He had always found the city to be an exemplar of beauty. Its fantastic topography had been built on with money, art and pretension, sustained since mediaeval times. But following the war's bombing, the car and concrete ruled. While there were good post-war buildings, plenty of cheap and outsize disasters had disfigured the centre. Yet the city somehow benefited from this philistinism: it could never be described as precious, encased in aspic, or self-regarding. Enough of the old survived to create a city-centre-size palimpsest where nothing was entirely real and any street could become a portal into a past dimension. Much of its atmosphere was sustained by the city's continued disregard for its own beauty.

After walking the perimeter of the square he cut through one of the side streets that was just such a portal, leading on to a cobbled dockside overhung with ornate Victorian warehouses on one side and a line of decorated houseboats moored to iron bollards on the other. He reached the corner of King Street and an impressive half-timbered mediaeval pub.

He couldn't get inside, because three old rockers and a young woman in worn jeans and a denim jacket were manhandling something the size of a dresser toward the wide door. The cumbersome flight case was equipped with wheels, but three steps down into the bar presented a problem. They laboured, heaved and wrestled, until the case reached the ground with unstoppable momentum, sweeping forward on its casters and taking a chip of wood out of the inner door jamb. One of the older men let out an exclamation and recoiled, massaging his right hand while the case rolled on nonchalantly towards a stage at the far end of the barroom.

The other rockers and the woman gently propelled it the final few yards, and when it was parallel with the stage they undid various butterfly catches and lifted the lightweight upper panels over the top, revealing the twin keyboards and ornamented wooden casework of a bulky organ console: Hammond! Matthew was spellbound. He moved into the doorway to watch. In his head he started to hear classic rock songs to which the Hammond organ had lent its unmistakeable grandeur.

The rocker with the grazed hand joined the others. His sharp movements and screwed up face showed both pain and annoyance. He was clean-cut and small, as was one of the other men, and the young woman was not built to lift heavy equipment. The last, tallest rocker seemed to be bearing most of the weight. The four of them, with obvious difficulty, manhandled the heavy console on to the stage. They unpacked another flight case and heaved out the organ's magic spinning-speaker cabinet. Matthew had heard of these Leslie cabinets, but never yet seen one. Organists should always be loyal to each other: any band that went to the trouble of shunting in a Hammond with its rotating speaker deserved proper attention. He would enjoy watching the Leslie's rotors spin in different directions within their enclosures and hear how that created the Doppler tremolo. But a poster announced that the Chloë Balducci Band, presumably made up of these people and their equipment, would not be playing till the next evening. Their gig would be part of a weekly blues series.

Matthew moved back to one of the picnic tables in the area outside the door, sat on its edge and lit one of Richard's cigarettes. He was still smoking when the woman in the jeans jacket emerged. He recognised her from the poster: the eponymous bandleader. As she emerged, she glanced at him, then at his cigarette. She looked as if she might speak. Matthew raised his pack to offer one, but then the smallest of the old rockers stumped out of the pub.

'I thought you said you had roadies,' he said angrily. 'Baz helped, but you and Merv were useless. I've messed up my fingers.'

The musician held up his hands. He was shorter than her but his movements were aggressive. He sported unusually long sideburns, their carefully tended curves displaying his vanity as much as his retro velvet jacket.

Chloë Balducci's posture became more defensive.

'What about my hands?' she said.

'I'm doing this gig because I thought I'd help you out,' he said. 'I shouldn't have to end up hurt. I'm going to charge you rental for the Hammond.'

'But it's part of the deal,' said Chloë.

'Not any more.'

'I never said we had roadies. I said we'd help. You were the one who wanted to lug it in tonight. I had to spend my time phoning Ian to sort out the access and everything.'

'If you want a Hammond, you need people to get it inside.'

'That's why I'm here. I've come in my own time to help you.'

He held up his fingers again. 'If the gig was tonight I wouldn't be able to play.'

'But it's tomorrow,' she said.

'Then I need a rental fee. I didn't think I'd have to lug it in myself.'

'My God,' she said, 'don't you enjoy cruising around with it? Why not just bring a Kid Keys under your arm?'

'How much are you making?'

'None of your business, but it's barely nothing.'

The man raised his arm and wagged his finger in her face. 'Then get Ian to give you more money.'

A movement caught Matthew's eye. Chloë was intent on the Hammond organist. Beyond her shoulder the cobbles extended towards the edge of the wharf, marked by a line of bollards. In front of these a temporary shack was selling burgers and chips. A tall, stooped figure had stepped away from the stall, as if in response to the keyboardist's angry gesture: a lanky man wearing a blue hooded sweatshirt lettered in yellow with 'UTK'. He stopped, mid-lope, and stood with his weight on one leg, his gaze fixated as if on Chloë's back. Matthew was in the man's line of vision, but could sense he was not the object of his stare.

'There is no more money,' said Chloë.

'Get Ian to pay you more. He's not just ripping you off, he's ripping me off, and he's mashed up my hand.'

'Look Pete,' she said. 'What about Baz and Merv? They've come down to help and haven't asked for extra money. They've done all this for you.'

'But they're not roadies, and neither are you.' The Hammond player stared up into Chloë's face. 'You need to get more from Ian. I'll bring a rental invoice tomorrow.'

'Hey come on,' she said, 'give us a hug. We're in this together.' She opened her arms.

'Nah,' he said. He stepped back, wiped his hands on his shirt and began to walk away across the slick cobbles along the quay.

Chloë lowered her arms, exhaled and shook the tension out of her body. Matthew had been sitting motionless, and must have blended into the picnic table. Now she noticed him again. Her face registered embarrassment, then a 'let's move on' smile.

'Sorry you had to watch all of that. I thought it was brass players who were difficult.'

She hadn't watched the Hammond player leave. Over her shoulder Matthew looked for the man in the blue UTK hood, but he had vanished from beside the burger shack.

'Those smell good,' she said. 'What brand are they?'

'They're Turkish.' He took out the packet. 'Fatima. Would you like one?'

'If you've got enough.'

'Yes, I've got enough.'

Matthew's own cigarette had almost burned down. He held it in his lips as he lit one for her, and in the brief matchlight was able to regard her features. She was about six inches shorter than him and slim. Dark hair pulled back, dark eyes, fine cheek bones and a sharp nose.

She inhaled. 'These are nice.' Her look and accent seemed partly American.

His cigarette was finished now, but he wanted to smoke with her. He took out a new one and lit it from the old. She watched his action with a glimmer of a tobacconist's admiration, but he wasn't a natural chain-smoker. He'd have to be careful in case the nicotine rush made him sway off the picnic bench.

'Are you doing the gig tomorrow?' he asked.

'Yeah, that's us.'

'What kind of music?'

'Blues.'

'I don't know much blues.'

'Come and find out what you've been missing. It's a big genre with lots of history.'

That was the kind of answer he might give if someone asked him about the organ repertoire. North Germany in the seventeenth century. England in the eighteenth. France in the nineteenth. He'd never thought of popular music in those terms. Was she a kindred spirit? He wanted to find out, but did she want to have such a deep conversation with a stranger sitting on a picnic table in the dark?

He said: 'Do you always bring an organ with you?'

'When we can. The venue's let us load it in the day before, which helps.'

The two other rockers – Baz and Merv, presumably – emerged from the pub. One wore jeans and a leather jacket, and the smaller looked dapper in slacks and shirt. Their demeanour suggested two more reasonable men.

'Is that all for tonight?' asked the taller, hairier, more weathered one.

Chloë's attention was drawn to them and their professional world. She moved to the two musicians, and they discussed the next day's repertoire. She told Baz, the tall one who was a guitarist, who would be doing which solos in which songs. She went through the tempi with Merv, the drummer. She was confidently in charge without bossing anyone around. Matthew watched her cigarette burn down. Then it was gone; his too. She was still talking to the band members. He wanted to talk to her more, but felt too awkward waiting.

'Good night,' he said. 'I'll try and come tomorrow.'

She turned and smiled sweetly but impersonally. 'I hope you do.'

He walked back to his hotel. He wanted to go to her gig, perhaps to celebrate. He hoped to have a new job by evening, although a niggling feeling told him this was wishful thinking. He had assumed Richard's funeral would be an occasion for the happy few to come together and send off a beloved fellow traveller. He had assumed this happy few would accept him naturally as Richard's successor. He had been wrong on both counts. The happy few hadn't materialised. The dean seemed to be in the process of giving Richard's job to Geraint.

Matthew steeled himself. If he believed he was Richard's natural heir, then he must put himself forward. In the morning he must persuade the dean to appoint him.

IV

Well-rested and purposeful, Matthew enjoyed a breakfast of bacon and eggs – relishing his native diet after years of salami, cheese and black bread. Outside it was crisp and growing lighter. He reached the cathedral in a few minutes and went in, feeling confident. Morning prayer wouldn't start until eight-thirty so he had time to admire the building.

He reacquainted himself with some of its details: the ogee-shaped alcoves in red, green and gold of the Lady Chapel altar, echoed by an ogee-shape within the massive east window above the altar, whose complex tracery flowed right into the vaulting. The vaulting itself had numerous virtuosic sprouts of rib that formed fanciful three-dimensionalities while holding up the roof.

An odd building, combining mediaeval and Victorian sections, it offered up its wealth with reserve and understatement. In his schooldays, Matthew had wished it had a higher and grander vault, but he had gradually learned to appreciate the building for what it was. Now he could accept it as somehow right, on its own terms. Right, too, for the new organ that he and Richard had planned for the Lady Chapel. The bountiful cathedral would have not one but two fine organs.

He imagined music, and music filled the silent building of his mind. Improvisation was a skill he had worked on feverishly since school, and it had taken him years of practice, but now he could improvise and plan new pieces of music within his head, without an instrument to play them on. Within moments he was lost in a musical exploration.

'When the wicked man turneth away from his wickedness that he hath committed, and doeth that which is lawful and right, he shall save his soul alive.'

The cleric's voice woke Matthew from his reverie. He realised the service was starting. Five or six people had assembled around him in the Lady Chapel, without disturbing him. They epitomised the Church's characteristic tolerance for the many eccentrics who stood around in its spaces, transported by their fantasies.

He took his place for the short service. He had hoped it would be led by the dean, in which case he might be able to talk to him before nine o'clock. But instead it was taken by one of the canons. Matthew listened to the words he had heard so often before. They were as much a part of the building as the pillars.

At ten to nine the service ended and he walked through the cathedral to the single remaining section of cloister. Where monks would once have paced in contemplation around four sides of a hollow square, only a single section remained. The other three had been razed, along with much of the old monastery.

Double doors opened into the chapter house. The sweep of flagstones led to the song school and tea shop. The cathedral office was halfway along. It used to open at ten, but the American dean must have revised that timetable; the florid and sleepy old secretary was already unlocking the studded door. He wore a black velvet mourning band round one sleeve of his pistachio suit. He didn't look up.

'We open at nine.'

'Derek, it's me, Matthew.'

Derek raised his eyes myopically. His hair was now silver and his physique had plumpened, but in spirit and demeanour he was unchanged since the thirteen-year-old Matthew had first met him.

'Saint Matthew? Is that you? The organist errant, the star pupil?'

'Organists errant always come home.'

They shook hands warmly.

'But Matthew, I don't know that you'll find the place as you expect.'

They went into the office, whose sturdy vault made the basic and well-used office furniture look temporary.

Derek would know everything. Matthew asked: 'What's been happening since Richard died?'

Derek lit a gas heater to dispel the cold. Without looking at Matthew, he confirmed that Bryce had appointed Geraint, though not yet permanently, to replace Richard.

'Richard's sister dropped off a letter for you. I asked her why she didn't give it to you in person and she said she hadn't seen you at the funeral.'

Matthew absorbed his invisibility to Richard's sister while Derek rooted around for an envelope.

'You'll want to read this in peace. Why not sit there while I get the office up and running?'

The envelope was addressed to him in Richard's distinctive italic, so Derek would know its importance. Matthew sat down and opened it.

A brief covering letter from Richard confirmed that the following papers were a copy of his will. Richard specified that a house he owned in Dorset should be sold and as much as necessary of the proceeds should be used by the cathedral to build the new organ for the Lady Chapel.

Matthew already knew – as did most of the staff – that Richard had bequeathed this. He had helped Richard design the instrument, which represented their shared ideals. What was the life of the artist but to make fantasy real? It would complement the main organ of the cathedral and be a superb resource for concerts, practice and teaching. Richard also left his books, music and instruments, currently in the organist's house, to the cathedral, for future organists to use.

The letter had one further final clause. Richard wrote that Matthew should succeed him as organist and director of music at the cathedral. There it was in writing, but did anyone else know?

Matthew read it all through again, then asked: 'Derek, did Richard ever mention me succeeding him?'

Derek looked at Matthew with kindness, as if trying to formulate an answer pleasing to him. But he remained silent.

'Never?' asked Matthew, wondering whether the position was indeed Richard's to will away. Derek shook his head as if in answer to both questions. 'What's happening today?'

'We have two accomplished young men, and in fact a young lady, applying for the assistant organist's position. The auditions start at ten,' Derek explained.

'But the posts have only been vacant a few days. They can't have been advertised.'

'Bryce is headhunting.'

Matthew stopped. There was no way someone as resolute as Bryce would be persuaded by Richard's will, let alone a few reported intimations made over a glass of cherry brandy years before.

'Can I borrow some paper?'

'Of course.'

Matthew sat down at one of the less cluttered tables and handwrote a CV and covering letter.

Fifteen minutes later Derek saw he was finished. 'Matthew, why not come over here and glance over my shoulder?'

Derek had spread out the CVs of the other candidates, as well as Geraint's. Matthew scanned them. Geraint had been assistant organist at Wells in the seventies, then staff repetiteur and occasional conductor at the Welsh National Opera, and he had also done solo piano work and bits of orchestral conducting. He'd never held down a job for as long as a decade. In short, he had broad experience but possibly lacked the saturation from long immersion in one field.

The three candidates for the assistant job were all in their third year of Oxbridge organ scholarships. They were more than half a decade younger than Matthew. He hoped his lengthier track record would be seen as an advantage, but this was not a given; he had seen many inexperienced organists given jobs, including every time he himself had been rejected. He guessed this was because green candidates were perceived as less trouble than more seasoned players who had developed their own opinions and habits. In the same way, he extrapolated that an older candidate such as Geraint could be attractive because he was in the last stage of his career and wouldn't behave in any way that risked the salary he needed until he reached retirement.

'Is Bryce in yet?'

'He's an American. He'll have been in since eight.'

Matthew held up his CV. 'Can you give him this?'

Derek nodded. 'We must get you to the front of the queue.' He took it through to Bryce's office and then returned.

'He's not there. I've left it on his desk. He can't be far. Why not have a look at this? It's the anthem the candidates will be given.'

Matthew perused the score which Derek had handed to him. Geraint was credited as composer. The piece was melodic and tonal; schmaltzy even. It was sight-readable, so he wouldn't have to worry about messing it up. He read through the score again. As he did so he heard it being sung, then an outburst of laughter followed by more singing. The choir was rehearsing it in the song school at the far end of the cloister. He followed from the score. After the music stopped he heard Geraint and Bryce talking in the cloister. Then the dean entered.

'Derek, are we ready for the candidates?'

'Yes, Bryce. Is there time for Matthew Marcan to have a word with you?'

Derek motioned to Matthew. Bryce didn't recognise him for a moment, then grinned.

'Matthew, good to see you in daylight. I enjoyed our chat yesterday.'

Matthew greeted him. They shook hands.

Bryce twinkled. 'I would offer you a morning glass of Madeira if I had some. Are you staying in town for a few days?'

'Yes. I hadn't planned to, but I'm happy to.'

'Has something come up?'

Should he say that yes, it had come up that Geraint had stolen his future?

Derek rescued him, telling Bryce about Matthew in complimentary terms and mentioning his interest in applying for the positions that were available. Bryce looked harassed and got up to go, but then he turned and said he would read Matthew's CV and then talk to him.

Matthew sat waiting for ten slow minutes. Then he was shown by Derek through to Bryce's retreat, where all traces of contemporary life were absent, aside from an expensive-looking computer. Many of the books on the shelves were bound in calf, the flagstones were carpeted in Persian rugs. The wheel window was glazed in rich colours. Matthew's CV lay on a substantial mahogany desk adorned with Gothic carvings and surfaced with green leather. No other papers were visible. Bryce rose and motioned Matthew to a board table with straight-backed chairs. They sat down.

'You've got good timing,' said Bryce. 'The auditions will be over by lunchtime.'

Matthew had expected more preamble. He found himself jittery. He'd had poor luck in cathedral job interviews so far, until Richard had guided his application to Bamberg. Was assertiveness a serviceable tactic?

'I'd like to be considered to replace Richard as the director of music, as Richard himself wished.'

Bryce blinked, as he'd done the day before when Matthew had talked about death.

'I thought this was about the assistant's job. In any case, we won't be advertising Richard's job.'

'Why not?'

'Why should we? We'll approach the people we're interested in.'

Bryce spoke with finality, but Matthew felt he needed to make his point.

'But that doesn't give everyone a chance to apply. Richard

and I had talked about the future. He said to me, in fact he wrote in his will, that when he retired he would like me to take over.'

This visibly shook Bryce.

'I don't know if he mentioned this to you,' added Matthew.

'No, he didn't.' Bryce's composure was restored.

'Derek just gave me a copy of his will. It was in an envelope left in the office, addressed to me. Would you like to see it?'

'No. It doesn't matter what he wrote. It's not in his gift.'

Matthew ploughed on. 'He must have been planning to discuss it with you at some point. He didn't know he was going to die.'

'Not even for an instant?'

Matthew froze. Yesterday's spiel about death seemed mortifying now.

'Sorry, I shouldn't be flippant,' said Bryce, 'but if we followed Richard's wishes, as interpreted by you, we wouldn't, as you say, give anyone else the chance to apply.'

This hobbled Matthew. Richard had wanted him to get the job because of his merit, but Richard holding the job for him went against meritocracy. Should he mention the bequest for the new organ and his involvement with its design? But this would make it worse, as if he was trying to use Richard's generosity to buy his way into the job. What could he say?

Bryce let Matthew stew, then said: 'In sum, he shouldn't have said that to you. And he didn't retire.'

'But if he wished it, shouldn't I be given a chance to apply?'

Bryce didn't look convinced.

Matthew went on: 'Let's put it the other way round. I would love to succeed him, and so I would love to be able to apply for the job.'

'Which job?'

'Director of music.'

'Okay, then let me ask you a few questions. If you were the director of music, what would your main priority be?'

Choral evensong hovered above a high altar, the acme of music and worship, the Church of England's gift to the world.

Evensong should happen day after day, year after year, century after century, to set the eternal clock of the cosmos.

But Matthew sensed this was not the right answer, so he said: 'Surrounding the congregation, the choir and whoever else comes into the building with wonderful music every day.'

'Nice idea, but what if most people don't share your view of what wonderful music is? They find church music, and most classical music, unapproachable, and they associate it with all sorts of negatives.'

Matthew felt a wave of anger. 'Then they're wrong. We should have the guts to tell them that. Who cares if no one comes? The service is beautiful in itself. We should stick to our guns.'

'Laudable, but, I think, naïve.'

'Were those people who kept Christianity going by clinging to rocks in the Irish Sea naïve? No one came to their services.'

Bryce inhaled sharply.

Matthew continued: 'Half the people who walk into this cathedral don't believe in God. Does that mean you should abandon Christianity?'

'Do you ask as a believer?'

Matthew was stymied. Did he believe? He could never say he was an atheist, as that word sparked a deep reaction: no, there was more.

'More so than not.'

'That's a musician's answer. Knowing God is fundamental. Your job is to bring people to God through music.'

'What relationship I have with God is because of music.'

'And what is your relationship with God?'

He had no personal relationship with God in Bryce's sense. Even with his purpose he was not on a godly mission; he couldn't make such a claim. What about the mission of education? He was living proof of this, having benefited so much from Richard's teaching.

'Surely education is a core mission? The choir draws people into the church, it finds able and committed boys, and soon,

I hope, girls, and gives them a strong education, musical and otherwise.'

'By 'otherwise' do you mean Christian?'

Did he? 'Yes.'

Bryce picked up Matthew's CV briskly, as if about to throw it away, then stopped himself and placed it carefully back on the desk. 'So the cart goes before the horse in the hope that eventually the horse overtakes the cart?'

Matthew almost stammered. 'Education, I think, is the best form of outreach.'

'I agree, but we do that already.' Bryce paused for just long enough for it to become uncomfortable, then tapped his fingertips together. 'Any more specific forms of outreach?'

'I think starting a girls' choir, as I mentioned, would double our outreach without watering down what we do.'

Bryce was now motionless. 'You would want to develop a girls' choir?'

'Absolutely. Salisbury's just done it.'

'Interesting. Some people are much more conservative.'

'I don't think being a cathedral organist is conservative.'

For the first time Bryce looked interested. 'I'm glad to hear that. From your CV, I would have assumed you had a rather conservative outlook. You must be the youngest person ever to have studied with Helmut Walcha. I know of him because my father had his recording of *The Art of Fugue*. Which I see you also play. You had an organ scholarship at New College. You seem to have more letters after your name than in your name. You have an enviable position in Germany. This Heinz-Günther Schmal must be lucky to have you.'

'I'm lucky to have him. And if I bring good musicianship, he deserves it. The assistant should be good.'

Bryce laughed briefly at a private irony. 'And what about Bristol, why do you want to come here?'

Matthew saw in his mind's eye images of this, his chosen city.

'I was a student of Richard's. I went to this school. I'm from near here – Dorset. My father's still there. I've always wanted to devote my life to music, and now the question is where I do that. I've been away for some years, but now I'd like to bring my music home.'

Matthew smiled. He felt he had given a good answer at last.

Bryce studied his fingertips, as if he for once needed to buy a little time. 'One last question,' he asked. 'Both music department jobs are vacant. In essence, music at this cathedral is a clean slate. Would you take advantage of this and change direction in any way?'

'I think the music here at the moment is beautiful. If we carry on we'll inspire other people to change their direction.'

A couple of minutes later Matthew found himself back in the cloister. Bryce had agreed he could audition quickly before the three candidates arrived. Matthew felt more confident about the audition than he had done about the interview. It was easier to conduct and play than to talk about doing so. He had found the interview bruising – not the genteel job-invitation he had often fantasised about.

He compared his experience to the way he imagined Bryce would treat the other candidates. A convivial chat with Geraint, for whom the top job seemed pretty much stitched up. Then the young would-be assistants. Bryce would be stern to convey that, if appointed, he wouldn't tolerate them being too independent.

Bryce emerged from his office and led Matthew to the song school, where twenty choristers, all boys between seven and thirteen, stood behind two rows of Bob Cratchit desks screwed to the parquet floor and arranged around a baby grand piano. They wore their cassocks but not surplices. The black cloth covered their temporality. They were already a coherent unit. The dean sat down near the door.

'I won't speak,' Bryce said. 'I'll just sit and observe you take the rehearsal, if that's okay?'

Was that his signal to start? Matthew sat down at the Bechstein Model B. The two rows of desks were ahead to his left and right. His back was to the window into the garden of peace. Richard was not far away.

'Good morning, boys. My name's Matthew Marcan. I'm looking forward to working with you today. Please turn to the anthem.'

Matthew rehearsed them as rigorously as he could, given the vapidity of Geraint's composition. He wasted no time in chat.

Matthew's credo for judging modern compositions was that they had to embody the century of hard thought and cataclysmic history that had passed since tonality had collapsed into atonality. You couldn't turn your back on this by writing too friendly a tune. His first inspiration, Helmut Walcha, had embodied this. When he'd met him, the German had improvised in an angular style as rigorous as the 'form follows function' of a skyscraper by Gropius. Richard and other important teachers, all Modernists, had articulated it to him.

Modernism derived its strength from this uncompromising stance. Geraint's anthem was therefore not to his taste. But he should give it a chance. He knew he wasn't always good at respecting other people's aesthetics. The choir might love singing it. Whatever they sang, it was their sound that turned the low-ceilinged rehearsal room into an artistic haven. He worked quickly because he didn't know when he would be interrupted, and sure enough, after six or seven minutes Bryce stood up.

'Are you ready?' the dean asked.

'Yes.'

'Good,' Bryce answered. 'Let's go up to the quire.'

The two men and twenty boys processed through the cloister. In the quire, the adult countertenor, tenor and bass lay clerks, all paid singers, were waiting in black in their stalls. Bryce sat down just out of view.

Matthew started the rehearsal with the *magnificat* from the Short Service by Orlando Gibbons, a piece he loved because it was one of the most melodic Tudor settings. It had been written in the 1600s before the rôle of the conductor had been established. Therefore all Matthew did was gently beat the pulse with his right hand. He didn't use his left hand to make expressive gestures or give cues, as he would for music written later. It was the singers' responsibility to come in correctly and shape their phrases and dynamics. Out of this calm the voice parts emerged and interlocked. Then the tenors missed their entrance.

'What are you doing?' Matthew snapped. 'You're late.' The men were paid singers; they should know their parts. The boys weren't making mistakes.

Flustered, Matthew looked down at his score to find a place to restart.

A tenor spoke: 'I was watching but I didn't see you bring us in.'

Matthew found he remembered him: 'Frank, you've got to bring yourself in.'

Frank Orme had been a lay clerk when Matthew was at the school. A countertenor who stood beside him also remained from that time, Roy Brunt. Frank still had pebble specs, Roy still kept his hair long, even if they were both now greying and thin on top. In essence they hadn't developed.

Matthew felt a trapdoor opening underneath him, a sensation he had felt before when his assumptions about the order of life met reality. Was the choir a dustbin for their lives? Had he himself developed? Was his whole mission in cathedral music an exercise in not developing? But he must pull the trapdoor closed. This was wasting rehearsal time. He was under the dean's observation. He had to keep the rehearsal efficient and disciplined.

'For Frank's benefit, let's go back to the top of page three.'

He sang the trebles their note and brought them in with an upbeat. He gave Frank and the tenors exaggerated cues and they came in at the right time…but now on the wrong note.

Matthew stopped everyone. He saw Roy smile conspiratorially at Frank, whose turned head exposed a calf's lick, somehow inappropriate in a middle-aged man. Were they trying to derail him? See how he responded under stress? He hated stress, and that made stress more stressful. He found himself trying to align his head to see Bryce in his peripheral vision. He snapped back to his music stand, but couldn't stop the intruding thoughts. Had the dean, or Geraint, asked them to make deliberate mistakes to test him? If he did nothing he could look weak, and if he was stern he could look quarrelsome.

He tried to make a joke of it: 'Roy, I know you're not paid much, but you are paid to get the notes right. Everyone, let's do it again.'

No one laughed, but after that they didn't make any more mistakes. Their melodies resonated off the vaults and the polished marble floor. It had been a few years since Matthew, under Richard's watchful eye, had conducted there. He remembered how the conductor's spot was where the choir sounded absolutely at its best.

Geraint materialised behind him. 'Time for the psalm?'

Matthew did his best to cover up a flare of anger. Why was Geraint speaking to him as if he was running the auditions? Matthew looked round at Bryce, who nodded.

Geraint handed him a photocopy of the psalm. 'I'll accompany. How do you want to do it?'

It was best not to be fancy. 'We'll just do alternate verses, alternate sides.'

'Is that all?' Geraint stared into Matthew's eyes for a moment. 'Well, you're the boss.'

Geraint went up to the organ loft and Matthew prepared the choir by getting them to sing the harmony to 'loo' a couple of times to get used to it. They then sang the psalm fluently, and Geraint actually played well. But Geraint's insinuation that he should have done more with his interpretation gnawed at Matthew. Should he have added more dynamics, solos or unison verses? He stood by his music stand uncertainly.

Bryce walked over. 'I guess that's it.'

Matthew didn't leave his position. He might never stand there again.

Geraint appeared from the organ loft. 'We should hear you play.'

If Geraint was asking him to play, auditioning him, was Geraint already permanently in Richard's job? What would he be playing for? The assistant's job?

'Yes,' said Bryce, 'Why not play for us?'

Matthew sensed the choir sitting up expectantly. They must know his reputation as a performer. 'I haven't prepared anything.' But he could play dozens of pieces without preparation, and had been working particularly on *The Art of Fugue* in Bamberg. He knew several of the movements from memory.

'Well,' said Bryce, 'it's all yours if you want to.'

Matthew guessed the undergraduate candidates would play complicated and outwardly virtuosic pieces pushing their techniques to the limit. But Richard had always told him it was more impressive to play less virtuosic pieces. You didn't show your limits and you could concentrate on a better interpretation of the music.

'Okay.' He turned to the choir to introduce it. 'I'll play the sixth fugue from Bach's *Art of Fugue*. This is where Bach combines the theme, or melody, at three different speeds, normal speed, twice as fast and twice as slow.'

Noticing one of the older boys listening attentively, Matthew addressed him: 'Changing the speed like this is called diminution and augmentation.'

The lad seemed to take this on board. Matthew caught himself wondering if he was taking instrumental lessons, and if so how advanced he was.

'He also turns the melodies upside down, which is called inversion.'

But he had to focus on his performance. This was his moment to make the stones sing and bring the cathedral to life.

He went to the doorway at the back of the organ and climbed the rickety stairway that ascended steeply to the level of the ranks of tin alloy pipes. He turned right along the tight walkway through the pipework and pneumatic machinery which was like the ganger in a ship's engine room. It led to the organ loft itself, the most exclusive space in the cathedral, a sanctum panelled in aromatic polished oak. While cramped, it contained the potential for lifetimes of creation.

The four rows of ivory and ebony keys and columns of stop knobs allowed for the invention of any number of sounds. The shelves of worn volumes contained an encyclopaedia of compositions. Like a small and plain cabinet at the end of an enfilade of boisterously decorated rooms in a palace, it was somewhere for private work and betterment, but it boasted an aerial view of the spacious quire and nave. It granted its incumbent the potential to turn inner reflection into rich sonorities that could fill the vast space and make the stonework vibrate, transporting everyone in it to a better realm. It was a uniquely consequential four metres squared.

He sat at the console and drew the stops he wanted. It helped now that he had identified an intelligent listener in the audience. That gave him an individual to play for, which made it easier to play well. He played the first theme and let the rest follow. His intelligence and emotions guided his limbs and connected with the instrument that plenished the cathedral.

He had worked on the piece intensively and knew it part by part. He loved its surface – intensity, grandeur, and above all, captivating beauty – but if you looked underneath you found the most rigorous application of logic and structure in fresh ways, and all derived from a simple melody. It was as close to perfection as art could get. His rôle as performer was simply to be true to the composition, to let the intertwinings of melodies flow out through him. And yet, even though he stood back from the music, it gave him power, and he felt and expressed its deep emotion. When the choir clapped at the end he hoped he had succeeded in bringing it to full life.

He came back down the stairs, through the door in the back of the organ and round to the quire. Bryce and Geraint were talking. He overheard Geraint: '…a good player, but I don't think he has a choir in Bamberg. He's lost touch with the Anglican way of doing things. He sounds too clenched.'

'I wouldn't necessarily say that,' said Bryce, 'but now's not the time.'

They turned to greet Matthew. Geraint gave him a nod and looked down at him. Bryce thanked Matthew and asked him to contact Derek the next day to find out if he had been selected. 'I guess that's all. We'll look forward to being in touch.'

'Don't you want me to accompany the other rehearsals?'

'I'm sorry?' said Bryce.

Matthew looked at Geraint, who'd clearly forgotten about their conversation the previous day.

After a moment Geraint started, as if he'd remembered: 'Oh, no, I can do that. We don't want to use up any more of your time.'

'Exactly,' said Bryce, who then turned to Matthew and said goodbye.

It was obvious Bryce wouldn't ask him to be the next director of music. Geraint already had the job. Matthew wandered round the city centre in angry turmoil. Was the trouble because he loved what he did and didn't want to change? What about all the skills he had refined over years of studious work? What about his devotion? Was he to be found wanting because he didn't have a coherent outreach policy, or a bold new direction into the shallows of banality? What about Richard's work, and all the people who had gone before him? Would it all be handed to the opera-buff Geraint? What terrible luck Richard had died before he could bring the new dean round to his point of view.

If that was how it was, then best leave them to it. Good luck to the cathedral. They seemed to be driving him away, so he should take the hint. He was better off without them. He stopped in a café for a cappuccino and a piece of walnut cake with cream cheese icing and tried to feel good. This might be his last visit to Bristol. He had to push the angry thoughts out of his mind. Try to enjoy buildings and spaces. He forced himself to embrace the city. He compelled himself to walk to his favourite places, those squares and terraces that were not just beautiful in themselves like Dowry Square, but also offered a hilly vista to the countryside or glimpses of the harbour and river.

There wasn't enough time to see it all, let alone get in and out of the various delights – the wrought-iron and glass covered market, various churches – before they closed, but he trailed around as much as he could.

In the late afternoon he would have loved to go back to the cathedral for evensong, but he felt banished. Instead he sat on a bench on one of the quaysides. He became angry again. It was a wonderful city. Just walking around made him feel good. Every direction he looked in held a building or vista of interest, even in the dusk. Why should this be his last visit? There was only one job he was meant for in the place, and they didn't want to give it to him.

The new organ upset him more. He and Richard had designed the instrument of their hearts, determining the scaling and voicing, the types of wood and the composition of the metal alloys for each of the forty ranks of pipes. All these attributes affected what types of music they would bring to life most exquisitely, and it would be perfect for his favourites: Bach and North German Baroque music. Most of all it was Richard's gift to Matthew. The cathedral would accept it because it was worth a lot of money, but they wouldn't accept the errant organist whose sense of aesthetics the instrument reflected.

Well, tough. He'd leave them to it and continue his career in Germany.

Similar ideas surged round his head, but gradually his anger wore down in the dusk. His pique began to be pushed aside. The blues singer he'd met the previous night had been hovering in his mind. She was alluring, even in her moment of drama with her Hammond player. Would she not therefore manage herself well on stage? He should go to her gig. It might be a relief to listen to her blues.

V

Matthew walked to the half-timbered pub on King Street. It was already filling up. The crowd of about fifty included a few leather-jacketed types, even an Americanist in cowboy boots and bandana. On stage, the Hammond and Leslie had been joined by a drumkit, amps and a couple of guitars resting on their stands. One was a red electric guitar with Fender written near the tuning pegs, the other a metal acoustic burnished with age. He hadn't known that metal guitars existed. A big genre with lots of history, of which this odd guitar was presumably an artefact.

If she was going to play an antique guitar, blues even had its own period instrument movement. If they'd bothered to bring such instruments, surely they would turn out to be good. Hopefully they could transport him far away from cathedral music.

Musing on this, he ordered a pint of Mendip Gold with chicken and chips. It was hearty, tasty and comforting. It was impossible to feel bad. He remembered the rhythmic exercise from childhood: titi-ta-ta, titi-ta-ta, chicken-and-chips, chicken-and-chips.

'Where's he gone? Why's he not here?'

Chloë Balducci was standing close to Matthew's table, speaking urgently to the tall old rocker from the night before. Baz wore a Hawaiian shirt and a trilby and already had his guitar shouldered. It took a few moments for Matthew to register her perturbed tone, but she was speaking with urgency:

'What are we supposed to do, wait for him?'

'All I can say is you should call him again,' Baz said.

Chloë glowered over at a payphone in the corner by the door to the gents'.

'One more time. If he's not here by the time I get on stage I'm impounding his organ.'

The Hammond stood on the left of the stage, the speakers in the Leslie cabinet ready and rotating. Chloë strode to the payphone, jammed a coin in, and dialled. She listened for the length of eight or so rings but got no response and slammed the phone down.

Two other musicians had now arrived. A black man of about twenty held a bass guitar. Merv, the dapper artisan in his forties, held drumsticks in one hand and a harmonica attached to a neck brace in the other. As the guitarist in the trilby was about sixty, the band therefore drew from three generations. They also had multifarious looks; standing between the Hawaiian shirt and the well-pressed slacks, the bass-player wore a shell suit. Chloë herself wore jeans, lizard-skin cowboy boots, and a turquoise pendant over her black silk shirt; her long hair was down. Blues allowed such disparates to play together.

Chloë marched back from the phone.

'Come on.'

She made for the stage and her band followed her obediently. She carried herself with a poise that presaged virtuosity or disaster. Matthew felt butterflies. He'd experienced the gamut of concert nerves and he could feel what she was feeling. His mouth dried. Her band rushed to plug themselves in to their amps. Matthew found himself nervous. Chloë was striking, even at rest, and this fiery mood enhanced her. Her dark eyes seemed to blaze inwards.

'Sorry,' she said into the mic, 'we were going to start with a stomp and get you into the mood but I can't stomp right now.

We're going straight for the heart. Here's a slow blues. If I don't play two or three of these a day, I want to jump off a cliff.'

She slung on her red electric guitar with its classic contoured shape, and in the same movement cut a melody out of it, teasing from dominant to tonic and bending the upper notes. Matthew's worry dissipated. She was in control. She was going to be good, because she thought in melodies, and her nerves hadn't clouded these. After her call the band responded with the stately chords of a minor-key blues march. Pathos and barely controlled energy filled the room as Chloë sang about tragedy.

> *My mama said, gonna take you to the doctor,*
> *See what's wrong with your head.*

The other guitarist filled in harmonies beneath her soloing, and the drummer blew furiously into his harmonica. He was a tour de force, a musician's musician, able to muster rhythm and melody like a one-man-band. Yet the sound was still lopsided. The organ sat in massive silence, taking up the whole left hand of the stage, removing a crucial weight from the sound. However well they played, they were one wing down.

Despite this, by the end of the tune they had relaxed. Chloë told the room it was time for the stomp. They confidently played the infectious dotted rhythm and people got up from their tables to dance. Her eyes relaxed and she made eye contact with the punters as she sang:

> *The man I love is kinda big and fat*
> *And I'm the kinda woman feels good like that.*

When she reached her guitar solo, she stood still and her dark eyes locked on some point in the beyond while she produced a melody of ornate sophistication. For the first twelve bars, that is. Then, as bass and drums careened into the next round, she turned towards the Hammond. Presumably the keyboardist was supposed to start his solo, but she'd forgotten he was missing.

Her look turned frantic. She carried on, but she'd lost the melody. Time slowed down.

Matthew could hear her searching for notes and repeating some of what she'd just played, piecing a melody together with difficulty, using little scraps of blues scale that didn't go anywhere. Her shoulders tensed. She looked down, then turned to the other guitarist with defeat in her eyes. Effortlessly, he picked up the melody and they got through the rest of the twelve bars. Then she was singing the next verse. The shame in her voice didn't match the jovial words.

As soon as the song ended both Chloë and Baz scanned the room for the missing organist, but he still wasn't there. They conferred, then they pressed on. From that point all the songs they performed trod a line between skill and stiltedness. The sections the band was able to play as they had been conceived and rehearsed summoned up their full emotional power, but odd holes appeared where a Hammond solo must have been intended.

Each time they caught Chloë in the same way and she couldn't break the pattern. She ploughed on with an expression of affliction, and while she wasn't able to fill the awkward musical gaps that kept appearing, her singing and soloing in the well-functioning parts of the set were always inventive, melodic and convincing. How could she do one but not the other? She must have prepared all her solos to the nth degree in advance, but wasn't able to create new ones quickly enough to fill the gaps occasioned by their missing Hammond mate.

The truth, revealed painfully and publicly, was that she couldn't improvise. Matthew himself had slowly developed a facility for improvisation, and now could do it fluently. But even if he at last had the skill to fill musical holes, he could well remember that utter, wretched mental blankness when he'd been supposed to play something – anything – and couldn't come up with a single idea. He knew the humiliation Chloë felt. He might never have been in exactly the same predicament as she was now facing, but his career was laced with incidents that were equally painful because they always happened in front of a crowd of music-lovers, at least one of whom would turn out to be an uncomfortably talented instrumentalist.

Part of him wanted to leap up on to the stage and fill out the chords on the organ to help her, but to do that was to become the annoying musical know-all whom he himself dreaded. Also, operating a Hammond would be different to a pipe organ and his contribution could spell disaster. He had to sit still and look positive. No one could mitigate the bludgeoning assault of emotions under which Chloë had to remain upright, in full view of the crowd, and keep playing.

She and her band made it to the end of the first set. Most of the crowd didn't seem flummoxed by the flawed performance. They clapped and cheered, though alert ones could probably tell she wasn't happy. She gave the merest of bows, cleared off the stage and disappeared through a swing door into the neon-lit pub kitchen. Was there a dressing room or refuge back there? Baz watched her go with concern, then left the stage to solicit some business at a table selling her tapes.

Not as many people were buying them as Matthew felt should have been, when they clearly had enough money to buy drinks aplenty. He went up to the stall and bought a copy of the album, *Havoc in the Old City*. The cover was a photo of Chloë looking relaxed and cheerful, sitting on one of the ship-tying bollards on the quayside with her metal guitar.

Empathising with her had dried his throat. Matthew wanted another beer. Most of the crowd had beaten him to the front of the queue. The throng happily chatted and purchased endless supplies of drink. The stage was low, so the Hammond was at shelf-height: a few blasé types rested their drinks on the organ while they smoked cigarettes and gassed away. Waiting for his turn at the bar, Matthew found himself beside a man in a sweatshirt and recognised the letters 'UTK'… It was the hooded figure from the quayside the night before. Matthew hadn't noticed him there earlier, before or during the band's first set.

The man was seated at the bar and his face was turned away, but he wore his hood down, revealing soft, pale flesh and short buzz-cut hair. He was writing on a schoolchild's pad, and had already torn off a few drafts that lay on the bar beside him. He was taking his time composing this text, yet his biro worked disjointedly – one moment stiffly manic, the next few moments drooping into stillness. Nonetheless it seemed as though a deeply considered letter was taking its final form.

'Mister, what do you want?'

The publican was addressing Matthew, who handed him his empty pint glass. 'Another Mendip Gold please.'

It was not normally in Matthew's nature to snoop, but his eye was caught by the overlarge, angular handwriting that was forced – cut even – deep into the paper. His attention was immediately held, and absorbed:

Found you at last, Klo, Klo, Klo. You know what I go through. 3285 drafts now. One a day, night night night. I need to say it. I need to ask it. Now. It's what I wrote with my boxcutter, but not how you think. Kit kit kit of kittens. I've screwed up already. I don't want this. Only you can be there.

The note was baffling; what sort of nutter was he? Was this 'Klo' supposed to be the singer? Did he actually know Chloë Balducci, or was he a fan who'd fixated on her imago at her gigs? Matthew couldn't keep his gaze off the letter. It radiated an unsettling power.

'That'll be one pound forty.' The publican passed him the full glass.

The writer looked up, realised he was overlooked, and immediately shifted his body so the pad could no longer be seen. Matthew put down coins for the beer and slowly returned to his table. The writer also moved, ripping the message off the pad, screwing up the discarded pages and sequestering them in the pocket of his UTK hoodie. Holding his note against a glass of whiskey he'd had on the bar, he shambled along the front of the stage and stopped near the Hammond. Three middle-aged blues fans were talking in the space in front of it. He simply stood by them, projecting his presence into their territory. Initially the trio blanked him, but when he went nowhere, looming as impassively as a monolith, they looked disturbed and gradually edged away.

The man then reached up with his spare hand to the top of the Hammond, and gathered a few empty glasses without minding if his fingers got wet or foamy. He swivelled round, depositing them on a nearby table. As he repeated this manoeuvre, never shifting his feet, people started to give him more room. The three drinkers looked ready to challenge him, before collegially deciding against it. There was nothing for them to do except move away. When the hooded writer had cleared the Hammond of empties he set his letter on the veneered surface, and placed the whiskey like a paperweight on top of it. Only then did his feet move, carrying him calmly back towards the doorway and beyond, out into the night.

Matthew watched all this from his table. But trying to engage with the inner life of this eerie letter-writer would be too much for him now. As he started on his fresh pint of Mendip Gold, he found his own emotional memories welling up instead.

As a school leaver, he had won the prestigious organ scholarship to New College, one of the handful of colleges at Oxford that, as a choral foundation, maintained a large choir of boys and men who sang for daily services. After five years of study with Richard at school, he felt prepared and confident, although being an organ scholar effectively meant that he had a demanding job on top of his undergraduate studies.

His first year had gone well. He had served as the apprentice of a senior organ scholar in his final year. The older student had both guided him through the easier music and taken on the more difficult playing for himself.

Matthew had at first offered his devotion to Dr Paice, the

director of the choir and a fellow of the college, as the keeper of his ideals. He desired approval, counsel and direction, but Paice simply gazed back wordlessly as if at a junior member of a different species. He gave no guidance to either organ scholar. Nonetheless he managed to convey speechlessly that he expected note-perfect performances to materialise out of thin air.

In his second year, the senior having graduated, Matthew became the only organ scholar and had to learn by himself all the music to accompany the many choral services. Six days out of seven, a blur of staves, clefs and ledger lines two feet in front of him produced a miasma of sound. Where was the pulse, tone, harmony and meaning in this cloud, and how did it relate to the pall of vowels and consonants rising from the choir stalls?

The repertoire seemed much more difficult than the year before, and this nourished Matthew's paranoia. Were they testing him in some underhand way? Why was it that the experience of his friends at other colleges was so different? Their organ scholarships seemed cheery, convivial and well-guided.

Service after service hurtled by. If he ever got the hang of a piece he immediately had to move on to the next day's maze. If only they could perform pieces more than once, so he could improve! Even if he played the right notes he was out of time. It was impossible to follow Paice's conducting and listen to the singing while at the same time playing the right notes.

The organ had been newly built in the 1960s, in convinced Modernist style with green and silver woodwork, rocket-like diagonals, and glass swell shutters that reflected the capacious mediaeval chapel. The instrument itself was the size of a three-storey building. The attempt to control it preoccupied him, leaving no spare attention for the choir or the conductor. When he looked in the mirror for Paice's beat, his mind blanked and he couldn't find his place back in the score.

He had to practise so much that he had no time left to work for his degree, and had to endure the scorn of his supervisors. Yet still the succession of chapel performances swamped him. He couldn't master the ever-replenishing stack of scores. Terrorised by Paice's belittling glare after a particularly bad evensong, Matthew packed a bag, left the college and strode to the station.

It was almost ten at night when he arrived outside Richard's door, leaning against it for several minutes while he summoned the courage to knock. The loser returns defeated.

But within seconds of tapping, Matthew found himself suspended by the comfortable springs of an armchair in the warmth and charm of the book-lined sitting room. He had no brainpower left.

Richard sized up the situation: 'We're going to have to get you a doctor's note. What do you think your illness should be?'

'Incompetence,' Matthew shot back.

'Rubbish. You're a good student. He gives you too much to learn and offers no help. Anyway, we can get a not-entirely bogus letter from the school doctor.'

Richard's vehemence and loyalty warmed Matthew. 'Was I stupid to leave?'

'No. You've got yourself two weeks' holiday.'

'Two weeks?'

'Yes.' Richard smiled. 'We're going to turn your playing round. We need a bit of time.'

'What about New College?'

'What about them?'

Richard smiled kindly, but Matthew's gloom returned: 'What if Paice's right? What if I can't play well enough?'

'It takes time to play well. Paice is arrogant. Don't let it infect you. Maybe he learns notes quickly and thinks that's all there is to it. Maybe he can sight-read big pieces, and maybe he could do that when he was your age. But has he ever gone any deeper? Someone who's arrogant won't reach their full potential. So don't let him stop you reaching yours.' Richard smiled again. 'And you're sure you want to go into cathedral music?'

Richard, his original teacher, *belonged*. With his unkempt grey beard and lived-in jacket, he looked eccentric, but wasn't. Matthew coveted that broad mind and kindly outlook, that lack of hardened childishness, selfishness and ego that marred so many musicians.

Matthew's own faults, whatever they were turning out to be, could only be reduced by the attention that Richard gave him. If only he could grasp correctly what he felt Richard to be saying. Was it that musicianship was delicate, subtle and complicated, to be presented in front of you for others to imbibe, rather than hoarded within? He wanted to follow Richard, not just into music but back to his own cathedral. The job brought daily music, importance and influence within the community, a house cocooning books and instruments, all in the city he loved.

He replied to Richard's question: 'Paice hasn't put me off cathedral music yet.'

'I'm glad to hear it,' Richard replied, before laying out the pros and cons of such a career.

'Be careful where you end up,' he concluded. 'You don't want to be silted up somewhere too remote, like Truro, or too small like Ripon. Even a town like Salisbury doesn't have what we have here. You need a good university, and a town big enough to provide an audience. Your playing's already erudite, so you'll need sophisticated people to work with. You'll need to be able to get to Europe easily. What about here?'

Matthew's heart jumped. Richard was allowing what he wanted. But he lacked the confidence to express that in words.

'I like it here,' was all he could venture.

'You love it here. I retire in ten years. I'd like to arrange it so you take over from me. It should be easy because,' and here he had smiled, 'they'll see New College on your CV and assume you're well qualified.' Richard looked around at the bookshelves and old furniture. 'It all depends on whether you'd like to succeed me. When the time comes I want there to be someone who'll appreciate the books and possessions I'm leaving to the cathedral.'

Matthew basked in the knowledge that he could be Richard's anointed successor.

After prescribing relaxation for a couple of days, forcing

Matthew to go out into the city for walks, matinées at the cinema and a couple of meals out, Richard took as much time as he could over the remainder of the two weeks to lead Matthew through the pieces on the New College music list for later that term. The exercise was to get used to playing with a conductor. Richard stood at the podium in the quire and conducted as Matthew played.

In a rehearsal with singers there is no time for the organist to reconsider their mistakes, but as the choir was not present, Richard could hone the bars where Matthew came unstuck, and rehearse them until they were right. Richard also told him which bars he had to memorise, so he could look at the conductor and then back at the correct part of the score. He divided all the pieces into manageable sections, which they repeated until Matthew was able to play them while watching the beat with confidence. Properly led, this didn't take him long. He went further with some pieces and practised them until he could play them with his eyes locked on Richard's beat all the way through. After two weeks, his confidence restored, Matthew returned to New College.

He was able to manage his workload and present an unbreachable wall of aloofness to Dr Paice. From that point on they saw each other daily in the organ loft mirror, but otherwise communicated only through occasional terse notes left in each other's pigeon holes in the porter's lodge, an arrangement that satisfied Matthew in his new guise until he graduated, left and never returned.

There followed three difficult years as a jobbing organist. Grinding travel around the English regions, church contracts that never lasted long, insubstantial teaching jobs and little paying work beyond these. He applied for nine coveted cathedral jobs as they came up, though none appointed him. But it was also exciting; he could listen to and learn what he wanted, and he devoted himself to learning big works far beyond the bounds of Anglican music. Then Richard, through his contacts, had learned about the job in Bamberg and suggested it:

'You need something less rat-racy, somewhere you can develop without worrying too much.'

As assistant director of music at the Bamberg Dom, the work had been similar to New College – rehearsing and accompanying daily services – but whether because of the skills he had now acquired or because Heinz-Günther was a more capable manager, he found it both easier and more gratifying. So the years had passed by, and a new skin of scar tissue grew over the old wounds.

Chloë emerged from the kitchen and marshalled her band. They looked around, but there was still no sign of the organist. She gave them a talk before gesturing them on to the stage and then following them on. She had regained her poise and was clearly intent to make the second set better than the first. She picked up the steel guitar and attached ferocious metal fingerpicks to her fingers. As she did so, the glass on its note on the Hammond caught her eye. Her expression turned so venomous at this intrusion that Baz scuttled forward and quickly removed them. Poor big man in the sweats. His letter, which she probably hadn't even realised was intended for her, was thrown away.

She stood ready and began. Her metal acoustic guitar had a much more countrified sound than the red one, and with its percussive strumming backed up by the drummer's harmonica, the band sounded as if they'd emerged from some hilly back-region of the USA. In this music, they didn't miss the spacy, eternal sound of the organ.

Chloë steered her band through a set of what sounded like original compositions that swept through blues and jazz techniques. There were no obvious holes: it seemed they had compressed the keyboard solo sections out of the songs. Then she led them into gradually changing chords underpinned by the young bassist, who wove in passing notes and inversions. She spoke over the chordal tapestry, her accent a local burr with Deep South around the edges:

'This one's especially played for everyone here tonight that's in love, to all of you that wished you had someone to love, and to all of you that wished you were loved by someone.'

Then the band reached the end of the twelve-bar phrase and she sang about love and the passing of time, letting the words fill a whole twelve-bar sequence.

If you're gonna leave me, why d'you leave yourself in me?
If you're gonna leave me, why d'you leave yourself in me?
'Cos I can't cut you out and run, though I want to be free.

Matthew was transfixed. Perhaps because of the adversity of the previous set, her voice was imbued with a breaking and hoarse quality as she sang of unredeemed love.

Love.

Matthew had had his share of unredeemed love.

Thoughts of romance welled up. He battled them down. She was appealing, talented and a fine musician, but she wouldn't have any interest in him. Yet she was singing about obsession and lovesickness, topics he had in common with her.

Then it was time for her guitar solo. She was commanding the stage and the absence of her keyboardist wasn't an issue now. She drew a strange melody from her guitar, using a metal bottleneck on her left little finger to bring out primaeval resonances and harmonies as she slid the pitch up and down.

Next, she led them through a final stomp, and that was the end of the gig. The audience gave enough applause to warrant an encore, but the band didn't return through the swing door from the kitchen. Then people were getting up, either to buy more drinks or to leave. Matthew smoked a cigarette at his table but the room was emptying and he felt self-conscious sitting still among the ebbing crowd. He didn't want to leave so he went outside and perched on his picnic table.

He tried to take in what he had seen: she was a youngish white woman from the West country, and yet she had managed to get into the heart of blues, a genre born out of the extreme human tragedy of another race on another continent. And she had done so with one band member down.

Soon the sidemen came bustling in and out with stands and cases. The older guitarist and drummer both had trolleys. The young bassist carried his heavy amp as if he wanted to earn his stripes. There was no sign of Chloë. Soon the gear was neatly piled on the paving stones, and the drummer went to pick up his vehicle. It turned out to be a reconditioned camper van, one of the diminutive Japanese models. They started to load it, putting the round drum cases in first.

Finally, the door swung open and Chloë appeared. She was flushed with indignation. 'Guys,' she said, 'thanks and all, but you know, you've forgotten something.'

'I don't think we've forgotten anything.' Baz, the guitarist, spoke with a note of trepidation in his voice. He knew as well as she did that a couple of large objects were still on stage.

'Merv,' said Chloë, 'will the organ fit into your van?'

The dapper drummer said: 'The Hammond's Pete's.'

'Exactly,' she answered. 'We can't leave it here.'

'I just think it's better if Pete comes and gets it himself. Tomorrow, the next day, whenever.'

'Whenever?' Chloë retorted. 'Is that his idea of time-keeping? Oh, you can hire me, but you have to pay me more, but I'll only play whenever I want to, not at the actual gig?'

'Pay you more? What do you mean?'

'He wanted me to pay a rental for the Hammond. I told him I'd barely break even as it is.'

'Look Chloë,' said Merv, 'you did brilliantly. It's not your fault he didn't turn up.'

'Brilliantly? It should have been, but it was rubbish. I worked my ass off, then he messes up the whole gig. It was a disaster, even in my career of disasters.'

The band members looked at their feet until Baz echoed: 'You did brilliantly. It's his fault.'

'I know. That's why he's not going to get his organ back. Do you want it?'

'Want it?'

'Yeah, the Hammond. Do you want it?'

'Me?' said Merv. 'I don't have anywhere to put it.'

'I thought you ran an antiques shop. You could sell it. Thomas, do you have anywhere?'

The young bassist shook his head. 'My mum's not going to want it in the house.'

'What about you Baz?'

'Don't look at me. I'd actually like it, but I don't want Pete coming after me.'

Chloë surveyed him. 'Well, I do want him coming after me, and finding nothing but a locked door.'

'Why don't we sort it out in the morning?' said Baz. 'Ian won't mind.'

'In the morning?' She raised her voice: 'Oi, taxi!' She waved at an Asian man standing beside a Mazda on the cobbles. 'Can you fit a Hammond organ into your cab? And a Leslie?'

The driver looked baffled. 'You what?'

Chloë pulled a wad of cash out of her jacket pocket. It was the takings from the door, about two hundred pounds in tens and fives. The band members drew away as she waved it at the taxi driver. 'Hey mister, I'll give you this if you take a Hammond organ to my house.'

The taxi driver took a step backwards.

Baz stepped forward. 'Chloë, don't worry. We'll take the organ.'

'At last. Then you can have this.' She offered him the wad of cash.

'Put it away Chlo, you've already paid me. That's your cut.'

'Yeah, because I'm not paying Pete. Why not take it? Ten pence a mile adds up.'

She held out the cash.

'Guys,' said Baz, 'let's go and get it.'

Relieved, the three of them went back into the pub. Through the window they could be seen dragging the hefty organ to the side of the stage and laboriously lowering it on to the base of its wheeled case, then doing the same with the rotary speaker. Chloë slowly pocketed her money.

'Would you like a cigarette?' asked Matthew. This was the moment for which he had stationed himself on the bench, but who knew where her mood would lead them.

'My God, did you sit through that?' she said without acknowledging the packet he offered.

'You were brilliant. The second set was like no one was missing.'

'Very diplomatic. So the first set was a train-wreck.'

Matthew didn't know what to say. 'A lot of it was really good. The rest was…'

She was close to him in age, lovely to look at, and was standing in front of him giving him her attention. Moreover, her talents were comparable to his own, they had plenty in common musically, and she had clearly put in the years of graft that can distinguish, or isolate, a musician from the mainstream. Most girls he met didn't know what C major was and, while he might be a little paranoid, he could feel them thinking him weird for going off by himself so far into the outer reaches of music. So he was always on the back foot romantically. Here was someone who had learnt the same language and should be able to make a connection, yet whatever he said to her was bound to touch off a landmine.

'…the bits where the organ was missing were…'

She looked up. A trace of humour battled the angry humiliation in her eyes. 'Were…?'

He girded his courage. 'They were weak.'

'Weak? Well, that's better than some other words I might use.'

'You just weren't able to fill in for him on the spur of the moment.'

'Are you a musician?'

'Yes.'

'What do you play?'

'The organ.'

'Oh God.' The humour had left her eyes. She was lost for words.

'Don't worry, I don't play the Hammond,' he added quickly. 'I'm a cathedral organist.'

'So you could probably have sat down at the Hammond and made something up. Baz was just itching to take over. Everyone I meet could do better.'

'No. And you did get yourself through it.'

'No I didn't.'

She began to speak, then winced. She tried to speak again but she'd run out of words and scrunched up her features.

She couldn't see that in the second set she'd overcome the challenges of the first. Matthew had given enough performances to know how much preparation went into any kind of poise on stage: practice, day-in day-out, for years. Even under pressure her poise had mostly held up.

He raised his cigarettes and again offered her one. 'Would you like one?'

'That's kind but I've got mine.'

The other musicians rolled out the organ case on its casters and set it by the camper. They went back in for the Leslie cabinet. She walked back to the door and lit one of her cigarettes and watched the band rearrange the amps and drums, then hoist the organ and speaker into the van. The suspension sank noticeably.

'Okay Chlo,' said Baz. 'Hop in. We'll take it up to your house.'

'Giddy up then. Just leave it outside the door. I'll get it in when I get there.'

'What, you're not coming in the van?'

'No. I want some space.'

'How will you get it inside?'

'It's on wheels.'

'It's four hundred pounds. Just getting it over the doorstep's going to be a nightmare.'

'I'll manage.'

'What if someone steals it?'

'I mean, (a), do you really think someone will, and (b), what if?'

With that, they said their goodbyes and the three musicians

clambered into the camper and crammed themselves on to its front bench seat. Merv started it up, pooped the horn and they chugged away over the cobbles. Matthew turned back to Chloë, but she had gone inside. She came back out after a few moments carrying a guitar case and a suitcase-sized amp and with her second guitar in a soft case on her back. Even granted that their weight had rounded her shoulders, hers was a posture of defeat. She trudged past him without meeting his gaze, and over to the taxi. The driver looked at her with some suspicion, but not enough to refuse the fare. The car bore her away, leaving Matthew already missing her presence.

Back in his hotel, Matthew forced himself to think about the cathedral. He sensed what was going to happen. They would offer him the assistantship. Though Geraint would prefer a drone straight from college, Bryce would have his cake and eat it by employing Geraint, the charismatic leader, plus an unusually experienced assistant.

What would Geraint be like as a boss? He couldn't imagine someone more unlike a cathedral organist, and it was clearly only Richard's death that had propelled him into the rôle. But then Geraint also didn't seem like someone who would step on an assistant's toes, so Matthew might well have freedom to work as he liked, especially using the new organ. The salary for an assistant was less, but that was the least of his concerns. He didn't need much money to live the way he wanted, and the assistant's flat above the song school was a fine place to live: panelled rooms, a grand piano and mullioned windows overlooking the garden of peace. It was only a matter of time before Geraint retired, at which point Matthew would naturally be promoted and move into Richard's house. Again, he imagined living there with a family. That was a future. Then he remembered the family was illusory, so he pushed it from his mind.

He should accept the offer when it arrived. Bryce was a shrewd judge of character. Matthew would be better as assistant.

He owed it to Richard to return. He also had to recognise that though Richard had been generous in his estimation of him, other people had no reason to share that view. So he must carry on and learn, even when he was tired of having carried on learning for years. Every ridge ascended just revealed another ridge beyond. That was artistry. Learning exhaustingly that you never reached your goal.

But what was his goal? Was not participating in the human drama he had glimpsed a part of it? The romance and excitement of going out with someone? The life he'd neglected in favour of his musical hamster wheel? The rich transubstantiation of conflict into music that he had just witnessed? In sum, would he see Chloë again?

VI

He was back in mid-air in the Berthier rooms in the palace in Bamberg. At night, alone, in bed, that was when the thoughts of the Other stalked him. He had fought the Other his whole adult life. Who was the Other, and which door of the magic theatre did she emerge from? Was she a composite of elements of his mother, or her friends, or other women who had dangled him in their arms when his infant mind was creating archetypes? She had taken human form at many stages of his life, indeed he was mentally promiscuous with Others. The student across the bar. The young German on the train whose book on the Romanesque was well chosen to start a fixation. These women had talked and some had accepted invitations for coffee or a meal, but after two or three dates they had always pulled away. This must surely be because he, propelled by emotions, was jumping the gun in a way that made clear his projections and distance from reality. His desire for intimacy perversely kept him from true intimacy.

And now, after years of invasion by the Other with a thousand faces, and just as he was gaining the self-awareness to read his own past actions, he saw with fear that the Other was taking shape again, holding a guitar. This musician, whose musical conflict he had witnessed and with whom he had shared a cigarette, was drawing the Other out of the floorboards into her own likeness. The real Chloë was distant and unattainable, so the Other stepped in to taunt him with her songs of unrequited love. Phantasie with an emphatic Ph.

Bryce did indeed offer him the job of assistant. Matthew told Heinz-Günther immediately. Despite his notice period of three months, the Domkirche allowed him to leave at the end of February after Ash Wednesday. He played with especial care and experienced the services in January and February, culminating in the ashing of a full cathedral while he improvised a set of chorale variations, with added poignancy as they would be his last in that job. When he left he felt he had reached a personal apogee in his standard of performance. He had also used these weeks to learn thoroughly all the music he would have to play during his first four weeks in Bristol.

His colleagues and the congregation were sad to see him leave, and on his second-last day, Shrove Tuesday, they put on a lunch in the Kaisersaal in the Bishop's Palace. As if the grated potato pancakes sizzled in duck fat were not enough, the older ladies of the congregation produced the most exceptional selection of *Kuchen* and *Torten* he had ever seen: sour cherry, plum, apple, raspberry, plus all the German berries he couldn't quite translate, several types of quark, plus a finale of chocolate, almond and fresh mint. He had seen much in his enthusiasm to comprehend the inexhaustible German genius for *Kaffee und Kuchen*, and this surpassed all. He left Bamberg on a high.

He returned to Bristol, and his new rôle as assistant organist, arriving for the first week in March, towards the end of the spring term. He entered the comfortable, if chilly, pillared gloom of the cathedral at three-thirty, an hour before his first rehearsal and evensong. He had just been to the office. While the secretary hadn't meant to be tactless, Derek's first comment had been to enthuse about Geraint's extraordinary performance, to mark the start of Lent, of Couperin's *Leçons de Ténèbre* with two opera-singer friends. Their sheet music still lay on the chamber organ with a mug containing an inch of cold coffee and smudged with lipstick.

Matthew climbed the rickety stairs and went through the wardrobe-like door into the loft itself, his inner cabinet where warm light reflected off the polished wood and ivory. A handwritten note lay on the console:

Matt, I've cancelled the rehearsal before evensong, but I'm sure you know the music already so we'll just do it live.
Thanks, Geraint

Thanks? Cancelled? What was Geraint thinking? Matthew's stomach turned. He had come back from Germany to make the stonework sing. While it might seem effortless, in reality it took lots of rehearsal, preparation and practice. Was his return going to be compromised by working for someone who didn't care? Was there a power dynamic he hadn't appreciated? Had he been deluding himself for these last two months?

He listlessly descended the organ loft stairs, but all there was in the nave were Geraint's Couperin scores and his singer's stained cup. Had Geraint busked his way through the Couperin and felt his talent validated by the resulting applause? Was the subtext: don't prepare; appear to play like a genius; don't tidy up? To his own annoyance, Matthew was still jealous of a man who had the skill to produce good results without effort. He wandered nervously down the cloister to the song school. It was closed and empty. Unable to focus on any productive practice, he could do nothing but nurse his anger and kill time. The forty-five minutes dragged interminably.

Finally, the choristers and lay clerks began to drift in, robe up and collect their music folders. Under happier circumstances he would have greeted them and chatted, but the weight of his feelings kept him seated in silence. If Geraint had arrived first they could at least have talked briefly in private about their impending collaboration. He'd never found much elation when thrown together to play with strangers. Was this all he could expect in his new job? Finally their leader swaggered in.

'Ready for action?' asked Geraint.

His tone was combative, but also indirect: passive aggressive.

Matthew responded as evenly as he could. 'Will there be a rehearsal tomorrow?'

'Yes. Boys at eight-thirty,' answered Geraint, without any hint that he was interacting with another artist.

'I meant before the service.'

'Don't worry Matt, we're at sixes and sevens today. You've got all the music? The anthem?'

'The anthem's unaccompanied.'

'No it isn't.'

'It isn't?'

Geraint brushed Matthew's arm. 'Didn't we send it to you? I'll give you a copy now.'

Geraint strolled to the shelves and back, twice through the choristers and lay clerks who were now robed and standing in line.

'Here's the score.' Geraint passed it to him. 'Olwen Goodenough. *And So To Fatness Come*. Do you know it?'

'No, and it's not on the music list.'

The title was odd for Lent, but he didn't have time to study the words. The score was a photocopy of a handwritten manuscript. The dense and complicated composition with an atonal and polyrhythmic middle section would be gruelling to sight-read and, without rehearsal, challenging to keep in time with the choir. He felt a wave of his New College harrowings.

Geraint chuckled. 'Interesting words by Stevie Smith. It's a good modern composition. Tackles the angst of the twentieth century. You'll like it.' Then he turned away to marshal the choir.

Matthew strode back up to the organ loft. Was Geraint mocking him? How did he know he thought modern music should reflect the tumult of the century? He looked again at the anthem. Maybe it was good. It was a shame to do it half-cocked, but there was no time to practise any of it. He tried never to play in public without preparation. The nerves alone could cripple him. He swore as he sat down at the console.

In the mirror above it he could see a few parishioners already in their stalls. Mr Quantock had finished his rounds with the taper, lighting the candles in their glass holders. Then the first choristers were processing in pairs into the building. That meant he had to play a short piece to accompany them; otherwise the service would begin without him. He closed his eyes and improvised slowly moving chords. The keyboard opened itself out. The music appeared to him. He opened his eyes and looked into the mirror. The choir was in position. He lifted his hands from the keys.

After the introductory prayers, Frank cantored the responses: 'O Lord, open Thou our lips.'

'And our mouths shall show forth Thy praise,' responded the choir.

The music Matthew had prepared in advance went well, but any satisfaction was lost while he nervously awaited the anthem, the last piece in the service. Geraint conducted without much clarity, and the choir didn't seem to be accurate either. The challenging organ part had several sections supposed to be played fortissimo. Most important was to keep going regardless of mistakes and tricky rhythms. Matthew blushed as he repeatedly mistimed chords and played wrong notes at full volume. Then a succession of grinding chords led into the final cadence.

The words *suonalo ancora* were scrawled after the last chord. He didn't understand them. They weren't standard musical terms. Geraint brought off the chord. There was nothing for an instant, then Geraint's reflection gave a downbeat. Matthew was caught off guard and did nothing. What was he supposed to play? Geraint stared at him and gave another downbeat. Did 'ancora' mean 'again'? Was there a repeat? Was this opera-speak? Matthew looked frantically back through the score to find the place he was supposed to go back to. There were no double dots, the usual repeat marks. Sweating, he glanced up into the mirror. Now the choir were gazing up at him. Geraint had frozen.

Then Matthew saw some more words in Italian written above one of the staves at the start of a section. He didn't know what they meant but he assumed it was the start of the repeated section. Geraint wasn't giving any more downbeats but looked up expectantly. He then heard Bryce stand up. He had to play before Bryce launched into the prayers. He started the first phrase, which was marked triple forte. At the same moment Geraint gestured to the choir and they sat down. Matthew looked back in the mirror while playing. Surely Geraint would make them stand up again? But all he saw was Geraint's bald patch as the conductor returned to his stall.

So after all this, they were abandoning the piece? Playing at full volume, cringing, Matthew played on for a couple of bars and then there was nothing else he could do but improvise the best cadence he could in the same style, and for this, luckily, his innermost musician didn't desert him. But that victory didn't outweigh the excoriation. It was like being back at New College. The sound seemed to take forever to echo away, his wounded dissatisfaction seeping slowly up the nave. Then the resulting silence dragged on forever, until finally the dean got up for a second time and said the Grace.

'…and the love of God, and the fellowship of the Holy Ghost, be with us all, evermore…'

'Amen.'

Matthew junked the movement from *The Art of Fugue* he'd prepared as the voluntary, the solo piece the organist plays at the end of the service. It would have been a special way to mark his first service. He pushed the music aside and mechanically improvised the shortest possible piece, ending the moment the last singer left the quire. He turned the organ off. Now his anger outweighed his mortification. He got up and marched after the choir. They were finishing the after-service prayer in the south side aisle. At the Amen, they trooped off towards the cloister and song school. The dean followed, taking off his academic hood as he walked.

Geraint ambled after them with one of the older choristers.

Matthew recognised him: he was the one to whom he had addressed the comments about augmentation and diminution back at his audition. Matthew caught up with them at the entrance to the cloister.

Geraint turned genially to Matthew. 'When I first arrived, I would just sit in the cathedral and soak up the atmosphere. Have you thought of doing that? It'll help you understand how to play the building.'

Matthew seethed at this irrelevance. 'I've spent a lifetime in here.'

'Should I soak it up?' asked the chorister. He was foal-like, all arms and legs. He spoke with the local accent. His voice was deepening and would break soon.

'Have you met Nick Hannon yet?' said Geraint. 'The head chorister.'

'No.'

The lad looked at Matthew. 'I liked the Bach you played at your audition.'

Matthew was pleased to hear this but his head was full of invective.

'Hannon, Mr Perryman and I are going to talk for a few seconds. We'll catch you up.'

Geraint and Hannon exchanged a glance.

'Hannon, sir?' The chorister looked as if he wasn't used to being called by his surname.

Matthew had to remember to try to adapt. He said sharply: 'Can you leave us alone, please?'

The lad smiled enigmatically and moved away towards the song school. Without waiting for him to be out of earshot Matthew turned to Geraint.

'Do you always drop the organist in it like that?'

'The assistant organist, Matthew. I'm the organist.'

'Well in future, don't.'

Geraint smirked. 'Don't what?'

'Put me on the spot. Give me music at the last minute, especially pieces like that. What happened at the end?'

'You tell me.'

'The repeat wasn't marked.'

'Yes it was. Don't you speak Italian?'

'No, Geraint, I don't.'

'Matthew, aren't you supposed to be able to cope with this sort of situation? The other candidates were all good at sight-reading.'

The words cut Matthew. Were his skills deficient? He must deflect Geraint away from this idea. 'Do you care about the performance?'

'Up to a point,' said Geraint.

'What does that mean?'

'It means it sounded fine to me, Matt. You shouldn't worry.'

'But it was sight-reading. How can that be as good as having prepared it?'

'We hire people like you because you can learn music quickly.'

'I'm not a sight-reading machine.'

'We have to work quickly,' said Geraint. 'We can only put in time if there'll be a big congregation.'

'You can't be serious.'

'Yes I can. No one was there. Did you count the congregation? There were six. Don't expect more tomorrow. So why worry?'

'Because it's evensong.'

'So?'

They reached the door of the song school. Geraint paused, and spoke as if making an announcement: 'Matt, is evensong the highlight of your day?'

'Look Geraint, I don't care if evensong's the low point of yours. I want you to treat me—'

A party popper exploded next to Matthew's face. He jumped as streamers showered across him. Hannon chortled through the smoke. He punched Matthew's arm.

'Welcome to the cathedral, sir.'

Around him the room was slurring into laughter. The whole choir guffawed at him, men and boys, drinks in hand.

He heard Frank: 'It might not be the high point of your day, Matthew, but would you like some sherry?'

The room rippled.

Geraint was beaming. He turned to Matthew and shouted above the noise: 'I'd heard you were fun to joke with. Have a drink.'

His chuckle was a chicken squawk. A lay clerk brought a tray. Geraint took just one plastic cup full of Harvey's Bristol Cream, the sticky local sherry, and pressed it into Matthew's hand. None for himself. When Matthew was at school the choristers were all given surreptitious sherries.

'Your health, Matt. Your rôle is to help me bring a bit of life into this staid old place.'

Matthew forced a smile and raised his cup. Geraint mimed raising a glass.

'Aren't you drinking?'

'Not me, no.' Geraint said nothing more, though the awkward silence was as expressive as his stilted tone and reddened cheeks.

Matthew took a sip of his over-sweet sherry.

'Well, drink up, man,' blustered Geraint. 'I'll give you an organ pipe full if you don't – all sixteen foot of it. If it was a dry sherry I'd be tempted to myself.'

Matthew sipped again.

Geraint considered him, steel behind the affable look. 'Didn't they do this to you at Bamberg?'

Geraint was testing him, though he couldn't comprehend why. Did he need to avoid projecting weakness? 'They didn't, actually.'

He thought of how the duck-sizzled potato cakes in Bamberg had been served with deferent, though certainly not joyless, politeness.

'Maybe they should've done,' Geraint retorted. Then he seemed to consider for a moment and added quietly, 'Well, maybe I've been in opera too long.'

Matthew said nothing. Just as the silence was starting to drag, someone shouted: 'To our new assistant!'

The choir hurrahed and raised their plastic cups.

Frank, caught in the middle of the room with the sherry bottle, rushed round the music desks to the grand piano and struck up 'For he's a jolly good fellow.' The rabble joined in.

'A jolly good fellow,' said Geraint to Matthew, and slipped away into the throng.

Frank stood up from the piano and raised his plastic cup. 'Three cheers for Matthew Marcan! Hip hip—'

'Hooray!'

'Hip hip—'

'Hooray!'

'Hip hip—'

'Hooray!'

Frank clambered on to the piano stool and stretched out his arms. The room hushed. Matthew looked down in embarrassment, relief and residual anger, but part of him acknowledged that the choir was attempting to welcome him.

'A few moments ago,' Frank intoned, 'some of us could be forgiven for thinking change was a-coming. Like a hero from the Wild West – this is after all west of Swindon – the new man in town came into the corrupt song school.'

Laughter and applause. A few gentlemen of the choir shouted 'Awright!' One, exaggerating the glottal stop, shouted 'Sor'ed!'

Matthew forced himself to look up. He blushed and tried to smile at those who were looking at him. He raised his plastic cup.

'Who is this mysterious stranger in our midst?' Frank went on. 'He naps in his flat directly above us but we don't know who he is. You do still take a nap, do you?'

The choir laughed. How did they remember these details of his life?

'Well, ladies and gentlemen…' Frank looked around as if scanning the horizon. 'Sorry, where are the ladies?'

An exaggerated laugh came from Roy Brunt.

'Nick, where's your mother?' someone called.

Then Frank hopped down and began an oom-pah rhythm at

the piano. Someone started to keep time with a pair of coconut shells. The choir began to sing their anthem:

> *We are from the west, from the wild wild west*
> *and a very wild west it is.*
> *But we are the best, the very very best*
> *When it comes to singing responses in evensong!*

Frank added extra beats to this bar before continuing. A couple of verses of twaddle passed by, and then finally the closing chorus:

> *Because! Because! BECAUSE!*

Frank rolled a fanfare on the piano, and everyone shouted:

> *This ain't Weston-super-Mare!*

He was back at New College. He remembered with a jolt the antics of the 'New Gentlemen', the male student members of the chapel choir who created a drinking-cum-close harmony group that – in an innocent way, compared to other student drinking societies – would have a glass too many and sing ribaldries.

Someone yodelled. The room boiled in laughter. Matthew forced himself to laugh. It was so different to the earnest reception with which the choir and congregation had greeted him in Bamberg. There they were knowledgeable about organ music and wanted to discover what he thought of their Haupt-orgel. His stomach had rumbled at the suckling pig, assortment of salads and local smoke-beer they had laid on to welcome him, even though he was merely a youth.

They had come together to celebrate an interesting turn in their communal musical life: the arrival of their young organist from England. Young. He'd only been twenty-four then, yet they'd treated him well. For the first time in his life, now, he felt too old.

He glared at Geraint, who was on the other side of the room, laughing with one of the boys. It was as if the humiliating evensong could be forgiven and forgotten simply because someone had set off a party-popper. The party didn't make up for being tricked into giving a dreadful performance.

Geraint turned and caught the sharpness in his stare. For an instant his red face lost ground, as if the brittle inhibitions were papered over a collapsible frame, but then he redeployed his features in a questioning, challenging smile as if to say: 'You over it yet?'

Matthew spun away. He wasn't going to smile and move on.

Hannon was looking over at him and seemed apart from the rest of the room. Was it a look of solidarity? Matthew moved over to him. As he did so Roy unlocked one of the cupboard doors.

'Hannon, what's he doing?'

'He's our photographer. Why do you call me Hannon?'

'Isn't that how teachers address pupils?'

'Not normally, Mr Marcan.'

Hannon pronounced it with an exaggerated Czech 'ch' sound.

'And we're normal?' said Matthew. 'By the way it's Marcan, as in Mark.'

'As in Matthew-Mark-an'-Luke-and-John?'

'Did they tell you that one too?'

Hannon tilted his head back and smiled.

'Okay, everyone,' came Roy's voice. Hardly anyone heard him, so he shouted: 'Quiet!'

The choir fell silent.

'Form up, everybody,' Roy commanded.

Two boys climbed on to the piano. Another sat on a desk, others leant into each other at angles or stood around parodying the people they had really been just two minutes before, now pretending they were at choir drinks. Props materialised out of the cupboards: a ring to blow bubbles through, a toy gun, a tennis racket. Music folders were held foppishly underarm. Everyone remained mute, miming conversations. Hannon moved into the middle and opened his folder as if singing a solo. Matthew stood beside him. Roy snapped a few pictures.

'He'll get them to make it sepia,' whispered Hannon without looking at Matthew. 'Like by the toilet.'

He nodded at a couple of prints hanging next to the door to the WC.

Matthew followed his gaze. 'I'm sorry I snapped at you earlier.'

'That's okay. It's the price I pay for my genius.'

'The what?'

Hannon started laughing.

'Stop laughing,' said Matthew. 'You'll ruin the photo.'

'He's finished.'

Roy lowered his camera and the company began to disperse.

'So how are you going to use your genius?' asked Matthew. 'Management consultancy?'

'No.'

'Law?'

'No. I'm going to be a cathedral organist.'

'A what?'

Hannon laughed. 'A cathedral organist.'

'What, like me and…?'

'No, not like you and Geraint. I'll be different.'

'You're sure you know what you're letting yourself in for?'

'Yes. Richard gave me lessons. I need a new teacher. Can you teach me?'

Matthew had plenty of time in his work week, his salary was perfectly adequate, and he enjoyed engaging with promising pupils. More than this, part of the vocation of the cathedral organist was to guide the education of the choristers. While they might be children, they were also accomplished young professionals with a need and often a desire to develop their skills, which they would carry to the next generation. He nodded towards Geraint. 'Doesn't he teach you?'

'The piano,' said Hannon, 'not the organ. He said I need to reach an advanced level on the piano before learning the organ.'

'Piano? What are you learning?'

'The Schubert G-flat Impromptu.'

'I don't know it.'

'You don't know it?' Hannon looked incredulous. 'It's lush, it's my favourite.'

Matthew had concentrated on organ music, especially the Baroque, to such an extent that the whole classical era was absent from his repertoire. Mozart, Beethoven and Schubert had written almost no organ music and while he knew their orchestral music from listening to his mother's records as a child, he had never learned to play any of their piano pieces. Would devoting precious time to them have diluted the intensity with which he played his favourite composers? Did turning his back on them really mean he played Bach, Weckmann and Buxtehude any better?

'So if Geraint's so brilliant, why do you want me to teach you?'

'Because of the way you play Bach. Geraint never studied in Germany. He never studied with Walcha. He can't play it like you do.'

Matthew glowed. The lad had actually found out about him beyond the residual gossip of the choir, and knew enough to tell the difference between different performers and methods. He wanted to hear more, even if it was flattery. 'So what's my approach, what do I have?'

Hannon looked at him evenly but didn't speak.

'That's not an answer, Hannon.'

'You were fourteen when you went to Walcha, weren't you?'

'Yes, I think. Did Richard tell you?'

'I'll be fourteen soon.'

Matthew was startled. Was the lad really just thirteen? And had he himself been so precocious at that age? 'So you need to get moving,' Matthew said with private irony. 'When do you want to start?'

'Right away,' said the lad keenly.

'Can you do Thursdays at three-thirty? We can get the lesson in before choir practice.'

'It'll take a few minutes to get here from school,' said Hannon.

'That's fine. What piece do you want to start with?'

Matthew asked this to test Hannon's knowledge of the repertoire, which hopefully the boy was exploring on record and tape.

'The Bach C major Prelude and Fugue,' said Hannon.

Bach had written several, all of which were major undertakings. But the boy was obviously familiar with at least one, and if Richard had already given him lessons, he would have covered the basics of touch, and hand-feet co-ordination.

'The smaller one?'

'No, the big 9/8 one,' said Hannon. 'I've started already. It's my first big piece. Did Richard give you sherry in lessons?'

Matthew snorted, but under the surface he was thrilled that the boy was already knowledgeable and accomplished enough to judge and choose demanding pieces on his own initiative. This echoed how Matthew himself had been at the same age, compulsively listening to tapes of Bach's organ music, cross-checking performances of the pieces by different organists on different organs, developing his own opinions about how the music should be played, marking his findings into his scores, and painstakingly learning to play the pieces himself, creating his own interpretations according to the theories of performance practice that he was developing for himself. Richard, his teacher, had not deflated Matthew's passion, but had allowed him freedom, only stepping in to coax a more orthodox performance out of him when the young Matthew produced a truly wayward interpretation.

'He gave me sherry,' said Matthew, fondly remembering his teacher, 'but that was years ago. Does Geraint?'

'Not always,' said Hannon, 'because it's not allowed. But isn't drinking in lessons the way forward?'

'It was when I was your age. Maybe they didn't think I'd do anything without it.'

Hannon pretended to look serious. 'I thought good pupils dragged their teachers after them.'

Matthew considered him. 'So what do your parents think of you becoming a cathedral organist?'

'Dad doesn't know. Mum hates the organ. She doesn't understand.'

'Can she be made to understand?'

Hannon looked determined. 'She's going to have to be.'

'Good,' said Matthew. 'I'll give you lessons. But if you want to be a cathedral organist that means an organ scholarship to one of the better Oxbridge colleges, and that means hard work from now on.'

'Yes, I know.'

'Harder than what you know.'

Matthew was thinking of Geraint: what piano pieces was he teaching the boy? What was it going to be like to teach Hannon the organ with Geraint sniping at him from their weekly piano pulpit? Geraint might offer negative comments about the pieces they worked on and every aspect of their approach. Today's practical joke was in essence a way to undermine him, and what if that continued? Even now, would Geraint crack a joke about him as he left the song school? Would there be a round of laughter for him to catch as he climbed the stairs up to his flat? Bitterness rose up in his gorge.

'If you learn the organ with me, you'll have to give up the piano.'

Hannon said nothing.

'There won't be enough time for both.' Matthew drained his sickly sherry. 'No more lessons with Geraint.'

It might have been a Tuesday in Lent and not even dinner time, but the lay clerks were partying like students. Upstairs, Matthew patrolled his generous flat: five spacious rooms, with ceilings twice his height. It had been fitted out by Edwardian joiners in the sturdiest woods. The capacious furniture had stood there for generations. The grand piano – a mellow-toned, century-old Blüthner – grew out of the sage green carpet. But the sturdiness didn't keep out the tinkling and revelry from the song school below.

He was too stirred up to cook his normal dull dinner for one: pasta with pesto or tuna and some boiled greens. Chloë Balducci stepped into his thoughts. The name of her tape was intriguing: *Havoc in the Old City*. He could do with some of that. He put it on and cranked up the volume.

The flat filled with aural warmth, a tangible sound created by fingers against metal strings on wooden necks, signals travelling down lengths of cable, valves glowing in amplifiers, needles edging into the red. Then archetypal chords, a stomping rhythm and her voice:

Pitter, patter, pitter, patter, I'll sing the blues for you.
Pitter, patter, pitter, patter, you'll want me to go home with you.

The tape was great, but it was no substitute for the real her. Her live performance was more intense – so, better – even if the tape made more sense because all the elements of her style were recorded, including her interplay with the Hammond. It made him want to see her play live again. He turned it off, put on his coat, sneaked back down the generously-hewn stairs and out through the cloister door. They hadn't even noticed. Outside, the laughter and piano-playing mushroomed into the vastness of the orange-lit ether until their revels were drowned by the rumble of the city. He allowed gravity to pull him down to the harbour. The waterside warehouses were now bars and an arts cinema. Happy couples might feel they were ambling along the covered promenade, but to Matthew they prowled, mocking his aloneness.

He drifted into the lobby of the Harbour Shed, a roomy bar on the quay. As he'd expected, a table was piled with leaflets advertising upcoming music and events. He found *What's On In Bristol* and leafed through to the section on live bands. Chloë was listed among the many gigs, playing in a couple of weeks at the Hogshead.

He floated into the bar, bought a pint of Bristol Bridge and found a table. He couldn't push away how much he had been struck by her. But the Other also stalked. He daren't even think of her real name, because she had, or would, become the Other, and he didn't want that. He wanted to break free from the Other and live.

In the back of his mind he knew he'd come back to the city as much because of her as because of his imperfect job. He could certainly never reveal that to anyone, because it was a truth that showed his true self. He was a true fantasist, to the point of upending his life to pursue a fancy. He hung his head. He'd given up a good life full of artistic satisfaction in Germany. Now he was alone. He'd moved to a city where he had no friends. He'd let his school friends drift away. He wasn't connecting with his colleagues at the cathedral. He didn't even view them as colleagues, but as adversaries. He might as well be swimming alone in the black waters of the harbour.

VII

Tendrils of music pulled him out of sleep. Scales and exercises from the song school below. It was some minutes past eight o'clock. Someone had started rehearsing the boys. It didn't sound like Geraint. The choristers met every weekday before school, arriving in good time for forty minutes of practice starting at eight o'clock sharp. Geraint and Matthew would divide these rehearsals between them. But if Geraint was always going to be late for his he would erode the choir's practice time. Was Matthew going to have to make that up when he took the rehearsals?

After breakfast Matthew went downstairs to the dean's office for an appointment with Bryce. They greeted each other and shook hands.

'You arrived okay?'

'Yes. Straight in at the deep end at evensong.'

They sat down. Bryce didn't make any further comment about the music at the service but, as Matthew was expecting, got straight to the point:

'In terms of who answers to whom, there's no canon precentor at the moment, and I'm happy for there not to be one, so you and Geraint answer directly to me. Let's talk about the direction we're moving in. I want to make sure that although we didn't give you the number one job, you're still on-side with what we're doing and feel you can contribute. First, I want to stress that I'm not a wrecker.'

'A wrecker?'

'Because I'm American. People assume I'll turn this place into a drive-through.'

Matthew laughed. He sought out vintage American films on TV, especially the ones shown late on Moviedrome. 'I've never been to America. I've never been to a drive-through either. But it appeals to my imagination. Maybe someone should drive their Pontiac up the aisle.'

'Maybe your enfilade of death could be a drive-through?'

Bryce's tone was gentle, but the joke jabbed Matthew. He wished yet again he had never come up with such an idiotic concept. No wonder he hadn't got the top job. He tried to respond to the joke as if it was good fun:

'Yes, the drive-through of death. You're not already asking me to drive through it, are you?'

Bryce chuckled and settled back from the table. 'Not at all. But you should certainly visit America. You'll find it's more than a land of drive-throughs.'

'Why did your family move there?'

'Not for any sentimental reasons. My family knows which side their bread's buttered. Have you read *Christ Stopped at Eboli*?'

'No.'

'Read it. That's my family. You'll understand why the happy and prosperous Volantés are in Nebraska, not Calabria. And now there's a happy branch here.'

Bryce eschewed 'ums' and 'ahs' and talked quickly for an Anglican clergyman. When he stopped talking there was a sudden hole. Feeling this, Matthew asked what Nebraska was like.

Bryce's eyes shone. 'The prairie's like being at sea. The breeze means it's never too hot. Have you read any Willa Cather?'

'No.'

'You should. I'm from the same town as her, a little place called Red Cloud.'

Bryce studied Matthew for a moment through his frameless glasses.

'What have you read?' he asked.

Matthew smiled defensively, as when Hannon had asked him about Schubert. 'A lot of musical scores.'

'Well, you've got a lot to discover.'

The remark warmed Matthew with its implication of potential new lives to live.

He noticed a framed photo of the dean and Richard. It hadn't been on display at his interview in January. The two men were similar in their bald beardedness and resembled a comedy duo: Richard the tall, droopy one, smiling benignly, a recessive physicality; Bryce the short pug, leaning forward purposefully, arms crossed.

'Why did you come to England?' Matthew asked.

'Mission. There's no less corny word for it. Now people come to England with the same spirit that English missionaries went to Africa.'

Bryce allowed a palate-cleansing pause to last a few seconds.

'But to get to the point, I am painfully aware, because of the churches I led in America, that this cathedral is moribund. For everyone who comes to a service, four tourists come in. And we don't have a lot of tourists. This isn't Salisbury. But the people who do come in never come back. They see what we're about, and they're not interested. My last church, in Tupelo, Mississippi, had a bigger congregation and a bigger budget than here. That was just an Episcopalian church in a small city. Here we get more of our money from tourists than from the congregation. They give nothing. They're completely unmotivated. I hear it every time they say 'Amen'. When I ask for them to say 'Amen!' as if they mean it, they look at me as if I don't understand English restraint. I know all about restraint, and when it is and when it isn't appropriate, and restraint is not an appropriate Christian response to the urgent problems of this world.'

Volanté paused for a few breaths. Matthew wanted more. He felt excited. Bryce had vision.

'First I want to discuss my approach to changing the music here, just in case you think it'll be all guitars and castanets. I love classical music. I love Bach, Buxtehude, Messiaen, Howells. We perform it well, and it's an important part of the liturgy, and it helps make God apparent, et cetera et cetera. And let's face it, the people round here need it. But no one comes and listens. We're not getting it across. Nonetheless, I want a Christian ministry of aesthetics, and music is a central part of that.'

Matthew absorbed this. Bryce was persuasive, and despite his own love of the music, he could see that the dean had a point.

'That's why I gave the job you wanted to Geraint.'

Matthew felt jabbed again. He was being persuaded by the dean's vision. Did Bryce's comment show that he didn't realise that Matthew was amenable to being drawn to common ground?

'But your position is important, too,' continued Bryce. 'We should move beyond the way it's been done in the past, with the assistant being a slave to the whims of the director of music, and all this nonsense about being a master of the poor choristers. I don't want you to be defined by your title. You might not be the best front person, but I want you to bring music to kids from the new and old estates in Southmead as if it was the Good News, and make them love Bach. Not just Bach, make them love Kuhnau.'

Matthew sat up mentally at the mention of Bach's obscure predecessor at the Thomaskirche in Leipzig. He found Bryce watching him.

'And that might mean presenting it with a bit of imagination,' Bryce continued, 'especially if we want them to come back.'

Again, Matthew wanted more. Even if his whole job was being rewritten, Bryce was making sense.

'I mean, that introit by Attwood you did yesterday. I'm not blaming you because it was your first service, but would the Anglican choral tradition really collapse if we put a bit less emphasis on pieces like that and a bit more on…?'

Matthew had to say something, but what? 'On…?' Despite his alignment with Bryce's ideas, he sounded defensive.

Bryce reclined. 'That's for you and Geraint to work out.'

'But on what? I can't create music that doesn't exist.'

As he said it, Matthew realised that he could indeed create music that didn't exist. His improvisations created new musical worlds. He regularly improvised in services to cover, say, the priest preparing to read the gospel. Could he work improvisation into accompanying the choir or communicating with the congregation? Should he develop his creative spontaneity and try to cross genres?

Chloë stepped forward from where she had been waiting in the wings of his mind. He saw her in the cathedral with her guitars, amp and band, her music blooming in the echo. His projection of her musicianship fitted the cathedral exactly. The bedrock chords of blues had the immutability of religious music.

Then his more rational self caught up. This vision might not be pure fantasy. He might actually be able to hire her to perform at the cathedral. Could he bring blues into evensong? Could she perform in a service? Were the traditions and personalities of clergy and musicians flexible enough to allow such a blend of cultures? Wasn't that what Bryce was aiming for?

Meanwhile, Bryce had said nothing.

'What about blues evensong?' said Matthew.

Bryce sniffed. 'Let's walk before we run.'

'But don't people like bands?'

'Bands, yes…' said Bryce. 'I'll think about it.'

'Okay,' said Matthew. It was safer to keep the focus on organ music. 'You talk about changing directions, but you're still accepting the new organ?'

'For the Lady Chapel? Yes.'

'The money's coming from Richard's estate.'

'I know. We're grateful.'

'Have you looked at the specification?'

'Yes, so far as I can understand it. It all looks fine.'

'Of course it all looks fine. Richard and I designed it. We laboured over it. It takes years to understand these details.'

'But how many other people will get the nuances you've spent years studying?'

'The nuances add up to beauty. Anyone can get that. Anyone can also notice, even if they're not trained, when a sound isn't beautiful.' Matthew paused. 'Look, I'll happily play Kuhnau till I'm blue in the face, but it makes me nervous to have to find an audience. Isn't that Geraint's rôle?'

Bryce didn't show any sign of being perturbed. 'You speak like a follower, not a leader. And it's a congregation, not an audience. And yes, I am getting Geraint to do just that. His *Leçons de Ténèbre* were fantastic. He's giving a recital next term, in May, a half-hour Max Reger programme at ten o'clock.'

'Ten pm? Reger?'

'Yes, yes.'

Matthew was amazed. 'Will anyone come?'

'Yes. We've done a couple already and had good attendance, and many of them come to compline beforehand. Not the usual crowd at all, as you'll see. I'll look forward to seeing you there.'

He would go, certainly. He loved Max Reger, whose challenging compositional style was treacherous technically but extremely expressive: the autumnal despair of the romantic soul overwhelmed by the birth of the modern world. Matthew had tortuously learned dozens of his pieces, including the hyper-difficult one called *The Inferno*. If Geraint was going to play Reger, it would give him the perfect opportunity to size up the opera man. But in the meantime Bryce had reminded him of his boss, and surely he had to have some sort of conversation with Geraint if they were to work together effectively? Matthew couldn't face another evensong like the day before, and the next one was only hours away. They couldn't just bounce from blah service to blah service.

'An individual needs six rooms to be civilised.' Matthew was surprised by the force with which his father's voice bubbled up. Jiří Marcan had told him this many times. Matthew couldn't stop or even dilute the memory of his father counting off his fingers: 'Sitting room, study, kitchen, bedroom, spare room and bath.'

Matthew's flat had five rooms. Here at the organist's residence in Dowry Square – Richard's old house and now Geraint's – there were twelve. Too big for one person, but the perfect size for a family. Five narrow storeys stacked up like a lighthouse.

He climbed the shallow front steps and pressed the doorbell. There was no discernible effect. He rang again, and then knocked. He rapped on the door a second time. No answer. He tried the door. It opened and he stepped into the familiar marble-papered hall. Geraint had strewn the flagstones with Doc Martens, sandals and running shoes. They contrasted with the antique cartoons still lining the walls. In the hush of the house he heard nothing more than what came in from outside, subdued traffic noise and the rustle of the air and the leaves. He climbed the dogleg stairs and reached the landing. The door to the first-floor sitting room was closed. Matthew stood in front of it and strained his hearing. He could hear nothing. He knocked.

A cup in a saucer tinkled.

'Who is it?' said a surprised voice from within.

'It's Matthew.'

He stood still, facing the closed door.

'What? Come in and explain yourself.'

Matthew turned the handle but stayed in the doorway as the door swung open. Geraint was propped up on the straight-backed chair he remembered Richard buying at an auction. Geraint's hair was dishevelled and he was wearing bright pink pyjamas under his silk dressing gown. He stared at Matthew in aggrieved surprise:

'Don't stand there like an idiot. How did you get in?'

'The door wasn't locked.'

'I rarely lock it. So?'

Matthew felt as if he needed to explain his presence: 'I thought I'd pop over.'

He moved forward into the room. His boss seemed hung

over, but he'd drunk nothing at the choir party, and nothing but a cup of weak, milkless tea sat on the buckled table.

Geraint surveyed Matthew: 'Why not sit down?'

'Thank you.'

Matthew lowered himself into the gently collapsing armchair to one side of the fireplace. The horsehair stuffing was breaking through the arms where the velvet had worn away. The chair had been angled to face an outsize TV, jarring with the spinet, virginals and harpsichord. Piles of newly published anthems in garish bindings, many no doubt by Geraint, littered the floor. Richard's scores, many of which were facsimiles of the original manuscripts, still neatly filled the shallow shelves. Geraint's presence wasn't yet so permanent that he couldn't be easily cleared out of the enchanted room.

Geraint's face softened into a confused smile. 'You're not looking at me. Are my pyjamas that risqué?'

Matthew forced himself to look at Geraint. Seeing him in clear light for the first time, the ruddiness of Geraint's cheeks and nose wasn't just red skin but derived from a tight network of broken blood-vessels. The eyes too were pinkened, though that didn't seem permanent, and they probed him with unfiltered intelligence.

'You're still recovering from evensong,' stated Geraint.

Matthew grimaced, then smiled. 'Let's hope today's goes well.'

Geraint looked at him in what was probably an even way.

'Before you get too comfortable, would you like a drink? I can send you on a mission to the basement. You need servants to make this house work. What would you like? Coffee, tea? Or a glass of wine? The cellar's still full. I don't drink, so it's up to you to empty it.' Geraint turned towards the window and back. 'I think you could say the sun's over the yardarm.'

'I'll have a cup of coffee,' said Matthew. 'What can I get you?'

'There's some ginger root in the fridge. Just put a slice in the bottom of a cup and add boiling water.'

'That sounds nice. I'll go down and make it.'

'Do you know where the kitchen is?'

'Yes,' said Matthew. 'Unless it's changed.'

He got up. The springs buzzed.

'Nothing's changed,' said Geraint. 'He lived in the past, didn't he?'

Matthew had reached the doorway. He turned and stared.

'Richard, I mean,' said Geraint.

'What's wrong with that?'

Geraint edged back in his chair, a tiny movement. 'Nothing.' He smiled to placate Matthew. 'When you're back with your coffee, I want you to tell me about what's-his-name.'

'Who?' asked Matthew.

Geraint sat forward again. 'Helmut Thingy.'

'Helmut Walcha?'

'Yes. He was blind, wasn't he?'

'Yes.'

Geraint beamed. 'You can tell me all about the blind leading the blind.'

Matthew turned and descended the two flights of stairs, declining from formality to lines of servants' bells, reed matting, a blue-painted larder with a glazed door. In the subterranean kitchen he slid the kettle on to the range. He hung his head and looked down at Geraint's bright new tea-towels. What a mess he had got himself into. Here he was, standing in the kitchen he belonged in, somewhere that could be a base for an illustrious career and a home to a family, and it was as far out of his reach as if he'd stayed in Germany.

He busied himself getting down the bone-china and slicing Geraint's ginger. The kettle reached the boil. The fragrant ginger infusion made his instant coffee seem ordinary. It wouldn't calm him. Why was he so jittery? He found a bottle of Richard's brandy at the back of one of the cupboards. He sneaked himself a glass and sank it. He felt stronger, warmer, more confident. He returned the bottle, washed the glass up, put the hot drinks on a tray and carried it upstairs. He couldn't help but pause in the hall. It was as if he was alone in the house. Geraint wasn't making a sound. He stood there and enjoyed the calm, the quiet, the sureness, all amounting to harmony. If only real life could have those qualities.

Upstairs, Matthew passed Geraint his ginger tea.

'Put it there, beside the other one. Did you bring biscuits? Oh, don't worry.'

Matthew put the tray down on the uneven table, which he knew to be by Hepplewhite, and passed Geraint his cup and saucer. Matthew's father had dreamt of owning a piece by Chippendale. The footstool would do, but he would never be able to afford a matchstick. Geraint, who didn't value any of it, had walked into all of this.

'So tell me about Helmut…'

'Walcha.' Matthew added. He returned to the velvet armchair.

'Yes, Walcha,' Geraint said. 'I saw him at the Festival Hall years ago, decades ago, when I was a student. I hate to say this, Matt, but I didn't find his playing very engaging.'

Matthew didn't know how to respond. In his best playing Walcha had rendered Bach with a grandeur and seriousness that made the interlocking lines of counterpoint come together to form an ideal of human art.

Geraint obviously didn't see that: 'You don't think his style's a bit out of date?'

'Of course it's out of date,' said Matthew tetchily. 'Totally out of date. I wouldn't dream of playing like him, note for note. His phrasing's all wrong, for one thing. But because he was blind he knew the music inside out and had an authority I've never heard in anyone else. It's the spirit of his playing that's so right. That will never date.'

'Spirit? Everyone I've talked to finds his playing boring. Well, let's leave it at that.'

'No, let's not leave it at that.'

Geraint pulled back. Matthew wondered if he had spoken too loudly. He lowered his voice and continued:

'You'll laugh, but Walcha believed that as players we're the custodians of Bach's music, keeping it in good shape and passing it on into the future. It doesn't matter how good a musician you are, and it doesn't matter what your circumstances are. Anyone can do this, even if they can only play a simple minuet. We're all links in the chain. Bach's here for everyone.'

'Very noble. And how's that helping you?'

'Why do I need help?'

'We all need help,' said Geraint.

'You don't agree with Walcha?'

'No. And what about Beethoven, Mozart, Schubert, Liszt, Brahms?' Geraint waved his cup around. 'Wagner, Chopin, Verdi, Mahler? Why's Bach better than them? He never threw himself into the Rhine in his flowery dressing gown, only to be plucked out by a boatswain who thought he was a carnival prankster.'

Geraint didn't seem to speak with any self-reference, but propped up in his chair like an invalid and wearing colourful pyjamas and dressing gown, was he telling this story as an allusion to himself? He'd talked at Richard's funeral about committing suicide over and over again. Repeatable suicide.

'Who did that?' asked Matthew.

'Schumann. Can you convey what was driving him?'

'I do actually play some Schumann, his six fugues on B-A-C-H. And I thought he wrote them because working on counterpoint helped him overcome his mental problems.'

Matthew felt he had given a reasonably good riposte, but the image of the silken Schumann, failed in his suicide, was indelible. Wasn't tragedy – suicide even – a gesture that was understood by an observer who had noted it? However desperate, it somehow proved that people were linked to one another. But Schumann's shambolic attempt seemed totally alone, within nothing but chaos and misunderstanding.

Geraint's snort brought him back into the conversation. 'And how's B-A-C-H helping my daughter?'

Matthew must have missed the first part of Geraint's statement. 'I didn't know you had a daughter.'

'Of course you didn't.'

'Geraint, if you can bring Schumann to life like that, how come your anthems are so…' He couldn't bring himself to say the word 'anodyne'.

'So bland?' asked Geraint.

'Yes.'

Geraint smiled like a buccaneer. 'Because they're for bland people. So what was Thingy like?'

'Walcha. Extraordinary.'

'How?'

Matthew was silent.

'Come on, how?' asked Geraint.

'Here's an example. When I was there he played me the Bach 9/8 C major prelude. It's on my mind because Hannon said he's learning it.'

'I know. It's too much for him.'

'Anyway, Walcha forgot I didn't speak German. He pushed me down the bench and started describing the themes as he played them – you know, the four distinct motifs you get in the first four bars. I looked up the words he used. The first one was 'singen', singing, for the rising triplets, then 'spielen', playing, for the fanfare-like motive. Then 'lachen', laughing, for the twittering semi-quavers, and finally 'tanzen', dancing, for the gigue-like arpeggiated triplets. He played the whole piece calling these words out, 'singen und tanzen' or 'lachen und spielen', and singing the themes as they went by. Speaking, laughing, singing, dancing. What a wonderful evocation of life.'

Geraint was considering him. Matthew grasped for words: 'He believed Bach is the only music that'll sustain you for a lifetime. If you know the music of Bach intimately, it doesn't matter what happens to you, because you'll always have an abundant inner life.'

Geraint sipped his tea. 'And you agree with that?'

'Yes.'

'It's a bit extreme.'

'Then I'm a bit extreme. But do you have a better philosophy?'

'Than notes, notes, notes?' Geraint laughed. 'No, and I don't worry about having a supernatural rôle. It sounds to me like your whole philosophy of musical expression is to make up for the fact that your life is deficient, but that's your business. I'm not changing the subject, but you've been here before, right?'

'To this house?'

'No, to Bristol.'

'Yes. I was at school here.'

'So you know it's an alright city. You can have a bit of fun here.'

Was fun the purpose of his life? Matthew sipped his coffee silently. Again, his eyes were drawn around the room. Geraint noticed.

'Maybe not fun, then, but it's a good gaff, isn't it? I wish it belonged to me. I started well. My mother bought me a place in Notting Hill when I was at the Academy. But the money's all gone. I've just had to put my flat in Redland on the market and move in here. Do you own property?'

'No, but I'm first in line for the family bungalow.'

Geraint smiled. 'The family bungalow? Where is it?'

'Chettle, in Dorset.'

'Very nice. Do you enjoy being from the country? Do you engage in country pursuits, whatever they are?'

Matthew had not involved himself with the countryside that he grew up surrounded by, though its aesthetics had impressed him. By the time he had formulated the idea, Geraint was speaking again:

'Richard was from Dorset, too, wasn't he? Maybe that's why he liked earning no money and living in someone else's draughty house. Have you tried sitting up against the storage heater?' Geraint raised his teacup with a flourish. 'Perhaps we could make a deal with the dean. You get the house, and I get more money.'

Matthew raised his coffee, wondering how serious Geraint was.

'So Richard wanted you to be the organist here?' continued Geraint. 'You and he were kindred spirits?'

'Yes. Richard wanted…' Matthew paused. 'He wanted me to replace him, ultimately.'

'I see.' Geraint made a sucking noise with his teeth. 'Then why didn't he get you to be his assistant?'

'Because I went to Germany. I would have come back in a year or so. But then he died.'

'Well, let's be glad Bryce has resolved everything. We have our rôles. I'm happy. I hope you'll be able to roll in the direction Bryce is propelling us.'

'I hope so too.'

'It's probably not where you want to go, Matthew. I know you're old school, Richard, Thingy…'

'Walcha.'

'Yes…'

Another awkward pause. Matthew looked around him at the room and its furnishings. It was all so beautiful. 'I don't care what happens to the music as long as evensong stays the same.'

'You can't bank on that if no one ever comes to it. Bryce thinks it's a waste of money.'

For a moment Matthew couldn't conceal his fear. Geraint added with seemingly genuine concern.

'Matt, we might as well pay you to put all your energy into that pyramid thingy in the graveyard. Should we really give you everything you want, for life, if your efforts bring no one into the cathedral?'

'Geraint, can I ask you a question?'

'Of course. Answer a question with a question.'

'Why are you a cathedral organist?'

'Matthew, titles aside, you're the organist, and I'm the conductor.'

Only the night before Geraint had asserted the hierarchy of organist and assistant. Had he forgotten or was he trying to confuse him? 'You know what I mean,' said Matthew weakly.

'If you were in my shoes,' said Geraint, 'you'd do the same. Not all Bryce's ideas are stupid. I'm happy to beat time. You have to loosen up.'

Matthew saw his vision of Chloë and her band playing in the cathedral. 'I agree. We could try out more popular styles of music in evensong or on Sundays, like a band.'

Geraint considered Matthew as if someone else had possessed his body. Then he sniffed. 'Take it from me, you don't have what it takes to play in a worship band. I've written stuff for that market, and if you think my choral music's bland, my worship music really bottoms it out.'

'But why does it have to be bad? There's blues, jazz, lots of popular forms that are good musically. I had this vision of a blues evensong. The music has a heft that would work well in a church setting, but it's recognisable enough to appeal to more people than what we do.'

'Blues evensong? Are you mad? Who's going to want to listen to you playing blues?'

'But I wouldn't play. We'd hire a band.'

'Only suggest songs you can play yourself. If you'd need to hire a band, we'd need budget-lines that aren't there. I know there are classical musicians who can do jazz, but that's not you.'

'Why can't we book a band?'

'Then why are we paying you?'

'But I specialise in certain types of music. If we wanted a band shouldn't we hire people who actually play in bands?'

'But we don't want a band, and even if we did they wouldn't need to be that great to satisfy the congregation, so I'd just round up you and a couple of others and maybe put one of the lay clerks on the drums and give you some of my music. Done.'

'But you just said not all Bryce's ideas are stupid. I'm trying to go along with you. I'm open to new types of music.'

'No you're not. Blues and jazz aren't new.'

'Worship music isn't new, either. And at least blues and jazz don't talk down to the congregation.'

'The congregation doesn't realise it's being talked down to.'

'Does that mean we can't do anything well?'

'This place doesn't demand it.'

'Then why are you in cathedral music? Why not something else?'

'Because I am. My marriage put paid to my concert career. This is cushier than repping or teaching. Do you expect me to live in a bedsit and be an artist? I'm too old for that. I'm here till I retire, Matt.'

'Please don't call me Matt.'

'Sorry. But it's natural for you to feel like you do. I don't have a problem with that. But I don't want you to hassle me, and I don't want to see you disappointed, and therefore angry at me.'

Matthew said nothing.

'Let's face it, society doesn't reward brilliance. We just need to find a niche somewhere where we can do our own thing, give them a bit of what they want, and then…'

Geraint grimaced dismissively.

'Then what?' asked Matthew. 'What is it you want to do?'

'I'm not obsessed by accomplishing anything, if that's what you mean.' Geraint sipped his ginger tea. 'I care about my daughter. She's twenty-four and is finding herself in Australia. She left as soon as she was eighteen. There's not much I can do, but I hope she comes back.'

'I'm sure she'll be back.'

'Sure?' shot back Geraint. 'How can you be sure?'

Matthew didn't know what to say.

Geraint continued: 'I've just been on a course all about facing up to things, admitting things.' He leant back. 'The truth isn't always polite. I was an alcoholic. I broke up a family. How do you swallow that? I just wonder why she didn't go that bit further – to New Zealand. If you look at a globe it's exactly on the other side of the world from me.'

Matthew had nothing to say; there was nothing similar he could draw upon from his own experience.

Geraint smiled. 'I can see you don't like to be too personal too quickly, but your spiel about Walcha was like an AA meeting.'

Matthew looked at the worn arm of the box sofa.

'If you're an addict, whether to alcohol or…' Geraint paused until Matthew looked up, and then stared him straight in the eye, '…to the correct interpretation of Bach's organ music, you just care about one thing at the expense of everything else. It's not healthy.'

'I don't feel unhealthy. I love what I do.'

'But Matthew, most of the time I didn't feel unhealthy either, and I loved drinking. My God, leaving aside those morning bathroom sessions, what's not to love about drinking?' Geraint looked at him expectantly but Matthew said nothing. 'Now I've learned to care about my family, people – all sorts of things, Matt. Real things. Things maybe you'll care about at some point.'

Matthew looked down, aggrieved. All sorts of counter-arguments about how the aesthetic foundations of his life were perfectly real rose in his throat. But he also knew Geraint was partly right. Reality. What was it?

'Geraint, I don't want to argue.'

'But?'

Matthew felt the trapdoor opening. 'Sorry?'

'You said, "Geraint, I don't want to argue." Normally a statement like that would be immediately followed by a 'but' followed by something argumentative. So let me have it. What do you want?'

'I don't want anything,' said Matthew. 'I don't want to argue.'

'So you just meant that you don't want to argue?'

'Yes.'

'Well neither do I,' said Geraint. 'Why bother saying that?'

Matthew studied the remainder of his coffee. He finished it, then put his cup down on the rosewood that somehow maintained its polished sheen while also acquiring the delicate warp and darkening of age. He found it beautiful. He found Chloë's music powerful, compelling and beautiful. How could it be that others found nothing? Art, craft, beauty. Was their power not obvious to all? Why did art become a subjective battle?

Geraint also drained his cup: 'I need to get on.'

Matthew did not say 'with what?'

VIII

Shortly before three-thirty Matthew walked through the cathedral. The undramatic nave and aisles calmed him. It was his domain of competence. He walked to the Lady Chapel at the east end. This area was big enough to be a church in its own right. The new organ Richard had bequeathed would stand against the stone screen between the chapel and the back of the cathedral's high altar. The medium-sized instrument would be endowed with a clear but rich sound, ideal for playing Bach.

Matthew clapped his hands to test the acoustics, which in that localised area were direct but resonant. He filled it with the music from his inner ear. He picked a chorale melody and imagined treating it in two parts, with a bass-line that fenced with the melody. It was a perfect space to spend the hours and days and weeks of his practice. And Hannon too, he hoped.

He walked down the north side aisle, through the panelled door and up to the organ loft. When he had been a pupil, Richard would already be playing when he arrived for his lessons, and to enter the organ loft was to be enwrapped in both rich sound and cosy light. Matthew would come in and start turning pages, familiarising himself with whichever piece Richard was playing. He resolved to be doing the same when Hannon arrived.

Thinking of Geraint's upcoming recital, he began a fugue

by Reger. Hannon was not only his first pupil here, but the first pupil whom he could teach with experience. He had taken on some pupils in Bamberg, and had learnt how to teach by teaching them. Luckily, they had been too young to notice, and the language barrier had helped preserve his authority. But he had loved teaching and relished teaching more.

'I did knock, Marcan.'

Matthew jumped. Hannon emerged into the light. 'That's Reger, isn't it?'

'Yes.' Matthew recovered himself. 'Do you recognise it?'

'Yeah, Geraint played it at one of his concerts.'

'One of the night-time ones?'

'Yes. Is it true you're part of an unbroken line of descent going back to Bach?'

Matthew was surprised: Hannon was alluding to a spurious idea from the nineteenth century that certain French organists were great-great-great-grandpupils of Bach.

'Do you mean like who taught whom?'

'Exactly,' said Hannon.

'Did Richard tell you this?'

'No. Geraint was talking about his teacher, who was French.'

'I think we're all part of that. You could trace me back to Reger, because Walcha was a pupil of Ramin who was a pupil of Straube who knew Reger. Anyway, let's get on. For your lessons, I'll always be in here playing a little early. When you arrive, come and sit on the end of the bench and turn pages for me until I've finished. That way you can see what I'm doing.'

'Richard did that too,' said Hannon.

'How many lessons did you have with him before he died?'

'A year's worth.'

'You're lucky. Now, I'll finish the fugue by Reger I was playing so you can hear the ending, then we'll get started.'

Matthew resumed the piece and Hannon turned pages to the end.

When he had finished, Matthew said: 'Now; your turn. Can you play the Bach prelude for me?'

He made way for Hannon, who moved slowly into the middle of the bench.

'I've learnt the whole piece,' the lad said.

Hannon pulled out some of the seventy-odd stops marshalled densely to each side of the four keyboards. He played through the whole prelude. Richard and Geraint had done a good job starting him. He had the foundations of a strong technique and had no difficulty co-ordinating his hands and feet. But he also hesitated and made plenty of slips. He used exaggerated articulation, almost staccato, and a lot of *rubato*, pulling and pushing the rhythm, yet the overall effect was wooden. He rushed the pedal point at the end before making a pronounced slow-down for the final flourish. Nonetheless, he looked happy. While it wasn't a mature performance, Matthew was happy too. Mastering the co-ordination for such a piece was an accomplishment in its own right, and in his own development he had taken years to combine natural fluency with a regular pulse. There was plenty of time for that to develop.

'See, I can learn a piece in a week.'

'You think you've learnt it?' asked Matthew. 'Play the opening theme.'

Hannon played it, again using an almost staccato style.

'Now, play the unison theme at the end.'

Hannon did, with melodramatic *rubato*.

'Okay, so first of all, Bach and all the composers who preceded him, and also the organ builders like Schnitger, all had their feet firmly on the ground. They were writing music to express a successful society ordained, as they saw it, by God. This was mainstream music. I don't think they'd have bothered with *rubato* like you use it, or an articulation as extreme. They'd have just played it as it was, with what they called *gravitaat*. Bam. So have the confidence to underplay. *Rubato's* often a way of pussy-footing around the music. What's the purpose of your articulation?'

'I don't know. Geraint did something like that.'

'Do you think it works?'

'I don't know.'

'What do flautists do every now and then?'

'Breathe?'

'Exactly. That's all articulation is. Just let a natural bit of space in where a flautist might breathe. In the eighteenth century a flautist called Quantz wrote in a treatise that every note should be separate, like a pearl. A pearl is opulent and fat, not mean and truncated. I want pearls from you.'

Matthew talked about Walcha's motifs: speaking, laughing, singing, dancing. Then they moved to the fugue. They spent time with Hannon playing the subject and countersubjects at various stages of the piece – the soprano here, the tenor there, to identify the thematic material. Matthew knew this fugue had more statements of the subject than any other by Bach, so they spent time trying to unearth them all. They found thirty-five, but there was probably at least one more lurking in the score. Bach, who liked number symbolism, would probably have opted for thirty-six because that number could divide in more ways and have more meaning.

'Okay. Now play it all again, but leave out the alto. Sing the alto, and play the other parts.'

Hannon tried, but his performance ground to a halt within two bars. Taking out one part made the whole unfamiliar, and he was essentially left sight-reading and sight-singing a new piece. Matthew slowed his tempo right down and set him to work through from the start again. It took many minutes with many stops and starts. By the end, Hannon played with more fluency, and his face was set with concentration.

'Will I have to do everything like this?'

'For now, yes. If you learn pieces like this you'll know them thoroughly. If not, there'll always be little things you never get completely right, and they may be fine when you play by yourself, but when you play in public those little hairline cracks become gulfs full of mistakes.'

'How much practice do you want me to do?'

'As much as you can. Can you manage two hours a day?'

'Mum keeps making me do other things. She wants me to do art.'

'Do you want to do art?'

'No.' Hannon looked evenly at Matthew. 'I want to play Bach like you. How did you discover Bach?'

'Records. My parents had lots of them. And an anthem, *My Heart Ever Faithful*. You probably know it. We sang it in choir at prep school.'

The music came back to him – the joyous D major tonality and the vivacious part-writing redolent of a universe where everything had its place and meaning.

> *My heart ever faithful*
> *sing praises, be joyful!*

Hannon said: 'And when you were my age you went to see Walcha?'

'Yes.'

'I've listened to some of his CDs. I don't like his playing.'

'Why not?'

'It's too slow, and too phrased.'

'You're from a different generation. But the point is, when I was your age I loved his playing, and that's why I visited him. You'd have gone to see someone else.'

'So what did you do? You just went to see him?'

'I wrote to him.'

'Did you go by yourself?'

'No, I went with my mother.' Matthew smiled. 'It was my mother who got me into him. She bought me a tape of his. But I was proud then, and I wished I had gone alone.'

'Would you have been allowed?'

'I don't know.'

Hannon pressed some of the thumb pistons, the buttons that controlled the stops automatically, boyishly enjoying shunting the stops in and out and getting the distant sound of the solenoids pushing the sliders into position deep within the instrument. Matthew felt he wanted to ask more, but might not because of his young age, so he decided to say more.

'We got the boat to Ostend and the train from there to Frankfurt via Cologne. I remember all the carriages were orange. But in the centre, with blue and white livery, there was this dining car which seemed impossibly romantic to me. I stood at one of the high round tables while Mum got sandwiches, and I felt like a real adult with a real purpose. The people were as far away as it's possible to be from the people in Chettle, the village I'm from. There was this pair of men in leather jackets, and I used them to imagine I was rumbling across America, like some kind of biker. Do you imagine things like that?'

'Sometimes.'

'Good. You'll benefit from an imagination. It takes you everywhere you don't get to go, and wherever you do go is more vivid. When we'd finished eating we walked down the narrow corridors of the carriages, past people sitting on foldout chairs or hanging their heads out of the windows. To the side of the corridor, each carriage was divided into compartments. The seats folded down into the middle of the compartment so it became a sort of enormous bed. There were five or six people. I can remember them. By the window, a young man and woman were busy exchanging glances. That seemed romantic, much more than anything I'd ever seen in the village.'

When Matthew was waiting for Walcha's reply to his letter, he would run out to the postbox to waylay the postman. One day as he approached from the field, Alice, oldest sister of Barnaby Pike, and called Fat Alice by his classmates, hovered in the bushes. Then as the postman's van came round the corner, she sauntered out to the postbox with a letter, arriving just as the postman got out of his van.

'Morning, Nathan. Nice day isn't it?'

'Yeah.' The postman tried to empty the postbox without looking at her.

'I was just coming up to post a letter.'

'Yeah.' The postman filled his sack.

'Did you come from Gannett's Cross?'

'Yeah.' He got back into his van and drove away. She still held her letter.

She swallowed, jerking like a cow regurgitating cud.

Matthew said to Hannon: 'I remember my mother whispering: "Matty, you mustn't miss this; look." Everyone else in our compartment was asleep. We were going down the Rhine valley. The river was massive, much wider than the Thames. My mother said: "You don't see topography like this in England. You have to come to Europe."'

Matthew remembered her hugging him. She was so far away, dead for so long. But she had hugged him. She must have loved him. He said to Hannon: 'Anyway. We got to Frankfurt and went to the Dreikönigskirche. I'd hoped it would be some Baroque pile suitable for the mysterious Walcha, but it was just a largish Victorian church.' Matthew smiled. 'Anyway, I was self-conscious having my mother there. At the arranged time this Mercedes taxi draws up. The driver got out and opened the rear door, and there was Walcha. He was about seventy-five, and his flesh was soft and white like a Czech dumpling. He was blind, as you know. He didn't wear dark glasses and his eyes just floated around. But he was dressed well, as if someone cared about how he looked when he left the house. He also had aftershave. Let's call it *eau de cologne.*

'I left Mum downstairs and we went up to the organ, which was on a balcony at the back of the church, exactly where it should be. It was the first time I'd seen a Werkprinzip case – you know, with each division of the organ having its own case within the case. And the towers of the organ case were arranged like the crowns of the three kings. It was so logical and mystical at the same time, like Walcha. He designed the stoplist.'

Matthew described Walcha's performance of the C major prelude, as he had to Geraint.

Then Hannon asked: 'Is there someone in Germany I should study with?'

'There's a lot of people. There's Heinz-Günther Schmal, my

old boss in Bamberg, and people in other countries too. But you have to find ones who matter to you. It's no use me telling you.'

'Would I be allowed to go?'

They looked at each other.

'It's not up to me. Times have changed. When I was your age my teachers had the attitude that parents were a liability, and the teacher decided, with us, what we did. But now we have to see if your mother will agree with that way of doing things. However…'

Matthew told Hannon about a masterclass coming up that would use the organ at the symphony hall in Birmingham.

'Perhaps we could go to it,' he finished. 'Let's see what she thinks of it. Hopefully she'll begin to see things your way.'

'She just doesn't hear what I hear when I hear the organ.'

Hannon was right. Some people were entranced by the sound of the organ whereas others heard an impenetrable wall of sound. Matthew relived his first cathedral service, the moment he had been hooked.

He was nine years old. Late in his first term at his Dorset prep school, Moultrie, the choir visited Exeter Cathedral to sing evensong. He had enjoyed singing, but it didn't engage him overwhelmingly. The organ caught his attention in the canticles and hymn. Then, as they filed down the nave at the end, for the first time he heard a well-played organ voluntary. The music began with a rippling opening section of feathery arpeggiated chords. Then a deep bass note was followed by chords of a sumptuousness that encompassed the aural spectrum from grandest bass to silverest treble. Matthew stopped dead. The boy behind jabbed him:

'Keep going, Marcan.'

Young Matthew kept filing, but as slowly as he could. He could hear all five lines of music snaking themselves into chordal magnificence, not like the triads he could pick out on the piano with the key note in the bass, but complicated harmonic mysteries. When he reached the vestry door he stopped and refused to budge as the others went in. The bass line was rising and rising and continued to rise, getting higher and higher in timbre until finally it reached a plateau and fell back to its proper register. The whole progression was created with inarguable logic and balance; it could only be the way it was and yet it was unique. The harmonies continued until another lengthy rippling section above a held bass note completed the piece.

Hannon was watching him. Had he drifted away again?

'Look,' Matthew said. 'I know how we can get your mother on side even before we go to Birmingham. There's a big schools' service next week. The cathedral choir isn't needed. So you can play one of the hymns. I'll start teaching it to you now. Ask her to come, and she'll see you playing in front of a packed cathedral. She'll be impressed.'

Matthew took the hymn book off its shelf and opened it to *Old Hundredth*. It wouldn't take long for Hannon to learn it.

The rehearsal and evensong following Hannon's lesson were lacklustre. Geraint offered nothing to inspire the singers, not even a beat clear enough to keep their singing in time. Afterwards Matthew needed to release this frustration. After everyone had left and the cathedral was locked, he let himself back in. He started playing the Bach *Pièce d'Orgue,* which was the piece that had overwhelmed him as a child when he first heard it after the evensong at Exeter. But it was too finely wrought for his mood, and the Edwardian organ was too woolly in sound for its clear texture. He needed to play music that suited the instrument's warmth, dynamic range and nebulous power.

He opened his Max Reger volumes and sought out the cataclysmic harmonic extremes at the opening of the *Inferno* fantasia, where the octatonic scales resolved into cliff-faces of harmony, and then dissolved into ghostly Modernist weirdness. The *Inferno* was of apocalyptic difficulty. While he had been able to perform it in Bamberg, he hadn't practised it for more than a year and he was no longer in technical command of it. But he didn't care, and shoved his way through the endless variety of discords, adding a few of his own. It felt great to press the button marked 8, or full, below each manual, hear the phalanxes of stops being pushed out, and dig eight, nine or even ten fingers and both feet at once into the keyboards and pedals.

The cathedral organ had benefited from all the advances of the nineteenth century and was bigger and more powerful than instruments suited to Bach. In this way the nebulous sound was an advantage, because it found its way everywhere. The Trumpet stops added a blazing fortissimo. He blasted the dark vaulted cavern.

Even if the cathedral could be visually and spatially underwhelming, when it was dark and empty and you listened from a good place – and luckily the organ loft was one such – the acoustic was sensational. The bass flooded around the building topped by a white cap of upperwork. The stones rang back and forth. Endless harmonics, from enormous to tiny, inflected unceasingly. The palette of the organ was immense in itself and infinite in its reflections and reverberations. Whatever temporal challenges his job might involve, it also gave him a seat at the Temple of Tone.

IX

A week of rehearsals and services passed. It was time for the service for the combined school choirs from the diocese. They'd all been rehearsing all term. The quire and nave were already packed half an hour before it was due to begin. The choirs were already in position, including the cathedral school's choir, which was made up of boys and girls from all the years of the school. Some of them came over to talk to Hannon. Matthew stood to one side. He wanted this to be Hannon's event. He didn't want the lad to be seen as a teacher's pet. But there was no danger of that; they were all relaxed and open.

Hannon joked to his friends: 'It's not my fault I'm playing. Blame Mr Marcan.'

Hannon looked young compared to his year group, who seemed to be well into the throes of adolescence. Perhaps he had been placed a year ahead. He seemed to exhibit a variant of Matthew's own paradox, being young in the way he carried himself and in his boyish keenness, but more advanced intellectually and musically than his peers. Still, he was young and uninhibited enough to lean out of the organ loft and wave at his friends.

Outwardly, Matthew looked at them from his rôle as a teacher, but inwardly he remembered his own year group, in that same school not too many years before. If he squinted, they were much the same, and just as real to him, though now he had more perspective to see how they mingled promise and naïveté, moroseness and irony, and gradually developing sensuality. He wished he hadn't been so shy and proud, face in his score all day. Was he just working through the then-new pain of his mother's death? Wouldn't his friends have commiserated if he had told them? He'd just added a new pain to the old – missing out on adolescent love.

Four-thirty rolled by and Geraint hadn't arrived. A thousand schoolkids fidgeted, filling even the aisles, transepts and Lady Chapel. Dozens of headteachers read their order of service for the umpteenth time. Matthew exhausted the stack of pieces he had prepared to play before the service. The weight of flesh and clothing deadened the cathedral's acoustics, taking a couple of seconds off the echo. Mr Quantock's long-staffed crucifix trembled with frustration. Bryce stood still and fearsome.

Then Geraint ambled into view. The service could begin. His leads were perfunctory, so the choirs came in by degrees. He did nothing to pep them up. He led with off-hand, can't-really-ly-be-bothered body language. He didn't stand up properly. He either didn't know or didn't care that the conductor's posture and breathing would be subconsciously imitated by the choir. For better or worse he was their puppeteer.

As a result the massed choirs' singing was slack and lost. Despite watching closely in the mirror, Matthew could barely come in on time. The openings of the choral pieces were shoddy. Therefore Matthew played more decisively than usual, maintaining a determined four-square pulse from which the thousand singers, and even Geraint, couldn't escape. But this approach to music was at best firefighting. Locking people into rhythmic grids was not the way to engender the symbiosis that led to a good performance. This was not the gracious wall-to-wall weave of the Anglican choral tradition, which was founded on generous musicianship. A thousand singing children and youths and their supportive families had come from around the diocese to attend. Were they to be denied the buzz that a good service can grant? Bryce led the liturgy as best he could, but by the end was dolefully surveying the squandered youthful optimism.

But the consolation was the final hymn. Hannon played it without error, jaw set, breathing to the beat, eyes fixed on the music. Matthew sat beside him, drawing the stops, tapping the beat and counting between verses. He didn't watch to see if Geraint was conducting. They would drag the singers with them. For the last verse, while Hannon played the four-part harmony at great volume, Matthew doubled the melody on the fourth keyboard on the Tuba stop, a high-pressure trumpet that was the loudest rank. It cut through the cloud of tone and overtone like a foghorn and added a brassy pinnacle to the occasion.

The service ended. As Matthew played the voluntary the congregation left in a milling, chattery chaos. Hannon rushed down to see his friends, leaving Matthew alone in the loft, serenading the multitude whether they liked it or now. Given how it had inspired him at his first evensong at Exeter, Matthew played the Bach *Pièce d'Orgue*. Perhaps among the thousand children there would be a young potential organist, to whom the artistry and gravitas of the composition would speak. If no one else had those receptive ears, then the performance was for Hannon. By the time Matthew played the final chord the cathedral had got its echo back. He gathered his music and peered out at the emptying cathedral.

Hannon was standing at the crossing with a striking woman with dark hair and youthful skin. She seemed young to be the mother of a young teenager, yet she moved with the assurance of experience and authority. She was pleased with her son, and they seemed to be reliving the elation of his playing in front of a thousand people.

Bryce was working his way around the stragglers, meeting and greeting. His posture revealed his gloomy anger. If this anger would take some form against Geraint, who had abused the preparation, timeliness and idealism of the whole congregation, all the better.

Then a graceful movement caught Matthew's eye. Also doing the rounds of the youths was Vanessa Johnson, the bishop's wife. Elegantly dressed, she switched her attention to Mr Quantock and his little team and helped them move chairs. He remembered her well from his schooldays. She used to come to evensong often, and she and Richard would exchange looks suggesting a secret understanding of the world. He hadn't seen her at evensong yet, which suggested that she had not yet developed any kind of understanding with Geraint.

Matthew went down to see her. 'Lady Vanessa.'

'Don't call me that,' she laughed. 'I was wondering when I'd see you.'

She wore an emerald-green suit, and her laugh-lines and the grey in her hair added to her aura of fun. They chatted and caught up.

'I'm sorry you didn't get Richard's job,' she said. 'Are you disappointed?'

'I'm getting over it. Do you know why they didn't pick me?'

'It made me so angry. We were hijacked by the dean. He did it so quickly.' Then she touched his arm conspiratorially. 'But you're here. That's half the battle, isn't it?'

'Not if I have to wait for Geraint to retire. That's a whole battle in itself.'

She rolled her eyes around the cathedral. 'It was always so effortless and harmonious with Richard. It's awful, how it happened.' Then she caught herself. 'It's not that I don't like Geraint. It's not really his fault that he was hired, or that he's in the wrong job.'

'I don't *not* like him either.'

'Yes, and we mustn't stand in the way of progress, must we? Though I did try my best for you, Matthew.' They looked into each other's eyes. 'He's not really one of us, is he?'

Matthew smiled back as best he could. Was she acknowledging that he was one of them, not just a loner trying to get in? After saying goodbye, he walked up the cloister towards his flat. Geraint was coming towards him, having stowed his cassock and surplice in the song school. Geraint called down the cloister as they approached each other.

'Matthew, have you had a chance to plan for the pseudo-bop?'
'The what?'
'Hasn't Bryce told you?'
'No.'
They reached each other and stopped.

'He phoned me a few days ago,' said Geraint. 'He wants a band for a youth event he's planning. It'll start the summer term with a bang. So we need to book a band.'

At the word 'band', Chloë Balducci appeared in Matthew's mind's eye.

Geraint continued: 'Bryce was thinking of hiring a consultant but I think doing this successfully could be a triumph for the music department. I don't know what to do. I might as well try booking a tennis match.' Geraint's eyes gleamed. 'But a young man like you would know the proper procedure. And Bryce did say it was your idea.'

Matthew had no idea how the world of bands worked – whether they had agents or managers, what fees they commanded, and what other conditions they might demand. But if he was given the chance he knew which band he would go straight to.

'It was my idea. I suggested blues evensong.'

Geraint swatted away the idea. 'As I've said, forget blues. This is actually going to happen. Bryce wants to do a Saturday evening event, a sort of Christian dance. Between us, it's nothing important. You just need to book a band.'

He could see Chloë playing blues in the nave. But would she be available?

'When is it?'
'April 14th.'
'But that's less than a month away. Will anyone be available?'
'People who are still available will be cheaper.'
'And what kind of band? Is it worship music, like at the family service?'

But he was thinking: if she's available, I'll book her band; surely Bryce would be impressed.

'This isn't a spiritual exercise for you,' Geraint said. 'Just book the first band you find. The quality and style are irrelevant. Just get it done, so Bryce can see the music department is operational.'

Matthew smiled inside. He could follow these instructions to the letter by booking her anyway, just not saying she was a blues player. Surely she could bend her style into whatever was needed. 'Are we operational?' he asked, so as to say something.

'Highly,' said Geraint with a smirk.

'What if Bryce doesn't like the band I book?'

'That's Bryce's fault. If he has a bad idea we can't turn it into a good idea.'

'Why don't you want me to do this carefully and get a good band?'

'Like who? Do you know someone?'

'I saw a blues band who were tremendous.'

'Why do you keep banging on about blues? Are you mad? Who in this city under the age of sixty has ever heard of blues? This isn't a young fogey event for you and your friends. They don't want to see some old josser wailing about pain. We need a Christian version of *Boom! Shake the Room*, but on a budget. And that's why I don't want you to do this carefully. You're too out of touch. It shouldn't be too sophisticated. I hate sophisticated pop. Just give them one jangly idea, get in and out and get paid.'

'Maybe blues is the wrong word. I've got a tape I could lend you.'

Geraint raised his voice: 'Why do you never take no for an answer? I'm your boss. I'm telling you what to do. So do it.'

Geraint composed himself for a few moments, and began to look as if he could talk without erupting in anger.

'Matthew, talking of bosses, ultimately you need to be your own boss. I don't want to have to micromanage you. So, book the first suitable band you find, or maybe the second if the first is really too naff. Anyway, I'll leave that to you. Au revoir.'

X

Matthew could see that Chloë's band would have to fit in with what the cathedral wanted. He had to be able to justify the choice professionally. He listened to her tape again, from start to finish. The rise and fall of its energy, no doubt carefully planned, sublimated his own feelings. He had hoped it would also leap out as a piece of youth-friendly popular culture that would prove Geraint wrong, but it was too distinctive and skilful an album to work within his boss's parameters. There was no disguising its bluesiness, and its subject matter was for people with an ear for songs of deeply lived experience. Matthew would have loved it as a teenager, but not everyone else would.

Everything that was good about it – the instruments working in counterpoint, the simple harmonic basis combined with myriad passing notes and chords, the melodic gift in the solos, the humanity of the voice combined with depth in the lyrics, the variety of tempi and key – all would wind Geraint up. Absolutely nothing about the music was bland. How could he ask her to change her style, ultimately to play blandly? Yet she needed to pass under Geraint's radar so he wouldn't guess that she was the old blues josser they had discussed. Could he ask her if she could adjust her style so it wasn't straight blues?

Why was he bothering with all these convolutions? Shouldn't he just ask her out after one of her gigs? Why was he trying to introduce her to the cathedral? But would she give him the time of day as a person? Was it not safer to meet her on a professional footing? These imponderables outlasted his day, but one became clear: art was rebellion. He saw that; she saw that; no wonder their work was at loggerheads with the world.

The credits-insert with her tape included a phone number for bookings, but in an attempt to see what other bands were available, or at least to see what wasn't available and therefore to justify booking her, Matthew searched through some of the city's record shops, both the big chain store in the centre and the three second-hand shops on Park Street and the Triangle. None had a section for Worship Music. What if there was a good local band right under his nose? How would he find it? He did find one promising second-hand record by an American Christian metal band called Isaiah 61. Perhaps he should spend the whole year's music budget on flying them in and see how Geraint and Bryce reacted.

If art was rebellion, the problem Matthew had with most popular music was that harmonically and melodically it didn't rebel enough. One of the choral scholars at college had ardently espoused the Sex Pistols as the acme of rebellion, and with him Matthew had listened to both sides of *Never Mind the Bollocks*. He laughed remembering the two of them, cassocks hanging nearby, analysing the music earnestly for the losses and gains of the twentieth century as their teachers had dinned into them.

The band's bluster certainly addressed big themes, but their melodies and harmonies were much less adventurous than the threatening atonality that classical music had offered up seventy years earlier. They couldn't deliver the free-floating chromatic progressions of Reger's chamber music that made it feel good to have multiple personalities, or the thematic concatenations of a potent Bach fugue. Let alone the tornado of jangling harmonic distortion underpinned by a bass-line that really was the seabed, in Messiaen's depiction of a shaft of holy birdsong so forceful that it parted the Red Sea. This was more powerful than any punk rock.

The films he avidly watched on Moviedrome were the

popular form that best represented the complexity of modern-day culture, not the pop music. And contemporary worship music reduced it all to absurd levels. How could someone stand up and sing religious truths over two or three dumb chords while Tallis, Gesualdo and Bach were looking over their shoulder?

Where did that leave blues? Why did he like Chloë's music, beyond her own allure? Was it that she played in a style that had grown up organically, complete in itself harmonically and with its own unique melodies? The pentatonic blues scale was a solution to the question of where to go with tonality in the twentieth century, as its melodies and combinations were fundamentally unlike what had gone before, yet it was grounded in eternal harmony. It perfectly reflected the joy or sadness of its lyrics. There was no question of the music either dumbing down the words, as in worship music, or not being up to the words, as in so much pop. He could tell how much vocal skill she needed to express the songs, let alone the percussive scratch of her fingerpicks on the metal guitar. Was he just thinking this because he found her attractive?

'Looking for *Bat out of Hell*, maybe?'

Matthew awoke to find himself standing by the bins of second-hand records in Side Tracked. A forty-something rock-fan dressed as if it was still the 1970s, and topped by well-conditioned if thinning locks, was looking at him with a doctoral expression.

'No. Do you have the Chloë Balducci Band?'

'She's certainly got a broad fanbase.'

'Do you have her tape or CD?'

'Yes, in the blues bin.'

Matthew eventually found it. 'Is she from here?' he asked disingenuously.

'Yeah, she comes in with the tapes herself. She hasn't been picked up by a label like the others.'

'Which others?'

The record-seller reeled off the names of local bands who were currently making it big nationally.

'She's off on her own, but if you like blues…'

'Yes, I'll buy it.'

Matthew was happy to buy a second copy, especially if the broad culture was ignoring her. He found himself feeling self-conscious:

'Do you have any worship music?'

The record-seller didn't blanch. He presumably dealt with every kind of customer.

'No, but we have a gospel section there.'

Gospel! Why hadn't he thought of this older Christian music? The few tatty but intriguing records must contain riches. Like blues, it had a cohesive aesthetic, and was absolutely not 'naff', to use Geraint's word. But was there a local gospel scene? The bands were all American.

Then it hit him: Chloë was musician enough to skip boundaries. He would ask her if she could play gospel music. The burden of working up new repertoire might be too much for her and her band, but it was worth asking. If she could do that, the event would surely succeed, and if she couldn't he would regretfully find another band.

Finally her gig came up. The Hogshead was an upper floor in what had once been a warehouse, the low ceiling of the wall-less expanse was held up by cast-iron pillars, and the club was ample for a dancefloor, tables, bar and band. Even with their weighty old amplifiers and the two guitars ready on their stands, the roomy stage seemed empty without the Hammond and Leslie. Matthew bought a pint of bitter and sat in the middle a few tables back, ready to absorb the performance of Chloë and her band. He felt relief as she loafed on to the stage, more relaxed than the first time he had seen her play. She started with the same stomp as last time, then played the slowly-shifting chords of a minor key slow blues, similar in mood to the one at the last gig. The simple harmonies gave gravitas, while the inventive bluesy melodies gave vitality. As she sang above it, she engaged the eyes of her audience, working her way round them:

Lord, tell me who's this me inside me, and what's it doin' in there?
Said Lord, who's this me and what's it doin' inside of me?
Gotta tell me Lord, 'cos this me's gonna take me away from you.

The chord progression reached its turnaround, and another twelve-bar phrase began. Matthew loved the spacious way the music developed, ostensibly based around only three chords yet filled with often surprising passing harmonies that formed above the walking bass-line.

When I meet you Lord, You'll show me who I am.
Lord it's gotta be You, who shows me who I am.
You'll put me face to face with me, in eternity.

Did her physicality embody the music's rich texture? The set of her face spoke of a quest for identity beyond her immediate reality, also attested by her embroidered western shirt, the dull polish of her Navajo silver and turquoise, the four-inch tooled-leather guitar strap and the cherry-red Fender that she alternated with her burnished steel acoustic. When her solo came she raised her eyes to an unseeable vanishing point. With ferocious confidence and nimble exactitude her metal fingerpicks tore the melody out of the guitar. None of the uncertainty of the last gig remained; she had resumed command of her mojo.

Musically, Matthew had certainly met his match. Melodies flowed out of her, and her poise suggested an inner world replete with peaks and abysses which might echo his own. She had the whole room entranced, from the biker types at the front to the tall hooded fan at the back with the bar staff. The hoodman wasn't writing anything, but had appeared after the music started, stood in the least visible spot for part of the gig, and vanished before it ended. But didn't his presence evince the power of blues?

Matthew had listened to and directed plenty of singing, and he noticed every nuance she added to the vocal line: melismas to embellish the main melody, bending the notes to enhance the effect of the chord changes below her, or using vibrato on extended notes. She thought in counterpoint. When her voice dropped into its rich lower range she added a frond of guitar above it. Assuming the songs were her own arrangements, he felt the pleasure she intended when one player's notes jostled their partner's, when the bass rose in thirds and sixths with the guitar, spinning the inner lines into passing chords. But he felt the absence of the Hammond, whose gap was still unfilled. Obviously, any band needed an organ.

After the set Chloë came to a table near the bar to sell tapes. As before, a few people bought them, fewer than her music deserved. Matthew was drawn towards her. She seemed much shorter than on-stage. He now had two copies of her tape, but nonetheless bought a third.

'What are your influences?' he asked as he paid.

She laughed. 'Life.'

She looked at him with recognition, but couldn't seem to place him.

'No, which blues musicians?' he asked

'They change every day.' She spoke politely, as if to a regular at her gigs. 'I'm in a Big Bill Broonzy mood today but it might be Memphis Slim or Alberta Hunter tomorrow. How about you?'

She looked expectant, as if he should come out with a list of blues names. He risked an answer she might not expect:

'Bach, Reger, Messiaen, Weckmann.'

She looked like she'd remembered their meeting. 'You're into classical ones. I like Scarlatti.'

'Scarlatti? Why?' This was unexpected. He loved Scarlatti too, but his music was psychologically complex and tormented in a way Bach's never approached. Her love of it revealed her character. But he lacked the confidence to put this into words so all he said was: 'He's somewhat off the beaten track.'

'So am I,' Chloë smiled, her staged innocence drawing attention to the depths beneath it. 'He was a manic depressive. I'm not, thank God, but it took him somewhere pretty wild.'

'Did you write the one about the me inside me?' he asked.

'Oh yeah. I write most of our stuff. Do you like it?'

'Yes,' he said.

'I like that one too,' she said. 'I wanted to call it *The Killer Inside Me* but my bandmates didn't get the reference.'

'I do.' He beamed in triumph, recalling an obscure Stacey Keach/Burt Kennedy post-western. 'I've seen the film.'

She shot him a sidelong glance. 'There's a book too. Do you listen to blues?'

'No. I will do, though.' He held up her tape. 'Do you play here often?'

'Yes. We all live in town, so here or there once or twice a month. But I've met you at one I think?'

'Yes. Outside the pub on King Street. I gave you a Turkish cigarette.'

'I remember.' She said it matter-of-factly. 'But that means you were at that awful gig.'

'It wasn't awful. It was exciting.'

'Hm. Do you have any more of those cigarettes?'

'They're all gone, I'm afraid.'

'Well, I have these.' She took out an American soft-pack of filterless Pall Malls and flicked it to edge out a couple of cigarettes. That seemed to dissipate her anger about the gig. She offered him his and lit them both. Her cigarettes were stronger and sweeter than his. Nicer.

'Did your Hammond organist ever turn up?'

'No. He's vanished; gone for good. No idea what I did to deserve that. Though I've impounded his organ.' She showed no awareness of her double entendre.

Matthew found himself blushing and his skin prickling. 'I'm one of the organists at the cathedral.'

'You said.'

Her tone suggested she didn't want elaboration, so he got

to the point: 'I need a band for an event at the cathedral.' He outlined the situation. 'I've seen you play and I love your music, but a blues band isn't quite right for this.'

He stalled, not knowing what to say next.

She was unperturbed. 'So you want a band to play worshipful music in a way that resonates with teenagers, without too much blues?'

She spoke as if she was reading from a script by Bryce.

'Yes, exactly.'

'Okay, that should be possible.'

'Do you play gospel music?'

'Yes, and I love it, but we can't make it sound like the 1950s.' She looked at him as if he, as an organist, hadn't realised that music had moved on from the 1650s. 'I'll drop by the cathedral and check it out. I might have a listen.'

'Well let me know if you do.'

'When are you doing some good music?

They arranged to meet after evensong on the following Thursday, one of the last normal services before Holy Week. If she arrived early and heard the choir, they would be singing *Like as the Hart Desireth the Waterbrooks* by Howells. If ever there was a piece of church music with a bluesy feel it was that: Howells used a pentatonic scale that was much the same as the blues scale, and the anthem forged beauty out of a sombre mood. He could then crown it with an impressive voluntary after the service, perhaps some Reger he could blare at the vaults.

He wanted to ask her out, not hire her for a gig. But while she was straightforward professionally, she didn't seem at all forthcoming romantically.

When the Thursday came, Matthew, on tenterhooks, waited in the cathedral for the choir to arrive. He wanted the performance to go well, but he assumed Geraint would be late and slack in his direction. Matthew was overreaching his rôle, but once the singers had arrived and Geraint had not appeared, he started the rehearsal. So far the choir had seen him humiliated, welcomed him at their party, and heard him play, but he had not got to know them well.

Once everyone was in their stalls he said, 'Let's start with everyone's names.'

As they said their names he tried to gauge them. The cathedral school, albeit fee-paying, was a day-school, and the choristers came from a broad selection of backgrounds. Matthew felt well-disposed towards the boys who had a West Country burr. There was a hint of this in his own accent, which he had always felt marked him out proudly as a scholar whose fees had been reduced.

He led them through the warm-ups and some of the responses. Then Geraint ambled into view. Matthew didn't wait to be shooed away, and went back to the organ loft. Hopefully he had instilled some extra focus into the singing, and indeed the rest of the rehearsal went well.

As Matthew played before the service he kept glancing into the mirror, and finally he saw Chloë. She bowed to the altar and sat in one of the stalls across from the organ. Nervous during the anthem, his playing felt stilted. The old terror of not staying in time with the choir returned. But he got through it. It was such a satisfying anthem to sing that the choir performed well and even Geraint couldn't make it listless. He peeked at the mirror and saw her listening closely. Hopefully she would appreciate this exhibition of artistry, and be able to comprehend the wall of sound engulfing her. How would she view the cathedral organist, who performed with his back to the congregation, when she was used to the shared experience of blues transforming an old warehouse into a juke joint?

After the service he played the Reger Fugue in D major, the same one he'd played to Hannon before his lesson. He didn't have to worry about following a conductor's beat or staying in time with the choir; it was much easier to play as a soloist than as an accompanist. He began the fugue, which started slowly and quietly. It was an intense piece, melding sumptuous harmony with growing intensity: it got louder and louder and faster and faster, until at the end it moved at twice the speed of the beginning, and then the final thundering bass theme came in at half speed, which had an effect like putting the handbrake on in a speeding car.

Performer, organ and cathedral combined into the Temple of Tone. Thunderous bass notes hurled themselves around the nave. The madness of Reger's infinite harmonic palette was held in check by the four-part counterpoint. Handfuls of chords spread the apocalypse. He lifted his hands from the keys as the final chord lived on for its seven-second reverberation. He looked in the mirror. She was sitting in her stall, her face combining reverence and disbelief.

He turned the organ off and went down to greet her. She stood in the middle of the crossing with the confident, assertive poise she maintained on stage.

'Hi Matthew. I wish I played the organ.'

She looked him straight in the eye when she spoke, and there was no hint of double entendre. Her eyes were deep brown, but this time he looked down into them rather than up to her on stage.

'Well if you want lessons…' he joked.

'Do you take beginners?'

'I don't think you're a beginner.'

Out of the corner of his eye he saw Geraint approaching. He found himself quailing. Was Geraint even real? Since their last meeting, all Matthew had seen of him was his reflection in the organ loft mirror, an entity that made distant gestures and could be heard addressing the choir. He was turning into Dr Paice from New College.

She hadn't taken note of Geraint and continued: 'Good singing, too. I liked the anthem.'

He found himself self conscious and mumbling as Geraint closed in. Why did the man have to interrupt them? He made himself look back at her face. 'I thought you might; it's quite bluesy.'

'I thought that too. Do you have a spare copy?'

'A recording?'

Geraint arrived and appraised Chloë. He looked as if he might lick his lips.

'Sheet music, if you have it,' she said.

'Matt,' said Geraint.

'Hello Geraint.' Matthew had to continue: 'This is Chloë Balducci. Her band might play at the youth event.'

'Available at short notice?' Geraint asked in what he seemed to think was an enticing way.

She had raised her hand but stepped back. He managed to shake it.

Geraint bowed. 'The pseudo-bop's a bit beyond what we normally do here.'

'The what?' Chloë managed to minimise her recoil.

Matthew felt himself blushing.

'Pseudo-bop. It'll be like a student bop, but minus the smuggled vodka. We're looking for someone to play some praise music. Just simple stuff that'll sound like the music they listen to. If your band's any good you'll be able to do it in your sleep.' Then Geraint smiled. 'Matt's my assistant. I had to stop him booking some old bluesman. If he asks you to be downbeat and howl away about pain, just ignore him.'

Matthew inwardly raged at the 'my assistant' and 'old bluesman'.

Her colour rose. 'Which bluesman did he want to book?'

'He can tell you,' said Geraint.

Matthew burned as their eyes swung to him. His mouth was drying up. His choice was either to lie to Chloë or inform Geraint he'd gone against his wishes.

'You,' he said to her.

'Me?' she answered. 'I'm not a man.'

'I know.' Was this going to be the end of any prospects with her? 'I don't know why Geraint thought you were an old man. I told him I'd seen a great blues band.'

Geraint stared at her. 'Do you play blues?'

She turned, met his stare with fire, but said nothing.

The intense silence was too much for Geraint: 'Does blues have an audience?'

'Who needs an audience? I just sing to people's arses as they play pool.'

Geraint tried to refocus. 'I just think three chords is a bit limited for teens.'

'Blues is about where you go between the chords.'

'There's a lot more than three chords in Chloë's music,' interjected Matthew. 'There's not just blues but jazz, and the passing notes make bits of it atonal. The blues scale seems to go anywhere.'

Chloë gave Matthew a peeved glance, as if boxing in her musical language took its essence away.

'Yes,' said Geraint almost under his breath. 'When Julia was five I'd get her to do black-note improvisations. Anything sounds good in the pentatonic scale.'

'Is Julia your daughter?' said Chloë. 'I'm sorry she was a better musician than me when she was five.'

Geraint stepped back. While he made remarks that caused offence, he seemed to retreat from their effect. 'That's not necessarily what I meant. Anyway, I just want to make sure the kids get something they understand.'

'Then tell Julia and the kids that it's lucky blues is the single biggest influence on popular music. Everything they listen to is influenced by it, and an old bluesman like me can play anything. In any case, it's going to be more like gospel.'

Geraint's demeanour changed. He began to melt away. He tried a smile. 'I'm sorry. I wish people were more receptive here. But I don't think it's right to force a well-intentioned, blithely ignorant Christian youth group to shoulder the dark story of the world's past as represented by blues. Let's just keep it light.'

'Light? I'll get them dancing. Blues is about wang-dang-doodle as much as pain.' Chloë took a breath but didn't say more.

Geraint was stopped by this, and a smile grew and then he chuckled. 'Frankly we should book you for evensong. I'm sorry I misunderstood. I didn't want an argument.'

Matthew sighed inwardly that his idea for blues evensong, first rejected, had now been assimilated as Geraint's own.

'Neither did I,' said Chloë evenly. 'Anyway, I was just telling Matthew how great I thought the anthem was. I'll listen to more Howells. I just asked Matthew for the score.'

'Why do you need the score? Can't you just serve it back up by ear?'

She looked away from Geraint and opted to say nothing.

A copy of the music was in the organ loft. If Matthew left them together while he went to fetch it, Geraint was probably more likely to go. She was under no obligation to engage him in conversation and he would find a long silence awkward.

'I'll get it for you.' He left.

He retrieved the browned score that hadn't left the organ loft since the 1950s. When he got back, Geraint was halfway across the nave. Matthew watched his boss cross the chancel and leave through the cloister door. Chloë also watched Geraint go.

'Is that what having a degree does to you?'

'I don't think he has a degree.' He handed her the score. 'He just went to music college, so he has a diploma.'

She raised her chin. 'Different levels of bull.' Then she held up the score. 'I won't lose this. I'll get it photocopied.'

'You can have it.'

'No, I'll give it back at the…' Her tone was drained, as if this wasn't the first time she had fought off adverse comments about her work. 'Why do you call it a pseudo-bop?'

'I don't. I think parties were called 'bops' when Geraint was a student. At my university they called them gaudies.'

'Gaudies? That's nicer.'

They stood in silence. How to get the conversation back on track? Matthew asked: 'And you're okay with me asking you to do gospel?'

'Yes.' Again, her tone was fatigued. 'A booking's a booking.'

'A booking's a victory,' he said. 'No one's booking me to give concerts.'

'This place has booked you.' Her voice regained some buoyancy. 'You're booked to play every day. No wonder. It was brilliant.'

'Did you like it?'

'God, I don't think I even said. It was gobsmacking. I was going to ask you if there was life and death in organ music, but I can see that there is. First the bluesy anthem and then the last trump or whatever that organ solo was.'

Matthew was silent. He'd wanted to play a special piece for her to establish himself as a fellow artist, assuming she might find his playing acceptable, but hadn't dreamed she might be so enthusiastic. His limbs tingled, partly with fear. If she liked him, she might move in closer than being a romantic projection. Where would that lead?

'Thank you,' he said. He had to keep talking: 'What if someone asks for your blues band for the same date?'

'Do you know much about the blues scene?'

'No.'

'I won't get double-booked. Blues isn't cool. Ask Geraint.'

'Isn't it?'

'We just don't have a big enough pack. Even successful local bands tend to just play to the same people over and over. Even the fabled Bristol Sound. My brother is the drummer in one. Their gigs are riots, but they always play to the same group. That's easy, comforting. And sure enough they got a record deal, though they were never able to come up with a second album. With blues you're on your own. Audiences don't want to confront the truth within blues. So I'm kind of stillborn from dead parents.'

Her macabre image entwined closely with his inner world. 'You should move into cathedral music.'

'I am.' She beamed around the cathedral. Her fatigue had washed into a charming spiciness. 'I'm glad to be playing Christian music.'

'Are you a Christian?' he asked.

'If I wasn't a Christian I'd be an axe murderer.' Then she twinkled, as if she was nothing but a sensible musician. 'So where will we set up?'

He was still thinking about her response. If she was a Christian, should he be one? Then he turned his attention to the practicalities. 'They'll put the stage at the crossing, here, and you'll face down the nave.'

'Cool. I've never sung in an acoustic like this. Is anyone around?'

He looked around. Geraint had definitely gone. The light was on in Mr Quantock's Gothic cubbyhole but he wasn't there. The choir and congregation had all vanished. 'No, no one.'

'Do you mind if I sing?'

'Go for it. What'll you sing?'

She smiled at him sidelong for a second. 'This is what Geraint expects blues to be.' She turned towards the west end and hummed a bluesy intro before singing:

The man he done got old.
He done run out of what he was put here to do.

Unamplified, her voice filled the nave and came back with the echo. Matthew had often found the best singers to be even more powerful than expected. She grew when she sang. Her singing thrilled him.

She grinned as she returned to her normal stature. 'Singing here's easy.'

'You never know, the dean may have ordered some pool tables. But I like the 'done got old'. Can you say that with anything, like, I done sung the anthem, or, I done my practice?'

'They do in Mississippi. But don't worry about me singing like some scratchy old 78. I'll do some old Mahalia Jackson, but it'll sound updated. The old records just have a piano mostly, but with a full band and a bit of swing it should have a bit of currency with the young'uns. Not that they're that much younger than us.'

Her using the word 'us' made him feel good. They talked on for a few minutes. Leaving aside her personal charm, as a musician she fulfilled his vision of what a church gig could be, but he had no idea how much her fee would be. Surely she and her band would be beyond their budget. He asked her how much her fee would be.

'It's a Saturday? Three hundred quid all in.'

He knew his budget was small, but her fee was even smaller. 'I'd planned for four-fifty. You can have all of it.'

'Okay,' she smiled. 'I'll send over a deal memo before you change your mind.'

She was a fellow traveller. In fact, she probably went beyond him. She'd obviously gone on journeys, real and mental, to outdo any of his German quests. She was like someone in one of the seventies' films he liked watching, and for a moment his life was like a film, the fantasies of communion through music becoming real, and the colour and lighting becoming more intense than reality.

What to do next? She was walking to the west doors. He followed happily. He didn't want her to leave, but knew she would be back because their agreement was like an elastic band connecting them. They said their goodbyes and she was gone. With her performing, the quality of the event was assured. That would strengthen his position. A step towards promotion and living in the house. But that wasn't why the stones of the cathedral were singing. He couldn't stop the vision swamping his mind: her and him living in musical bliss in Richard's house.

Two days later, Bryce called Matthew in for a meeting in his office and explained about the upcoming youth event. Matthew realised that while this event had already absorbed much of his own attention, Bryce hadn't yet mentioned it to him.

'It's to bring young people to Christ,' said Bryce. 'In the diocese we have a good track record of ministry to children. We have plenty of church schools, and parents often attend the midweek school services, even if they never come near us on Sundays. Most parishes have effective Sunday schools. But we lose young people in their teens, when they start to question the world. They come to assume that Christianity is at odds with both the scientific and cultural worlds.'

Bryce looked meaningfully at Matthew before continuing.

'The clergy have to make sure that children are given answers more sophisticated than: God is an old man sitting on a cloud; you float around Heaven with your pets when you die; and the universe was created in six days six thousand years ago. But that's my problem. Your problem is the cultural dynamic. They want to listen to the music of their time. Didn't we all? What they hear at church isn't exactly Nirvana. We need music that is worshipful, but it can't just be safe and bland in comparison to whatever they're listening to in the real world. And what greater drama is there than the Christian life?'

Bryce held up his hands as if his point was indisputable.

'Now, Matthew, you've gone to great lengths to tell me about your musical discernment. I want you to apply that to contemporary popular music and find me a properly Christian band that stacks up musically. Sorry to bring you on board so late, most of the arrangements were made ages ago. But when I spoke to Geraint about booking a band, he said you would be the person. If you can book one at this notice, then kudos to you.'

Bryce leant back and put his fingertips together, a genial pose and twinkle in his eyes belied by the combative silence.

Matthew played his card immediately. 'I've already done it.'

Bryce sat up.

'You've done it?'

'Yes. Geraint asked me to move forward and book a band, so I did.'

'Who are they? Are they good? Will they fit into what I've just said?'

'Yes. They're within budget too.'

This time it was Matthew who initiated a silence, in which Bryce swam for some moments until saying: 'Well, tell me about them.'

Matthew did so, and also outlined some of his aesthetic reasons for choosing them. Bryce listened carefully, but never lost his initial blanche of amazement.

'Matthew, you might actually turn out to be good at this.'

XI

Easter passed, with significant services and demanding music every day of Holy Week. Matching the events of the Passion with appropriate music, and performing sometimes in daylight, sometimes lit by a flood of candles, and sometimes in darkness, was one of the best parts of being a cathedral musician. Geraint and the choir managed to deliver solid and at times lovely performances. There followed a week of holiday before the new term started, during which Matthew rested and enjoyed exploring the city. He was musically satisfied, and he knew that he would see Chloë. The weather was improving and every tree seemed to be in blossom.

A week into the new term, she and her band arrived at four-thirty to set up for the pseudo-bop. Matthew recognised the sidemen and remembered their names – Baz, Thomas and Merv – but realised they would have no memory of him. He drew back with shyness, and an uneasy feeling of being much younger. But he forgot his nerves once Chloë and her gang started to wheel in their flight cases and amps with even-footed pragmatism. On a second trip they also rolled in the outsize case that belonged to the venerable Hammond organ.

'Have you got your organist for tonight?' asked Matthew.
'Yes, though he doesn't know it yet,' said Chloë.
What did she mean?

'Here's your score,' she continued, handing him his copy of *Like as the Hart*. 'Or should I say, your scores. Here are the charts for three of our songs.'

He couldn't quite believe her inference. 'Do you want me to play?'

'Yes. It's very simple. All you have to do is count.'

There didn't seem to be room for debate.

He helped them set up. Never having played in a band before, he took careful note of the positions of each instrument and amplifier. He felt a frisson of incompetence when Chloë pointed out that the Hammond didn't work on regular drawstops, but controlled its tone with sliding bars that varied the strength of particular harmonics.

'Or you can just use these black keys.' She pointed at the lowest octave on each of the two manuals. 'Push each one down to give you a ready-made preset sound.'

'Like pistons,' said Matthew, out of his depth.

He had only a few minutes to try out registrations while his bandmates – what a mad thought – fine-tuned their own sound. He immediately started experimenting with the spinning speakers in the Leslie cabinet – treble and bass units that rotated in opposite directions. It was great to watch them. All it took was the flick of a switch and they went from a slow twirl to a fast rotor-blade spin, and this generated an extraordinarily physical vibrato. The two rotors in the cabinet accelerated and decelerated at different speeds, so when you switched settings the treble and bass vibratos collided aurally with each other. If you flicked the switch at the right moment this became beautifully expressive. He could feel a weird recklessness overtaking him.

When they had fully checked their sound Chloë led them in a rehearsal of the three songs he would be playing. The first two were hymn-like gospel numbers. The paper chart wasn't like a musical score, but simply showed chords and numbers of bars. The chords included the augmentations such as sevenths, ninths or thirteenths, which was helpful, because he wouldn't find it easy to pick them out by ear. Everything was uneasy, his feet dangling idly, and no mirror to look at for cues. And he wasn't accustomed to being seen while he played, so sitting at this Hammond on a stage, even in the empty cathedral while they ran through the pieces, made him additionally self-conscious. He felt he had to do more than just fill in the chords, so he added passing notes and melodies, as in a psalm accompaniment, anything to make him feel that he looked as if he were doing something. Chloë sang these run-throughs with full-throated abandon, not holding back to save her voice. If it was a rehearsal technique to inspire her band, it worked. Her usual bandmates played brilliantly and Matthew knew he couldn't make stupid mistakes.

'Bit more Wellington?' said Baz, the guitarist.

Matthew located the spindly swell pedal. It offered his foot no resistance, unlike the two cathedral swell pedals that physically activated ropes and pulleys to open a hundred square feet of shutters on each of the swell boxes. The Hammond produced red-hot distortion. Then a tap of his foot, and a creamy, celestial shimmer swirled around him. A lovely sound to hold in reserve for quiet spots, to give a change from the power and volume of the guitars. Chloë signalled to run the song again. Was it because his Hammond playing was wayward? Matthew focused relentlessly on the beat. The placement of the amps and Leslie meant that much of the time he couldn't hear what he was playing in the mush of cymbals, which was strange since they were each making so much noise. But he had spent much of his career not being able to hear aspects of organ or choir properly, so he could make it work.

He watched the other musicians, particularly Thomas the young bassist and Merv the drummer, who were used to playing together and locked in to each other's beat. Reading the charts was easy; what needed thought were the musical embellishments to turn mere chords into an interesting texture. He had to remember the pentatonic scales in various keys. He ventured an extemporised run. Both Baz and Thomas turned and raised their eyebrows at him. Was this acknowledgment and appreciation? He was encouraged.

The third, most complex, chart was labelled *Like as the Hart*. Reality was transcending phantasie. He had influenced Chloë's musical direction. As he played he recognised familiar harmonies and a haunting, bluesy melody recalling the Howells anthem, but simplified into a repeated chord progression. The beginning was quiet, there was a more tempestuous middle section, and then it died into stillness.

'Good. There we are,' said Chloë, again not inviting any debate.

So that was it. What a musical director: challenging, trusting, leading by example. And he was playing in her band.

After the rehearsal he gave her the fee in cash that he had insisted that Derek withdraw before the event, then invited them out through the cloister for food. Bryce had organised a barbecue in the car park for the couple of hundred teenagers who were happily eating burgers and hotdogs. Matthew tried to steer the band to the front of the queue but they insisted on taking their turn for their free food. When they had got their burgers he sat next to Chloë at one of the folding tables. As they ate he asked her where she was from.

'Here. I grew up up the hill in Montpelier. What about you?'

'Dorset, but I lived here when I was a teenager. Where did you go to school?'

'Up another hill, in Cotham. What about you?'

'I went here, to the Cathedral School.'

'Here? A private school and all.'

'Yes,' he smiled, 'though I had a scholarship.'

'I thought Cotham was rather urban and tough until I travelled.' She laughed. 'I'm living in Clifton now, so I've gone up in the world.' She paused. 'So you still work where you went to school?'

'Yes, though I went away to college, then worked in Germany for the last three years.'

She smiled. 'So you have left home?'

'Yeah. I came back after my old teacher died in January. I wanted to take over from him as director of music, but the assistant job came up too and that's the one I got. It's nice being close to him.'

Though as he spoke he realised he didn't think of Richard much now.

'I can understand that.' She looked around. The solid masonry of the school was ahead of them, the south transept of the cathedral hung over their shoulders. 'I was in the choir at Christ Church Clifton when I was a kid. A bit happy-clappy at times, but happy days. I still go. Even rolling the gear in here fulfils a kind of fantasy. Being asked to play somewhere meaningful. Music being part of life.'

'So you have those fantasies too?'

'Maybe. Where did you go to college?'

'Oxford.'

'Crikey. What was that like?'

'It was okay,' he began, but there was no point in obfuscating. 'No. It was awful. What they did to me was one step away from child abuse. They took my boundless loyalty and ground it into my director of music's Aubusson carpet. It wasn't a university. It was a boarding school to create quick-thinking automatons with no depth or expression. Musically, that meant play the right notes or get spiritually broken. It's only luck that I've made it this far.'

'Yeah, you're steering clear of being embittered,' she laughed. 'So it's okay that I didn't go to college?'

'Of course. Maybe you had a lucky escape. Where did you learn the guitar?'

'I had a normal guitar teacher at school. But I watched a lot of people.'

'Like who?'

'As many of my heroes as I could find. They're not necessarily guitarists. Big Mama Thornton, Albert King, Freddie King, Jimmy McGriff. I caught up with the dead ones on vinyl. Professor Longhair, Mahalia Jackson, Nina Simone especially, because she's so smart. Some of them are dead, though I met Son Seals and a few others.'

'Have you been to America?'

'Oh yeah. I was like, if I want to learn the blues I should drive a tractor in Mississippi.'

'I want to drive a tractor. I want to find out about life.'

'Watch out, you might get more than you bargained for. Anyway, I went on my travels. That was my education. The irony being some of the blues players I went to in the name of authenticity had masters of music degrees from places like Berklee. I have this fantasy vision of my destiny. I want to hack my way into the tradition that I feel a part of. That's American blues. What about you? You probably don't use the word hero. Who taught you?'

Matthew told her about Walcha.

'He had to memorise everything he played. First his mother, and then his wife, played it to him, bar by bar, part by part. He put it together in his mind. No one else has done that. No one else knew the music that thoroughly. He could refer to everything that Bach wrote: all the cantatas, the passions, everything. It must be one of the great feats of the human memory.'

'So he was married?'

'Yes.'

'Then he must have been pretty engaged with at least part of the world. I know a woman's rôle in Germany fifty years ago would have been a bit limited, but I doubt she was just his servant. Did she play herself? I mean, above and beyond playing phrases for him?'

'I don't know.'

'That seems to be the lot of the best women.'

They ate without talking for a while. Afterwards Chloë took out her filterless Pall Malls. He couldn't hide his look of interest. She offered him one and they lit up.

'Where did you get that metal guitar?'

'In a pawnshop in Knoxville, Tennessee. Resonator guitars were big in the twenties. Before amplification, I guess.'

'Did you bring it tonight?'

'No. It's not really a gospel guitar.'

'Do you compose on it?'

'Changing the subject from Bach to Balducci,' she laughed. 'Yeah, and on the piano. But I've also got Cubase on my computer.'

'So you don't record directly on to wax cylinders?'

'No,' she laughed. 'But you're saying what everyone says: blues has to be authentic. But it also has to be original. People are seduced by authenticity. Like if they dredge up some old guy from Mississippi, then they'll think he has it. And you can't really argue with that. He would be authentic. But just because he's authentic doesn't mean he'll be really good. Because to be that you have to be original, and originality's a bit more hard to come by. That's what I try and add when I write. Or I play songs that are so unknown they might as well be original.'

Soon it was time for the gig. Matthew's three songs were in the middle of the set, so he watched from the side of the stage as the band started. Most of the earnest teenagers were young enough still to divide by gender. Boys stood along one side of the cathedral, girls along the other, a few brave minglers in between. Teachers stood at the back. The event wasn't open to the public, but posters had been up around the cathedral. Chloë's diehard fan in the UTK hoodie had made it in, and stood uncertainly at the west end, as if he didn't know he was welcome. Chloë gave a bluesy introduction that led into the gently swinging chords of a gospel tune, and sang:

> *I shall fall asleep one day,*
> *From this earth, I'll pass away.*
> *But I shall wake in glory,*
> *And sing redemption's story.*

Physically she wasn't big; could she really produce that tone? Her voice was redolent of mysteries outside his experience. Her voyages in America sparked his imagination: Biblical themes shot through with hot nights and hot blood.

When my weary eyes are closed,
And I've sunk to sweet repose,
Singing glory hallelujah,
Singing glory Lord!

The cathedral negated the tinniness that afflicted the sound of pub bands. Its space allowed the drumbeats and amplified instruments to grow with depth: Thomas's bass notes sauntered down the nave like flying cheeseburgers. The band tapped into the sad chord sequences that transcended the anguish and faith of slaves. The teenage audience had little if any connection to the world that created the music, yet surely it would touch them.

And above all sailed Chloë's guitar. She took about half of the solos and each was a fluently constructed expression of her melodic gift. Then it was time for Matthew to join them. He sloped over to the Hammond as invisibly as he could. The stage stood where the nave altar usually was, and a lighting bar with some coloured spots had been hung above it. He was both dazzled and barely able to see the keyboard. As before, all he could hear were drums and bass. He suppressed his panic and forced himself to follow the chart slowly and stick to the beat, which was usually slower than nerves made it feel. He managed to lock his playing into the band.

Was this audience, cathedral and band real? Was he actually there? He had somehow interjected himself into Chloë's life. During his three songs he used his vantage point on the stage, whenever he could look up from the music, to watch her hold court in the centre stage. She stood anchored by her mic-stand, but her body moved gently with the music. When Baz took his solos she stepped back and deflected the attention to him. She sang sometimes with her eyes closed, her expression somehow both relaxed and intense. He tried to enfold her singing in his chords, but not swamp her. As he inserted a melody above his chords she opened her eyes and looked straight at him. It was the most physical look he'd ever experienced. They were joined in space and music, and time stood still. Then she blinked and she was looking away again.

His trio of songs flew by, and he had to leave the stage. She introduced her final tune, an upbeat and apocalyptic stomp called *God Almighty's Gonna Cut You Down*, by saying if the end's coming you might as well dance. The teenagers laughed, and some even danced, if bashfully. Then it was over. Her hour must have passed. She strolled off the stage. A happy Bryce took the microphone for final announcements and farewells. The teenagers and the various adult chaperones milled towards the doors.

Matthew helped Chloë and her band members manhandle their gear. It took all their effort to heave the Hammond organ from stage to trolley. They then had to gather and coil cables, and fold away stands, until everything was ready for rolling out towards Merv's camper van, now with a trailer attached. The sidemen packed it all in, she paid them, and they drove off. Chloë was still there, in her light jacket and carrying her Strat's soft case and a colourfully woven satchel.

Could time stop, please? Did she have to go? An unstoppable force was going to drag her away from the cathedral. Booking her had brought her into his personal orbit, but now she was leaving and if he didn't do something she would never come back. They walked round the cathedral and on to College Green. The usual cider-drinking crusties looked on at the occasional remaining teenagers, some of the younger ones scurrying in front of the cathedral's floodlights and creating expressionist shadows on the masonry.

Smoking would keep her there for three or four minutes. He didn't always have cigarettes but he'd bought a pack of ten in anticipation. He offered her one and she accepted. He reached forward with a light. For an instant he saw her face warmed by the flame, as with the Turkish cigarette. Matthew was not used to intimate proximity, but he was connected through fire to her. He drank in her expression. The second stretched on, then the match went out. He inhaled. It wasn't as nice as the

Turkish ones, or hers, but it was nonetheless pleasurable to be inhabited by the smoke. He watched as she exhaled through her nose and mouth.

He should say something. 'I thought your version of *Like as the Hart* was lovely.' Lovely was an understatement. Powerful. Resonant. Deep. Those were better words but he wasn't confident to use them.

She asked, 'Did you improvise the melodies you added to the chords?'

'Yes,' he said.

She went silent. Improvisation was a contentious topic for her, but he wanted to find out more about this.

'Do you improvise your solos?' he asked.

She looked wary. 'No, I work them out in advance.'

'And you can remember them all?'

'I have to,' she said defensively.

He could see he had to speak carefully. 'Do you work the whole set out and memorise it?'

A snobby part of him, annoying even to himself, was testing her musicianship and memory.

'Yeah.' She didn't invite a response, but with that one word she'd passed whatever test his annoying side was trying on her.

He inhaled, grateful for the cigarette that gave him something to do.

'Do you find improvising easy?' she asked.

'Now it's easier.' It was the wrong moment to reveal that losing himself in complex improvisations had been one of the deepest satisfactions of his life for years.

'What do you do?' she asked, 'Jazz?'

'No, I improvise in classical styles.'

'Classical improv? I didn't know you could.'

'Well, I do.'

'And styles? Like, how many?'

He'd never counted. Again, it was the wrong moment to reel off North German pre-Bach Baroque, Bach, French classical,

German post-romantic, Modernist, even spoof avant-garde and the many other styles he could conjure up.

'Mostly I embellish hymn or chorale melodies. But I can also improvise in the style of Howells.'

'Like what we just did? Off the top of your head?'

'Yes.' He added hurriedly, 'It's not as good as the real thing though.'

She looked at him with both defeat and admiration as she smoked the last of her cigarette. She had looked at him from the stage with confidence because they were within her music; this was the underside of that look, as if to say: I guess you think my composition wasn't worth much if you can improvise like that.

'Improvisation's an illusion,' he said. 'It's taking ideas from someone else and bolting them together in a way that's different enough to sound like a different piece, but not different enough to be original. It's a new version of something done by someone else.'

'Then why can't I do it?'

'You can, because you can compose. The best improvisers are composers. You just need to…'

He trailed off. Was what he was saying true? Was pastiche not real?

'I just need to…?' Her look of panic turned to anger for a moment. 'Do you have perfect pitch?'

'No,' he said.

'Can you hear melodies in your head, and play them?'

'Now, yes.' He hadn't been able to make sense of that awful miasma of sound when he was at Oxford. 'Not always.'

'Then why can't I? I can hear them, but I can't play them. I can never find the notes.'

He could see Chloë thought he had a magical talent. But what he had wasn't talent. It had taken years, decades, slogging away. It had only clicked in his Bamberg years. It was a combination of accumulated practice time and spending the last three years in an environment where he wasn't overwhelmed by his insecurities.

As he thought this through he heard his mother, Fiala,

singing those Kodály melodies over and over, counting and clapping. He hadn't said a word about his mother's rôle. He grasped, for the first time and with forensic clarity, that she was the source of the skills that allowed him to improvise, and he had never yet recognised her contribution.

'It's not talent…'

He told her how Fiala had been taught using the Kodály method at school in Czecho. Kodály had been horrified by the poor aural skills of most professional musicians, and his method was based on singing simple melodies to infants, marching and repeating rhythms and developing the inner ear before starting to play an instrument. And so, Fiala had marched her son around, singing and clapping, over and over again. This was from when he was only a day old, she later told him. Music was part of learning to walk, speak, eat and sleep. He now discerned he had been Fiala's project, and whatever he had achieved had been based on what she had so painstakingly drawn out of him. Without the skills she had given him he would have never got beyond musical frustration.

'It's like what you were saying about Walcha,' she said. 'Another woman behind it all.'

'I know. Melody by melody, part by part. We had our own mother-son version of speaking, laughing, singing and dancing. I only realised that a minute ago.'

'My mum is a secretary and never did anything like what you've said. But I can't bring myself to blame her.'

Oh my mother, he cried inside, Mum, why have I been motherless for so long, where are you? She'd insisted on his boarding at Moultrie because she wanted her son to be well educated, but sending him off aged nine had broken the connection between them. She must have felt that brutally.

'Show me,' she said.

'Show you what?'

'How you improvise.'

Reality was becoming ever more unreal. Chloë, the woman of his inner world, the Other of Others, was asking him to give her a private concert. He unlocked the wicket gate with the outsize hand-cast key that outweighed all his others. He could feel her reacting to the key's presence. It was an object that signified the dignity of the cathedral in the same way the leather and steel and rosewood of her instruments dignified the notes she played. He led them into the now empty nave. She walked purposefully towards the organ. He opened the wardrobe-like door and stood aside. She left her guitar inside the door and went up. He followed, turning the lights on, and she stood beside him at the keyboards.

'So Howells was using a pentatonic scale, and basic harmonies in a minor key, chords one, three, which is the relative major, four and five. So here's a slow pentatonic melody, and I'll only use those chords to harmonise it.'

He did.

'Now here's the illusion. I want to build up, but I don't really know how to do that in the spur of the moment, so I'm just going to repeat the same general idea, but with more stops, thicker chords, though they're basically the same, and an octave up, and I'm going to end on chord four. So the old recipe will sound new.'

He did.

'And now for the middle. Howells liked an arch shape, with the loud bit in the middle. So I'm just going to waffle loudly using that melody and those chords, and I'm going to modulate to the dominant which will make it seem like I've got some direction, but as soon as I get there I'll tail off and get quieter. Every line of chords I use is something I've worked out in advance before. When I was learning I filled notebooks with them. I use them on a daily basis. I'm not creating anything.'

He made the most of the many ranks of pipework and used the brash Tuba to give some blasts of triumph. He finished the piece with a diminuendo, down to nothing. He was downplaying the techniques he was using to set the dark cathedral afire with sound. He turned to her. She looked ravished. Whereas every woman he had managed to get close to had ultimately looked at him in disappointment, she looked as if in that moment he was what she wanted. No one had looked at him like that.

'Why am I cut off at the root?' she asked. 'I can see and feel everything you did, and I can hear and understand it, but why can't I express it, and why can you? All my life I've met people with lots of talent and they make me want to smash everything in sight. I could pull every pipe out of this organ and hurl them into the darkness. Like the first gig you came to. It was a disaster, and then I talk to you afterwards and you basically tell me all the things I got wrong and how I should have fixed them. In the kitchen there they have this enormous walk-in fridge and I just wanted to lock myself in there and slit my wrists in the milk buckets. Why did God give me so much vision if he gave me no talent? Why do I find it so difficult?'

She stared out into the diffused orange gulf of the choir, from which the statues of the altar screen peered but offered no answer. Whatever words Matthew now chose could not be commensurate with what she had expressed.

'Because it *is* difficult,' he said.

She sighed into the darkness. It was as if their warmly illuminated organ loft with its polished wood and ivory floated in outer space. She turned back to him. 'Well thank you Matthew, that was really kind of you to book us. It was a good gig. And then you did the encore.'

Was she going to leave his orbit? They left the organ loft. He should ask her out.

'Thank you for playing,' he said, not sure of what to say. 'You were super.'

'I didn't play,' she said.

'Yes you did; you just gave a concert.'

'Oh, I'd forgotten. Well, no disasters this time.' They'd reached the north-west porch for the second time. 'I'd better flake. I have your number. I might ask you for a lesson.'

At the cathedral door he wanted to kiss her on the cheek, but bottled and instead reached forward with his hand. She was surprised, but she shook it warmly. Then, unplanned, he raised her hand and kissed it. For an instant their eyes met.

'You could become a fan,' she said.

'You've got masses of fans.'

'Oh really? People with too much time on their hands?'

She spoke flirtatiously for the first time. Maybe something would happen?

'I'm not your only fan,' he joked. 'There's at least one other person who's come to the three gigs I have.'

'Maybe an outpatient at the mental hospital?'

He wasn't imagining it. She was flirting. Not much. She held herself firmly in reserve. But she was definitely flirting. He found himself edging forward, a fraction of a fraction of an infinitesimally small distance, but he felt welcomed towards her.

'No,' he said. 'He looks like he might have a job. Drives a forklift truck maybe? You've probably seen him at the back. He's the tall guy in the UTK hoodie. '

She blanched. Her eyes widened then her face froze. Any hint of flirtation vanished: 'UTK?'

He'd said the wrong thing. Not only that, but he'd stepped into an obscure world where those initials had some terrible import. Was the trapdoor about to open? He stepped back.

'Yeah,' he said.

'Which were the three gigs you came to?'

'The one where your organist never turned up, then the Hogshead, then tonight.'

'He was there at the gig when I fucked up?'

Matthew wanted to erase the conversation and rewind to where she was starting to flirt, but he forced himself to think back. 'No, I didn't see him there, but he was there the night before when you loaded in. He was eyeing up your Hammond player.'

Her mouth opened in what looked like horror. 'He was eyeing up my Hammond player?'

'Yeah.' He'd walked into a minefield.

'How so?' she demanded. This was a steely inner her that

wouldn't be revealed in a normal conversation or on a date. She wasn't looking at him but was searching as if in her mind's eye.

'I'm trying to remember.' That wasn't true. He could see it clearly in his memory. He should just tell her. 'He was standing behind the burger shack watching. I noticed him because he stepped out when the Hammond player…what's his name?'

'Pete.'

'He came out when Pete raised his arm at you, wanting more money. And then when Pete refused to hug you and wandered off, I think he might have followed him. In any case, he'd vanished.'

'Vanished?'

'Yeah. But he'd kind of locked on to Pete.' An implication was dawning on Matthew. 'Do you think he followed him away?'

She stared through him. If her features were motionless, cogitations were whirring within.

'And you saw him here tonight?' she asked.

'Yeah, he was at the back at the start.' He paused. What he was going to ask was a rhetorical question and therefore seemed stupid, but he had to ask it: 'Do you know him?'

She swallowed. 'Can you come with me?'

'Where to?'

'We're going to Pete's house.'

'Now? Where is it?'

'Not far. Just come.'

Pete must have inherited his Victorian terraced house from his parents, as it still appeared as if a previous generation lived there. In the sickly streetlight, the door and woodwork appeared to be painted in an unfashionable chocolate brown, and while the thick gloss still had depth, it had not been touched up for years, and was flaking round the edges. Even more unfashionably, the single-glazed, fragile-looking windows were hung with net curtains. All the windows were dark – a three-dimensional darkness because all the inner crinkle-fabric curtains were open.

A pot of half-dead geraniums stood on each side of the front door. Surely they pre-dated his ownership of the house. Pete's career as a musician, and his abrasiveness, were founded on a rent-free life.

Chloë stood in the cover of the doorposts as if gunshots might be fired through the front door and rapped it quickly with the back of her hand. No answer. She rapped again, then noticed the Bakelite bell handle beside her face. She turned it and a metallic drilling came from inside. No answer.

She smiled. 'You're not into house-breaking, are you?'

'If something's happened to him, maybe we should break in.'

'Why do you say that?' she said.

'You haven't explained, but I don't think we'd be here if you didn't think something might have happened to him.'

She pursed her lips. 'Hmm.'

She led him to the end of the road and then doubled back via an alleyway behind the house. Garages and sheds opened on to it. She was looking over the fences and lean-tos at the backs of the houses, gauging where his would be, when they came across a car covered by a tarpaulin.

'This is his stupid Ford Capri.'

As they approached it a sodium-bright security light came on. The wheels and mirror-polished hubcaps were all that was visible of the funky 70s' coupé under its fitted cover. It was parked on gravel blackened by a previous generation taking the ash out. No garage blocked the route into the garden. The picket gate was unlocked. Chloë slipped through and down the unkempt but intrinsically ordered garden to the back of the house, which, like the front, lay in darkness. She peered in through all the windows of the back extension and the back room, which was down a further little alley beside the extension. She came back.

'He's not home,' she said. 'It's spooky, but it looks normal.'

'Do you want to call the police? They could look. Or a locksmith?'

She looked up into the orange sky and leant against the car

and its tarpaulin. Then she looked down at what she was leaning on. Her face changed. She reached for it as if to raise its skirt, but then stepped away from it. The car was obviously an extension of Pete, and when viewed like that, it was as repellent. He could imagine what was beneath the cover. Presumably bright red bodywork and chrome lustrously polished. Tinted windows. Some priapic object dangling from the rear-view mirror. Anyone looking at the car, especially its proud owner, would see themselves reflected in its narcissistic sheen.

Then she forced a smile.

'This car was the only thing he loved.'

But she kept looking at it. What was she imagining?

'Someone's got a grim sense of humour,' she said. 'But Matthew, Pete's clearly not here. Let's walk back.'

'Okay.'

What was the connection between her, the tall man in the hood and the Hammond player? Where was Pete? Did she know, or have any inkling? He wanted to ask her, but her silence was impregnable. He didn't want to ask any question that moved him even further from the earlier moment of happy flirtation. There was least risk if he said nothing and followed her. But if he did that he was also tacitly ignoring whatever the situation was. It had been drastic enough to transform her mood and propel her across the city. If she was involved in some intrigue, how would it change his view of her? Despite these questions he could sense himself being drawn to her further.

They reached the city centre and stopped at the foot of Park Street. The dark cathedral was back to his left, across College Green. Her route to Clifton would presumably take her up Park Street.

'Well thank you Matthew, that was a great evening.' This was a thank you by rote; her face was clouded and her eyes downcast. 'Sorry for a bit of a wild goose chase to end with.'

'That's okay,' he said. 'Let me know if I can help.'

The elastic band that he had felt linking them was no longer present. Despite his having played in her band and wowed her with his improvisation just an hour or so earlier, they seemed to have reached a place of no connection.

'Okay. I'll see you around,' she said.

Surely these were the least romantically promising words she could utter. He tried not to reveal his disappointment. He was about to say 'bye when a question popped up.

'Chloë, what does UTK stand for?'

Her face turned harried for an instant, but then set as if she decided answering, not evading, the question was best. 'University of Tennessee at Knoxville.'

'You know him.' This was a statement, not a question.

'Well now…' She smiled, gave almost a bow, and added a little southern inflection to her accent: 'That would be telling.'

A break in her voice conveyed that she wasn't being flippant. It was a matter of life and death, even if she wasn't going to say any more. They said their goodbyes and went in separate directions. He felt that an inner part of him had been torn out and taken with her. He already longed to see her again.

XII

'Matthew, for a long time I've wanted to apologise for that afternoon. It was just a bit of fun. Nothing to take too seriously.'

Matthew awoke from the world of his visions and preoccupations. He was surprised how nice Geraint was being. The two of them were sitting in the little office adjoining the song school. As well as a desk that Geraint never used, it housed the kettle, instant coffee, teabags and a stash of Plymouth porcelain. He had just put the kettle on. They had met at Matthew's instigation to go through the following month's music list.

'What afternoon?' said Matthew.

'When we gave you the Fatness anthem.'

'The Fatness anthem?'

'Your first service.'

'Oh, that.' It seemed an eternity ago.

'Didn't you realise? Hadn't anyone done that to you before?'

'No. I'm not good at things like that.'

'Well, I'm sorry.'

They sat in silence for a moment, illuminated by the fresh light of the graveyard.

'Anyway,' Geraint said, 'let's move on.'

'Yes. How often do you want to repeat settings?'

'Not more than twice a term. Does that sound about right?

We can always fall back on plainsong. Is there anything you want to do?'

'Some Howells. But it's up to you.'

'Let's see how the Gloucester service goes tonight.' Geraint laughed uneasily as a hush fell between them. 'Do you know, I met him?'

'Who, Howells?'

'Yes. Johann Sebastian Howells. He visited Salisbury when I was a treble. He was wonderful.'

'Are you from the West Country too?'

'No, Anglesey. My father was a soldier. Royal Welch Fusiliers.'

'You're joking.'

'No, I'm serious.' Geraint made his sucking noise. 'He was a bit of a snob, you see. His ideal was to be able to carry a fifty-pound pack for forty miles to the door of the In and Out Club and then order the right vintage with his meal. He sent me to Salisbury Cathedral School, not realising it was a musical school. He thought it was monks and cold showers to prepare me for Sherborne. Obviously, I was already finding my way on the piano, but he was quite a sport when I was put into the choir. I wasn't exactly a disappointment, but I didn't live up to him and become a commando. When I met Howells, he seemed to pick up on this. He lost his own son, you know. He was a sad man. He never said anything, but he understood me, insofar as you can in a few moments. I never got that from my father.'

Matthew hadn't assumed he and Geraint would ever become friends, but he felt the early shoots of friendship and confidence. He needed friends.

'What did your mother do?' he asked.

'Nothing. I was sent off to school, he was away with his clan-like violence, she lived alone in the country. She had help keeping house. She did nothing. I've never understood that kind of set-up. The part I can understand is that she drank. And it didn't prepare me for marriage with someone who wanted to be – who was – equal. Actually, my family was a terrible example.'

It occurred to Matthew that the death of his own mother meant he had even less of a proper role model for a relationship than Geraint. He wanted to ask more, but would Geraint tell more?

'My mother was the brains in my family,' Matthew ventured.

'Maybe you can marry someone with brains.' Then Geraint blushed. It was an odd reaction but Matthew liked him even more.

The electric kettle reached the boil. Matthew made two cups of instant coffee using the Plymouth porcelain. He poured the milk from the mini-fridge. These diminutive comforts meant the office could become a homely place to work in if they spent more time there. When he passed the coffee, Geraint avoided his eyes.

'Matthew, there's something else I've been meaning to say. I don't feel completely happy about the way things have started between us. I think we've both got off on the wrong foot, and I think we both assume a lot of things about the other person. But from now on I see no reason why we shouldn't work productively together.'

Matthew looked into himself and again saw he wanted the seeds of friendship to grow. 'Yes. I feel the same way.'

'But anyway,' Geraint said, as if backing away from something. 'What other music would you like to do?'

'How about something straightforward like Dyson in C minor, so Hannon can accompany it. The sooner we get him playing in public, the better.'

Geraint pulled a face when he heard Hannon's name. 'Your star pupil.'

Matthew felt the atmosphere grow hostile but said nothing.

'Are you enjoying teaching him?' asked Geraint.

'Yes.'

'I don't know what you're teaching him, but I told him that in my opinion, music is about empathy. The composers wrote down their innermost, most important dreams for us, and we have to channel them. They didn't do that just to get involved in someone's practice timetable. Being able to play the notes is secondary.'

'It was Hannon who asked me for lessons,' said Matthew.

'I don't even know if I'm being paid. I just assumed it would be helpful.'

'Yes.'

Another pause.

Matthew tried to sip his coffee, but it was too hot.

Geraint stirred his repeatedly. 'There is one thing. Nick's been trotting over to my house once a week for his piano lesson. They can be quite fun. One of the few work-chores I look forward to. But last time he turned up…' He looked into his coffee without desire. '…he told me he wanted to give up the piano. I was surprised, because he's perfectly okay at it and it gets him out of double chemistry, and I asked him why. He said you'd told him if he learnt the organ with you, he'd have to give up the piano. He had made his choice. It was all rather earnest and painful. Matt, did you say that?'

Matthew caught the acrid smell of the instant coffee. 'Yes, but maybe I got a bit carried away.'

'I think you did. In more than one respect. We can't make a musician. A musician is born being able to do certain things. Teaching them isn't about giving them skills, like pedestrian people think. A musician brings that themselves. It's about drawing out their overall vision. I think Nick has been born able to do a reasonable amount. We can draw that out of him, but when we get to the limit of what he can do, we can't drag out any more. He just doesn't have the talent.'

Matthew thought: if that's the case, then Nick can work even harder. He said: 'People told me I never had any talent and look what I've managed to do.'

Geraint stared at him as if what Matthew had managed to do was wanting, then said, 'Of course, when he gets into the big wide world he'll meet someone who wants the same thing but doesn't have to work as hard, or who does work hard but makes twice as much progress. Ten times as much. And what does little Nick do then? It'll be a big disappointment for him to become an accountant then, after he was misled into thinking he could be a musician.'

Geraint drifted into another silence. He had spoken in a loaded tone, as if you could as well substitute the word 'Matthew' for 'Nick'. Was he saying that Matthew was now at the point where he should realise he had been misled into thinking he could be a musician?

The silence went on. Matthew grew tired of it and snapped: 'I just want to make sure he goes as far as he can as an organist.'

'What, all the way to 1750?' Geraint shot back. 'And I take it the modern piano isn't a worthy musical instrument?'

Matthew didn't try to answer. He put down his coffee cup. Otherwise he might spill it or crush the bone china.

'Well, let's just leave it at that.' Geraint was in control of himself once more. 'I'll go on teaching Nick the piano. I think it's good he's starting the organ. You're welcome to give him lessons. Just don't give him too much to learn at once. I don't want him to be spread too thin.'

Matthew felt rebuked, but also relieved the argument seemed to be over. 'I'm sorry Geraint, I had his best interests at heart.'

Geraint flinched. Within a second or two he had his face under control. Then his face contorted again. 'Do you think I don't have his best interests at heart?'

'No.'

A strained pause.

'Go on,' said Geraint. 'I think I deserve more than one syllable.'

'Look,' said Matthew, 'there's no need to go over this. I just think it's important Hannon learns to play Bach, from the outset, in a historically informed way. Of the two of us, I think I'm the one to do that.'

'You think I can't do that?'

Matthew leant forward, though inside he was leaning back. 'You seem to focus more on romantic repertoire.'

'Just romantic repertoire?'

'Well…'

'And how are you going to teach him historically informed Bach on that Edwardian organ?'

'There's the new one arriving,' said Matthew.

'Wouldn't it be a shame if the boy thinks that the profound legacy of western art music is notes-notes-notes?'

'There's more to me than notes-notes-notes.'

Geraint said nothing further for half a minute. When he spoke again it was quietly: 'What pisses me off, Matthew, is from the moment you arrived here you've been looking down your nose at me as if I'm some kind of philistine. Let me tell you, it's not *not* in Nick's best interests to study with me.'

Geraint put his cup down roughly, spilling coffee into the saucer.

'Also, it's not *not* in this piss-pot cathedral's interests to have me as the organist and master of the choristers.'

Matthew shrank backwards.

Geraint continued icily: 'Firstly, I actually care enough about Nick to have found out his first name, and I care enough about the cathedral to want people to come to the services. Secondly, I love all the same music you do, and I can play it better than you can. Thirdly, I can play all the music you can't play, and I can play it better than you could, if you could.'

Matthew looked at his coffee cup.

'In fact, Matt, you should ask yourself whether it's in Nick's best interests to study with you. Are you the man to show him how to interpret the inner worlds of great composers?'

Inwardly, Matthew trembled. 'I know you're better than me technically.'

'And technique is just empty virtuosity? It's not the result of refined judgement, natural geography of the keyboard, exquisite aesthetic mastery? You think it's just shallow finger work?'

'It depends.' Matthew looked at his knees, expecting further evisceration.

'Matthew, you little prick, I've bent over backwards welcoming you here, and all you've given me is disloyalty. You're an ingrate.'

Matthew didn't move. He kept silence.

'I'm not sure it's going to be right here for you in the long term. You can't subvert a perfectly good music department to fit your own narrow tastes.'

Matthew tried not to let his dismay register on his face. Was he being fired?

Geraint continued: 'There're a lot of cathedrals in this country. Fifty or so?'

'Forty-two Anglican ones.' Matthew found he could still talk.

'Trust you to know. But several of them are round here, within striking distance of your father. That is why you want to be back?'

'Yes, of course.' Matthew had a guilty flash. He had not yet contacted his father. Had he mentioned his desire to be close to him to Geraint? If not, Bryce must have told him.

'There are several close to him. Wells, Exeter, Salisbury, Chichester, Winchester…' Then with a gleam: 'Portsmouth.'

'You're suggesting I should apply for other jobs?'

'Look, Matt, no one wants to boot you out on to the street, but let me tell you why you're never going to be the director of music of this cathedral. We need to attract people. To do that we need to communicate, which involves sensing what other people need. And you'll never sense anything about anyone other than yourself.'

'What about the pseudo-bop?' Matthew faltered. 'That was a success, wasn't it?'

Geraint looked at Matthew with incredulity.

'Don't get impressed with yourself because you played a few chords. The band went down well because they weren't you.'

Then he held up his right hand and waved his fingers at Matthew.

'You know, I'm going to start doing some finger work. And then it's goodbye from me…' He turned his finger waving into a full wave. '…and goodbye from you.'

'Sorry, but I have a contract.' But Matthew knew cathedrals were notorious for firing organists on a whim.

'I have a contract too,' said Geraint. 'And I intend to remain here till I retire. I like a bit of spunk from an assistant but not so much that it'll give me an ulcer. You do as you wish, but know that there might not be a future for you here.'

Matthew got up noiselessly and left. From the cloister he dragged himself up to his flat.

He paced around his sitting room. He should never have been an organist, devoting himself to something that made him so vulnerable. But what else could he do? Aside from childish desires to be a dashing Uhlan, this had been his métier since the age of nine. But did that mean he could do nothing else? He was still young enough for a change. But a change to what? And if he should leave, where to? Return to Bamberg? Someone else would have his job by now. The prospect of life as a prep school music teacher opened before him. He thought of Moultrie. The music teacher there hadn't been spared from supervising games, changing rooms and showers. No, that was not the life. Then a wave of opposing thoughts hit him. How could he turn his back on music just when he was starting to hit his stride? What about *The Art of Fugue*? He might have neglected it recently, but he could restudy it.

The sun worked its way past the corner of the building. The even light made his eyelids heavy. Within minutes he was sitting on the sofa, a few more and he was lying. Then a female form, Lassitude, came for him. He woke up to flourishes of Chopin wafting up through the floor.

Yes, Geraint was right. What about the composers he had ignored? Schumann had thrown himself into the river. How would he ever know why?

Remembering evensong, he sat up with a shock. He hadn't overslept. He had two hours. Relieved, he lay back again and listened to the pianist rehearsing some phrases before playing a whole section mellifluously. He closed his eyes. Chloë appeared next to him. Was there not release in her embrace? No, because while his imagination could beguile him, the real Chloë had gone.

The damn piano tinkled away. Geraint was mocking him.

Matthew pulled himself up again, then got up and prepared himself for evensong. He remembered something Walcha had said. Romantic music was like someone in front of you eating bread and jam and then holding their mouth open to reveal the chewed mess. Walcha had been wrong. He couldn't pass those blinkers down to Hannon. What made Geraint's intrusion more painful was the beauty of the music. He played so well.

He had to repair his relationship with Geraint, otherwise he could lose job, flat and livelihood. He descended into the cloister. Swathes of music were tumbling in from the song school. Peeping in, he saw Geraint at the piano. He was lost in the music. Normally so tense, Geraint's features were relaxed, his head and upper body moving naturally with the music, his starchiness vanished. His eyes were closed, he was playing from memory; he was in his natural element. If he went on like this, he could erase Matthew and everything he had ever done.

Then Geraint slumped into the next phrase. His head flopped down then up and his eyes opened. Matthew embedded himself in the stonework. Carefully he peered round the monolithic jambs. Geraint was looking towards him but his bleary eyes weren't seeing anything. He looked sloshed.

Matthew retreated to his flat. Ninety minutes later the choir gathered in their stalls for the rehearsal and evensong like a dumb Greek chorus. Matthew waited in the organ loft, his eye on the mirror. Geraint strode to his podium. Gone were the jokes and asides, gone was the air of impenetrability, gone also was any discernible effect of alcohol. He stared at Matthew as a superior at his flunkey. Nothing was forgiven.

'We'll start with the hymn, just as a warm-up. First to "loo" in harmony, then verse two. Matthew, the opening chord.'

Matthew knew he was playing for his career. His hymnbook was already open at the right place. Since the first evensong he had compulsively prepared the music he needed to play long before each service. He promptly sounded the gathering note. Geraint brought the choir in. For the first time, Geraint controlled his beat. Gone were the symphony conductor's outsize movements. He was neat, precise and economical, commanding the choir rather than being dragged behind it. Matthew smudged one of the bars. In the mirror he saw Geraint glare at him while maintaining the beat, an admonishment that made his palms sweat.

After they had sung the hymn Geraint said to the choir: 'Tonight's psalms are favourites.' He scowled at the mirror, then back at the choir. 'Nick, listen with at least half an ear to what Mr Marcan does. A psalm's a good test of an organist.' His voice sounded more natural than ever before.

When the rehearsal ended the choir left to robe up and the congregants shuffled in. Matthew began a series of quiet pre-service pieces. As he played, he glanced in the mirror above the console. Vanessa walked in and sat down in the back row of stalls, an addition to the Greek chorus. Lit by the soft candles and shaded bulbs, her reflection hung above him in the mirror. He observed her kneel for more than two minutes. What was she praying about? Could she pray for him? Was she really a power in the establishment? If so, he must play for her.

Then the two lines of choristers curved into the quire and Matthew put his mind to the coming service.

'O Lord, open thou our lips.'

Frank raised his standard too, and cantored well. The responses were crisp and to the point, clearly enunciated and well-tuned. Geraint's hands were on top of the beat.

Matthew checked the piston settings of the organ to make sure all the stop combinations for Psalms 93 and 94 would be correct. Then they were upon him.

When the ungodly are green as the grass,
and when all the workers of wickedness do flourish:
then shall they be destroyed for ever;
but thou, Lord, art the most Highest for evermore.

Matthew used all the different sounds of the organ to express the words of the psalm, a grand sound for the first two verses, but soft stops for the third verse, which told the listener to put his faith in the Lord. He played the tenor line an octave up on the sweet Harmonic Flute, and felt pride in his hard-won ability to invert the harmony while following the words and keeping an eye on Geraint's beat. When the words turned dark he made the choir stalls shake gently with the 32-foot pedal pipes.

As if in competition, the choir responded to Geraint's every movement, and sustained a magnificent crescendo:

> *They smite down thy people, O Lord:*
> *and trouble thine heritage.*
> *They murder the widow and the stranger:*
> *and put the fatherless to death.*
> *And yet they say, Tush, the Lord shall not see:*
> *neither shall the God of Jacob regard it.*
> *Take heed, ye unwise among the people:*
> *O ye fools, when will ye understand?*

At the end of the psalm everyone fell into an electric hush. At Geraint's signal, the choir, usually now so ragged, sat down in formation. In that avid moment, Matthew felt satisfaction. If Geraint was getting serious, becoming a real cathedral organist rather than a hack mourning his wasted talent, then he was shifting towards him. By challenging him, Geraint was giving in to him, because it was better to work for a demanding superior than to fill in for a deficient boss. If Geraint produced psalms like that every night, the years up to the man's retirement would fly by. Matthew would be a happy underling.

After the first lesson, well read, came the *magnificat*. Geraint directed the choir to stand. Matthew watched him intently in the mirror, already in position, hands and feet above the notes, ready to play. Geraint deliberately gave a vague upward motion and then started beating the first bar to catch him out, but Matthew was with him.

The music began quietly with the boys on each side of the quire singing a different melody, then built inextricably as

Howells's eerie lines intertwined themselves above the sound spectrum from the organ. Matthew had rehearsed exactly what stops to use where, and while he was playing he was pressing thumb and toe pistons and changing manuals to alter the organ sound from moment to moment so it formed an aural tapestry.

When the canticles were over, Matthew had little left to do. The rest of the responses and anthem were unaccompanied. Just the hymn and then the voluntary. Geraint kept up to his newly found standards, and the choir rose to meet him, enjoying the new competitiveness between Geraint and Matthew. Even Frank's reediness was now well-timbred rather than annoying.

At the end of the service, Matthew replayed the Bach *contrapunctus* from his audition. As he worked through its augmentations and diminutions he saw in the mirror the choir file out, all except Hannon, who moments later stumped up the organ loft stairs to the console just in time to turn the first page. He perched on the end of the stool and turned pages for the next five minutes, a welcome oasis in such a conflicted day. The fugal texture built to its interwoven climax. The echo of the last chord died away for its seven seconds. The building returned to a dusk diffused by its thick glass.

Hannon was talking excitedly. 'That was really good. Better than last time.'

High from his performance, Matthew basked in the compliment. 'That's kind of you.' He should acknowledge openly rather than be mealy-mouthed: 'Yes, it went well. Thank you.'

As they followed the choir to the cloister, Matthew's heart sped and he felt himself trembling in anticipation of whatever Geraint would say.

'Matthew.'

But Geraint hadn't spoken. The woman's voice came from behind him. Matthew turned to see Vanessa bumbling down the steps from the transept. She arrived in a bundle of tweed, brooches, soft old skin and amused eyes.

'Matthew,' she went on breathlessly, 'that was marvellous.'

'Thank you,' smiled Matthew.

She looked beyond him. 'Geraint, that was tremendous.'

Matthew turned to find Geraint in the song school doorway. Now the focus of the service was past, he looked overwrought and sweat stood out on his brow.

Then the dean emerged from the vestry. They all met.

'I'm glad things are coming together,' said Bryce.

Matthew could see he was holding himself back. He had clearly enjoyed the service.

'I thought the first few weeks would be hesitant,' Bryce added, 'but that was quite assured. You're working well together.'

Vanessa cut in: 'What Bryce means is you seem like you've been playing together for years. The psalm was wonderful. Matthew, it must be the pent-up frustration of all that Lutheran harmony.'

'Yes.' Geraint loured at Matthew. 'Too much of it.'

Then Vanessa turned to the dean, and added: 'They make a brilliant team, don't they?'

'A team of donkeys, perhaps?' Geraint said quietly.

Vanessa didn't seem to hear, but Matthew was astonished. Did Geraint not realise she was the bishop's wife?

Bryce didn't seem to have heard either: 'I think if standards stay high, we could build a regular congregation at evensong.'

Geraint looked at Bryce with condescending incomprehension: why does this clergyman care about the mortals who attend evensong? What am I doing working among such lesser people? Geraint's eyes swung to Matthew and his expression lost none of its stab. He spoke quietly but fiercely:

'Verse three of the psalm. You started with the second-half chord by mistake. Why did you do that?'

Had he done that? Matthew couldn't answer.

'Then you tried to show off by inverting the tenor and alto. Didn't you notice you ended up with consecutive fifths? If you invert a fourth it becomes a fifth. Haven't you learnt that?'

'Steady on, Geraint,' said Bryce.

'Didn't you hear any of this?' asked Geraint.

Bryce and Vanessa looked at him in confusion.

He glared back. 'If you don't have ears, don't congratulate my assistant. It undermines the work of my department. In the *nunc* Matt played the second section on the wrong registration and the chords in bars 32 and 33 were out of time. Should I go on? An assistant should be able to get through a service without cocking up every piece.' He turned directly to Matthew. 'Every piece. Just because you're a lackey doesn't mean you should play like a lackey.'

Bryce looked as if he was formulating a response, but said nothing.

'Nonsense,' said Vanessa, but no one registered.

Matthew caught the whiff of alcohol. Not alcohol on the breath, but the laboratory-like smell a serious drinker gives off when accumulated alcohol is exuding from their pores. He looked at Geraint in panic. He was difficult enough to deal with. Was he now going to be turning up drunk? A tide of humanity surging by stopped him thinking further. Pressure had been building up behind them in the song school doorway. The choir, not wanting to interrupt the combat, were trapped inside. But sensing a moment of stasis they swept forward. Twenty boys and a dozen men funnelled past. Geraint tutted, held up his chin and allowed himself to be carried away by them.

Bryce still said nothing, but gave Matthew a pained if significant look, then walked slowly to his office. Vanessa touched Matthew's arm and spoke quietly:

'I'm not going to be told how to think by that little Welshman.'

XIII

Matthew found his limbs shaking. He couldn't do anything to stop the involuntary reaction. The argument repeatedly ran through his head, each time the dialogue rejigged with words he should have said to advance his points and rebuff Geraint's. The shakes passed, but his mind was still full of the conflict throughout the next day. Reality offered no respite in the brittle rehearsals led by Geraint. What would happen next? Why, in the midst of this, did he feel a hint of sympathy for Geraint?

All his emotions were confused. He had been alone for most of the time for most of his life, but for most of that he hadn't been lonely. Now he felt loneliness in the blank hours outside his cathedral timetable, pacing round his outsize flat or, if his energy had vanished, lying on his sofa or bed.

Chlo, Chlo, Chlo. God, he was quoting that letter. Did her 'see you around' mean 'I never want to see you again'?

His life had been derailed by that maniac in the hood. Who was he? And why was he covering for him? How could anyone write such a mad letter, with its three thousand two hundred and eighty-five drafts? The number appeared to him often in the day or night. What kind of lunatic would write so many drafts? But every time Matthew asked himself this question, a force within him gave him pause. Wasn't the answer uncomfortable? If he looked into himself, couldn't he see that in the wrong circumstances, he also could have written those thousands of drafts?

But the hoodman was still a weirdo.

Weirdo, weirdo, weirdo. Like primary school. Nezzer Ayres had called him a weirdo. That pillock from Temple Farm whose life was mapped out, and whose putative children and grandchildren's lives to the umpteenth generation were mapped out too. Seven hundred acres, confident, rich, in-bred, bird-netting for brains and filled with malice.

'Werdo'. That's how he'd pronounced it.

And now a werdo in a UTK shirt stood between him and Chloë. Why? And who was Chloë? Why was Matthew covering for her, and was she worth his confidence?

The next morning he walked to Pete's house. The brightness of the day dispelled the spookiness of the night-time trip, but he still felt queasy. The house was the same, with its scuffed chocolate-brown gloss and now fully dead geraniums. From the ashy back alley he could see the garden – and noticed that it was growing wild. He stared at the car under its cover. A voice told him that if he looked inside it he would find Pete.

Well, if Pete was inside the car, surely he could not be alive. Matthew shuddered. And if he wasn't alive, it was impossible that he could have re-fitted the tarpaulin without the agency of another person. Who was the other person and what had they done? Did it have to be the obvious?

Matthew thrust aside each question only to find another question in its place. They got more dire and led to questions about murder. While he'd seen hundreds of murders on TV, he'd never considered what it actually took to murder someone: what happened when you allowed your ego to expunge another person. Looking at the car brought murder out of the notional and into the real. It must be an all too physically intimate process – the crushing of a windpipe or penetrating with a blade. Cutting a steak could be tiresome, what about human flesh? What would make another person take on that intensity of action? What kind of person would cut through all their lifelong and elaborate socialisation to force themselves into another person's life and then tear it from them?

Did Chloë know the answers to some of these questions? Was he, now, consciously deciding that he knew nothing? Was the reward for his purblindness going to be 'seeing her around'? What was she feeling? Was she a femme fatale or a woman in danger? By doing nothing, was he covering for her, or letting her off? Did she need support? Who was he to offer her support?

The sun shone down on the Victorian alley and answered nothing. He opted to know nothing, turned, and walked home.

One of Chloë's gigs was advertised for the following week, so he retrod his steps to the half-timbered pub. The place and its inhabitants were the same as before, but her two guitars weren't resting on their stands on the stage. The amps weren't the vintage models she favoured. The drumkit looked cheap. Sure enough, when the band took the stage it wasn't her group. Would she appear later? Matthew stuck it out for as long as he could, even after it was obvious she wouldn't be appearing. Without her, the three-chord music sounded ham-fisted. Blues must be a genre where the skill of the performer was transformative, leaving just a dull shell if the musician didn't have the ability to soften the blunt melodies with nuance and add the multiplicity of passing notes that brought sophistication to the harmony. When he got home he phoned her, but there was no answer.

Days passed. He called a couple of times again but still no answer. His trepidation grew. He was falling into a familiar pattern of love-sickness that he wanted to be able to mature away from, but couldn't overcome: the dreary passing of days as her call didn't come in; the creeping recognition that what he desired wasn't going to happen; the crippling confirmation of the fatalism he carried in his heart; surely it wouldn't work out because it would never have happened anyway. Did the patina of fatality make his emotions selfish?

Listlessness spread into his routine. Where should he go

now? Walk to the same dull park he'd seen a hundred times and pretend it signified how urban design happily influenced the society that in actual fact ignored it? But he went for his walks anyway, in the hope he might bump into her. He saw her in his mind's eye at every corner, but the real Chloë was nowhere to be seen. Go to a film, or even the film section of the library or bookshop to wallow in what is just a substitute for life? No wonder the masses ignore modern cinema, they have lives to lead. Ditto for classical music, and no surprise that hardly anyone turns up for evensong. What was life, and was it even a part of the physical world? The inner world was so much more powerful.

Had she done a runner on him, securing his silence by saying she would return? Or was she in trouble somewhere, next on Mr UTK's hitlist? Or had they eloped? Could he forget her and move on? His fantasy world was stuck to the inside of his skull. Could it be swilled away? The staff of the Nervenklinik Bamberg walked into his mind.

The Domchor had visited the hospital to sing to its patients, and were rewarded by a tour that included the kitchen and its new dishwasher, forty feet long and containing sections, proudly pointed out, that rinsed, lathered, scrubbed, sluiced and dried the crocks of hundreds of convalescents and staff in record time. The machine was powerful enough to batten down the wildnesses of the German romantic imagination. Did his imagination need to be scoured?

He washed his face in the bathroom. The large taps and trough-like sink recalled the orderly world of the Edwardian organist and his occasional bath. No upsets of the heart there. He sat on his mullioned window-seat built for a thousand years. He had mahogany furniture, a wardrobe lined in cedar, a Blüthner grand. None of it was his. Was any of it even real?

At the beginning of May, the date for Geraint's 10pm Reger concert arrived. The lay clerks took Geraint out for a pre-concert curry which, while displaying confidence, seemed to be doing things the wrong way round. Matthew went up to his flat to cook a dinner that was meagre in comparison, and returned at five to ten. The cathedral was dark except for golden pools around the quire candles and the bulb in the organ loft. The windows with their acre of glass glimmered orange with the nightlight of the city. Perfect for the *Sturm und Drang* of Max Reger's music. Perfect also for him to get a sense of Geraint's mettle, to see how high up Mount Parnassus the opera-buff could climb. Matthew sat in his favoured spot directly across from the organ, where he would experience its best sound.

Hannon entered and took seats in the front row with his mother. The audience was growing. A dozen or so emerged from the Lady Chapel after compline. Most of the lay clerks were there. In addition to recognisable organ-music types, there was a be-dreadlocked, patchouli oil element to the audience, perhaps gathered in from the crusties who drank cider on College Green. At ten, Geraint appeared at the crossing. With a jaunty turn he acknowledged the applause, which continued sporadically until he reappeared in the organ loft, silhouetted by the music lamp.

Very maestro. Though as Geraint played the programme from memory, Matthew couldn't *not* feel admiration. It grew through Reger's *Phantasie in D minor* from 1916, a colossal piece that ranged from *pianissimo* to *fortissimo* and was built out of waves of sound. Far from trite, Geraint brilliantly brought off the drama and turbulence of Reger's *furor contrapunctens*.

The nave was an upturned ship filled with an ocean of trembling air. Individual notes set off vibrations: here a large window would buzz, there a choir stall would shake. Another note made a bone in Matthew's arm quiver. The cathedral became the Temple of Tone.

Chloë had asked if there was life and death in organ music. There certainly was here. Reger was near death when he wrote it, and even if he didn't know when the end would come, he must have known his drinking, the two-hour steak feasts and week-long composing highs would bring it soon. And the Germany of

1916 was steeped in death, a thousand boys every day between Verdun and the Somme. Reger must have felt that. Geraint did too, but only until the fugue. He hurled himself into it too fast and lost its sombre and haunted mood.

Until then lost in enjoyment, Matthew was pulled out of the inner world of the music. Why couldn't the man feel the force of death in the eight slow crotchets of the angular subject, that day-to-day terror that becomes beautiful in art? Was Geraint all about live and let live? Was he running away from death? Had he not found the aesthetic value in dwelling on it? So Geraint and he were opposite poles, but did that mean they were centred on the same core?

Then the last chord – D minor at its grinding grandest resolving to the major. Before the echo had died, the forty or so in the audience stood up and clapped. Some even yelled and cheered as if it were an opera house. Bryce was on his feet, grinning, hammering his hands together. Geraint's previous behaviour was forgotten.

Why couldn't they see the virtuosic evasion of Geraint's playing, that his phenomenal technique led him to miss the point of the music? Could they not see what Matthew offered was deeper? Why were they always blinded by people like Geraint, who played too quickly and added complication when it wasn't there, to make themselves look more adroit?

Geraint was a musician because it was his easiest option. He could just do it really well. He didn't need to because of inner compulsion. He didn't strive. Facility just oozed out of his fingertips. On that level, Geraint was more of a musician than Matthew himself. But what was the point of that kind of musicianship? And it was double-edged. It was musical arrogance, and he agreed with what Richard had said about that. If Geraint's skill-soaked arrogance meant he wouldn't fulfil his potential, he was at a disadvantage. But the crowd still preferred him.

Geraint descended from the organ loft, where he was gathered up by the lay clerks and other audience-members. Matthew watched him take in their comments: 'I didn't realise people wrote music like that for the organ.' 'Can you play it on the piano?' 'God, if it had drums…' 'It's like the whole cathedral comes to life.'

Mr Quantock was already extinguishing the candles and seemed keen to get away. Hannon was taking his mother to look at some part of the interior.

Then a crusty asked Geraint: 'So you're like, the organist here? What do you do?'

'Not much.'

Everyone laughed.

'No, it's true,' said Geraint. 'There's a service most days, the odd gig like this, and I've got the rest of the time to myself. What a job.'

Everyone laughed. Matthew gritted his teeth.

Geraint continued: 'My predecessor wasn't like that; he took it all very seriously, but he's in the graveyard now so we can lighten up.'

Everyone laughed. Matthew's anger rose at the gratuitous jibe against Richard. How different it would be if he, Matthew, were the director of music. But it was all Geraint's, and even as the man was dissing it, his choir and even his dean were standing around congratulating him.

Geraint was beaming. He clocked Matthew and gave him a stare as if daring him to respond. 'I met Richard once. Nice enough. But I don't want to carry on sleeping in his bed. I rebel. If I'm not allowed to sell it all I suggest a bonfire in my garden – all his books – and we can put that box-of-bones harpsichord on top.'

They laughed. Matthew plunged away from them towards the cloister. He wanted to tear something to pieces. What could he do? He was too disturbed to go home; his flat would be like a cage. He needed to pace. Maybe he could go out into the garden of peace. Would a cigarette help him? At the other end of the cloister the light was on in the song school, no doubt left on by Geraint. He went in to turn it off. Geraint's Barbour hung on one of the music desks. It breathed insouciance. He kicked it, but it was like kicking air. The pockets gaped open and revealed all sorts of rubbish. Geraint's hefty keyring leered at him. No doubt it carried all the keys to Richard's house, where he spurned all the gifts Richard had left.

Natural justice would be them swapping jobs. What difference did it make to Geraint if he was conducting, playing or doing nothing? Geraint didn't care about Richard. He didn't want the house. He didn't need those keys. Matthew couldn't look away from them. If only he could just take them. He would happily swap his own for them. Or should he just go there, claim squatter's rights? He didn't even need the keys to get in. Did Geraint know about the unlocked scullery door?

He felt his heart-rate rise. Did Geraint know how treacherous those basement steps were, especially in the dark? Could Geraint be led down those stairs? Could Geraint be pitched down those stairs? He relived his own fall and how closely the octagonal handle had swum in his vision. Could Geraint fall all the way down them and smash his head into that unyielding brass?

If he took his keys, when Geraint reached his front door and found himself locked out, he might decide to try the basement door. If so, he might pitch forward and enfilade himself on that door to another world. He reached forward for the keys. But to take them was theft, let alone the crime his darker motives implied. He willed himself to take them. Loads of keys were attached to a cylindrical metal tube about the size of a bullet. Keys for the cathedral, the song school, the organ, car keys, lawn-mower keys maybe, to cut him down like a flower, and then the house keys which he recognised. And if the maestro didn't know about the unlocked way into his house, let him be locked out and catch a chill on his doorstep. He could go the way of Henry Purcell.

A burst of voices and laughter swept in from the end of the cloister. Matthew dropped the keys back into Geraint's coat pocket. Footsteps approached. He glanced around the song school. The light was still on, everything was as he had found it. He didn't want to be caught in there but there was no way out. He backed into the little adjoining office. He left the door behind him ajar. It always was, so he shouldn't shut it. He could stay out of sight in the shadows.

A couple of people entered the song school. Frank said: 'You're so boring, Geraint. You're almost as bad as Matthew. Just one drink. Everyone else wants to. We can't go without you.'

'Okay,' said Geraint decisively, and Matthew felt for him. He didn't wish anyone to have to parley with Frank. 'But just a mineral water. Is there somewhere en route to my house?'

Your house? thought Matthew.

'No,' said Frank with some triumph. 'So it's Ritzy's.'

'Okay, you gather everyone up. I'll meet you in the car park.'

'You're on.'

Frank skidded out of the song school and up the cloister. He joined the other voices and the rabble stomped into the carpark. Matthew listened as Geraint seemed to stand still, collecting himself in some way. It was just the two of them, the walls were immaterial, so was the visual world. It was calm and both of them were close. Did they both feel it? Then Geraint sighed.

'Ritzy's.'

He put on his jacket, which jangled with all the metal in it. He strode out, turning the light off and latching the door.

Matthew relaxed. His hands had been clenched. In the short time he had gripped them the keys had indented themselves into his palm, which smelt of metal. He emerged into the song school. The whole place was dark now, rather comforting. The air was perfumed. At what point in life did you start to wear aftershave?

He let himself out through the cloister and into the peace of the garden. The tentative warmth of the day had dissolved into a crisp evening; the breeze rustled the fresh leaves. He felt half-elated, half-jittered. The graves surrounded him: his forbears; little Orlick Strange; all the others. Was Richard alive in the sound of the choir now Geraint was leading it? If not, would he wake up to it if Matthew took over in the future? He lit a cigarette and moved through the graves to where the churchyard bordered the alleyway leading up from the old docks past the east end of the cathedral.

He reached the low wall topped with railings and stood against it as he smoked. He could almost see College Green. Maybe he would be able to see Geraint and the others go past the end of the alley. He climbed on to the wall and leant out as far as he could without impaling himself. He could just glimpse the green. At some point they must cross his field of view.

'Sir.'

The pure voice cut through the night. Matthew almost overbalanced into the alley. He managed to turn and look behind him. The stone cherubs looked on with their opaque eyes, but there was one cherub too many.

'Hannon, what are you doing here?'

'I'm not doing anything.'

Matthew tossed his half-smoked cigarette into the alley. 'Then why are you here?'

'I was in the cathedral.'

'But what are you doing here?'

'It's how I get in and out. Through the triforium window. That is what you're looking at?'

The triforium window? Had he climbed out? 'Why not use the door?'

'Mr Quantock's locked up already. This is our secret route.'

Matthew looked back to the cathedral. The lowest panel in the nearest large window had hinges and was slightly open. Using the wall and the railings, anyone moderately fit could clamber up to the window ledge and through into the south aisle of the cathedral.

'It's really cool,' Hannon continued. 'You should try. My mother's up there.'

'Your mother's up there?'

'Yes.'

'Now?'

'Yes.'

'Is she okay?'

'She'll be fine. Mum, it's okay, you can come out now.'

Hannon's mother emerged from the window. She was supple

and elegant, only about ten or twelve years older than Matthew, but with the fuller physical command that the bloom of parenthood conferred. She wore it well; other people might simply weigh more. In moments she was down on the grass without having caught or even ruffled her dark blue dress and light jacket.

Despite her being the trespasser, Matthew felt naughty, as if a prefect had descended. He recovered his composure and greeted her. 'I came out for some air and saw the window open, I'm glad it's you and not burglars. You must be Hannon's mother.'

She looked surprised. 'Yes, Jane Hannon, Nick's mum.'

There was enough light to show her pale eyes, milky skin and well-maintained black hair. Celtic colouring. She was in her late thirties. She wore the practical dress of a nurse, with a watch facing outwards from one of the pockets.

'I'm Matthew Marcan.'

'I know.' She nodded at her son. 'I've heard all about you.'

They talked, then Matthew asked Hannon if he had enjoyed the concert.

'Yeah, it was great.' The boy spoke automatically. He was over-tired after a full day of school and a programme of demanding music.

'Do you want to meet at lunch tomorrow?' Jane asked Matthew.

'Lunch?' Matthew felt himself bumbling. Was she asking him on a date? 'Maybe. Where?'

She considered him, and he grew more confused.

'At the canteen. Where else? Have you been for your free food yet?'

'No.'

'You're staff?' she asked. 'At the school?'

'No, not at the moment.'

'Look, take it from me: you're staff.'

'If you say so, and I'd love to try it. I haven't been there since I was at the school.'

'At the school?'

'I went there. As a pupil.'

Her eyes widened. Was there some pity in her look, as if he hadn't got far in life? 'So you won't need a tour,' she said, 'but I can give you the combinations for the gates. Those are new since you were last here.'

'Do they let parents know them?'

Again she looked at him quizzically. 'You don't understand, do you?'

'Understand what?'

'I work here, silly. Of course I know the combinations.'

'I didn't know. What do you do?'

'I'm the school nurse. Don't look so horrified. Have you heard the expression "due diligence"?'

'Is that a legal term?' Matthew was now prepared for the conversation to go in any possible direction.

'Yes. My husband uses it a lot, but when it came to it, I'm the one doing it.'

'I don't quite follow.'

'I needed a job,' she said, 'and working here, I get to see what Nick's school is like from the inside.'

'If this was a boarding school you could come and live with him.'

She pulled a face. 'If my husband had his way that's what I'd have to do. Anyway, we've got to get away. It's past his bedtime.'

'It's past my bedtime, too.'

'Well don't oversleep. I'll see you in the playground at one tomorrow. Is the cloister door open?'

'It should be.'

'That's good. Last time we had to climb over the railings.'

She flashed a smile, whether flirtatious or condescending he couldn't tell in his heightened nervousness. As they left he couldn't control a rising image of a family. Nick would be a lovely son, but he didn't imagine Jane as the materfamilias. This woman who climbed in and out of cathedral windows had clearly attained a level of self-direction beyond any of the Others. And wouldn't she find Matthew wanting, asked his innermost self? Seeing her in the bed of his mind's eye and imagining her expectations terrified him, but also gave him a moment of excitement. Then Geraint's spectre flooded over him. He'd wanted to send him on a journey towards the octagonal door handle. He felt jitters.

He smoked another cigarette as questions popped into his mind. He found himself imagining Geraint falling. Or perhaps he would have just walked down the stairs without falling. In any case, the thoughts were madness. He had put the keys back. Surely he should just go inside and upstairs.

He couldn't sleep but there was nothing to do in his flat other than go to bed. He woke with a start in the middle of the night, so he must have dropped off. What had happened to Geraint? Nothing, the keys were still in the man's pocket. But if Matthew had succumbed to temptation, and taken them? He imagined Geraint leaving Ritzy's, walking the long stretch beside the harbour outflow, and approaching his house. Then he would feel for his keys. A moment of panic. Then, knowing about the unlocked basement door, he would venture down those perilous stairs. And then… He remembered his own dizzying fall. But Geraint might have avoided descending them. He might never have known the basement door was unlocked. He might have a spare front-door key hidden somewhere. He might come back to the cathedral to look for his keys.

It was past three o'clock. Every fifteen minutes the cathedral clock chimed, and each time it brought with it the image of Geraint plummeting down those stairs. How badly would he hurt himself? Would he crack his skull? Would he die? And then Matthew felt Schadenfreude. Geraint had usurped him, humiliated him, stolen Richard's house and legacy. Now the house he didn't deserve would get its own back.

Except it was all the delusion of a weak man who had not taken the keys.

Matthew eventually fell back into a fitful sleep. He woke early and was up and dressed long before choir practice. The morning added a sheen of absurdity to the night's fantasies. In the privacy of his mind he felt like an idiot. He wished he hadn't seen the keys and set in motion absurd mental activity and a sleep-deprived night. Then it was eight o'clock. He listened for the sound of the piano. It was Geraint's turn to take the rehearsal. He heard no scales or arpeggios. For five minutes he sat paralysed. Had his deranged fantasies really knocked Geraint out? Then he decided to go and find out what had happened. Just as he stood up the piano started. He relaxed. So Geraint was okay. Everything had been imaginary.

The morning dragged. He spent a listless few hours until meeting Jane for lunch. His thoughts went round in circles. His return to Bristol from Germany had left him beached, but somehow he had to make the best of it. He was relieved when it was time to go and meet her and talk about mundane things as they walked to the canteen. She told him the combinations for the gate and the various locked doors, and pointed out the staffroom. The school maintained the same atmosphere that he remembered from when he was a pupil, even if details such as doors, paint, carpet squares and lino had been renewed; but now it seemed pinched. It had never had much space, so the canteen still doubled as the second gym and wooden climbing bars were folded against the walls. They chatted through their lunch. Matthew found Jane watching him as he ate his pineapple sponge with custard.

'So you believe in institutions?' she asked.

'In a way. Do you?'

'So has Nick told you he wants to be a cathedral organist?'

'Yes.'

'And what do you think?'

'I think it's great. If he wants to do it, he should do it.'

She laughed hollowly. 'I know. I want him to do what he wants, too. That's the problem.'

He looked down at his bowl. He had enjoyed his dessert, but could see she would not like to imagine her son as an adult eating in a school gym. They talked fitfully until they got up to return their trays to the racks. Matthew looked around him. Maybe she had a point. If you peeled away the elaborate music and Gothic architecture, it was a pretty basic world he lived in. It might be good to escape.

'Next Saturday there's a masterclass in Birmingham. Nick might have already told you. I know the person leading it and he's not a cathedral organist. He's a recitalist, he gets to travel the world. There are some advantages to playing the organ. It'll be good to go to it.'

'Should I take him?'

'I was thinking of going, too,' he said.

She laughed. 'A school outing? Well, let's do it.'

Ostensibly they discussed the logistics, but to Matthew it felt as if they were fencing. Was she trying to find out about him, for some more personal purpose? Could she be considering him? Should he consider her? While attractive, she was unnervingly direct and, as a mother, experienced in ways beyond his understanding.

She was looking at him expectantly. How long had he been lost in his vision for?

He had to say something. 'You're here too, Jane.'

She looked surprised. 'I don't understand.'

'I think over lunch you've been saying you don't want your son to lead the life I'm leading. But you're leading that life too, to some degree. We're both here, now, in the school, and we both ate the same lunch.'

After a moment her incomprehension melded into a girlish and charming smile: 'Yes, but I'll leave.'

'What, when Hannon leaves?'

'Of course. I'm not here to fulfil any ambition.'

'What is your ambition?'

She looked cornered, then recovered. 'Ambition is childish.'

XIV

'Why are you wearing a trench coat?' asked one boy.

'Why are you wearing driving gloves?' asked the other.

They were ten or eleven, only a year or two older than him, but they might have been adults speaking a foreign language. Why had his mother given him those outsize gloves and long coat to keep out the cold and grey? He had no idea. He looked down and eventually the boys stopped demanding answers.

Matthew had arrived at Moultrie, his prep school, only weeks before the service at Exeter. His first impression was a smell of baked beans and sausage rolls. This engendered dismay: he was in for a diet that even at nine he could recognise as juvenile. He'd always eaten what was put in front of him, including his vegetables. His first weeks were a jumble of attempts to comprehend the mini-adult conventions of boys from the wider – if ossified – world of the upper-middle class. Reeling and listless, he loved the physical surroundings of the Neoclassical hunting lodge and the remains of its park and gardens. Clumps of grass grew out of brickwork in the ha-ha; wasps nested in the rabbit holes. He was used to this side of the school. His first memories of childhood were strong and natural and close to the dewy plants and mucky earth, mowing down phalanxes of nettles with his stick and scuttling through gaps in the hedges.

Raised on the religion of the Big House, he fitted naturally into Moultrie's lofty rooms scented by continuously polished panelling. He could sense the loss of the original furnishings when he surveyed the lines of rickety desks and plastic chairs. He disdained other boys' needs to humanise what to him was already a gracious country house with beanbags and cork noticeboards for their family snaps. But everything he saw was through a sheen of tears. He was one of a hundred and twenty-six parentless children regimented, but abandoned, within. He cried for weeks. The tears never let up. Why had his parents sent him to boarding school?

He auditioned for the choir along with everyone else, and though he didn't understand what was asked of him and couldn't sing with any beauty, he could repeat all the notes, rhythms and intervals that the choirmaster played, and he was accepted. The morning of his first choir practice a matron roused him forty minutes before the other eight in his dormitory. She told him not to wake the others, who lay asleep in childish poses. Now empurposed to be a little adult himself, Matthew dressed in the light from the hallway. The choir didn't have to line up like the others and pass by matrons who inspected their hands, ears and teeth. They flitted down the blue-painted corridors of the Georgian house, now neon-lit and floored with synthetic carpet squares, to rehearse in what had once been the drawing room of the house. If three of them had stood on each other's shoulders they would not have reached the cornices.

The piano's tone might have mellowed over the generations, but it was the only ten-foot concert grand Matthew had ever seen. Their sleeping classmates could have what they talked about: cars, bikes, following their fathers to serve in the army, even bottles of port being laid down for future birthdays. The choir gathered him from his disoriented wanderings and gave him a justification. No one asked him about his coat and gloves again.

Games, as sports were called at Moultrie: why put a thin nervous ten-year-old into the back of a rugby scrum? He didn't know the other boys' first names but he knew how they smelt.

The showers had been communal, referred to as 'the wallow'. Four shower heads spat into a tiled dip with no stalls or divisions. Two boys shared each shower. Going through this the first time had been a shock, though he soon adapted to it. Mr Chomley, an ageing master with one leg shorter than the other, stood by the outsize taps every day in case of accident. After washing, every boy would have to get out and stand in front of him, arms out like a crucifix, and turn around in a circle, to show he was clean.

One afternoon Mr Chomley was nowhere to be seen. Mr Deverill, the lanky northern music master, brought Matthew and the rest of Third Game in early from cross-country. The boys lined up for their shower. Mr Deverill corrected the water temperature and sat on a bench in an empty corner of the changing room.

Matthew followed the slower boys towards the shower. The first rank got out and dutifully waddled dripping and naked over to Mr Deverill. They lined up, arms outstretched.

'What the hell are you all doing?'

'I'm coming through, sir,' ventured the first boy.

'Coming through? Is that what this is called?'

'Yes, sir. To show I'm clean.'

'Well, don't bother. Go and get dressed.'

The line of children rushed off.

After his shower, Matthew got dressed in his cords and checked shirt. When he had pulled his Guernsey jumper over his head, he went over to Mr Deverill.

'Now then, Marcan.'

'Sir, I want to be an organist.'

'What?' The young teacher looked doubtfully at him. 'I suppose you'll be wanting an organ scholarship, from a good school like this and all.'

'An organ scholarship?'

'I shouldn't have said that. To Oxford or Cambridge. Or Huddersfield, perhaps.'

Matthew remembered a classmate declaiming he would be

'going up' to somewhere called Christ Church, Oxford, which he called 'the House'.

'Should I go up to the house, sir?'

'Whose house is that?'

'Christ Church, Oxford, sir.'

'I don't think so, Marcan. That's a choral foundation. It's a cathedral. You wouldn't stand a chance.'

'Well where should I go?'

'Marcan, the people who apply for these things are pretty advanced.'

Matthew was tortuously learning a movement by Clementi. It seemed pretty advanced. 'Where were you, sir?'

'No one's asked me for a long time. I was the organ scholar of Trinity College, Cambridge. I had my FRCO even before I arrived. Very grand. Look how far it got me.'

'I could try Trinity?'

'You don't want to end up disappointed.'

'But if I do a grade a year I'll be at Grade Eight in six years.'

Mr Deverill snorted. 'That's not good enough.'

'How much practice do they do?'

'It's not just a question of practice, Marcan.'

'But how much do they do?'

'A few hours a day. Four, maybe.'

'Then I must work harder, sir.'

Matthew meant it ironically. They had recently discussed *Animal Farm* in English, but Mr Deverill didn't smile.

'And sir?'

'Yes, Matthew?'

'Why doesn't my teacher give me pieces by Bach?'

Mr Deverill looked interested for the first time. 'You're the one who was all starry-eyed at Exeter.'

'Yes.' said Matthew. 'What did the organ play afterwards?'

'That was the *Pièce d'Orgue,* by Bach. I haven't played it since Cambridge. Probably never will.'

'Why not?'

At that moment Mr Chomley bustled in.

'Why isn't anyone supervising them?' He swayed over to the controls of the showers. 'Right, you've been in there long enough. Come on, make room for the others. Come through.'

The next afternoon Mr Deverill lifted Matthew from games and drove him in his shabby Datsun to the nearby village church. With easy, lazy musicianship, he improvised a piece building from the quietest stops and ended with everything the organ had, though this plenum was tinny and underwhelming.

Matthew noticed this. 'It doesn't sound like the one at Exeter.'

'It's a different kind of organ,' Mr Deverill said. 'There are only a few good organs, and half of those are in the wrong place or the wrong building. If this one wasn't stuck behind an archway, it might sound a bit better.'

Matthew's long devotion to his musical vocation had borne fruit. The construction of the new organ for the Lady Chapel had been underway since shortly after Richard's death. While no one was anticipating Richard's fatal heart attack, Rüdiger, the organ builder, and Richard's sister and executor, Agnes, both knew what would be expected when the time came. The specification and all the detailed drawings necessary for building the instrument had been completed years before under Richard and Matthew's supervision. Agnes set Rüdiger and his team in motion with a phone call a fortnight after her brother's death, long before Richard's will reached probate.

So by the time Matthew had returned to Bristol in March, the instrument was taking shape. The woodworking team were creating the windchests, the most complex and expensive part of the instrument. They were each the size of a dining table or two, six inches deep and accordingly heavy, and peppered with hundreds of holes, into each of which sat a pipe. Each windchest contained hundreds of hand-made wooden moving parts that allowed air to flow into the pipes and make them sound. The pipes were arranged in ranks, each rank controlled by a drawstop knob. The rank, or stop, contained fifty-six pipes, one for each note of the keyboard, all of similar design. Each rank of pipes sat atop a slider, controlled by the movement of a drawstop, that turned it on or off. There were two-dozen stops, and each one had a type and shape of pipe that was slightly different, to produce a different sound. Each stop could be used separately or combined with any or all of the others, allowing a multitude of beautiful and characteristic sounds.

Some of the pipes were wooden, but the majority were metal. The metalworking team operated in the way their forebears had done for centuries, casting their own sheets of metal by pouring molten lead into a wooden container that they drew along a hollow table filled with perfectly levelled sand. They then cooled, cut and hammered these sheets into shape, soldering the resulting pipes with an antique iron heated on a Bunsen burner.

Matthew phoned Rüdiger once a week; from his tone the organ builder didn't especially appreciate the disturbance, but Matthew wanted to be part of the process. He was pleased therefore when the master organ builder invited him to come and see the progress thus far. Matthew duly took the train to Swindon, where the workshop was housed in a former engine shed. It was tall enough for the organ, and indeed much bigger instruments, to be built without coming close to contact with the glazed ceiling. The instrument stood like an open, upended coffin; its proportions and outer walls were clear, but its innards were as yet missing. It would be filled with pipes and the moving parts of the action, then when completed it would be disassembled and moved to the Lady Chapel.

In his sixties, a Rumanian Volksdeutsche in dusty clothes, Rüdiger had an unbathed smell of musk about him and a habit of reaching for his genitals like a child. Also as proud as a child, he pointed out all the details of his workmanship and mastery. As a fourteen-year-old apprentice he had helped wrap in straw the pipework of the Schnitger organ – which Bach himself had played – of the Jacobikirche in Hamburg. It was then hidden in a vault, where it survived the firestorms of the war. He had subsequently been recruited for the defence of an unimportant bridge. He left his Panzerfaust, a bazooka shaped like a Schalmei pipe, and managed to surrender to the British. He came to England as a prisoner of war and never left. With him, he brought the lush sound of the German Baroque as passed from peasant to peasant. For the umpteenth time he was unpacking that tradition, creating a music machine that would have belonged perfectly in a Transylvanian church three hundred years before, and which would now enshrine German musical philosophy within an English cathedral. There it would speak with clarity and opulence. There it would express Matthew's devotion.

XV

It was a blowy day on the cusp of summer; puddles from the night's rain hadn't yet dried, but the sun was lancing through. Matthew was out early, ready for the trip to Birmingham, pacing around the cathedral end of the deserted College Green. A mediaeval gateway with upper storeys and towers stood near the west end of the cathedral, between it and the city's central library, beyond which was the school car park. It had been part of the original abbey, but now stood by itself. Hannon had suggested they meet at what he called the Great Gate of Kiev. This was the only gate he could see. He felt self-conscious as he waited. Was he in the wrong place? If so, would Jane make some comment? Would she find him staring in the wrong direction, confirming her probable prejudices about him?

'On the wrong side of the tracks, Marcan?'

Hannon came up the rise from the car park. He was wearing street clothes, the first time Matthew had seen him out of school uniform.

'You didn't say what side you wanted to meet on.'

'Don't worry. I'll come out.' Hannon came through the gate. He moved with ease, no jerky movements nor bookish awkwardness. He'd had Jane as an example. However much he projected his own young self on to his pupil, Hannon was a different person, from a different background.

'So why do you call it the Great Gate of Kiev?'
'Come on, Marcan, you're the musician.'
Matthew shook his head.
'*Pictures at an Exhibition*. Don't you get it? I thought you were a kindred spirit.'
'I hope I am. Where's your mother?'
'In the car. Let's go.'

Hannon led them back through the gate and down the hill to where she was waiting in a Vauxhall Astra with the windows open.

'Hop in,' Jane shouted from inside.

Hannon got into the back and buckled himself in. Jane accelerated away even before Matthew was settled in the front. She had pulled back her black hair simply and wore subtle make-up. A hint of perfume. She wore a cashmere jumper and dark blue jeans. He looked back out of the window as the cathedral and its surroundings receded behind them. It felt exhilarating to be getting away from its intense world. A male life, in which Jane was exotic. Would she still be exotic if his life was less rarefied?

'You're miles away, Matthew,' she laughed.

'No, I'm right here,' he said. 'In the here and now. Same place as you.'

'Is this a day off for you?'

'It is now.'

'Are you dressed in cazh? Mufti, as it were?' She nodded at his suit jacket. 'You're not tempted by the running shoes and Rugby shirt look? That's what the other young teachers wear on their days off.'

'Why would I be tempted by that?'

'No, you wouldn't be, Matthew. You're an original. I'm genuinely fascinated. You're not at all like other young fogeys. There's much music, excellent voice, in this little organ.' She nodded at him to make clear she was alluding to him.

'That's poetic,' he responded. 'Do you always speak like that?'

'No. Do you get the reference?'

'No.'

'It's Shakespeare. Have you read any?'

'A bit at school.'

'See, you have missed out,' she said.

She was certainly attractive, and the sparring was exciting.

He said, with intentional absurdity, 'So you don't think you've missed out because you don't know Bach's organ music intimately?'

She blinked: 'No. Do you like trip hop? Ska? Local bands? How about Mother Samosa?'

From Shakespeare to trip hop, none of which he knew well. Was she making a point about his ignorance? She slid a tape into the car's player and an upbeat song came on, with Jamaican rhythms and subversive lyrics. 'Is this your thing?'

'Actually I like it.' He wasn't lying. 'The words are good; he's got a good voice; I even like the harmonic development. It's a lot better than a lot of the alternatives, so what's not to like?'

'My God, we're in agreement,' she said. 'Do you know why I like it?'

'Why?'

'Because these bands are the first things I've ever come across that I actually like and respect from this totally backward, provincial city full of yokels. For the first time I can feel proud to be from here. Now my friends in London talk about the bands from here. That's never happened before. Not changing the subject, but do organists eat breakfast?'

Nick piped up immediately: 'Mum, can we go to a Little Chef?'

Jane sighed. 'No Nick, Mr Marcan might want something a bit nicer.'

'No he won't,' said Nick, 'don't you sir?'

Matthew liked that kind of food but, caught between Jane and Nick, didn't know how to answer. The lad was persistent, and it was funny how he could go from a mature appreciation of musicology one moment to a childlike demand for motorway food the next. Finally Jane rolled her eyes and agreed.

They found one of the diners, neon-lit despite the sunshine, and enjoyed a cooked breakfast in one of the booths. Matthew also enjoyed the private irony that the baked beans, sausages and fried bread that Jane and Nick evidently enjoyed could easily have been served up in the school canteen.

A couple of hours later they walked into Birmingham's brand new halogen-lit concert hall, their feet sinking into the carpets, their voices bouncing just discernibly off the imported wood of the acoustic panelling. The organ took up much of one of the walls of the huge auditorium. Its case design incorporated a fad of the German builders: some of the prominent pipes were put in upside down above pipes the right way up. From a distance this made the pipes look longer than they were. The case therefore had a strident look, like the grille of an American truck.

'Matthew Marcan. I was hoping you might be here.'

Andy Comiskey, the leader of the masterclass, bounded over with hand outstretched and greeted them. He was about ten years older than Matthew but didn't seem it. He looked as if he worked out and wore, alongside a designer shirt and jeans, red-framed glasses. Would Jane approve?

'Hello Andy.' Matthew shook his hand. 'I didn't think you'd remember me.'

'Of course I did; I saw your name on the delegate list.'

Andy glanced at Jane and Hannon. Matthew introduced them.

'Hi Nick,' said Andy. 'I see you're on the list of players.'

Matthew added: 'And this is Nick's mother.'

'Jane, don't worry about the Mrs.' She reached forward and shook Andy's hand. 'Nick's been looking forward to this.'

'Great, good to meet you. What are you playing Nick?'

'The Bach C major fugue.'

'Fantastic. I haven't heard that for a while. Why did you pick it?'

'Because it's like a big crescendo; it's cool.'

Andy laughed and turned to Matthew: 'Like teacher, like pupil. What have you been doing? You're back from Bamberg? They didn't let you take over from Richard?'

'No. I was gutted at first but I'm over it now.'

Jane interjected: 'Did you apply for Richard's job and not get it?'

Under her quizzing stare Matthew felt unsure how much to admit.

'It's only a matter of time before Geraint wears out, then you can have his job,' said Andy. 'I'll never work in a cathedral again.'

Jane's eyes swung to Andy. 'Why not?'

'Eight years of torment.'

'Torment? Why? Where were you?'

'Coventry.'

'Does a new cathedral even have an organ?' she asked, putting stress on the word 'organ'.

Matthew tried to catch Jane's eye. More people were arriving and a jam was developing in the entrance to the concert hall. 'We should take our seats.'

'Yes,' said Andy. 'Nick, sit at the front. I'm looking forward to hearing you play.'

Matthew and Jane followed Hannon to the front row. Other students, parents and teachers also took their seats. At eleven o'clock sharp Andy strode on to the stage and introduced the event.

Jane nudged him. 'So, Matthew, would you say Andy's a fashionista? Pretty trendy, eh?'

There was so much irony in her voice that Matthew didn't know how to answer.

'So who is he?' she continued.

'He was the organ scholar at King's, in Cambridge. He cut a bit of a swathe through the chapel because he was from a state school. He came and did a recital at New College, which was where I met him.'

'So he's better than you?' she whispered.

A dagger penetrated Matthew, but he offered an even-keeled response. 'It doesn't matter who's better; we're all links in the chain.'

Walcha's wholesome philosophy didn't stop him feeling jealous as Andy easily guided the six students through the masterclass. He gathered everyone who wanted to watch round the console. When Hannon's turn came he sat down confidently and selected stops including the 32-foot Contrabombarde. Andy chuckled.

'Let them have it, Nick. Give them the whole nine yards – why not?'

Hannon played through the piece, then Andy made comments about the articulation of the main theme.

'Nick, what's the time signature?'

'Four four.'

'No.'

Hannon looked again. 'Oh, two two. What's the difference?'

'It's two crotchets per beat, two beats per bar. With the bigger beats the music will flow more, like choral music. And really milk the suspensions, there are so many of them. Let's do this bit here; play from here.'

Hannon applied this and played lovely chords that resolved into each other. Matthew realised he should have told all this to Hannon.

'Good,' said Andy. 'Really go for it with this. It's so expressive, and people are going to want to hear the beautiful scrunches. Try it again.'

Hannon did so, and the result was more expressive.

Matthew compared Andy's teaching with how he had been taught. Andy was upbeat, and intent on vivifying the music, making it dramatic, accentuating the rhythms and clashes. That was good and right: '*plus vif,*' to quote Messiaen. As the class went on he backed himself up with scholarly, textual and historical arguments and certainly knew his stuff, but he didn't analyse the counterpoint or expect the pupils to know it deeply. Matthew felt lucky to have experienced Walcha's approach, but recognised that his playing missed the verve that Andy drew out of Bach's scores.

The day passed quickly. After the class, lecture and a short recital by Andy it was tea, cakes and éclairs – *de rigueur* for any gathering of organists. Andy circulated to them.

'Your playing's really good, Nick,' said Andy. 'Do you want to do music at university?'

'Am I good enough?'

'If you think you are, you are.'

Matthew heard a voice in his inner ear retort: 'and if you think you're not, you're not.'

'But you don't have to do music,' Andy went on. 'The singers and instrumentalists I did concerts with all seemed to be reading astrophysics and theology. I felt very conventional doing music. I would've done something else if I'd been any good at anything.'

'Do you teach?' Jane butted in.

'Yes, in between travel,' said Andy.

'Travel?'

'Yeah. Believe it or not people ask me to come and give concerts.'

'Where do you get to go?'

'Well, last year I went to Germany, France, Iceland, America, Singapore and Australia.'

'No?' Jane's eyes widened, as did her insight into the life of an organist. 'Was that a normal year?'

'Yes. Sometimes there's more.'

'They pay him, too,' said Matthew, trying to sound both tongue-in-cheek and serious. This might change Jane's perception of the organ for the better.

'And are you the world's most successful organist,' she said with full charm, 'or do other organists get to travel?'

'There's plenty of work. What you need to understand is that everywhere you go, there's a community of people who like the organ. You can find this niche anywhere. You could quite easily get a job overseas, because people value the way English organists are trained.'

'Then we should come up for a lesson with you.' Her demeanour was as positive as if she were planning a dinner party for her best friends. 'Where are you based?'

'Windsor, but I usually teach in London.'

'Well that's easy.' All difficulties were banished by her tone. 'I've got a friend in Windsor so we can combine the trip. And we can see the castle, Nick.'

Matthew said nothing. He was aware of Hannon watching the exchange like tennis; the boy wanted to go but didn't want to be disloyal to his main teacher. But it would be good for him to have the odd lesson with Andy. Matthew smiled at him:

'Sounds like a good trip for you. You should do this.'

Yet that dagger still stabbed. Was Andy the better musician? Would Matthew always be the terminal second?

Andy glanced at him and then winked at Jane: 'You can always pop him on a train and see how far he gets.' Andy gave Hannon his card. 'Ring me whenever you like.'

Jane smiled through the return journey. About half-way back she suggested stopping for dinner.

'You've made the whole thing possible,' she said. 'This is my treat.'

'Could we go back to where we had breakfast?' asked Hannon.

'No. Mr Marcan might want something better. And you'll get fat if you eat like that every meal.'

They turned off the motorway on to the A road, and threaded south through pretty Cotswold villages and towns. These were noticeably more prosperous than where they had come from, or where they were going. Jane's instincts led them to a Georgian coaching inn. Mouldings, woodwork, stone flags, a distressedly original bar. The food and beer looked excellent but more expensive than anywhere Matthew would go on his own. Hannon sat down at one of the tables and Matthew accompanied Jane to the bar.

'Don't even think of paying,' she said. 'This is on my husband.'

Matthew perched on a barstool while she bought the drinks. He caught his reflection in the tall, calcined mirror behind the bar. He saw himself as she might see him, a man with an undeveloped chest and thin limbs, lacking seniority and presence. His jacket didn't fit neatly. Because of his round-shouldered posture, cavities formed beside the lapels. Yet he carried such mighty art within him. He stood up straight and the cavities disappeared. If he slouched forward they reappeared. He tried to maintain a good posture.

'Do you always call him Hannon?'

Jane was staring at him.

'I suppose I do. Would you rather I called him Nick?'

'Yes. You can't hold him down forever. He's a teenager now. Do you think it's a good thing for a teenager to do all this music?'

'Yes. The skills can help with other subjects.'

'Other subjects. I thought he could do a bit of piano, that's all. But he doesn't want to do piano any more.'

Matthew was silent. He shouldn't have given Hannon that ultimatum.

'Anyway,' continued Jane, 'he should carry on piano with Geraint. He can balance you out. And, as I like the idea of trips to Windsor, we'll hire Andy every now and then.'

The barman passed over the drinks and they took them to the table where Nick was waiting. They clinked glasses. She spoke over the rim of hers:

'I went to an eye-gougingly competitive girl's school, and it left me with this idea that you pass with Quadruple As or whatever, and that means you've climbed a plateau and are set for life. But having children taught me the opposite. We're all on a journey. Not too long ago Nick was crawling among the dust bunnies, putting electric plugs in his mouth and shitting himself. Sorry, is my language too strong?'

She directed the question at Matthew, but Nick responded: 'Whatever.'

'Well, that's life,' Jane carried on. 'Now look at him. He tries things out. His perception grows. He's in a music phase now, but even if he passes Grade 8 that doesn't mean he's learned all there is to be learned. He's still crawling, and he's crawling around the organ loft, and once he's thrown the sheet music into the nave and put the stop knobs in his mouth a few times, he might decide to move on and do something else. And you're on a journey too. It's not like you've made it once you get to be a cathedral organist. Andy's allowed the journey to take him somewhere better. You don't want to get stuck fast in cathedral organ concrete.'

None of her truths scored a direct hit, but it was like a near-miss from a battleship.

'What's so incomprehensible about music,' he responded, 'is that it's so natural. Everyone feels it and wants to do it. Yet to do it you need to practise and practise and practise. I don't know why it's like that. Bach sounds so natural. Surely anyone should be able to play it.'

'Why? Bach doesn't seem very natural to me. Even Andy was talking gobbledegook in that class. Nature is something different.' She took another sip of her wine. 'But travel, I can relate to that. How far afield has *your* organ playing taken you?'

Matthew, remembering her eyes widening, had to construct his answer carefully. He had never travelled as extensively as Andy. The arrival of their dinner gave him some time.

'Well, it got me out of my village. I had a provincial upbringing. I'd been to France on a couple of holidays, and we'd done one trip to Czechoslovakia, where my parents were from. I was sent off to school, but aside from that my life revolved around a village in Dorset and the little towns where we would go for our more adventurous shopping trips. Music took me out of all that, starting with my big trip to Germany to see Walcha.'

Jane asked with interest about Walcha, drawing answers out of him as if what he said was more important than the finely cooked dinner. Matthew presented the rôle of Fiala, the mother in the narrative, in a good light:

'My mother also saw it as an adventure. Her travelling days came to an end when she married. Before that, she had lived all over Europe as a student. Not all women of her generation did that. I think she saw this trip as a last hurrah. She was very helpful to me. Even when I was a toddler she took me to lots of music classes. They go back as far as I can remember. She gave me lessons herself when I was at primary school. And she let me play her records. She had piles of them. Most of the symphonies and concertos of Haydn, Mozart, Beethoven and Schubert. I left all that behind when I discovered Bach, but it's still in me. I associate it with what I was reading at the time. When I hear the *scherzo* from Beethoven's Ninth I'm Sherlock Holmes flying over the Reichenbach Falls.'

Jane twirled her glass. 'Your mother probably had more time than I do.' She tousled her son's hair. 'Does your dad let you play his opera CDs?'

'I don't like opera,' said Nick. 'I like absolute music.'

'Absolute music?' sighed Jane.

'I was also keen to establish myself as independent,' Matthew went on, 'so I made her sit downstairs while I had my lesson with Walcha. I had wanted him to think I had got there by myself.'

'What did he say about your playing?' asked Hannon, who was soaking up the conversation.

'I couldn't understand all of what he said because he didn't speak much English. But he made me play without any of the stops pulled out, so all I could hear was the rattle of the tracker action.'

'I'd have liked to have seen your mother's face then,' said Jane.

Matthew continued to Hannon: 'It told me I was playing too hard. And then he made me take the music to pieces, like playing the alto and bass, leaving out the treble and singing the tenor, like I make you do. Of course, as you found out, it totally fell to pieces. But I learned the real test of whether you know the music. If you learn a piece like that from scratch, you know it from the inside and you never seem to forget it.'

'Are you sure?' said Jane. 'I thought Nick'd taken ten steps backwards when he brought his piece home.'

'No, he's taken ten steps forwards,' said Matthew.

'In everything, or just the organ?'

Matthew dodged the question: 'Would you let Nick go across Europe for an organ lesson?'

'I'd want to come along for the ride. Would you mind your old mum being with you, Nicky?'

'Of course not,' said Hannon sportingly.

'Then let's go and see Walcha,' she said.

'He's dead, I'm afraid,' said Matthew, 'but there are plenty of other teachers. Any of them would take out a few days of school.'

'Yes, and in the meantime we can take out the odd school day with trips to Windsor.'

Matthew felt a stab of territorial jealousy. Hannon, his pupil, was being hoisted out of his orbit.

The city announced itself. First the countryside became harsher, hedgeless and dry-stone-walled. Then the villages ribboned into each other. The neon of streetlamps and chippies punctuated the dusk. The car-centric post-war outer suburbs, if dystopian, then ushered in the Victorian precincts, the glories of regional builders who never ran out of ideas. Then the glowing office buildings sprouting from the centre, which still retained its mediaeval and Georgian atmosphere despite the ring road and the Brutalism. Jane picked a route through the middle of the city that avoided the cathedral.

'I'll drop Nick off first. It's quicker, and it's past his bedtime.'

Had she deliberately skirted the cathedral? It was news to him that Nick lived elsewhere from her. What was she planning? He didn't speak up because of both his polite side and his gambling side – this latter that went against whatever sense of caution he had. Part of him wanted to see what happened next, come what may. That made him think of Chloë. Had he given up hoping for whatever would happen next with her? Jane drove up the hilly streets from the centre to Redland, and drew up outside a spacious Victorian semi-detached house.

'You've got your homework?' said Jane to her son.

'I've done it,' said Hannon.

'No, you've got to spend proper time—'

'I do it in the lunch-hour, Mum. It's not important.'

Matthew sensed that the exchange could have become an argument, but Jane was holding herself back.

'Okay,' she conceded, 'you know best.'

'Thanks, Mum.' Hannon got out, then looked back into the car before he shut his door. 'Bye, sir. See you on Monday.'

Jane watched as her son went up the front steps and unlatched the door. No Mr Hannon came to greet him. Without a word she released the handbrake and they moved forward, but after a couple of junctions it was clear it was not towards the cathedral.

'His father'll notice he's back at about noon tomorrow.' Then she threw back her head and laughed. She took her eyes off the road and on to him for longer than was safe, her face illusionarily pale in the fleeting lights.

'I'll tell you what,' she said, 'why not come back to mine for a quick cup of tea? No strings attached. I think it's nice to unwind after a day with Nick. I love him, but parenting is more work than work ever was. Having to concentrate on everything he says is exhausting. Sometimes I wish he wasn't so clever.'

Matthew didn't know what to say. She was driving him to her house. Was it seduction? He had nothing to add to her comments about bringing up children. That was unknown to him. But he liked listening to her.

'His brother and sister were much easier, even when they used to bicker. That phase was endless, but at least the only words I needed were 'be quiet'. Now I have to listen to everything Nick says, and respond knowledgeably about swell boxes.'

Jane piloted them through the Georgian terraces of Clifton, slavery petrified into elegance via pyramids of sugar, and in one of the sudden leaps of the topographically enchanted city, they soared across the glacier-cut gorge on Brunel's suspension bridge, its cables hung with industrial-scale fairy-lights. The other side was rural and they plunged into the dark hedges. With both an anticipation in his groin and a fear in his gut, on he went with her, clambering out meekly when she parked in the driveway of a charming cottage and following her across the threshold into a warm home strewn with old coats, a dog basket, remote controls and Nick's books. Clutter spilled over the kitchen table. Once she had made tea her eyes gleamed as much with malice as pleasure as she selected a CD from what was likely her husband's highly categorised collection of expensive boxed sets: Messiaen's *Quartet for the End of Time*.

'I'll get to the nub of it.'

She swung her legs up over the sofa armrest, revealing their extent, and looked around the room as she talked.

'We lived in a flat and owned the other one upstairs. We rented it out. Andrew, my still-husband, started having it off with the tenant, a student. That's cost him everything you see here. He's had to buy this place for me, and he'll be paying my mortgage for years. But it's cost me something inside. I haven't found my student. Yet.'

She turned to Matthew, her movement betraying nervousness. She was the senior partner here, but still was pitching a man she didn't know well, who might have his own ideas.

'Don't think I'm bad because I'm direct and there's no commitment. I've raised three children. Why should I want anything to do with anyone who is in any way dependent? I did say there were no strings attached, but if you don't want it, there's no lift home.'

She disappeared for a shower. Was Matthew to acquiesce? He didn't want to, though he also didn't want to assert himself and say no. While the movie-watching, darker side of him was keen to drive forward into the impending experience that would surely be as existential as any film, the greater part of him was saying no. It wouldn't work. She had made clear romance was not on offer; just bare mechanics. Could he stand up for himself within her husband/tenant psychodrama? The feeling in his groin had vanished and his stomach tingled.

The seconds were ticking by till she would emerge from the shower, possibly in an alluring arrangement of towels, then lead him upstairs to her bed. What she was offering was a dream for someone less burdened by his fastidious body, for someone who wouldn't care about the absence of emotional intimacy and passion. He'd discovered the difficult way that his body stubbornly yoked sex with an unattainable romantic ideal.

Was it all set by what had happened the first time, and the lengthy preamble leading up to that experience? He had arrived at college with his first essay already completed, ready for meaningful work and study as organist and musician. The real reason why that had all gone wrong was nothing to do with Dr Paice and the voluminous workload. The first days of college had gone fine, navigating the academic and social meetings, until the evening of the matriculation dinner, after which he went for a walk with a third-year. The older student had asked about his love life. Surprised that a student whose business was surely learning would ask such a question, Matthew mentioned an infatuation with the girl who had been the then incarnation of the Other.

'Did you fuck her?' asked the third-year.

The membrane that had protected Matthew from reality in his adolescent years was punctured. Till then he had happily assumed that while sex took place in more daring works of fiction, such as the sixties' and seventies' films he already stayed up late to watch, it did not exist in reality. His parents had certainly shown no evidence of having a sexual life beyond his conception, which was pre-history. The artistic life to which he aspired was intellectual, theoretical and desk- or keyboard-bound. Other artists were surely fellow travellers. Sex belonged in a realm of otherness even beyond the Other, among those strange throngs who lived in the ideal city but whose business was banality, not art.

But hindsight is instantaneous, and his new friend's words revealed as strippingly as the shockwave of a bomb that his years-long ideation was a sham. Of course sex was part and parcel of life. Everyone he now saw, from the third-year walking next to him to passers-by in the street to, worst of all, the scores of his contemporaries in the college, were privy to a secret he didn't possess and couldn't unlock. They knew the language and actions that allowed them and their someone else to enter a world from which he was excluded.

Now, almost in the here and now, Jane's nakedness, her cavities, and his efforts to meet her expectations, would not arouse him, in the same way that he hadn't been aroused in the past.

He had endured three self-hating years as an undergraduate, denigrating himself for failing to see what was so obvious to everyone else. Surely every other person in the world was surfeiting on happy sex. He was failing to do what was so natural to everyone else, failing to feel what was so vivid to everyone else. After graduating he set off into the world disabled by an incompleteness so essential that surely he had F for Failure scratched on his forehead. Desperation led him to a prostitute in Germany. At first he was filled by confidence; even if it was legal there, he was breaking boundaries and taboos and following in the footsteps of innumerable romantic artists who had sought the demi-monde. He was overcoming the voice that told him: 'it'll never happen to you.' But when she bent over in front of him and pulled down her tracksuit bottoms and held her knickers aside, he felt no arousal. Even he could not romanticise the transaction.

'I'm sorry,' he had said.

'Don't be sorry about me,' said the *Strassenmädchen*.

It seemed to be the same voice as Jane's: 'Oh, you're one of *them*.'

He must have told her that he wasn't going through with it.

She continued: 'You didn't even get far enough to see how easily I come.'

He expected her to ask him to leave, but she didn't. 'I've never been turned down before,' she said.

He felt tired from the soles of his feet to the edge of his soul, but he nonetheless felt perfectly comfortable with her. With the wryness of glancing sex, a wryness he remembered from that *Mädchen*, they could still bumble around and make small talk as he gathered his jacket and left. It was an hour's walk home. He peered into the gorge as he crossed the suspension bridge. Sheer slabs of rock, the harsh glaze of the muddy river. No teeming life. It might as well be a moonscape. But it wasn't. That again was romanticisation. It was a river. He was a little person in a big city.

XVI

After too little sleep it was choir practice, to be followed by the Sunday services. If only Matthew could descend through the floor to the song school, instead of having to get up and then wearily collapse down the stairs to the cloister. Far from stopping, as with his paralysed memory of Fiala's funeral, the reel of life spun manically. Chlorophyl light flooded in through the bee-buzzing herbaceous border of the graveyard. The boys now resembled perturbing cherubs. As corrupt and sensual as innocent and pure, they sang with skill but as soon as the music ended, giggled, fidgeted, farted and conspired. One now looked as if he had been plucked from his playpen and inflated. And there was Hannon singing away, knowing nothing about his mother's previous evening.

Matthew reached back and opened the window behind him. The ground outside was higher than inside, so the buzzing bees and gently rippling stalks and Technicolor petals were right there. The fresh air took away the main hazard of children, that school smell following them wherever they go as a group. Any teacher knows it. He started them singing the day's psalm. His mood rose with their voices. Their identities were subsumed and they became a wonderful collective. But once the rehearsal and services were over, his energy seeped away again.

What was the point of experience and self-knowledge if all it left was a sense of exclusion and inner desolation? Back up the widely-hewn stairs, Jane entered his fantasies. This time he was all man and did everything she wanted. Capable. Desirable. Release. Not true. He was left energyless in his thousand square-foot flat under fourteen-foot ceilings.

That evening he chewed his pasta with tuna and tomato sauce, a meal he'd eaten alone a thousand times. His large kitchen was evenly lit by a skylight that caught the sun all day, and furnished with a freestanding stove, fridge, various wooden cabinets, a table and two benches, all painted white. For the first time, he felt its starkness. He had added nothing. Perhaps he should put up a calendar or some pictures. His food was similar, a home-made version of what you might be served in the canteen. Impossible to cook incorrectly, and easy to eat. There was nothing of him in it. And he ate that sort of meal every day.

What would someone else think of all this? He could see why he was seeing himself from another point of view, and who that someone else was, but he didn't want to name her in his thoughts. She just hovered there in Otherness. What would she think of his almost-tryst with Jane? Given that blues was about experience, she might approve, but what was the point of imaginary approval? Who was he communicating with in his fantasy of being looked at? Was his Other actually an aspect of himself that he was struggling to understand? If so, why was she garbed in the appearance of a woman? What would she value in him? What should he value in himself?

The questions were still there the next morning. He didn't have to take choir practice. He lay in bed without the energy to get up, feeling trapped. His job came with accommodation and enough money to provide what he needed. But it was a womb in which he swam. What did going into the world without this support system involve? How would he pay for it and deal with the practicalities? Finally he got up and phoned his father.

He had to wait till the next Monday, his day off. There was no route by train. His immediate urge to ask Jane to borrow her car was spineless, so despite the expense he rented a car. He reached Zigzag Hill, where the road ascended the steep edge of Cranborne Chase, opening a vista on the Blackmore Vale, a knotted carpet of villages, copses, hedges and dairy farms bordered by high ground on three sides. It had rained earlier, but shafts of sun were now breaking through the clouds. In the haze the glistening landscape spread out to infinity. Passing the view point had always meant reaching home for him. His spirits soared as he took in the natural beauty, even if it hid darker human realities.

It was also a vale of isolation, boredom, ignorance, prying, bullying, all escaped by smoking listlessly outside the village shop as occasional trucksful of scared sheep shuddered by on the way down and Range Rovers purred by on the way up. Those were heading for the pheasant shoots that demarcated social boundaries while bringing some money and jobs to the Chase.

Vanishingly few people refused to conform to the social hierarchy. A stubborn refusal to advance your own development was a form of conformity. Yet the area certainly looked beautiful. Turning off the main road, the lanes became narrower and overhung, and soon he was within the bowery and thickety confines of his home village. The clay-lined pond in the centre sat in a depression at the middle of a starfish configuration of lanes. He stopped and got out and smoked a cigarette. No person, vehicle or animal beyond birds and squirrels. The water was covered by bright green algae, seemingly a continuation of the grass. This had fooled Matthew as a child: he'd walked into the water.

'Go on, it'll hold you.' That had been Darren Osmond, the bowl-haired son of the roofer.

The weathered cottages in the centre of the village had walls of flint held in place by brick corners and lintels. The post-office cum shop, a corrugated-iron adjunct to one of these, was painted army green, as if to camouflage it. It could be removed at any time. He got back in the car and drove past the flinty church. It contained a meagre organ where he had practised during the school holidays. At night the music desk was illuminated by a single electric bulb, making the nave beyond its reach darker.

Past the church, cow-parsley clipped the mirrors on both sides of the car. After two hundred yards he slowed down. Because of the hedges he could only see up to the bungalow when he stopped in front of what had once been a neat archway of wild rose. Now it had subsided and thorny branches threatened the unwary. Through this, Matthew saw the stooped back of his father working among the lupins and foxgloves. The flowers still had droplets hanging from them from the earlier rain. Years before, at this time of day, his mother would be working in the kitchen, looking out through the windows facing the meadows at the back of the house.

Matthew watched. The engine hummed. Then Jiří straightened, turned and saw the car. Matthew felt a tremor in his heart and stalled the engine.

'Dad.'

He restarted the car and manoeuvred it into the layby. He got out quickly into the garden. His father met him on the path and they hugged.

'Hello, Dad.'

They kissed. Matthew caught the tang of his father's BO and the grease of his hair; not necessarily unattractive smells, like those of a favourite animal.

'Matty, how are you? It's been two years since you were here.'

'I've been in Germany. There was no time.'

'You know, you are welcome.' Jiří spoke tentatively.

He had been over forty when Matthew was born, and was now well into retirement. He looked reduced and frailer than when he had last seen him, and sported a tinge of white hair. It was like the halo a harpsichordist creates by keeping the keys down so their sound doesn't die. Everything else was the same: the tweed jacket too tight for his shoulders-back posture, the nylon tie, check shirt and Cornish-pasty shoes demonstrating a frugal expression of his aesthetics.

'So you're back?' Jiří almost pronounced it 'pack', with the strong consonant and the shortest possible 'a'.

'Yes.' Matthew began to relax.

'So you've come home?'

'Yes.'

'So you've stopped?' The vowels were so short, it was almost 'stppd'.

'Yes.'

'You have to stop somewhere, Matty. When I first saw the big house, I stopped.'

'But you didn't stop there. You stopped in a bungalow a few hundred yards away from it.'

'Sensible people stay in one place.' Jiří's hopeful smile undercut his tone of mathematical certainty. 'Well come in,' he added. 'The lunch will be ready.'

'What are we having?'

'Fishfingers.'

Jiří waited for a reaction. Matthew repressed it. Jiří held open the plain wooden door leading through to the sitting room.

'Just joking.'

Despite windows framing countryside extraordinaire, it felt claustrophobic and airless. Matthew opened a window. Behind the sitting room was the kitchen, and to the left a corridor led to the three bedrooms and bathroom. As he looked around, he saw his mother for an instant. Fiala was framed by the door of the kitchen, cutting vegetables on the chopping board, the sun forming a golden parallelogram on the whitewash behind her. She wore a plain summer dress emphasising her thinness. Her still mostly chestnut brown hair was severely cut. She looked up and saw Matthew, and after a second's surprise her face brightened and she became overjoyed. It was too much of a reaction for a self-conscious adolescent.

'Would you like a drink?'

Matthew sat down on an arm of the sofa.

'No thank you, Dad.'

The smell of the house caught him: the freshness of the

country air and the aroma of roasting lamb and mint from the kitchen, the fragrant basil in pots on the sitting-room windowsill. They didn't eradicate, but overlaid, the hint of musty fabrics, the dry smell of nineteenth-century books, and the smell of his father, indescribable like any person's scent.

Jiří's voice faded away.

His mother greeted him for the last time at home when he returned from his first year at the cathedral school in Bristol. He was fourteen. Atypically for a cathedral school, it was a secondary school starting at eleven, not a prep school for children aged seven to thirteen. Having been at Moultrie, which was a prep school, he turned up, aged thirteen, to join a year-group who had already known each other for six terms.

His career as a chorister was truncated as his voice broke during his second term. Richard had kept him on first as a countertenor, then tenor and finally bass. He never had a beautiful voice, but he could follow the inner parts as skilfully as the adult lay clerks.

It wasn't a boarding school, not like Moultrie where he had been sent when he was nine. But his parents, not moving from Dorset, arranged for him to lodge with an older couple they knew from the GB-Czech Club, whose own children had grown up. They cooked for him and helped with domestic details, but after four years boarding at Moultrie he could already meet many of his own domestic needs. In those terms he was a little adult. He had to go home to Chettle for the holidays, but family life now seemed a charade. How could they expect him to submit to their authority if they had sent him away? In any case he was well-behaved.

Fiala opened her arms and laughed wide-mouthed. He saw a flash of tonsil.

'Hello, Mum, how are you?'
'You're just in time for dinner.'
She had roasted a duck for what turned out to be their last

proper meal together. The cancer killing her was already past curing, and she was poised above the descent to hospital and then to hospice.

'Jiří,' she said, 'do please make us your orange sauce.'

His father persisted in the kitchen, fetching ingredients and stirring them over the range. The result was somewhat inadequate but Fiala swilled it over the helpings of duck.

'Matthew, you'll have some of your father's orange sauce.'

'Matthew.' It was his father's voice. Matthew forced himself to focus on what his father was saying.

'Would you like a scotch and soda? A gin and tonic? Sherry?'

'No, thank you.'

'Have some tea at least.'

'In a minute.'

Fiala had kept the sitting room immaculate. Parts of it were now dusty and forlorn. Out-of-date newspapers and bags of milk-bottle tops lay piled against one wall. But the precise habits of his father were discernible in the often-wiped coffee-table and its clean array of remote controls, dictionary, TV guide, glasses case, and a pile of books, all within arm's reach of the orthopaedic back-support positioned on the sofa.

Jiří brought a tray with crackers, some topped with whole fish, less than half the size of sardines and less pungent, the rest spread with a rich mushroom pâté. Matthew was amazed by what – in this context – was gourmet food.

After eating a few, he started up: 'You know, Dad, I thought about you the other day. Richard left all his stuff in the organist's house. It's all still there. Geraint's put his own stuff around but hasn't really altered anything.'

'You must be loving life in your new house,' Jiří said. 'To me, Matty, the English terraced house is the best combination of economy and flair ever.'

'Yes, Dad, I know you think that.'

'The architect, he makes the theatre for people's lives. He

improves their lives, and if he's really good they don't even notice. He civilises the uncivil. That's why he's the greatest artist. That is not a knock on music. You must know this in your new house.'

'I know Dad, but I don't live there. Geraint does.'

'Who's Geraint?' asked Jiří.

'The new organist.'

'But why aren't you the new organist?'

'Well, it's complicated.'

'What do you mean?'

Matthew didn't answer. After a pause he said: 'Anyway, let's not talk about it now. All Richard's things are still there.'

'But they should be yours.'

Matthew raised his voice. 'Dad!' His father was right, but that didn't make it easier to listen to a hectoring parent.

After a moment Jiří's eyes brightened, as if trying to appear unbothered by his son's abrupt manner.

'Does he still have the Hepplewhite table?'

'Yes, and he's still got the Hepplewhite pattern book too.'

'And he still has *Vitruvius Britannicus*?'

'Yes, all the volumes,' said Matthew. 'They're all lined up on the bottom shelf.'

Jiří's eyes glowed. 'Well, well, Matty, that really is something. Did you look at them?'

'No. I don't think Geraint's noticed them.'

'Look at the title pages, see if he has the original two-volume set, and if the others are just added on. You can't tell by the binding; they were probably all bound at the same time, much later.'

'You've told me that hundreds of times.'

Out the window the people-free fields extended in undulations punctuated by lone trees or copses of riotous boughs, leaves and twigs. How did a person fit into such a view? Did his wariness of other people and his romantic fixations on Others – did that stem from his father, in whose customary view another human could only be a threat, even if it was a mere dog-walker threatening his concentration? Would his father always be a circumspect exile, and was that his inheritance? If so, the feeling had been inculcated young. At school he'd reversed the concept; he'd self-consciously taken on a vocation that ran parallel to, and excluded, the shallows of contemporary life.

'So how does it feel to be the organist?'

Matthew shied his head away from the window. Countryside: loneliness; sadness; unfulfilled lives. Alice courting the postman in a poisonous minefield disguised as the picturesque. Alice had died after picking deathcaps from under Herrod's Oak. Had the boys from the village persuaded her to? The spores extended beneath the ground and pushed up a yearly crop of mushrooms. It was a horrible death. After the initial stomach upsets receded, all seemed well for three or four days. At that point Alice's father had made an appearance in the pub. 'She's over the worst of it, thank God.' The final onslaught was yet to come. The mushroom's poison was already destroying her liver and kidneys. There was no cure.

'So you're now the organist?'

'Dad, I'm the assistant organist.'

'The assistant?'

'Yes. Geraint's the organist.'

'And who's Geraint? Why has he got your job?'

'Geraint? He's some maestro with a big technique.'

'But you've got a big technique.'

'Not big enough for them.'

Matthew was overwhelmed by a burst of sadness. His father certainly believed in him. He tried to keep any tremor out of his voice. 'Whatever you're cooking smells lovely.'

'It's from Mr Waitrose. I don't shop at Mr Gateway when you're coming. Do you still think you're cathedral organist material?'

'What?'

Matthew looked up to find his father eyeing him.

'You must not bank on things. Your plan to succeed Richard was always a little…' Jiří reached into the air with his fingertips, as if feeling a grape. '…a little arch.' The 'r' was hard.

'Arch?'

'Yes. The food will be ready.'

'I don't care about the food, Dad. What do you mean?'

'Fidelity. What was it that Walcha said?'

Despite correcting him endlessly, Jiří mispronounced Walcha, saying 'Wolsher' with the correct Saxon soft 'ch' but without the German 'V' sound.

'Fidelity to the written note.'

'But couldn't you see? These bishops and these deans, they never cared about that. And all your teachers. The man at Moultrie, those people at Oxford. None of them cared; only Richard and you. You were always faithful. Do you remember that song you sang when you came back from Moultrie?'

My Heart Ever Faithful.

'Exactly. That's you, and yet you put all your trust in a bunch of idiots. It was never going to work.'

'Dad, what are you saying?' Tears welled.

'You demanded too much of careerist mediocrities who never understood you.' Jiří talked as if what he said was incontrovertible.

Did sureness of tone mean he was right? Forget the trapdoor, the room was lurching. 'Why didn't you tell me this years ago? Why have you kept this from me?'

'I've told you hundreds of times. You always told me to shut up. Anyway, the food will dry out.'

Jiří forced the conversation away. Matthew, fixated on the word 'arch', tried to steer it back but during the three courses Jiří happily prattled on about everything but that. Carrot and coriander soup, tasty but straight out of a carton. Roast lamb shank, well-cooked in the Czech manner, with green beans and courgettes from the garden. A pre-made jam roly-poly with custard. When they had finished, Jiří directed Matthew back to the easy chair. Coffee bubbled in the kitchen. Jiří came back proudly hoisting an aluminium espresso-maker.

'Would you like some coffee?' A grin paralysed Jiří's face as if induced by an exotic poison.

'Yes, thank you.' Matthew stared at the coffee-maker.

Jiří poured the coffee. 'Pretty good, eh?'

Matthew sipped it. 'Yes, that's pretty good.'

'It's a pretty useful machine, isn't it?'

'Yes.'

'Guess where I bought it.'

'I've no idea.' Matthew looked up at his father, who was determined to keep this going for as long as possible. 'Where? Salisbury? Blandford?'

'No, not even London.'

'Then where did you get it?'

Jiří enjoyed his son's impatience.

'Where did you get it?' demanded Matthew in a burst of adolescent anger.

Jiří's eyes flashed. 'Naples.'

'Naples? What were you doing there?'

'I went to view the ruined temples.'

'What, the ones in the Filippo Morghen prints?'

'Exactly.'

'And you weren't mugged?' Matthew asked.

'Your grandfather was in the Czech Legion. Naples was never going to intimidate me. It is knee-deep in Baroque palaces.'

'And you managed to get to Heathrow?'

'I flew from Bournemouth. Small airline.'

Jiří sat down and took an expressive sip of his coffee.

'But first I had to book the tickets. Nice lady at Far Horizons in Shaftesbury helped me.'

Matthew settled down into the easy chair as his father continued.

'You know, you who frittered away your grand tour when you were young, I knew exactly what I wanted to see.'

Jiří described the ancient and Baroque buildings of Naples.

'Can you imagine something built today still standing in two thousand years' time? There'll be nothing left in a hundred years even.' Jiří caught Matthew in his glance. 'You never listen to me. You never have.'

'I spent the first eighteen years of my life doing nothing else.'

The haloed face turned helpless. Disingenuous? 'What do you mean? You weren't even here after you were nine.'

'Well, you talked at me all through the holidays. Day after day, hour after hour.'

'Well, you never told me anything, ever,' said Jiří.

'Why should I have?'

'Maybe it's my own fault. After Mum died…'

'Don't call her Mum.'

'Why not?'

'She was my mother, not yours.'

Jiří sighed. 'After your mother died, I had to be both parents at once.'

'Then why did you never tell me my plan was arch?' asked Matthew.

'I did tell you.'

They glared at each other in silence.

'Matty, don't take this the hard way. You need to find people who are faithful. Not in a constrictive way.' Then Jiří settled back with the complacent smile of a man's man. 'The only type of fidelity people now can grasp is sexual.'

Matthew felt a twinge of his time-old embarrassment. But Chloë also snapped into his mind. He tried to banish the romantic images by asking: what on earth would she be like with her parents? He imagined her with them, all getting on in a mature, civilised way, able to discuss matters of the heart. He wished he could talk to his father about her, but surely that would be impossible.

He found his father looking at him with enjoyment for having made him retreat into his inner world.

'You and your thoughts,' his father needled. 'You're like a submarine without a periscope.' Jiří softened his voice. 'You must find someone faithful to the things you value. Faithful to art.'

Matthew's first reaction was anger, but he managed to swallow the forceful evasions erupting in him. What his father had said was personal, and also, dare he admit it, profound.

'I'm curious about your reasoning.' Matthew spoke carefully, restraining his urge to push the conversation away. 'What about my new boss, Geraint?' He described Geraint, mentioning his alcoholism. 'So he isn't faithful to art?'

'From what you say, no. He's too Bacchic. His playing's too instinctive. It's a bit superficial, yes? Art isn't just the brutal release of pent-up talent. He doesn't use his brain enough.'

This was insightful. Should he ask about Chloë? No. When Jiří warmed to his theme he became inflexible and smug. And as for Jane, would he be able to tell anyone?

He had to say something. 'Are we bright?'

'English is my fourth language, but we're not talking about me. As for you,' Jiří sat back, enjoying the moment. 'Aside from music, you're only surface-educated. You have a feeling about music, and by extension, art, but it's immature. You've no philosophy.'

'Philosophy's just Mittel-European claptrap.'

'No it isn't.'

'Well, I do have a philosophy. Fidelity to the written note.'

'No you don't. That's Wolsher's. You have to mature into your own.'

'Why should I?' Matthew spoke like a fourteen-year-old. He tried to be more considered. 'I'd be living according to your view of art, not mine.'

'You don't have a view of art.' Jiří sat forward and reached for his coffee, enjoying the last few drops. 'To have a view of art, you have to engage with life. Fully. Remember, Scarlatti was the greatest gambler of his age.'

Why were the important people in his life quoting Scarlatti at him? But if this was the moment to play his hand…

'Dad, I need money. Geraint has said I should look for a new job. I need security. I want to buy a flat.'

'What would you do with a flat?'

'Live in it.'

'But you have a house?'

'A house?'

'Richard's house.'

'No I don't. Geraint's living in the house. I have a flat.'

'You don't have the house?'
'No. I told you.'
'Then play ferociously until they give it to you.'
'Dad, I don't have any money.'
'I don't have any money either.'

Matthew gestured at the house around them. 'How did you buy this place?'

'I had inherited enough for a large down-payment. That's how we beat the inflation.'

The injustice, as it seemed to Matthew, rankled. Jiří inherited when he was young enough to benefit properly from the money, while his own patrimony would be used up by his father's old-age trips to Naples. But his inner fastidiousness stopped him expressing this.

'Did Mum have any money?'
'She left it to me, and I brought you up.'
'Some of it must be left. Was half the house hers?'
'What should I do, sell half and put myself out on the street?'
'But isn't some of it my patrimony?'
'That's an old-fashioned word. I suppose I am your patrimony.'

Matthew could think of nothing to say.

'Matty, you would not fulfil yourself living in a flat that you own with money from me. A gambler takes gambles. Asking your father for money is not a gamble.'

'Could you give me ten thousand pounds?'
'For a gamble?'
'Yes, it is a gamble from your perspective. Put it on me.'
'No.'
'Why not?'
'A donation is not a gamble. You have no odds.'

Jiří put down his coffee and changed the subject. He seemed to enjoy rebuffing his son's efforts to push the conversation back.

After leaving the bungalow, Matthew didn't want to drive straight home. Even with the window open, the little car would feel too claustrophobic. He turned from the centre of the village and drove up the track along the boundary of the big house. He parked next to a copse where farm machinery had been rusting since his childhood. The young lime leaves fluoresced and the fragrant wild garlic overwhelmed the dusk. The scent of the damp long grass crushed by the car's wheels was fecund with a reviving pungent freshness that invited you to bury your head in it. Would he lie in the aromatic grasses with Chloë? Would she like Chettle? Would she like Jiří? What would she think of his own relationship with Jiří, his lack of self-reliance, his failed request for money?

Jiří Marcan was not an ideal, but was any father? Fatherhood was too arbitrary. But one could pick surrogates. There, he was lucky. Richard had given him a past and a future and a model. Who had selected whom? Who had made the first move, so welcomed by the other? Matthew swelled: Richard had selected him. That was something, as his father would say.

But how would Chloë judge his turning Richard into a surrogate father figure at the expense of proper intimacy with his real father? He absolutely must get on better with his father, especially if Jiří started talking sense, however painful that was.

How would Chloë judge him fantasising about her when she had left to wherever she had gone, and he was alone?

He walked through the trees past the No Trespassing sign and climbed the metal fence. He peeped across the lawns towards the Queen Anne house Jiří deemed the most beautiful in Dorset. Malleable and delicate, the centre was a coved, three-bay projection. To either side was a flat elevation, again three bays, leading to rounded edges. It had no corners. Was it ridiculous to claim that contemplating this house as a child had influenced him deeply? Had it given him the sense of proportion allowing him to interpret Bach?

Jiří, buffeted as a child from country to country with a label round his neck, had been evacuated to the big house during the Phony War, and had settled in Chettle later because he had loved its architecture so much. The big house was his talisman. Did the disproportionate importance of an artistic object, and the inability to find the aesthetic in the warm and complex currents of real life come not from the house, but from the man who had so ardently espoused it?

What about fantasy? Was that what had been passed from father to son? Phantasie. His father had spent his life imagining living in the big house, and had arranged his life to further his phantasie. His patrimony was this, not money, and there was no escaping it. The power and pungency of his inner world must have taken centuries of phantasists to nourish and raise, sired by some hunter-gatherer dreamer of time immemorial.

He retreated to the car and drove out of the village. In the gloaming, the cottages were returning to nature, melting into the dusky foliage, thatched roofs blending with hedges, flint walls mingling with the chalk, except where warm squares of bright light cut through. The paint was dulled, the cars no longer glistened, the post office had vanished. As a child playing outside, he had loved this time most. If he looked at things right, the entire village disappeared.

Then the old village vicar, Dr Weyman, appeared in his mind. He was drawing out and amplifying the words of the prayer book as he had done at Fiala's funeral and half a thousand childhood matins. 'The sacrifices of God are a broken spirit: a broken and a contrite heart, O God, thou wilt not despise.' What did it mean? Could he disappear himself, and reappear as someone born again?

XVII

Stanford in G was on the music list for the coming Thursday. The famous *magnificat* included a soaring melody for a skilled and confident treble soloist. As head chorister, Hannon should be assigned this solo as a matter of course. The organ part was challenging, so Matthew had already ensured he could play it, even if Geraint chose an improbably fast tempo. Matthew had to make sure Hannon's solo got the attention he needed, even if it provoked antagonism, so he had suggested meeting his boss in the little office. He passed the score over.

'What's this?' asked Geraint.

'Hannon's solo.'

'What for?'

'Stanford in G. It's on the list.'

'List, list, list,' said Geraint. 'Why do you assume that Nick will have the solo? I might have other ideas.'

'He's the senior chorister.'

'Senior, senior, senior.'

An emptiness robbed Geraint's tone of its power to stab. There was a confusion behind his eyes. Was he drunk?

'I will give the solo to whom I like, and when I tell them to do it, they will do it. They will need to do nothing more than sing it through on the day, as they should be able to do.'

Matthew said nothing.

Geraint focused on him: 'And why did you take Nick to Birmingham?'

How did Geraint know about the trip? 'It was a worthwhile trip. The masterclass was good.'

'I'm sure. Andy's a bit up himself but he's an alright player. I conducted him in the Poulenc concerto once.'

Geraint looked deliberately around the room, then out of the window as if following a bluebottle. Without returning his eyes to Matthew, he said:

'The head asked me to speak to you. Students aren't supposed to be taken off by teachers without telling the school. I'm nothing to do with the school, and neither are you, so it means something if they've dragged me into this.'

The cathedral school, although supplying the choristers, was indeed a separately governed institution from the cathedral. Geraint held up a typed letter and addressed the wall behind Matthew. 'It's they who've written. The letter's right here.'

'But his mother was there.'

'I know. She's notorious for meddling in her son's education.'

'Notorious?'

He had heard her travails of raising three children and been offered the softness of her skin. She hadn't been cruel to him when he had backed out. Geraint's word conveyed none of this; Geraint, and the school that took her working hours, had not got the measure of her.

Geraint continued: 'How many mothers are nurses here? She interferes in everything he does. I gave him a glass of sherry in one of his off-on-again piano lessons, which wasn't exactly going to kill him. He, the young innocent, then tells her proudly, and I get an earful from her.'

'But if she's his mother, surely it's okay to go with them.'

'Yes, but that's not the point. I don't know what the point is. If you want that, speak to the head or to Bryce. But I've been asked in writing to relay the matter to you, so I'm doing that. That's all. Don't shoot the piano player.'

Frank and Roy were in charge of the music library, making sure that everyone's folder contained the correct scores. Matthew realised he was the only one who needed to keep track of the music list because he was the only one not to have a folder, having instead a set of organ copies of the choir's repertoire in the loft. Geraint's folder never deviated from its journey between his two stands, in the cathedral and song school, and while Matthew had assumed Frank and Roy only dealt with the singers, perhaps they also made sure that Geraint's folder was up to date.

All their leader had to do was turn up and open his folder and direct whatever was in front of him. His sight-reading prowess would get him through pieces when his residual knowledge of the repertoire failed him, so he had no need to worry about what was on the music list. With the exception of the occasional self-chosen oddity by Olwen Goodenough, he probably had no idea what music was planned. If his eyes fell on Stanford in G, he knew it well enough to guide the performance, and he would pass the solo to whoever was in front of him.

Therefore, rather than plan the performance, the best course would be to make sure Geraint's eyes fell on Hannon at the key moment. Since they probably wouldn't rehearse it properly, the lad would have to be prepared outside the rehearsals. He didn't relish seeing Jane, but she would have to be involved. He phoned her.

'You know that Hannon's got a big solo coming up next Thursday. Will you come to hear him sing it?'

He said 'Hannon' with a humorous inflection.

'Sure,' said Jane. 'He hadn't mentioned it.'

'That's our lad. He just gets on with it. But I'm worried that Geraint won't give him enough rehearsal time. I wanted to have a session or two with him, and also ask him to practise at home with you.'

'Why don't we combine that? Come round for dinner.' He heard her raise her eyebrows. 'We can re-establish normal relations.'

He had expected her cooking to be within his frame of normality – perhaps roast chicken or lasagne – but when she opened her front door an aura of spices washed over him. A world opened, beyond what he realised people did in the course of normal home life. He heard the cracking of presumably spice pods cooking in oil as he banged through the *magnificat* with Hannon. Luckily the lad had heard the solo sung by previous head choristers, so he didn't need much coaching. Jane placed a glass of Asian lager on a coaster on the upright piano. Caught by the sun, it questioned the priorities of his life. Work, work, work, notes, notes, notes. Where had fun, fun, fun been? What about family, friendship, holiday and joy, let alone speaking, laughing, singing, dancing? *Plus vif*, indeed. He stepped out from within himself and surrendered to the joy of the rich treble voice singing a beautiful melody beside him. He forced himself to forget about his fingers and just let the piano play itself, which somehow it did.

Then it was time for the feast. Jane served a duck curry with side dishes of vegetables and scented rice. No wonder she found the cafeteria inadequate.

'I like the idea of singing,' she said. 'It's a broader front than just an instrument. It seems more to do with his personality. More expressive. You agree, Nick?'

'I just want to get it right.'

'We'll prepare it properly,' said Matthew, 'and then the muscle memory'll get you through.'

In any dependable musical environment the lad would be supported. Didn't the congenialities of family, fellowship and society rely on people behaving in a dependable way? What was proving to be a lovely way to learn the Stanford would be wasted if Geraint's eye fell on the wrong treble on the day.

'Hannon, when Geraint decides to rehearse this, whenever that will be, we've got to make it inarguable that you'll be the soloist. Don't say anything like "can I do it?" or "would you like me to?" Simply step forward and say: "what tempo are we doing it at?" or even better, "this is the tempo I've prepared".'

Hannon said: 'He doesn't want me to be prepared. I'll say "this is the tempo I want".'

'Even better.'

Jane sat forward: 'Is Geraint going to give the solo to someone else?'

'Not if we don't give him the choice.'

'You and Geraint should go to a marriage counsellor,' said Jane.

'Let's just get through the service. We'll drag him along with us.'

After dinner Jane brought out some family albums and showed pictures of Hannon and his siblings as they had grown up from babyhood. Matthew's residual fear of babies and their trail of saliva, goo and finger marks lessened. Her idea of the journey of life was potent. He saw a lad on his on the way to becoming not just the pupil he knew well but also a co-professional, or a young man qualified in another field. Who knew which future would claim him?

Matthew's own life was undocumented, beyond Fiala's few photos. But that didn't mean it wasn't a journey too. It hadn't ended, however much he wanted to have completed his development into a finished product with a concrete list of attributes and accomplishments. He'd got far enough in music for some of his most noteworthy feats, such as mastering the *Inferno* by Reger, to have already slipped away from him. He wouldn't be able to maintain such pieces unless he kept relearning them. Pieces didn't stay mastered. Nothing stayed still. Music was a journey not just forward towards those wretched recurring ridges, but also with only a limited distance visible in the rearview mirror.

He had phoned Chloë a few times over the previous weeks, with no answer. Hopefully if she dialled the code to identify recent callers, she wouldn't be annoyed to find his number. Then a padded envelope arrived at the cathedral office. Derek usually sorted the cathedral mail by putting the envelopes into the staff's pigeon holes and leaving parcels for collection on the oval table. But this envelope he passed by hand to Matthew, eyes keen in his florid face, as if expecting an explanation for this anomalous parcel.

Matthew remained tight-lipped as his heartbeat increased. Upstairs he opened it carefully. Inside was a mix-tape, but no letter. The tape therefore must be intended to speak for itself. He studied the neatly handwritten list of songs on the insert. He had not heard of either the artists or the songs, but lost no time in listening to Chloë's curation. The songs passed through moods and styles, tempi and even a surprising range of keys. Best of all was a minor-key slow blues. It was the model of what she had played that first night and the spoken words were the same:

'This one's especially played for everyone here tonight that's in love, to all of you that wished you had someone to love, and to all of you that wished you were loved by someone.'

The sadness in the man's voice had worn through the fragile leather of the song. It was the most compelling non-classical performance he had ever heard. No wonder Chloë had travelled to America in her youth to bathe in such a culture. He played the tape over and over. What was the message? The sad slow blues with the spoken introduction dominated the other songs. Was he to infer something about unrequited love? And if so, why should the love of a woman as appealing as Chloë be unrequited?

The next day Matthew watched Geraint from the outset, and noted his bemusement when he opened his folder in the quire and found Stanford in G. He looked around the choristers, as predicted. Hannon stepped forward as prepped.

'This is my tempo, Mr Perryman.' Hannon beat the pulse that he wanted.

'Yeah, okay,' nodded Geraint. 'Let's run it.' He started beating at the same speed as Hannon and looked up at Matthew, who started playing immediately. As he did, he realised the arpeggiated nature of the organ part meant that he, not Geraint, controlled the beat. Once set in motion, the piece could run with the mechanised routine of the Nervenklinik Bamberg's multi-section dishwasher. The choir would have to stay with him. Therefore he gave no more attention to Geraint and concentrated only on his own part which, however many times he had played the piece, he still found a challenge. He gave all the support he could to Hannon's soaring treble.

'That's fine,' was all Geraint said about Hannon's vibrant singing. 'Let's do the anthem.'

It was a relief. Hannon had done plenty of preparation, and it was better for Geraint to add nothing to the performance rather than mess it around. Matthew descended from the loft for the short break between rehearsal and service, but found Geraint waiting in the crossing.

'Stanford in G is too high for the choir today. We'll do it in F sharp major. You can transpose it?'

Matthew was stupefied. The finicky organ part was filled with swift modulations, inversions and enhancements. It might be possible to transpose it well with practice, but to do so at sight would lead to calamity. All the preparation – his and Hannon's – would be wasted. Jane would be turning up to see the train-wreck.

Was Geraint drunk? The laboratory-like smell was coming through his pores, but was it yesterday's drink simply soaking out of him? In his manner Geraint seemed sober, and the more dangerous for it.

'Can't you transpose?'

Matthew raised his chin against the gratuitous belligerence. Geraint knew that, like any trained organist, he could transpose straightforward pieces at sight. But it was picking a fight to ask him to transpose something difficult without warning and having already rehearsed it as written. Geraint held his stare like a goat. Matthew found himself shaking but managed to keep his body and eyes taut. Images welled up that he hadn't seen for weeks: Geraint slipping, tripping, falling, grasping thin air in desperation, hurtling downwards towards the octagonal handle and thumping into it. Matthew's inner vision glowed red. He glared into Geraint's eyes.

'Of course I can do it.'

He slammed off back to the organ loft. Playing it in six sharps would be navigating a minefield. Any harmonic enhancement or modulation would become baffling. Sharps became double sharps and flats and naturals were still sharps. He would have to have faith in his fingers following the patterns. He stared at the score, but he didn't know how to prepare himself. Should he play it through? His fingers found the opening keys.

But…! F sharp major? F sharp major didn't really exist. It was always set out as G flat major. He looked from his hands to the score in disbelief. Reading G major as G flat major was relatively uncomplicated. All he had to do was imagine the key signature had six flats. The notes were laid out on the staves in the same way in either key. There would still be funky accidentals but broadly speaking it would be straightforward to read the piece in the new key. His fingers would have to find the right notes but at least his eyes and brain wouldn't be baffled by translating the entire score into a differently-delineated key.

Didn't Geraint know this? Wasn't his grasp of theory stronger? Didn't he know that the supposedly dastardly test he was setting his assistant showed up his own lack of grip? Didn't he know that he was going to have to stand through the exam test while his assistant actually passed it?

In the performance, inevitably he slipped up numerous times. But these were split notes, not cataclysms. After playing the first bar in anger, the challenge took on its own exhilaration. Trying to apply the muscle memory of his fingers to a new key at sight in public made his senses hum. Patterns, abstraction, stencilling on to a new key, all at speed. He got a buzz of being more than alive as he flew through the fast piece. Every correct note was a victory, and the mistakes got fewer, though his worst was last. Having sensed the safety of the end of piece, he forgot to transpose the first chords of the *Nunc Dimittis's Gloria*, which therefore sounded jarringly a semi-tone above the choir. Rather than adjust, he ploughed on. The choir had to join him a semitone up. So the Stanford ended up being in two keys. But that was Geraint's fault for making such an abusive demand. It didn't detract from him successfully undertaking the challenge.

Geraint didn't criticise him after the service, perhaps sensing his assistant was ready to fight, so when Matthew came down from the loft he felt as if he had resolved the conflict. He had stood up to Geraint and given a performance that was as creditable as the circumstances allowed. Few other professionals could do better.

Jane was standing in the nave. Good for her, she'd supported Hannon's solo. Then he remembered his pupil. He'd barely registered the boy's voice above his own travails.

'What were you thinking?' demanded Jane.

'What about?' asked Matthew to buy a few moments. How had the transposition affected Hannon's performance?

'You and Geraint should have your heads banged together. This was Nick's big day. And you changed the music. It sounded different. You messed with the chords, and he wasn't able to sing it well. He was getting the tune wrong. What did you do?'

After a moment of shamed blankness, Matthew explained.

'You what? You bang on about muscle memory in my own house, and then you two change the key. Why?'

He stared back at her as the familiar trapdoor opened. He had let down his pupil, and was so thoughtless he hadn't even realised. He should have just said no, or not said anything and simply played it in the correct key. Geraint could have done nothing. But he, Matthew, through some solipsistic flaw had been unable to say no to the challenge. 'I didn't change the key. It was Geraint.'

'Are you a five-year-old? You stand up to your little boss, and you say no. But no, you get off on proving you can do it, even if you mess half of it up. Even I could tell bits of it were in the wrong key. Where did that leave Nick? I know you…'

Jane took a deep breath.

'Okay, it would be unfair to say that because I know you better than the other teachers, I could inject some of what I think is your personal story into all this, but you have to learn that there's more than one person in life. It's not just you and your psychodrama. If you were less focused on yourself you'd be more…' She looked away and then round the cathedral, obviously trying not to blurt out words that were clear in her mind. 'Whatever happened with me is one thing, but don't take out your ego on my son. Sort it out with Geraint, and next time if he wants it in F double sharp diminished whatever, say no, we'll do it as we agreed in G.'

The acknowledgement of his thoughtlessness made Matthew feel bad all evening and all night, but the gravity of Jane's words gave him the perspective not to be demolished by the messily handwritten page that he found crammed into his pigeon hole in the song school the next morning:

Matt: yesterday's mistakes, in order:

Psalm, unsuitable registrations in verses 4 and 5; treble line error in verse 7. It was unsteady throughout and sounded like you were indisposed. Were you?

Magnificat: Too slow. Too deliberate, weak transposition skills, not following the subtleties of my beat. Registration too loud in the first section. Mistakes in bars 2 (can't we even get a couple of bars in before your first mistake?), 4, 5, 11, 12, 16, 21, 22, 23 etc. In bar 31 the pedal sounded for three quavers longer than it should.

Nunc Dimittis: out of time with my accelerando. Gloria in wrong key.

Hymns: not repeating repeated bass notes, sounds old-fashioned.

Should I go on? If you continue to exhibit this lack of professional ability I shall ask for you to be removed from your post.

The letter was unsigned, and possibly contravened even the fief-like laxities of ecclesiastical employment law, but it still fuelled Matthew's insistent feeling that Geraint was more musically gifted and his main criticisms might be correct. This was reinforced by what Jane had said about his personal deficiencies. He sat in despondency for hours. Then he thought about Chloë. Talking to her would make him feel much better. She'd sent the tape, so hopefully she would be receptive to talking to him. He phoned her. Miraculously, she answered.

'Hi Matthew, how are you?'

'Fine,' he said.

'Did you get my tape?'

'Yes, it was great. How have you been?'

After a pause she said: 'I was going to phone you. I've only been back a week. I had a tour that fell into my lap. Playing guitar in somebody else's band.' She sounded guarded. 'It just happened and I had to go.'

This was probably not a full explanation of why she had vanished. If she'd been back a week already, she hadn't rushed to phone him. But then she'd made and sent the tape. Perhaps she was treading carefully. But speaking to her felt so good that he didn't care. She was back. She was on the phone. He was in her aura. She asked how he was again and he mentioned the situation with Geraint's notes.

'What an arse.' Then she lapsed into a silence, yet he could tell she was thinking. Then she said: 'How about we call him out? He's a bully and bullies don't like being challenged. I'll come to the cathedral and watch the music closely. Except I won't be following you, I'll be following him, and the effect he has on the choir. Like weak cues and unclear beats that stop them singing well. I'll note it all down and send a letter to him, or better still, to the bishop.'

'The dean would be the person.'

'Whatever. The point is, none of them know I've got cloth ears. I'll write a pretty persuasive letter, and then he'll get his comeuppance.'

'Cloth ears?' he asked.

'You know, Matthew. Don't make me say it.'

'Say what, that you're brilliant?'

'Say that I've got all this inside me and I can't get it out in the moment. It takes me so long to work it out.'

The next day Chloë turned up for evensong, and happened to arrive as Matthew was crossing the cathedral on his way to the organ loft. He stopped and nodded at her to wait. Geraint was still fussing around his music stand. When Geraint finally stalked off to the song school to put on his surplice, Matthew gestured to her to follow. Why should she sit in the stalls? He could hide her in the organ loft. She moved out quickly from the shadows, through the wardrobe door he held open for her, and up the rickety loft stairs. Once inside the double-fronted organ, she was invisible if she didn't emerge into the loft where the console was, but remained shielded by the walls of wooden and metal pipes.

'Reporting for duty.'

She spoke with playful innocence. It felt natural to talk and smile, and the subterfuge felt good too. His feelings for her surged back as if she hadn't been away. He was with her. He could overcome Geraint. They could be together. Whatever her situation was, it didn't matter.

She found a gap between casework and pipes, and during the music she stood looking down, a silhouette except for a rectangle of light glimmering on her from the quire. She followed the music closely, but during the prayers and readings she stepped back into the gangway in the U-boat's engine room, or sat down against an open wood pipe. As the service went on she began to shake her head after each piece.

Geraint, by contrast with the last two services, had lost his concentrated poise. He often reached forward for the support of his music stand, and his beat was vague and inconsistent. Gone was the focus and rigour. At times he looked seasick. The choir sang valiantly; they'd been on good form since Geraint and Matthew's clash had produced excellent results. Nonetheless, organ and choristers couldn't stay together because the beat wasn't there to follow. Bryce watched the debilitating drama play out with face set, and read the liturgy as quickly as he could; he rushed through the Blessing and then the choir were ready to file out.

Matthew played the voluntary; Chloë sat in her in her dim hiding place and watched him. It was wonderful playing in front of her. At a couple of points he was able to snatch a look away from his music to her, and drank in the view: the surreally suggestive image of her surrounded by pipework and lit by rectangles entered the spool of his magic theatre.

Their subterfuge no longer seemed necessary. Matthew's playing was hardly at a lower level than his boss's conducting. Even if he had won this pointless competition, he felt weary. At the end of the service he walked into the gangway where, among its pipework, Chloë had risen to a kneel. But it was the wrong moment to dwell on that. She stood up and showed him a densely annotated piece of paper.

'Have I done okay, teacher?' she asked.

'You certainly did. Was he really as bad as this?'

'He was all over the place. Miss Blackham at Fairlawn Primary School was a much better conductor.'

Then she laughed. 'Anyway, this is what I'll write: "To the Dean of Bristol Cathedral, I was aghast to attend evensong and to be subjected to a performance of veritable slackness from the conductor, who derailed the choir and organist with his random beat and terrible posture. I enclose a full list of his errors. Surely this incompetent reprobate should be removed from his post forthwith. In fact, as dean, you should consider your own position. Outraged in Tunbridge Wells, Chloë." How about that?'

She laughed as artlessly as a child. She was comfortable with him, and opening up in intimacy. But Matthew found himself stepping back within himself. Was she the same woman who in some other life was so closely knitted up in the mystery of her organist Pete's destiny?

Downstairs, their route out of the otherwise deserted cathedral was blocked. Geraint was swaying in the crossing, staring at one of the pillars, mouthing inaudible words. They froze. Geraint focused on them and smiled, but said nothing. They accelerated past him and out. Despite the bitterness of the previous days, he could now see Geraint was in trouble. He felt compassion for him, and told Chloë as they left through the north-west porch.

'I don't,' she said. 'He's a tool. He oppresses you for two days and then starts talking to a pillar as if we should feel sorry for him. If I had the word of God and a two-handed sword I'd stab him, pillar and all. Sorry, I've been touched on a nerve. I'm a blues singer. He was so rude to me. He needs his comeuppance.'

'He just doesn't know anything about blues.'

'He's a coward. He put you through that and then wants sympathy. That's not the rules of the game.'

They lapsed into silence. He wanted to ask about the missing Pete, and her own absence, but didn't want to bring up contentious subjects. A harried look in her eyes suggested she knew he wanted to, but didn't want to bring it up either.

He ventured: 'Because of our trip to Pete's house, I now read the *Evening Post*. But nothing seems to have been reported.'

For a second she was motionless, then she laughed with irony. 'I do too. It's amazing that Pete was such an arse that no one's noticed he's not around.'

She started to speak a couple of times, but couldn't find the words.

Then she said: 'You saw *Candyman*, right?'

'Yeah.'

'It was good, wasn't it?'

'Terrifying, especially dubbed in German.'

She laughed, and held her hands in front of her eyes, at the welcome distraction from their seriousness. Then she looked through her fingers at him and lowered her hands:

'That film's a kind of metaphor. If you look in a mirror and say "Candyman" five times, what you're looking for might come and find you. I went searching in my life, and…'

She ran out of words again.

'Look,' she said, 'I've got to bounce.' She didn't move. She was looking down and frowning. Then she looked at him as if to ask if he was alright.

It was nice to be looked at. He smiled. 'Would you like a cigarette?'

'I would,' she said. 'Why not have one of mine?'

She flicked out a Pall Mall for him.

'Thanks,' he said. 'They're nicer than mine.'

'I know.' She lit them up, and in the moment of flame he caught her fleeting smile.

They smoked without saying much. It was awkward, not speaking because of the subject they were avoiding, but nonetheless they were together.

'Matthew,' she finally said, 'there are things in my life I need to clear up. I'm not really around at the moment.'

He didn't know what to say but looked at her with what he hoped appeared as understanding.

'That said, I've got a gig coming up,' she continued. 'I know you like coming to them, and I like you being there, but for this one we might have to do things differently. It might be my turn to give you an assignment.'

'Okay,' he said.

'I'll phone you when I know what to do.'

They stood in silence.

Finally he asked: 'Will you want us to see each other when it's over?'

'Matthew, you've made no demands, you're the most polite person I've ever met; all I can say is that I hope you'll still enjoy meeting me when you know a bit more about me.'

Matthew found that he enjoyed being led by Chloë. He could imagine what was in the shrouded car, which presumably had a bearing on whatever was happening with her, but he felt excitement, not dread. What were her hidden depths? Surely the revelation would not be sordid, but would relate to a romantic, artistic nature wanting more from the world than it customarily offered, even if that involved matters of life and death.

'Chloë,' he said, 'I truly have no idea what's going on, but I'll say one thing. As far as I'm concerned, we went to Pete's house to look for him, and he wasn't there. There was no suggestion that anything was out of the ordinary or that he might, in any way, shape or form, still be there.'

She registered what he said, but couldn't find words to express herself.

'It's okay,' he said. 'You don't have to say anything.'

The glowing end of his cigarette was in danger of singeing his fingers. He took one last drag and threw it away. Blue clouds loomed over the cathedral, tinted orange by the streetlamps coming on. The usual crusties sat on the Green. The coals of their spliffs buzzed in the dusk. A girl in combat fatigues was bent over a drum, intoxicated by her rhythm. He could just hear the tapping above the street noise, lagging behind her motions. A bus pulled away from its stop, swamping everything with the noise of its engine and a blur of neon. He pulled his eyes back to Chloë. She had still to finish her cigarette, and the centimetre or so of it remaining marked the time that he would have with her. She finished it, they said goodbye and she walked slowly away across College Green.

Chloë's words about Geraint rang through Matthew's head all night and the next day: 'he needs his comeuppance'. Surely she was right, but why did he still feel compassion? He made an appointment to see Bryce and outlined what had happened. The dean had already formed his own conclusions:

'I'm not going to sack him yet, but I don't like this drama going on in the music department. As such, I am disbanding the department, and both cathedral musicians will work independently from each other and answer directly to me. Geraint will be Director of Cathedral Music, but he will only be responsible for the choir, not the organ or organist. I want to create a new position for you. You will be Cathedral Organist. It's just a couple of words, but titles are important. To make it official, the pay will be higher…' Bryce smiled with the closest to scorn a dean in the Church of England could decently reach. '…by thirty pounds a month.'

The pay-rise was a token, but Matthew sat back, satisfied and happy. His new title endorsed him and signalled a new relationship with both Bryce and Geraint. It also signalled permanence and professional respect. For the first time he felt established and secure in his working life at the cathedral.

'There's one more thing,' said Bryce. 'As you know, the new organ is almost finished and it will be installed soon. While building a second organ isn't something I'd ever have advocated, it's arriving and I want to make a success of it. You are in charge of it. We need an event to mark it. I've let this slip somewhat, but if it's being delivered imminently, then I want you to plan an immediate concert that will put it on the map.'

'It doesn't have to be immediate, because it will take a bit of time to assemble it and then they have to voice the pipes. That could take a month.'

Matthew was thinking as he was speaking. He was the wrong person to give the concert. He would love to play *The Art of Fugue* on the new organ, but he needed more time to prepare it. He didn't want to be burdened with the extroversion of putting on a popular programme and communicating the music to the satisfaction of a crowd. It should be someone else. Having booked Chloë at short notice, he wondered if he could pull off another such booking.

'Wouldn't it be better,' Matthew asked, 'to book an organist from outside, rather than me or Geraint? Someone of the highest professional standing. I think I know someone who could do it at a month's notice.'

'Whom would you invite to play?'

Matthew answered confidently: 'Heinz-Günther.'

XVIII

The gates at the west end of the cathedral, with their avant-garde ironwork and inch-thick glass, were swung open. Mr Quantock, hair perfectly greased, used a boathook to pull down the bolts. He then watched critically as the rental truck reversed into the doorway. Wearing dungarees, but rather clean-cut, three aging men unloaded the frame and case of the Richard Galvin Memorial Organ, and started to assemble it against the back of the altar-screen in the Lady Chapel.

It had been built over the past few months in their workshop, then taken to pieces for transport and reassembly. The unstained oak was light, but would darken over the ages. Closed on three sides and to the top, the case was like a speaker cabinet, directing the sound out of the front, though the side-walls were hinged and could be opened for tuning or repairs. The façade of the instrument took shape quickly over the next few days, but the demands of the fiddly mechanical action, tuning and voicing meant that the installation would take several weeks overall. Matthew doted over every detail.

First in was the heavy electric blower, a reverse hoover, the only part of the organ that couldn't have existed in 1700. Authenticity wouldn't involve hiring beggars to pump the folding leather bellows, but they could also be pumped by hand if the electricity failed. Then the mechanical key action, hundreds of narrow trackers, like wooden threads, to connect the keys to the windchests. The rollerboards that allowed these trackers to change direction were as ingenious as railway marshalling yards. The pipes arrived in sets of drawers on wheels, each shallow drawer being lifted off vertically to reveal another layer of pipes. The odd-shaped pipes were installed first, at the back of the case. These pipes would never be seen by anyone, aside from the tuner who mounted a ladder and could peer into the case. The Krummhorn with its rifle-grenade-shaped resonators, the dumpy Vox Humana, the square wooden pipes of the pedal Violone, the Rohrflöte with its narrow tube protruding from each sealed pipe-top. The metal already looked dim and ancient.

To the master Rüdiger, the spirit of the Baroque was an ornate vessel running over with biotic sensualism. So he voiced the pipes as warmly as possible, accentuating the rare colours of the Quintadena with its heavy twelfth overtone, and the sour Viola. So the instrument's voice emerged gradually, for Rüdiger's appreciation of ideal tone meant he was not a fast worker.

Matthew had estimated the timescale correctly. The whole process would take almost a month. He watched as much as he could, and asked Hannon to as well. How many times would they have the opportunity to watch this age-old craft in action?

One person was not around to observe, but she dwelt in his thoughts. He had forged a real connection with her and yet now she was relegated to being an Other. He hated falling back into such a fantasy world. He wanted life. When he saw a poster near the Harbour Shed for the gig that she had mentioned, he felt a pull of eagerness in his chest.

The last poster had been merely functional, a photo of the band with their name and the date of the gig, slapped on to the wall in the half-timbered pub. This one was more artistic. The words *Killing Me Killing You Blues* were skilfully lettered around an alluring drawing of Chloë standing with her back to the artist, looking back over her shoulder. He didn't know what it meant, but it seemed both scary and redolent with hidden information that must relate to the situation with Pete and the man in the hood.

She'd said she would phone, but the days passed without her calling. He couldn't phone her because to do so would be to pursue her unduly. If you fancied someone, weren't you supposed to play it cool? Doing so was even more difficult, because his desire for her wasn't dampened by the aura of danger. He felt weighed down, even in his normal day-to-day life. Again, he found himself pacing and raging in his flat: werdo, werdo, werdo. Finally she phoned.

After a little small talk he said: 'It's a great poster. Is it some kind of message?'

'Yes,' she said. 'Someone might come to the gig. You'll recognise him – it's our man from UTK. You see, once upon a time, I had a friend in Knoxville. He's called Troy. I haven't seen him for nine years. Now, he's come to pay me a visit. God, I wish he'd just come up and said hello at that first gig.'

'But he did, he wrote you a note.' Matthew described what the man had written, how he had left the note on the Hammond under the whiskey glass, but then in the heightened emotions of the gig Baz had removed it.

'Chlo, Chlo, Chlo? Three thousand? But he's going to think I'm blanking him. He doesn't know I didn't see that letter.'

The line went quiet. He could imagine her eyes focusing on a world that wasn't there or then.

Then she said: 'He doesn't know where I live, and I don't know where he's staying. But I need to communicate with him, which we can only do like this. Hence the poster. It's not exactly subtle. But if I meet him, I just might like to have you around. Here's the plan…'

She outlined her vision of what the evening would entail. The venue for the gig was the *Thanatos*, a music venue on board a retired coaster permanently moored in the harbour. The gangplank was the only route on or off. Matthew would wait outside the venue, noting the arrival of Troy and keeping an eye on him. If Chloë and Troy left together, he would follow them discreetly, and she would aim to manoeuvre herself and Troy so they were always visible.

'He's going to know who I am,' Matthew said, 'because he saw me play at the pseudo-bop.'

'That might keep you safer.' Then her voice turned incredulous. 'Going back to the letter, he said it was the three thousandth draft?'

'Three thousand two hundred and eighty-fifth. The number's etched into my mind. It's so totally insane.'

'But he's not at all insane,' she said bleakly. 'What's happened?'

The nights were getting longer and the appointed evening was warm and the sun hadn't yet set. Matthew walked to the *Thanatos*. Bands played in a long bar whose portholes curved along the side of the ship. He sat on a bollard a hundred yards further up the quay, from where he could see the vessel. Chloë would play a short acoustic set on her metal guitar, opening for a more well-known soul band. That was all according to plan. What seemed a disconcerting omen was that this other band's crowd didn't seem at all interested in her. They stood on the quay smoking and chugging their drinks, abandoning Chloë's set to the bar staff inside. The audience certainly didn't want to confront truth in blues, but would Troy want to go inside and be an audience of one? From his vantage point Matthew couldn't hear the music, and no tall man in a UTK hoodie – nor anyone else out of the ordinary – seemed to appear.

Was she even inside playing? The elastic band tugged at Matthew, but he stayed resolutely on his bollard. What was she singing? Was she singing songs written for this man? If so, he didn't envy her having to sing carefully composed songs to an empty room.

The forty-five minutes allotted for her set passed, during which the funkily-dressed members of the next band emerged and started pressing the flesh with their fans on the quayside.

Matthew wanted to push them into the harbour. Then they reclimbed the gangplank and descended below decks. The audience began to knock back their dregs and file on board. When Chloë emerged with her guitar case it was on to an empty quay.

They both knew that the other was there, but she didn't look at him. Was his assignment over? Had their man not turned up, or was he somewhere unseen? She collected herself for a moment, then headed off along the quay towards the corner with Welsh Back. He decided he would shadow her around the harbour, but once she was beyond it, and beyond where their man could know where she was, he would peel off.

So he followed her in the twilight around the U-shape of the harbour until he could turn back on himself into Queen Square. The sky was light but the buildings were dark. There he cut through the cobbled lane between the Queen Anne merchant's houses aiming for the diagonal main road that passed through the middle of the square. As he reached the square he looked back. His heart lurched. A loping figure detached itself from the shadows and moved towards where he had left Chloë. Matthew's hair stood up and he felt weightless. He turned fully around carefully, knowing that if he moved too quickly his limbs might prove uncontrollable. Slowly and carefully, he retraced his steps back towards the quay. He could now see the hooded figure ahead. He reached the corner of Welsh Back, up which the hoodman had turned, and a hundred feet beyond him he could see Chloë walking ahead.

Would Mr UTK follow her home? A protective voice insisted that this interloper mustn't find out where she lived. Matthew himself didn't know, beyond her remark that she lived in Clifton, where there were a hundred possible streets. But as she reached the mouth of King Street, she must have felt her follower's presence. She slowed and turned. Did she see one or both of her followers? Then she resumed walking, heading into the Georgian centre of the old city.

She walked calmly. The hoodman padded on patiently. Their

plan had gone awry. Did she know she was being followed? Perhaps she did, because she wasn't leading him towards Clifton and she couldn't have picked a more atmospheric route. She skirted the empty covered market and walked down the narrow street towards the church spire built into a gatehouse in the old city wall. Once she had passed through the gateway she crossed Quay Street into Christmas Street, then angled left along Rupert Street. Matthew surmised that she was aware of being followed, and guessed where she would force an audience with Troy, her hooded acolyte. It would be Christmas Steps.

Sure enough, her route took her to the mediaeval stepped alley that ran up the hill from the centre towards Kingsdown. Matthew clung to the shadows at the foot of the steps. It wasn't yet dark, and the ancient lamp-posts were already alight, so the hooded man had no choice but to ascend in full view after her. When she was about halfway up she turned, her guitar case hanging like a teardrop Norman shield, and looked straight at him.

Troy stopped. They both stood still. They didn't rush together like estranged but still-interested lovers, which made Matthew glad. She simply stared at him. Then she raised her left hand and allowed him to advance. She was brave. The alley might be an assured stop on any tourist's walking tour of the city, but it was currently deserted. Troy stopped a couple of steps below her, but their faces were level, as he was almost a foot taller. She waited for him to speak, and then responded to whatever he had said. After a minute's talk she stepped aside and he climbed the last couple of steps, then they fell into a walk together, slowly, about five feet apart, each hugging their opposite sides of the alley, but close enough for wary conversation. After a moment, in keeping with his air of menacing politeness, Troy offered his hand. She extended her arm briefly across the gulf between them, giving him the guitar case to carry.

They emerged at the top of the steps and made their way left, cutting back diagonally downwards along Colston Street and then bearing right on to Trenchard Street into an odd area: once-debonair, now-worn Georgian houses, mostly converted to offices, sat next to wayward Brutalist blocks including an enormous multi-storey car park.

The intersection of these two forces was The Nightshade, a nightclub in an eighteenth-century basement from which steps ascended into a concrete forecourt separating it from the neighbouring student hall. Benches were placed around a paved space, and fairy lights and even a Chinese lantern hung in two substantial trees, enlivening the falling night. The bass and drums of a band were audible from the basement. The Bristol Sound swung, and the area teemed with school and undergraduate revellers. Chloë and Troy prowled through them, far enough apart that they passed either side of several groups.

The benches were all taken. Troy and Chloë stopped under one of the trees and its adornment of lights. Occasionally party-people flitted between groups, to the bar, to the music, but the two conspirators remained static. Matthew advanced as far as he thought safe, standing behind the second tree. Chloë was keeping her distance from her devotee, but nonetheless it seemed their intense discussion had been picked up from the day before. Not that this intimacy boded any agreement. They were at loggerheads: he was beseeching, she was saying no.

The minutes passed. Had she led them to a place where he could safely approach? Matthew saw a spot from which he might be able to overhear them. He carefully moved closer to them, into a sealed former doorway that was now an alcove, and into which the fairy light did not penetrate. He hugged the wall in what he hoped was sufficient darkness. He could hear their talking now. The man spoke in a gentle American southern accent, undulating with long vowels.

'Do I have a sign on my head saying "don't take me seriously"? That man. I was so angry. He didn't respect you. He was so arrogant. He didn't take me seriously. When I cuffed him he mocked me. So I punched him out. I guess I punched him too hard. Then I had to finish it. Chloë, I'm scared.'

'Don't get scared. Think clearly and leave.'

'I don't want to go back to jail. I don't want to be one of those pasty geriatric dudes in black and white.'

'What are you talking about?

'I was in the pen.'

'Where?'

'The penitentiary.'

'My God, what did they get you for?'

'Statutory rape.'

Her eyes widened. 'But haven't you always been…'

He shifted uneasily. She paused and neither of them spoke for a moment.

'You know I couldn't have done it,' he said. 'You're the only one who knows me.' He stood more firmly. 'It was that Van Vries girl. You met her.'

'That goth who was still at high school? Who stared at you through those big kohled eyes?'

'But I didn't do anything. Her father wanted her to be normal. Saw me and pulled strings and stitched me up. They wanted me gone, Chlo. And then I saw things and did things and had things done. But I wrote you every day. Every day the same. For nine years.'

She stared at him with concern, pity, fear, horror, feminine derision and many other emotions – all in all a kind of love.

'Three hundred and sixty-five days times nine,' he said. 'Every day. Three thousand—'

'Don't!'

'You saw my letter.'

'No, I never got it.'

'I left it on the organ.'

'I know. I only just found out. It got thrown away.'

'How do you know?'

She stopped. He let her writhe for what seemed an age.

'It's okay he told you,' he breathed. 'Your second boyfriend's sweet, isn't he? Talented.'

'What second boyfriend?' she rejoined. 'How could I ever have another boyfriend after what you did to me?'

'You just need someone with a broad mind.'

'Where is that person? I'm unlovable because of you.'

Matthew was craning forward, and had to repress an urge to advance on them. What had he done to her? How could she be unlovable? Her mind, voice, spirit, lungs and fingers, her personality, all amounting to the body that she was. Her music! What about her could be unlovable?

Troy spoke, completing Matthew's thoughts: 'Chlo, you embody everything that's lovable for the man who can grasp it.'

'Who do you think you are? A penny-Nietzsche? People who can grasp it don't exist. It's all in your mind.'

'But if it's in my mind, why are you offering yourself to me?'

She tremored, caught between wanting and not wanting him.

'So you can live,' she said. 'Live and move on.'

They had reached a place of extreme intimacy together that would surpass most people's experience. If the goal of life was to find another soulmate and seek out the furthest boundaries of what was possible, no wonder Troy didn't want to move on to someone or somewhere else that, by comparison to Chloë, would be insufferably dreary.

'I don't want to live,' he said.

This made her yell: 'Yes you do.' Then she got her voice under control: 'I can give you what deep down you really want, not this nihilism shit. Everyone wants it. I'll give it to you. Isn't that better for everyone?'

'I won't feel anything.'

She was silenced.

'And you won't, either,' he added.

'I can pretend. You can pay me if that makes it feel right for you. And then you'll be better.'

'And you trust me?'

'I'll always trust you. I know you'll never touch me. I mean, not touch me. You can, if you want, I mean…' Even her breathing was confused. She drew in enough air to whisper: 'I meant, never hurt me.'

'Touch you,' he sighed.

'Troy, you had your chance. I lay at your feet.'

'And now I'm lying at yours,' he said. 'Help me.'

'You can have one night, but then get on a plane and leave.'

'Only if you come with me.'

'I don't want to live in Knoxville.'

'We can go anywhere,' he said. 'You choose, as long as it's Stateside.'

'I don't… I'm here… My life is here now. '

'Do you think blues players would play blues if they had life?' he asked, sounding reasonable. 'Are you going to put your life above your music?'

'Leave me alone, Troy. You know how much I struggle.'

'If you don't want to get comfortable, come with me.'

'It's too late.'

'No it isn't. You're just beginning.'

'No. I'm old. Already. I know how to play blues. You have to leave me alone.'

'I can't.'

They were now gearing towards a full argument. But the young people all around them were intent on their own fun and didn't notice or care.

'I'm not going with you,' she insisted.

'If you won't come with me then you have to do it,' he said.

'Do what?'

'You know.' His voice grew quieter, but still audible. 'You'll be the last person I see. And you'll watch me so I know I existed. And when I'm done and gone you'll just walk out and leave. You're the only one, Chlo, always and always, you have to be there, you have to.'

Matthew tried to comprehend what he was hearing. Was Troy proposing her involvement in his death? But how could that…? He couldn't even articulate the implications.

Chloë was shaking her head, mouthing, searching for

words. Finally she spoke: 'Troy, I'll give you everything I can for a night.'

'I want more night than even you can give me.'

'No.'

'It's my only way out, and only you can do it.'

'No.'

'Why not?' he asked. 'No one'll ever know.'

'You can't expect that.'

'I thought you were going to live outside society. Like me.'

'That's juvenile. I was eighteen. It was summer madness. I'm not like that now. I've grown up.'

'I've always been grown up. I'm as tall as a tree.'

'What does that mean?' she asked.

'You won't have to do anything. Just be there.'

'I won't do it.'

'You don't have to. Just watch.'

'I can't. I won't. I don't want to.'

'You have to. In recognition of me.'

'I do recognise you,' she insisted.

'No you don't. Not yet.'

'Troy, you don't have to.'

'I want to.'

'I want doesn't get. Just go.'

'I can't.'

'Go or I'll tell the police,' she shouted.

He stopped. His voice dropped: 'You wouldn't.'

'I don't want to.' She spoke quietly but firmly. 'If you go I won't. But if you stay I will.'

'I'm not going back to jail. I wish I was dead nine years ago.'

'Then go.'

They stood staring at each other. They had garnered the concerned looks of some of the clubbers, who were probably the age Chloë and Troy had been in Knoxville, and were probably even now building their own formative experiences of heady music and the gamut of emotions. Ultimately these were more important to the clubbers than a pair of strangers tiffing, and they turned back to themselves.

Troy took a step towards her. His voice almost vanished to a seductive purr. 'You don't want to find out what it's like? What I now know? What I did to your other organ man?'

'Don't turn it around on to me.'

'I'm not. You know I'd never harm a hair on *your* pretty head.' He paused significantly as the import of what he said sank in. 'But what about other heads?'

Matthew wrestled with the implication. Troy had already killed Pete, so was capable of murder. Were other people going to die? Was he, standing just a few feet away from Troy and Chloë, risking immolation?

'No,' said Chloë. 'No one else.'

'It's up to you. If you don't want them to be…touched, then you have to do what I want.'

Tears were in her eyes. 'Troy, you're going loco. I can't. I won't.'

'Then I can't stop myself. Because you have to do what I need. You're the only person in the whole wide world who I can come to.'

'Troy, I don't want to be a crone in a jumpsuit any more than you do. I love fantasy – the darker the better – but this is real. You've got away with it for now, but it has to stop. You have to go. Get on a plane. Tomorrow. Go.'

'My happy love, you make it sound so easy. But only you can stop it. Bury me in the darkness where I belong. Only you.'

'I'm not going to. You have to go. Promise me.'

'But I bring something into your life that you need.'

'What?' she almost sobbed.

He sounded so clement. 'Death.'

She balked, but wasn't able to offer a riposte. The drinkers round about were now actively avoiding them, though not disturbing them. Troy reached up and, though she cowered away, she let him gently touch her face.

'A like mind is like a rare animal.' His hand lowered a little and he caressed her neck, just edging his thumb round her windpipe. 'Difficult to find, hard to tame, and almost impossible to keep.'

He took her right hand with his left and raised it to his neck and held it there.

'Don't you want to know what it's like?' he asked.

'No I don't. You will go.'

'I can't.'

She snatched her hand away from his neck. 'Then I'll make you go senile in stripes.'

'You wouldn't,' he shouted, the sudden power of his voice breaking the terrifying intimacy and turning the heads of everyone around.

'Give me my guitar,' she shouted back, wrestling for the case.

He was tall, heavy and held it solid. 'It's from Knoxville. You are too.'

'Then keep it.'

She broke away and ran, not a well-controlled sprint, but the erratic flailing of a woman whose muscles were water.

Troy stood and watched her tortuous progress for what seemed a minute, as she ran out of the club precinct, around the curve and up the incline on to the foot of Park Street, where she turned right and was obscured by the buildings. Then he swung around and locked eyes with Matthew, who took a step backwards in surprise and terror and banged into the pebbledash behind him.

Troy reached effortlessly up into low boughs of the tree and unhung the Chinese lantern, then carried it forward. Matthew found himself closing his eyes and looking down like a child. He forced himself to look up at the man who approached him. Troy stared blinklessly, the reflection of the lantern flickering in his pale eyes. Then the hoodman smiled and his face crinkled.

'What are you doing here, Mr Organist?'

His inquisitive expression was that of a reasonable man, an embodiment of mildness and sadness as much as terror. Whatever was going to happen was going to happen, and they didn't have to make it unduly unpleasant.

Matthew's knees quaked and arms shook. His fingers were useless. It was all he could do to stay upright.

Troy carefully placed the guitar case on the broken concrete paving stones. 'It's hers. You give it to her, so she knows that you were privy to our conversation.'

He nodded in valediction, put the lantern down on a table and loped away in the opposite direction to Chloë, past the interminable stretch of cheap concrete, bricks and tiles of the offices and car park that represented the drab life from which he so recoiled. Then he vanished.

Matthew lurched forward a few steps and collapsed on to one of the picnic benches. He gazed at his feet as if winded.

After a few minutes a girl with a beer and cigarette, who was certainly underage, asked if the guitar case was his. She and other clubbers had been stepping around it. She brought it over to him. He thanked her and remained sitting. He didn't want to go home. He didn't want to take the guitar and give it back to Chloë. To do so would inevitably invite a post-mortem discussion, and he didn't know how she would react to his witnessing the full intimacy of her exchange with Troy. Was eavesdropping on their fearful death-bargain more than his allotted assignment? But thinking ostensibly about the guitar case dilemma might give him time to come to grips with the moral and passionate complexities of what he had just seen. He lit a cigarette. The cigarette didn't help him come to any conclusions. He remained sitting, and then lit another.

'Is that your guitar, mister?'

He knew the voice. He looked up into Chloë's eyes.

'You saw all that?' she asked.

He nodded. A wave of compassion overwhelmed him. She thought her relationship with Troy made her less attractive and arresting, when the reverse was true. She couldn't see that she was a pathfinder, a flare fired into the dark vale of his life.

'Are you my guardian angel?' she asked.

Guardian angel? He had to come back to earth. 'Not really.' He found himself speaking in a bland tone to minimise what had happened: 'Troy saw me and knows who I am.'

'Well, you're part of the family now.'
'That's where I want to be.'
'Let's call each other,' she said.
Was Troy waiting somewhere to accost her? 'Are you safe?'
'Yes.'
'Am I safe?'
'I've told him to go. He has to. He's got no choice. He must.'
This was not the moment for blandness. He allowed all his passion to flow into his voice. 'Chloë, whatever happened with Troy, you did what I wish I'd done. I've never done anything. You're not unlovable. You've lived. And it makes you so attractive.'

She looked dazed, then she beamed, radiant relief creasing her face with laugh lines and glowing more than he could imagine to be justifiable. She stepped forward and then sat in his lap facing him. He was shocked. She looked straight into his eyes. She'd been crying, which added to the lustre of hers. She leant forward and kissed him on the lips, opening them with hers, forcing her tongue into his mouth. His being and body responded, feeling her hips against his, the warmth of her crotch against his thigh, her breast within the arc of his hand, her soft, hot, wet… Then she was on her feet standing in front of him holding the guitar case.

'Matthew…' She held up her finger and drew a suggestive slit in the air. 'Nothing'll come of nothing.'

She strode off with the guitar. He was left with his fluttering heart and half a cigarette.

XIX

Chloë phoned and suggested dinner. This was to be a bold step into a carefree life. They met at an Italian restaurant in a time-warped half-timbered building near the pub on King Street. Her normally slouchy walk was springier. His was too. Eros had escaped the traces. Both of them had years of pent-up erotic frustration. He could feel it, and could feel that she felt it too. Where would it lead? Could he stop himself being a spectator in his own life…and grasp it?

The waiter, Galeazzo, knew Chloë and sat them at a table upstairs.

'He's a friend of my brother Paul. Part of the pack who all went to the same gigs. This'll all be reported back to Paul, assuming their everlasting cloud of dope smoke isn't too thick, but the food actually makes it worth it.'

Both floors of the restaurant were made up of what were once several rooms interconnected with neck-height doorways, but the wattle and daub had been taken out from between the tinder-dry beams, so the area was opened out without losing its cosy, crowded feel.

'Sort of like a cage,' said Chloë as she sat down. 'How was your day?'

Her tone was that of a co-conspirator. Their lives were intertwined.

'If you really want to know, I was practising the Bach mirror fugues today.'

'What's a mirror fugue?'

They had been sitting together for only a minute. He felt the incident with Troy hanging over them, but she didn't seem to. Should he launch into an intense musical discussion and ignore the world?

'Walcha introduced me to them,' he said. 'They're only two, in *The Art of Fugue*. Bach wrote two pairs of fugues where, in the second one, everything from the first one is upside down. So a melody in the treble going up in the first becomes a melody in the bass going down in the second. The first pair is pure and sombre, the second energetic and joyful.'

Galeazzo appeared, touching Chloë proprietorially around the shoulders, and they ordered. A carafe of wine arrived with a platter of artichoke hearts and different types of salami, ham and cheese. It was a proper Italian menu with a pasta course and then a meat course, though with a hint of West Country in the detail. Chloë suggested they share a plate of nettle ravioli, and Matthew enjoyed the closeness that brought. Then she went for carpaccio and he for osso bucco. Wine flowed and they chatted. The world was a long way away and couldn't touch them.

'So do you think,' she asked, 'that your mirror fugues reflect life?'

'Like can I be your mirror please?' he found himself loosened up by the wine. 'I hope I find my mirror. Isn't that what we're all looking for, the other half of a perfect pair?'

'If such a person exists. Is a tarnished version going to work?'

'Sounds like a mirror image,' laughed Matthew.

'You, tarnished?' she asked. 'You organists are bolted into society. You're part of these big buildings. It gives you a stature that's… Can I say this?' She lowered her eyes then looked back at him. '…That's quite intimidating.'

She must like him. The food arrived. Good timing. He felt the protections of his normal life had been burnt off. The Other, who had held him aloft over the years, had dropped him. He was falling hundreds of feet through the sky. Like Icarus. No, that was too obvious. How about like Steuermann Alfred Mühler, cox of a stricken Zeppelin? Under the sixteen-foot ceiling of the library at Moultrie, Matthew had read about how Mühler had survived falling eight thousand feet in his gondola as the rest of the airship blazed above him. Even if the evening ended now, he had experienced enough to judge the totality of his life.

They ate their main course and talked through dessert, though not about deep subjects.

'How about,' she said self-mockingly, 'a digestif, perhaps?'

'What, like Crème de Cacao or something?'

'Yes, exactly.'

'Okay. But you'll have to choose what type,' he said.

'Let's have grappa.'

'Isn't that like ninety-eight percent?'

She blinked at him. 'So?'

Then a hollow feeling overcame him. Chloë liked him, and she treated him as if he was a normalised and integrated person. But if she knew the doubts he felt, his worry of inadequacy, sense of apartness and cut-offness, his creation of Others, if she was warned, then she couldn't blame him later if…

'You know, I don't…' Then his voice turned sarcastic. 'I suppose an ideal man would be super-experienced, super…'

He couldn't finish the sentence.

'Matthew… Matty, can I call you Matty?'

'Sure.' He thought of his father.

'Matty…'

Matthew regretted opening the subject, but now he had started he had to say something that made sense. He looked down.

'I've been pretty focused on music. I haven't…'

He had to go on.

'I've missed out on…' For a long time he didn't know how to finish the sentence. She waited politely and didn't press him. Finally he said: '…Life's more humane experiences.'

'So you don't fill up your bath with champagne every night and live a life of the senses?'

He laughed. What a considerate way for her to rescue him. 'No.'

She put on a mocking voice. 'But if you're by yourself you won't get any memories.'

'That's what I worry is true.'

'Don't worry. That's what someone said to me when I said I wanted to go to America by myself. Since then I've discovered I have plenty of memories.'

'Yes, me too.'

Her hands lay just across the table. He edged his fingers forward. He touched her fingertips. They didn't move away.

She attracted Galeazzo and asked for grappa, which he brought in brandy balloons. They raised their glasses and drank. She inclined forward. 'So, Matty, what's the wildest thing you've ever done?'

His heart sank again. Should he tell her about his experience in Germany, which broke the terms of conventional morality and was therefore wild, yet surely would come across as lonely and sordid? There must be something he had done or seen at college that was both wild and funny.

'I remember someone snorting vodka at an organ scholar dinner. So there!'

'Snorting vodka? How does that work?'

'I don't know, he just did it.'

'And what did you think?' she asked.

'He looked sophisticated.'

'Matty, did you snort vodka?'

'No, I had choir practice the next morning.'

'I bet you had.' Her eyes filled with wildness. 'Matty, what have you got tomorrow morning?'

'Choir practice? Actually, tomorrow I don't.'

'But the stage is still eerily similar.' She leant in and whispered: 'Sod tomorrow.'

She took a spoon from the table and poured some grappa into it from her glass.

Matthew whispered: 'Grappa's much, much stronger than vodka.'

'Oh, like ten times as strong.'

They looked around. No one was watching. She passed him the spoon.

'Chloë, I can't.'

'Matty, think of what your guy Walcha said about knowing the parts thoroughly. This is part of life. You need to know it thoroughly.'

Her intent brown eyes emboldened him. With a flourish he took up the spoon, blocked one nostril with his thumb and snorted the grappa. He recoiled, holding a hand out as if to catch the liquid, though none came. He felt as if he was going to sneeze blood. There was nothing to swallow via the back of his throat. The liquid had vanished. All the veins in his nose were tingling and burning in a combination of pain and euphoria.

'Wow!' She beamed. 'That was epoch-making.'

'My God!' He took out his handkerchief. His eyes were watering too. 'I done lived.' He tried to blow his nose but that didn't help. 'Has anyone noticed?'

They looked around the restaurant. The diners were absorbed in their meals.

'No; no one,' she said.

He sat blinking.

A surge of laughter gripped a table in the next section. They both turned, as if busted. A pair of families with teenage children were just in from the theatre, but they weren't laughing at them. Had Galleazzo noticed? The sounds of family life pierced Matthew. Happiness. What was it? He turned back to Chloë.

'Are you from a happy family?' he asked.

'If it was just me and my parents I might have been,' she said. 'I kind of hope Galleazzo did see, just so he tells my brother, just so it makes him shut up. They put so much pressure on me to come back from America because I'd abandoned them, then they don't exactly cherish me while I'm here. My sister usually sides with them.'

'What do your parents do?'

'Very straight. My dad works for an insurance company, and

my mum works in admin at the Royal Infirmary right near here. In America I saw families that actually show affection to each other. Even that "Big Daddy / Princess" stuff can be nice. But absence makes the heart grow fonder. I left home when I was seventeen, and everyone in the family knows that. What about your parents? How's Fiala doing?'

He couldn't remember when someone had last referred to her by name.

'She's dead.'

'I'm sorry. I was hoping to meet her.'

He felt a new closeness to her. He had rarely talked about his mother. People either seemed to know already that she was dead, and avoid the subject, or they didn't know. He never brought her up because in the past it had been a conversation-stopper.

'When did she die?' she asked.

'When I was fourteen, but it's taken me this long to see how little I knew her, and…' he delved into the blackness '…and how much I should be grateful to her. I've turned not knowing her into an art form. I pretend it's darkness, when it's actually just not recognising that without her I wouldn't be a musician. And even now, after we were talking about it, I relate to her by saying she was like Walcha's mother. She wasn't. She was my mother.'

He looked up at Chloë.

'It's funny,' he continued. 'There's something attractive about having this gulf in your life. This sense that somehow you're in touch with the greater darkness, in touch with death. You see, that's better than facing up to the reality, which is, she just vanished. I don't have much of a relationship with my dad. I get around that by fixating on idealised teachers who are now dead, as if that cements my relationship with death and gives me understanding of life.'

He reached across the table and took her hand. Again, it didn't move away. He felt her warmth and vitality.

'Really, Chloë, I don't know anything about life. Vacuums are just vacuums, and darkness is just darkness.'

'Nothing is just nothing.' Then she raised her eyebrows.

Dare he hope that the two of them really were mirrors? Her hand was still within his hand.

'I—' he began.

'Shhh.' She squeezed his hand.

'What I—'

'Shhh Matty, shhh.'

'No, I need to try and finish. I used to think music made up for the fact that I didn't have much else.'

'That's a self-fulfilling argument, isn't it? It justifies not doing anything.'

'I know.'

'When it comes to it, you learn by doing things. That's all you need to know. But you're fixating on what you think I think of you. Don't you think I might be thinking, what's he going to think of me? When he knows me. When he sees me.'

'But I can see you.'

'No you can't.' She smiled. 'Not yet. I know what I think. We're both cut off at the trunk in different ways. Matty, do you know what I've done?'

'What?'

'I went down and bought some of the Kodály Method books for infants and children. I'm teaching myself all the melodies, exactly the way you'd do aural training for infants. I've had to take some knocks in terms of pride to start giving myself pre-primary music lessons, but I'm doing it, and it's working. After a big swathe of Kodály I tried some diploma-level ear tests, and they'd got easier. It's possible to go back to the beginning. In all senses.'

The restaurant was emptying. Galeazzo approached and ostentatiously made sure the bill was only for Matthew, who felt satisfaction paying for a meal that was more expensive than any before. The chunk of his weekly salary represented a step into a new life.

'You're heading for Clifton?' he asked when they were outside. Matthew was swaying and while he wasn't seeing double, the edges of objects did seem to have grown a little.

'Yeah.' She was standing rather more carefully than usual.

'Do you want to walk as far as the cathedral together?'

'Why there?'

'I live there, above the cloister.'

'What, you live at work?'

'Yeah.'

'I didn't realise. Do you have a fireman's pole?'

After a second they both got the unintentional joke. In an upswell of laughter they stared at each other. Then they were quiet but flushed. It was almost as if they might have kissed.

'Wouldn't you like a taxi?' she asked.

'I think I need the walk.'

They walked. The wine and grappa had robbed Matthew of most of his spatial awareness. College Green appeared too quickly.

'There're taxis over there,' he said. 'Let me walk you to them.'

'You can barely walk, Matty. Should I drop you off at your cloister?'

'You could if you like,' he said. 'But let me drop you off.'

'But I live a mile away.'

'So? I insist.'

There was a pause, then she said: 'Okay. Drop me off at my door.'

A taxi took them up Park Street and over the Triangle, past the fountains in front of the sandy portico of the Victoria Rooms. Floodlit, they floated past like a back projection of the Trevi Fountain in Rome. The two of them snuggled into each other. They kissed, hot and wet. This time it just happened. He felt elated, joined to the world. The taxi stopped. Matthew reached over her and opened her door.

'If I could move, I would help you out.'

'If you could move, would you like to come in?'

He paused. Everything in him wanted to go with her. Fear still held him back, but he could only grin.

Chloë spoke hot breath into his ear: 'I'll show you my hobbit feet.'

Matthew paid the driver and staggered out. They turned

to the left up one of the alleys and then flowed with it down a stone stairway into what had once been a quarry, latterly filled in with artisan's houses in a graceful Regency style. Of course she would live somewhere perfect. A moment later they stood before a stuccoed cottage.

'We're home,' he said.

'I'm home. You're far from home.'

She led him through her front door and through an inner screen of beads. He stooped through them into a compact living room.

'You know what I'm thinking,' she said. 'I saw an old Don Siegel film where a cowboy cop goes to pick up a convict in New York. He meets this girl – a hooker, I think – who's all into beads and shit. Very sensual. You're the cowboy, aren't you? Lone rider from the past, come to pay the world a visit. Well, welcome.'

He got the film reference as he looked around him. The sofa was draped with a Cajun-looking shawl. Potted spider plants multiplied in one corner. The guitar case promised its big genre with lots of history, but it rested on the closed lid of the Hammond. Despite being pushed almost into the wall, the organ's heavy mahogany crowded the modest room. An arch led through to a kitchen with a worn black-and-white linoleum floor and a Belling stove. The house had been done up last in the seventies. A steep nautical staircase climbed upwards into a realm that might free him from his past.

'We're both free,' he insisted.

'I've always been free. Would you like a drink of water?'

'Water?'

'Yeah, the champagne's for the bath.'

'Sorry, a glass of water would be very nice.'

He followed her into the kitchen area.

'Don't look too closely. You might see the algae growing in the draining board.'

She filled two glasses at the tap.

'I'll carry these. You bring the guitar. Do you want to go upstairs?'

So this was it. No more evasion was possible. As they went up to Chloë's bedroom he thanked God he was drunk. What better excuse if his body didn't perform?

'Come on, silly. Keep going.'

The bed was covered by a gold counterpane with a peacock-feather pattern. Shelves housed books and hundreds of neatly arranged tapes, LPs and a few CDs. A framed photo of a decades-old guitarist hung above the fireplace. He didn't know who she was, but the questing wildness in the woman's expression explained Chloë's fascination. There was a table by the window with a hard straight chair drawn up to it. He put the guitar case down.

She came in after him and touched his back. She pointed him towards more personal photos on the mantelpiece.

'So that's my mum, and that's my dad. There's my fabled brother. There's my sister Jen. She's a dental hygienist. You take the chair. I'll stand.'

'Stand? Are you sure?'

'Yes. So I can look down at you.' She removed the clothes hanging on the back of the chair. 'There, the chair's all yours.'

'Is that you?'

A nine-year-old with secret knowledge held behind pursed lips.

'Yep. That was when I wanted to be a horse smuggler.'

'What about this?'

Chloë was about eighteen and proudly wearing an American baseball jacket. 'Now I can see my prized jacket was too big.'

Matthew shuddered, remembering his past selves. Awkwardness. Work, work, work. Unrequited idealism. Luckily his past had been unrecorded. No images unless snapped by happenstance in someone else's photo. He would never be stalked by past selves. He was glad his history had receded into the gloom. There had never been a happy teen off to find out about the world in an American jacket who merited a photo. Did his past even exist?

'What are you thinking?' she asked.

'This place is lovely,' he said. 'How long have you been here?'

'I bought it two years ago.'

'You're a home owner?'

'I'm going to be thirty in a year or three, Matty. Five years ago I realised my parents wouldn't help. I saved. I'm here now, and with every month's payment I get closer to my goal.'

'What's that?'

'Being unshackled.'

That, he could learn from. 'I've got it all wrong. I thought a mortgage was being shackled.'

'Assuming the oil doesn't run out, you get a sort of freedom.'

He tried to focus on the trim woman, straightforward and honest, original and independent, who trod wider paths than he.

'If you promise not to laugh,' she said, 'I'll play for you.'

She lifted the steel guitar out of its case and sat on the end of the bed. He watched every movement of her fingers as she adjusted the tuning and put the metal finger-picks on her right hand thumb and fingers and a slide on the fourth finger of her left.

'This is a river blues by Big Bill Broonzy.'

'This isn't really happening to you,' said a voice; 'it'll never happen to you.' But enough of Matthew knew that it was happening and that the voice was wrong.

The river blues was jaunty with lots of slide. Matthew sat transfixed. She was using most of the fingers of both hands. Each finger had a life of its own. The guitar responded with its abrasive but arresting tone.

Then she made the blues slower.

'This is a new genre; bedroom blues.'

'Could you sing too?' he asked.

She looked at him. 'I have to think of something.' After a few moments she began a country tune and sang:

> *So it's good-bye, children, I will have to go*
> *Where the rain don't fall and the wind don't blow*
> *And yer Ulster coats, why, you will not need*
> *When you ride up in the chariot in the morn.*

She put the guitar on a stand. 'Come on,' she smiled.

'Where to?' he whispered.

'I don't sleep standing up.'

In the bathroom, he used the toothbrush she offered. He took as long as he could, but the hollow pain developing in his stomach didn't go away. When it was her turn he waited on the edge of the bed, his shirt open, but otherwise dressed. She returned in orange and red shot-silk pyjamas, logical in a home brimming with colour and texture. She'd buttoned the jacket all the way to the top. He was relieved she had acknowledged his reticence, but glad to be in the realm of intimacy where he could sense the softness and shape of her body beneath the loose and thin fabric.

She tossed him a T-shirt. It advertised her band, extra-large size, much too big. 'You can wear that.'

He put it on and took off his trousers, and they got into bed primly. Then she nuzzled into him, her face so close it distorted in his view.

'Where does the name Marcan come from?'

Matthew pulled back. 'It's Czech. It should be pronounced Marcan with a 'ch' sound. My dad always said after a while you get tired of travelling and stop and put down roots. So I decided to Anglicise it. I've put down roots.'

'Yeah.' Her voice was sleepy. 'Roots are interesting things.' She kissed him, then turned round, pushing her back against him. 'Is it comfortable if I lie like this?'

'Yes.'

He held her and felt the life of her body. She was thin and there were only sheens of silk and skin between him and her ribs and heartbeat. He had never felt so close to another person. Love was actually physical and straightforward. Not the emotional heart-rendings and mental-romantic fantasies he had a tendency for, but a worldly and conscious intertwining with another person. What he had felt with Chloë up to that point was more about him, an intense hope she would join with him and satisfy a gap within him. But now he could see the next stage to which he would have to grow, where he would be able to think about her.

'I'm going to take this off.'

Would he have to fantasise about her while being with her to engage his body? Would he be able to make the inside of his head realise he was in bed with her in real life?

She unbuttoned and took off her top, only showing him her back. As she stretched away from him to drop the top, the moles against the skin of her neck were like an after-image of stars. Then lower down there was pink scar tissue gouged into her skin. It formed a rough word, as if scraped in sideways with a razor or the blade of a pair of scissors:

'Nothing.'

Matthew blinked. When he opened his eyes the word was still there, written in weirdly fresh pink regrown skin. 'Nothing'. He blinked again. He was now fully engaged in the here and now with the physical reality of her back close to his body.

'Chloë, why's "Nothing" written on your back?'

She was staying still, obviously letting him look fully. She turned back at him over her shoulder. 'Because you want to be my mirror.'

He couldn't decipher her meaning. Slowly she slid back into position and spooned against him so her back was invisible.

'You thought I was getting my tits out, but if you want to be my mirror you need to see my back.'

'What does it mean?'

'Nothing.'

It took a second to try and work this out. 'Who did it?' Then he regretted the bluntness. Had she been the victim of some outrage? Then he remembered her comment about her unlovable body. Of course, Troy must have done it.

'The Nothing Man did it.'

Matthew knew well the sensation of a trapdoor opening beneath him, but now he felt it more than ever before, and with the added sensation of a drop beneath so dark that it was impossible to imagine what bedrock he would strike or when the noose would snap tight. Comfortable intimacy had vanished, replaced by intense and dangerous intimacy. But wasn't that what intimacy was?

'Who's the Nothing Man?' he whispered, though he already knew the answer.

She took a deep breath. 'Troy.'

A picture of her situation appeared in his mind. Troy'd branded her.

'Tell me about him,' he said as neutrally as possible. He couldn't let any tone in his voice imply what she would perceive as the wrong reaction. 'Or tell me about you – the two of you?'

'In some respects he was pretty normal. I met him on my travels, in Knoxville, same place I got the guitar. Rugged but beautiful town surrounded by freeways on the banks of a big slow river.'

Matthew felt the stars on her back open into a universe. She was going to impart her life's secrets. He was a good listener. In that way he could fulfil her. His body might be unreliable, but it bore a soul filled with mighty art that could connect with hers.

'In his own way, he was my first lover. He's still the yardstick, and my back is his way of testing my potential boyfriends.'

'Did anyone pass the test?'

'No one got to take the test. I've never shown anyone my back.'

Matthew wondered when someone else had last seen his own back.

'I've never gone to the beach,' she continued, 'or been in a swimsuit, or a backless dress. I've never wanted to face the moment when someone might ask, let alone when a man might ask.'

She stopped, but it was clear what this had cost.

Matthew had moped about his own perceived lack of romance and experience, but she was more hobbled than he was. Yet she had carried herself forward so far. He was flooded by admiration and compassion. What a woman – and he was with her in her innermost sanctum.

'Tell me everything. Why's he called the Nothing Man?'

'I named him after a Jim Thompson novel, though when I

met him he was reading *The Demon* by Hubert Selby. Troy's a nihilist, I guess. He was convinced he'd have to kill someone at some point, and that by doing so he would find out what it really meant to reach the bottom of the abyss.'

'I guess he was serious.'

'Yes, though it doesn't seem to have worked because he's still falling. I think he saw me as a protégée.'

'You weren't in danger, were you?'

'No.'

'Did you want him to write that word? Did you let him?'

'Oh yeah.'

'But weren't you frightened? Didn't you want to run away?'

'No. I was at that teenage point of wide-eyed openness, innocent and more open-minded than I've ever been, thirsting for wild new points of view. In that context he didn't seem like he was giving me a real walk on the wild side. I hadn't set my margins. I was only eighteen. I was a virgin. He was too, and he didn't do anything about it with me. He couldn't have. Sex would have made him too vulnerable. He was my foundational sexual experience but he never undressed. He only penetrated the skin on my back. I bled into my clothes for a week but I was so proud. It was my red badge of courage, by the Tennessee River, thousands of miles from home, on my own, with just him.'

The light was still on. She detached herself from him and fetched the photo album. 'You might have seen him go past but I didn't point him out. That's him.'

The Nothing Man was indeed Troy: fresh-faced and in his early twenties, gangly, dressed in black sweatshirt and tight jeans. His buzzed hair mingled with his stubble. His smile didn't seem that of a mad blade-wielder, but it was single-minded, with the same mildness that Matthew had seen in person.

'He looks like an organist,' he said.

'He looks relatively normal, but it's his manner and what he said, making darkness seductive, that was most people's problem. You can see why the Van Vries family got him put away. And now he's older. His whole nothing schtick has led nowhere. Nothing to show for life but bruised romanticism, and no way out.'

She raised her arm and touched her back. Whether she had forgotten she was naked from the waist up, or was conscious of it, she had advantageously revealed her breasts. Whatever she was looking at wasn't there. She lowered her hand and returned to their closeness, pushing her back against him.

'Some eighteen-year-olds look so gormless, and I can't believe I was so young. Even if I was an innocent, I'd sorted out my own travels across America. '

Matthew heard in his mind: 'Did you fuck her?' The dismissive question from his third-year friend when he was a fresher. The voice raked through him. Here she was telling him about a visceral sensual journey she had taken at eighteen, and not only had he been incapable of this when he was that age, but if he'd met her then, he would have ignorantly assumed she had simply experienced a boringly routine sex-life and was happy and satisfied. He showed ignorance on all sides and at every depth.

'What Troy never realised,' continued Chloë, 'and I never said, in case he conducted a fatal experiment on me, but which I spotted even at seventeen, was that falling to the bottom of the abyss doesn't mean killing someone, it means allowing someone to kill you. I'm very much alive, but I can understand that desire.'

Matthew remembered wishing Geraint dead, though that now seemed infantile. Geraint himself drank because he desired repeatable suicide. That was closer to what she was describing. And he himself had a fascination with the moment of death as imagined as his enfilade.

'Masochism's a sign of intelligence,' she continued. 'I don't know that I'll ever feel what I felt when he was moving his boxcutter through my flesh. And Troy's changed. He wants to be the one who dies. He's come closer to my way of thinking.'

'Where does it come from,' he asked, 'your way of thinking?'

'It's just there. I was never abused or anything. I didn't have formative experiences that gave me a taste for it. Nothing is just nothing. Nothing comes from nowhere.'

'It's not nothing, though.'

'I know, but we need a word for it. The Nothing Man himself – his father was a capable guy in insemination. He drove round Tennessee and up into the Midwest with a big bull pumping up cows. That might be Freudian but it doesn't explain his son being the Nothing Man. Some of us just have it. Do you?'

Did he?

'You've gone quiet,' she said. 'Have I shocked you?'

'No. I just feel like an idiot.'

'What, for dating me?'

'No, my God, no. For having lived a life that never had anything in it like what you've described.'

Was that a lie? What about the woman in Germany? That was an attempt to plumb the well of nothingness. Could he tell her? He took a deep breath and did.

'It's not that I'm not surprised,' she said. 'I did think you must have done something. You've been alive for x number of years. But I'd have done a better job than she did. She wasted your money. I'd have made you realise that you don't need to worry, because it's all in the mind. Your brain's your sexual organ, and you've got a nice big one.'

The *Mädchen* and his fifteen minutes with her were indeed less real than what was in his head. He told her about the Others, and that she was the Other of Others.

She turned round, consciously revealing her breasts, arching her back for full effect. He was comfortable enough to look fully.

The inner voice telling him that being with her wasn't real was held in check by her voice: 'Just wait till I tell you about my inner life.'

'What, you haven't already?'

She smiled. 'There might be a couple of other small details.'

She reached back for the light switch. With a click, darkness, then her voice: 'I say beware of mirrors, because he might be your mirror, not me. Nothing and eternity.'

Her fingers massaged his cranium. She pressed her forehead next to his.

'Sex is a con. How can it ever live up to the amount of time we imagine it? But if you and me can get into the cabinet of mirrors together, maybe we'll fulfil each other.'

XX

Rüdiger and his colleagues had worked quickly and completed the assembly of the new organ in the Lady Chapel in time for Pentecost at the end of May. The voicing of each of the fifteen hundred pipes was well under way. The summer half-term holiday, with no choral services, allowed ceaseless attention to detail. Matthew coaxed the craftsman into working more quickly so he could play for 'a friend'. Rüdiger was direct and pragmatic, though a sparkle in his eye suggested he understood that the friend was special.

'I can have twenty of the thirty stops voiced by Friday. Invite your friend then.'

On Friday, in the summery early evening, Matthew waited for Chloë by the Great Gate of Kiev. They'd talked on the phone a few times but this was their next set-piece date. She rounded the corner of the council building. The city was warm and bathed in late sun, and she was wearing a light dress. It was traditionally cut, with a high neck and sleeves almost down to her elbows, but it was a more feminine look than he'd seen yet. So this is what it was like being lovers. He greeted her with a nervous kiss. She looked up at the west end of the nave, where every carving was picked out by the reddening light.

'It was all dark last time I saw it.' Then she laughed as if what she had said was inconsequential.

He unlocked the cathedral. She gazed at the big key. He had

a moment of listlessness: she's here, I'm here, what do we do now? Should he give her a tour? It would give him something to do while in her gaze. He could get used to her again over a few minutes while following a script. He would show her the cathedral's most beautiful attributes so he could admire her. He would perform his lines waiting for the moments when she asked questions and he could enjoy her voice.

So he showed her how the east end had been built in the fourteen and fifteen hundreds; it boasted some quirky and even unique sections of vaulting, including a quasi-Baroque 3-D section built with ribs but no panels. It was the first English cathedral to be a so-called hall church, so he pointed out how the quire and side aisles were the same height. The nave and west end were added in the nineteenth century. Chatting as if they were architectural critics, they agreed that it was good pastiche style. But regardless of what they said, it was nice to hear her speak.

They ended up in the Lady Chapel. Matthew turned on the powerful lights Rüdiger had left in place. With a smell of burning dust overlaying the tang of newly assembled woodwork, the Lady Chapel shone as brightly as a film set and she was as beautiful as a Golden Age star.

'I only want to hear you improvise today,' she said. 'Nothing written by anyone else.'

Matthew didn't want to think about anyone else other than her. He had practised extensively to prepare a programme for her, but if she wanted improvisations, he would happily conform.

'The melodies will be by other people. I'll improvise chorale variations.'

It had taken more than a decade to learn to improvise like this, struggling to learn how to play the melodies he could hear in his head, then struggling to harmonise them, then struggling to turn the basics of melody and harmony into fluid counterpoint. He had made the journey himself without a teacher. He'd once asked Dr Paice for guidance, who'd replied only, 'If you were musical you'd be able to do it.'

'When I visited Walcha,' he said to her, 'I watched him improvise using chorale melodies. So from then I knew it was possible, and wanted to do the same. It was in Germany that I really put the time in.'

He showed her the rudiments of how to improvise variations on a chorale melody. He handed her a German hymn book from Bamberg.

'So, theoretically it's possible to improvise on any of these tunes?' she asked.

'Yes. Pick one, and I'll improvise some variations for you.'

She picked *An Wasserflüssen Babylon*. Matthew laughed. 'Bach improvised on this in a famous concert in Hamburg. I'll do it but it'll just be a sort of dim echo of what much greater people could do.'

She sat a few rows back where the sound was more blended. He turned his back to her to face the keyboards, so he couldn't see her: the eternal curse of the organ console. He would have to communicate with her purely through the music. He improvised seven variations, concentrating on the harmonic possibilities of the chorale melody and using technical devices to divide up the melody and then have the parts imitate each other in a way that made it as expressive as possible.

He tried to emulate the steady and optimistic pre-Bach counterpoint of Scheidemann and Buxtehude, composers who had mastered the most difficult compositional skill of all – writing music that was satisfied, content and yet also deep. That was harder than expressing tumult and crisis, frenzy, anger or disjunction. He started with a straightforward four-part harmonisation. This was the simplest movement, but to him the most profound. All the others would spring from it.

For this he used just one stop, the eight-foot Principal. In his design of the organ, although most organ pipes are built of tin-alloy which creates a bright sound, Matthew had insisted that almost all the pipes were made from almost pure lead, in the early North German manner. This gave them a sonorous, dark, sad sound that you didn't hear often, because most of the old German organs were bombed, 'improved' or otherwise destroyed. This lead sound was suffused with the grandeur of eternity. He tried to make his improvisations worthy of that sound.

He pushed his mind as far as it would go. For the second movement he forged a decorated melody against a bass-line to create a sombre bicinium. Then a spirited, light trio. Then a measured, calm prelude with each phrase of the chorale being developed and then soloed in augmentation. Then a dance-like consort, using the reed stops. Then an inventive, surprising fantasia with a highly-decorated melody. Finally another harmonisation, with grander harmonies. He used a different combination of stops for each movement, showing her the most beautiful sounds the organ could make. He played for about fifteen minutes. The whole series of movements showed everything he loved about the organ and music. His soul sang.

At the end he let the echo die away, then turned round gingerly, unsure of what reaction to expect. She gazed at him with tears in her eyes, musically ravished. It was more than he had seen before, and had craved to see again. He hadn't dared to assume she would feel the powerful expressivity beyond words that he was trying to convey through music. He felt awkward peering at her over his shoulder so he got up and sat down next to her, by which time she had collected herself. She clapped, then let him enfold her in his arms.

'Matthew, that was brilliant. You made it all up?'

'In a way. It's all already there. I just drew it out of the melody you picked.'

'Well, I think you deserve a drink. And luckily…'

She wriggled free and took a bottle out of her satchel and gave it to him. It was a Kentucky bourbon called Rip van Winkle.

'I was given this in Knoxville. It's been ageing on my shelf for years but I haven't got round to drinking it.'

'Rip van Winkle. He fell asleep, didn't he?'

'Yes, and when he woke up he didn't recognise the world.'

'Well here's to that. Let's drink some. I can get glasses from my flat.'

'Your flat?' She held up the bottle. 'I still don't know which wall it's through. But no need.'

She opened the bottle and passed it to him, gesturing that he drink. He took a sip of the bourbon's caramel strength, then passed it to her and she raised it and drank like a veteran.

The whiskey enhanced the chapel; Matthew could picture the vanished vibrancy of the mediaeval polychrome. He proffered cigarettes, but as he was hoping, she got out her Pall Malls. He lit them up, getting a thrill from smoking in the cathedral. She blew smoke upwards towards the vaulting, showing the delicate form of her chin and neck.

'At the Festival Hall there was a Bakelite sign saying "Absolutely no smoking at the console". Cool, eh? Very 1950s.'

'Matthew, you're wild in your own way. What should I do with the ash?'

'Just knock it off into the corners somewhere. Try not to get it on the organ.'

They drank and smoked.

'Do they pay you enough to live on?' Chloë asked, 'or do you need a day job?'

'They pay me enough, especially with the flat. I actually feel well taken care of.'

'Is the flat like this place? Does it have Gothic ceilings?'

'Almost. It's big and spacious. The real prize is the organist's house, where Geraint lives. When Richard was here I would stay there. It's where I want to live.'

How would she react if he said he fantasised about living there with her?

'But Geraint'll be living there for a while,' she responded, 'unless we get him sacked. Can't you just buy another house?'

'How did you afford to buy one?'

'I saved up and got debted up. I stood and smiled and sold a lot of other people's merch. My own stuff doesn't bring in much.'

'Doesn't it? What's merch?'

'T-shirts. Records. I can't live off my gigs, so I've got an alternate life. I know the clubs, so I do booking and tour management and merch for other people.'

'What, for other blues bands?'

'Not just blues. It's like having ten jobs.'

She elaborated. Most of her bands were American. She arranged European tours, with herself often playing in their band or supporting with her own to earn both money and experience, and get the gigs she couldn't get by herself. She ran the merchandise stall and liaised with the record labels and promoters. When there were spare dates she booked her own band to step in.

'You make nothing from your artistry and have to do all that to earn a living?'

'It's a pretty staid world, isn't it?' she laughed. 'All this art screaming away and no one notices or gives us money. I tell myself that being overlooked makes my music better.'

Matthew had a glimpse of a life beside this newly discovered part of Chloë. How would that play out, day by day? Could he imagine it all in a different house, in a new world away from the cathedral? He found her looking at him. She must have seen him drift away. She took another tip from the bottle of bourbon.

'Okay, here's the plan,' she said. 'There's a great blues scene in Germany. I've got some gigs there coming up. Now, some bookings are good and support the whole tour. Others just pay for the night and the hotels. Others lose money but you take them for some reason, like it's a club you need to play but they'll only give you a Monday night or whatever. Anyway, I've taken one booking that'll lose money, but it's in an interesting place.'

The pew between them was expanding. He sensed where she meant.

'It's somewhere you've told me about,' she continued. 'You, like me – we're provincial – and this place sounds like the very best of provincial.'

'You mean Bamberg, don't you?'

'Of course I do.'

'You've found a club there that's booked you?'

'Yeah.'

He felt his love for his other most beautiful city in the world. 'Chloë, you know, Bamberg's so beautiful. That's what all Germany was like before it was all bombed, and Bamberg survived. You get this vibe out of the buildings. You'll love it.'

She laughed. 'I hope so.'

'When are you going?'

'Me?' She leant forward. 'Or we? You can come, Matty. Come on tour with us. We can have a trip to Germany. You don't have to do anything. I've booked a roadie who'll drive. The rooms are already booked. The band is doubling up but I've got one to myself. You can crash with me.'

He had observed since teenagerhood the female propensity to plan a couple's future. Surely that was the female equivalent of the male *grand projet*. But he'd only seen it from outside, watching other couples. Now it was happening to him. This was one of life's consummations. He was on the inside track of a woman's life plan, of which holidays, travels and tours were the centrepiece. He could escape aspic for life.

'If I can find cover I'll come. I'd love to.'

His vision iridesced and his hearing rang. In his mind the stones were singing.

She brightened: 'You'll be pleased about this. I brought the books along.'

'Which books?'

'The Kodály ones I told you about.'

She took three worn second-hand mini-hardbacks out of her satchel. The cover drawings showed children and friendly animals gathering around staves, notes and rests. The images brought back his childhood. He smelt the polished parquet of the church hall, and heard the clap of heels on the wood. He was marching round in circles, singing the little ditties translated from Hungarian, that had bequeathed him fifths, fourths and thirds, and ultimately major and minor sixths and sevenths.

Look goat look,
Look goat look.
Nanny reads a book,
Nanny reads a book.

Chloë, not his mother, was singing, laughing and repeating exercises for a child with the voice of the blues. With a physical shock he felt her journey. She had been a newborn, then a child, then a would-be horse smuggler. For long hours, days, weeks, months and years she had played, learned, related to the unfamiliarity around her, giggling, crying, exploring. If she had children, their bouncing youth would be answered first by the ripening of satisfied maternal femininity, then gradually paid for by her decline. Her face would weather with her body; the intoxicating character and physicality that he wanted to keep the same forever would decline and fail. Ultimately she would die.

A woman on this vivacious journey wouldn't want to move into a house owned by an institution and newly vacated by a drunk. She wouldn't want a birdcage. Life did not stand still, he was learning.

'I've known this one for years,' she said, 'but I didn't know it was a way of learning thirds.' She sang:

Ain't I rock candy
Ain't I rock candy
Ain't I rock candy
Alabama Gal

Footsteps rounded the luxuriant carving of the altar screen. Geraint squinted at them in seeming surprise. Matthew found himself standing up, but Chloë stayed in her seat. Caught singing her ditty, she blushed puce to the roots of her hair. She looked at Matthew in panic. Geraint took in the whiskey and cigarettes.

'Are you having your own bop?'

'No.' After this curt word she said nothing. Her face was burning.

After not knowing where to look, Geraint gave his attention to the bottle. 'That looks like more than communion wine.'

She exhaled smoke in slow motion, but it didn't make her blush less.

'Is it rye?'

She stayed silent.

'Why, it's a Kentucky bourbon.' Geraint's southern accent was surprisingly passable. Had he been there? He aimed the remark at her as if he was determined to make her speak.

She was still flushed but managed to speak in a peeved way: 'I brought some bourbon as a gift because Matthew just gave me a private concert. We don't have any glasses.' She held up the bottle as if it was a hatchet; she knew he was an alcoholic. 'Would you like a few inches?'

Geraint leant forward, drawn towards the bourbon. Then he planted his feet. 'No. My wife loved mint juleps and whiskey sours. But I shouldn't.'

'Hm,' she said.

'In fact, Matt,' he went on, 'it's actually easier to apologise in a group setting. I'm sorry about those notes I sent you. I was drinking again. I was knocked over by our argument. I don't like conflict. I never have. It knocks me off the wagon.'

Surprised by his candour, Matthew couldn't resist the only answer he could come up with: 'I can drink to that.' He smiled, took the bottle and raised it.

'I'm sorry if I was rude.' Geraint was inclined towards Chloë, but he'd closed his eyes. He opened them and looked at a space between Matthew and Chloë. 'Can I sit down?'

Matthew looked at Chloë.

'Yes,' she said.

He sat. After some seconds of terse silence, Geraint nodded at the organ and asked Chloë what she thought of it.

She laughed, releasing some of the suppressed tension. 'It's the best thing since gunpowder.'

Matthew laughed.

Geraint looked from one to the other of them: 'Gunpowder.

I like that. My father used to tell me that I would be the loudest thing since El Alamein.'

Chloë and Matthew went on laughing. Geraint laughed himself.

'I mean,' said Chloë, 'I always liked the Hammond, but this is the real thing. I've realised what volume of sound actually means. It's physical presence taking up space.'

'You're sure you're not an organist?' Geraint asked.

'Maybe I'll take lessons.'

'Maybe I should play more,' said Geraint. 'I've always been a bit ashamed to be an organist. People think they're weirdos. But maybe we should get it out from under its bushel. Sorry for mangling the grammar.'

This Geraint, the sober and engaging one, was so pleasant Matthew found his sense of compassion stirring again.

'Bryce has asked me to organise a concert,' Matthew said. 'I've asked Heinz-Günther to come and inaugurate it. But we can have more. Why don't you give a recital? We all know you can pound out the Reger on Big Bertha back there, but why not play some Bach or…'

Scarlatti sprang to mind. Chloë and Matthew's father both loved him: the great gambler. Geraint would be a natural conduit for his music's neurotic energy.

'…or some Scarlatti?'

'I play all of Scarlatti, hundreds of pieces, but I'd never play it on the organ. I play it alone, at home.'

Matthew caught Chloë sighing at Geraint's solipsism, though Geraint didn't notice. He was still speaking:

'But Heinz-Günther will have his own ideas. What's he going to play?'

'North German Baroque. Buxtehude; that sort of thing.'

'I'm not going to row back on anything I've said about the organ,' said Geraint in the manner of an after-dinner raconteur. 'There's no Haydn, Mozart, Beethoven, Schubert etc, but some of the organ-bore composers managed to write one or two pretty pieces. Buxtehude, Bach of course. Do you play the Bach *Passacaglia*?'

'Of course.'

'Do you know what it means?' Without waiting for Matthew to answer, Geraint addressed Chloë. 'It's Spanish, *pasar una calle*, to walk on a road, to go on a journey. There are streams of *passacaglias* by Spanish composers that I've played through. People have said the form came from Africa via slaves to the New World and then back to Spain in the 1500s and 1600s.'

'African dances came to Europe from South America?' asked Chloë.

'Yes, and then fed into dance forms used in mainstream classical music. Sometimes they have a back beat.'

'I want to see you play them,' she responded, looking surprised with herself for responding warmly to his agreeableness.

Geraint was behaving like a new person. He no longer seemed to antagonise Chloë. He was no longer directly in charge of Matthew, and while he maintained his air of superiority, it seemed to have been redirected into his research. Had the alterations to his rôle made him more relaxed? Or was it his walk on the road? Matthew couldn't begin to comprehend fully life's great trek, its great *passacaglia*. Billions of people in constant motion and development over the centuries. Why couldn't life be a frozen moment, with everyone held complete, having reached the goal for which they had striven, no longer needing to grow, able to enjoy their completeness for the span of a perpetual instant? Why did life have to be this damn never-ending drudge?

Geraint looked at Chloë.

'You've been teaching him how to improvise?'

'Me?' she said. 'No, I can't.'

'Why not?'

'I've got cloth ears.'

'No you haven't,' said Matthew.

'Yes I have.'

Geraint looked kindly at Chloë: 'Let me tell you a secret. Talent and art are two different things. The artists are the ones who often don't have the most talent; they struggle, but because they have a vision, they struggle on and produce art. I have talent – oodles of it. I can recognise any note. I heard some of what Matt was playing to you a few minutes ago, and I could sit at that keyboard now without any effort and play it back to you.

'Yes, Matt, I'll take you up on your offer. I'll give a concert. I'll dust off a few pieces and I'll play them brilliantly, but it won't mean anything, and that spooks me. All it makes me is a parrot. I realise now that in my whole career I've never actually said anything worth saying with my talent. Talent's a burden because it forces you to face the limitations of your vision.' He smiled at Chloë. 'Drink to your cloth ears, because if you'd been given better ears you might just be a dumb session player putting your talent into someone else's art.'

'Did you listen to my set at the pseudo-bop?' asked Chloë.

'Yes, I could hear it from my little office. Your journey's actually leading somewhere. Keep going.'

Matthew was thinking about talent. If his mother hadn't sung and tapped and marched with him for those formative years, he would not be able to express anything musical, despite being filled with musical desire and vision. But he didn't accept that Geraint had nothing to express. How could Geraint's fluid brilliance be entirely empty?

'My God, is he Jekyll and Hyde?' asked Chloë.

'What?'

'You didn't notice, but he's gone. He said not to disturb the visionary's vision. But he was really nice today. No one's called me an artist like that. Who is he?'

'Who are we, Chloë? I don't know.'

'You guys are arse over tit,' Chloë said. 'You talk about art but when it comes to your services, you don't join hands and go for it. I love hymns. I sang them all when I was a child. You play these wonderful hymns but don't believe them. Then you improvise and open a door to heaven when the cathedral's empty, but in the services you fuss about split notes. Then when your new organ arrives you tell him to give a concert. And what you really care about is his house.'

'What should I do?'

'Give a concert, but play like you play to me. Open whatever floodgate that is. Play that piece Walcha memorised, and memorise it yourself, like he did. Then play it for the world. You'll wipe the floor with all of them.'

She made it sound so easy, but nonetheless her words were galvanising, Matthew got out his score of *The Art of Fugue* the next afternoon and planned to practise in the Lady Chapel that evening, once the organ builders had finished and the cathedral was locked to the public. He could earmark this wonderful space and time for practice most days. At the end of the week Rüdiger was due to finish his fine-tuning and drag himself away from his completed masterpiece back to his workshop. Then the instrument would also be available during the daytime.

But that evening, as Matthew strode up the south side aisle towards the Lady Chapel, he sensed he was not alone. He slowed his purposeful walk when he heard the whoosh of the bellows. He tiptoed forward and peeped round the statuary of the altar screen. At the console of the new organ Geraint was hunched in introspection. Two shallow piles of music lay on the bench to each side of him. Even from a distance Matthew could recognise the bindings of some of the scores: collections of Baroque music from various schools and countries.

Geraint might look perplexed now by volumes of unfamiliar styles and forms, but his mercurial intelligence would ultimately bring him victory. Vision or no vision, Geraint could eclipse him entirely if he started playing Baroque music brilliantly on the new organ. Yet Geraint claimed to have no vision. But if he was so easily eclipsed, could his own vision be any more substantial than Geraint's? *The Art of Fugue* was not easy to interpret. Did he, Matthew, have a vision to forge into it?

He retreated to his flat. He was in *Art of Fugue* mode so he started playing the fugues on the clavichord. The twenty pieces bewitched him. They were everything music should be. Surely he must be bringing something to the music if he loved it so much. He couldn't look through the score without pausing to play favourite moments.

It was the middle of the night before he stopped. On a high, he poured himself a glass of Chloë's Rip van Winkle, lit a cigarette, and planned a practice regime. He knew the work well, but he needed discipline to complete memorising it.

If he gave the concert in September, he had more than three months. He would try and complete his work in two, and leave a month for living with it. He would have to memorise as much as half a fugue a day, as well as perfecting his technical grasp of them. But he was building on a deep and long familiarity: he had started memorising the fugues in Bamberg, if haphazardly. Now he had to memorise them systematically as Walcha had done, part by part, soprano, alto, tenor and bass.

He would have to sing a single line for a few bars at a time, then play it, then sing it, until he could repeat it from memory. Then he would add it to the next. He would then try and play it while singing another part, or sing a part while playing all the others. It would be painstaking, but he'd done it before with other pieces. If he put the hours in he could do it, and it would make him happy – what all-consuming, joyous work, and what a goal if he could please Chloë and justify her empowering belief in him. Please her? No; ravish her; get that look from her again.

XXI

The Lady Chapel was brimming for Heinz-Günther's concert. Matthew had invited sympathetic listeners from the wider city and beyond, as well as from the cathedral and school. In a consummation of his nervousness, many had turned up. Agnes Westmoreland, Richard's sister, sat in the front row, approvingly surveying the florid lettering of the programme that Derek had assembled using coloured paper, scissors and the edging from photocopies of antique title pages. Matthew grinned at her when he sat down, but drew only a formal smile. Chloë sat on his right. Geraint sat beyond her. Hannon sat next to Matthew on his left, with Jane on the other side. As the music progressed, Hannon sat intent and followed from his scores, occasionally pointing out a detail to Matthew.

Heinz-Günther played with his customary effortlessness, virtually motionless as his fingers darted as if of their own accord. He used pieces by composers such as Scheidemann and Bruhns, all favourites of Matthew's, to show the variety of beautiful sounds the new instrument could produce.

Before the final performance of a praeludium by Buxtehude, Heinz-Günther paused and half-turned on the organ bench to Matthew, who stood to speak:

'Everyone, it really is a pleasure for us to be here tonight, and to welcome Heinz-Günther Schmal. I was lucky enough to work with him in Bamberg for three years, and we hope our association with the Domkirche there continues. The other point to mention is that this organ is given to us through the generous bequest of our previous organist, Richard Galvin. Richard was, as we all know, a fabulous musician and his loss is felt by all of us.'

There was a murmur of assent. Matthew paused and surveyed the room. This was his chance to say something meaningful and go beyond generalisations. Geraint, at one with his rôle and looking military in a handmade pinstriped suit, nodded in agreement.

Matthew found he was able to express his feelings fluently: 'He was a lovely man – always kind, always encouraging, always hard working. Heavens, I wouldn't be here if it wasn't for him. This wonderful new organ is like having a part of him here, forever.'

There was a rustle of approval and some clapping. Matthew caught Agnes's eye: a glimmer showed he had managed to touch the deeper truth that she and Richard had been children together: playing, laughing, singing, dancing. Life.

Heinz-Günther turned back to the keyboard for the resounding final praeludium. Afterwards the audience adjourned to the coved vault of the chapter house. Here the evening sun emboldened the polychromatic glass. A riot of wyverns, maniacs and green men jeered down from the corbels at a satisfied audience that, seen from above, must have throbbed. The school's kitchen staff, pressed into starched white, proffered Dornfelder and crackers with smoked trout pâté. Matthew heard snatches of many conversations, all pleasingly focused on early music performance practice.

'Yes, there is a Terzian mixture…' 'Purely mechanical…' 'Wedge bellows…' 'I think the tone of the Piffaro is wonderfully coarse…' 'Yes, yes, the rhythms *are* dance rhythms…'

Matthew and Chloë accepted glasses of wine, then found themselves sucked by the throng towards Heinz-Günther. Matthew envied the German's ability to accept with unabashed satisfaction the many congratulations offered him. He could recognise his achievements without hauteur or pride, false modesty or doubt. Then Matthew, Chloë and Heinz-Günther were together. Matthew felt proud to introduce her as his girlfriend.

'Enchanté,' said Heinz-Günther. 'Well, Matthew, how is your new job?'

The question made Matthew look at Chloë and imagine the possibilities of the future. His happiness welled up. 'It's going really well. The new organ makes all the difference.'

'You should perform *The Art of Fugue* on it,' said Heinz-Günther. 'You've been working on it long enough. You should do it from memory. That would give them all something to talk about.'

Inwardly, Matthew was radiant. Heinz-Günther had validated his private ambition. Chloë nudged him.

'Playing here will do your music-making a power of good,' said Heinz-Günther. 'The sound is so warm and generous. Do your practice, then have a glass of wine and feel good about yourself. Music is innocent, rather juvenile, really, in the good sense. Even your man Walcha – he could be like a child. I want to see you toast that. To the child in you. Prost.'

They raised their glasses.

'So now that's decided,' said Heinz-Günther, 'when will you give your recital?'

'I don't have a date yet. It'll be after Geraint does one.'

'Can Geraint play this type of organ?' asked Heinz-Günther in surprise.

Geraint had been borne along in the crowd right behind them. He turned to face the German. 'Did I hear my name?'

Heinz-Günther wasn't flummoxed. 'Geraint, we haven't met. I didn't realise you played on historically informed organs.'

'It's got keyboards. Why not?'

'There are people who put years of study into the minutiae of these instruments.'

Geraint stood straighter. 'There are people who can't see the wood for the trees.'

Heinz-Günther retracted. 'Perhaps we Germans divide our curricula into schools and periods a little too respectfully.'

'Whatever.' Geraint gazed into his fizzy water.

'Do you know what you will play?' asked Heinz-Günther.

Geraint met his eyes with his buccaneering smile. 'I was thinking of starting in Spain in the 1640s, with a *chacona* by Juan Arañés. Heard of him?'

Heinz-Günther looked lost. 'I've heard the name but he's outside my specialism.'

'I don't have a specialism,' said Geraint. He reached across to the tray of a passing waiter and changed his water for a glass of wine. 'It would be my own arrangement for organ – it's originally for vocal and wind consort. Then I would play one or two of the North German descendants of this style of dance, a *chaconne* by Buxtehude, the Bach *Passacaglia* if it's not too obvious. I want to blow away a few cobwebs, and play them in a way informed not by dry old specialists like you, but by the original wild dances that came to Europe from South America.'

'I know that there's a history of musical reception between Spain, England and the Netherlands and into Germany,' said Heinz-Günther.

Geraint ignored him and took a long draught of Dornfelder. 'I think the whole concept of variation becomes more interesting if you look at it from the perspective of musicians who had to keep a dance going, rather than from an academic standpoint. So I thought I'd end with the most academic variations I can think of and play them like a dance. Do you know them? Forgive my German, but *Es ist das Heil* by Matthias Weckmann.'

Geraint put a who-won-the-war spin on Heil and deliberately pronounced the name in the most Anglicised way: Mathious Weckman with an English 'th' and 'w'.

Some of Heinz-Günther's wine went down the wrong way.

Geraint didn't wait for him to recover: 'Do you play the variations?'

The German looked panicked: 'I would only learn them on a thirty-two-foot organ.'

'You don't, in other words.'

Matthew could only blink at this exchange. Even he, the votary of the German Baroque, had not yet summoned the courage to learn Weckmann's enormous, tough and taxing set of variations, the Mount Everest of North German organ music.

'And may they bring you great pleasure.' Heinz-Günther raised his glass. 'Once again, prost.'

Matthew followed suit and drank, but Geraint paused lengthily before raising his glass and draining it. Then he turned to Matthew. 'Look, Heinz-Günther's got an early flight tomorrow; let's leave him to pack.'

Like a teenager, Geraint tugged Matthew away. Chloë followed. The admiring crowd immediately filled their places around Heinz-Günther.

'That's what I hate,' said Geraint when the three of them were at the other end of the room with fresh wine. 'Early music is basically a refuge for people who don't have good techniques. It allows them to look out of their arses at real virtuosi. I intend to set that right.'

The three of them talked and drank. Matthew was not used to so much wine and began to feel the effects of it. Then Hannon appeared out of the crush and was pulling him by the arm.

'Mr Marcan, Mr Marcan…'

Matthew allowed himself to be pulled along. 'Where are we going?'

'Just follow me.'

They passed through the thicket of happy music lovers, through the empty cloister, and out through the open door into the garden of peace. It seemed like a happy graveyard, the gorgeous end of daylight harmonising with the warm illumination issuing from inside. Chatter floated out, the wine-drinkers visible if distorted through the coloured and wavy glass. The stonework and monuments still irradiated warmth from the now-set sun. Matthew found himself studying the delphiniums and lupins; the plants thrust themselves into three-dimensionality with amazing complexity.

'Do you have a lighter?' asked Hannon.

The boy produced a slim cigar not much more than three inches long. He removed it from its cellophane wrapping.

'Hannon, what are you doing?'

'A friend of mum's gave it to me. She doesn't know. Smoking in lessons is the way forward.'

'Okay, just don't inhale too much. In fact don't inhale at all to start with.'

Matthew lit the cigar for Hannon. The lad breathed in carefully, managing to do so without coughing, and immediately let the smoke drift back out through his smile.

'It's nice.'

It was like going back in time to when Matthew had been the same age, and he sensed the thrill the lad must feel, a combination of rule-breaking in what was still almost daylight, and the genuine pleasure of tobacco.

Hannon took a couple more puffs, and inhaled a little bit of the smoke on the last. He tilted his head back and exhaled smoke directly upwards. Then he looked at Matthew like a younger child, as if he'd reached the extremity of what he dared to do: now his attention needed to move on to whatever was next.

Hannon passed Matthew the cigar. 'You finish it.'

Then Hannon ran back in. Matthew smoked a bit more of the cigar, then returned inside. The room was starting to spin a little, but the conversations were so interesting that he took another glass of wine. Agnes passed on her way out. Matthew tried to tap her elbow but perhaps ended up grabbing it.

'You know that I was your brother's student?' he slurred.

She turned and tried to place him. She still didn't seem to remember meeting him at the funeral. Then she smiled. 'I know exactly who you are. You were sent down from the House.'

'You don't know who I am at all,' he thought of saying. Then he actually said it. It felt good to say what he thought. 'I went to New College, not Christ Church,' he continued. Then he imitated the life-sapping way his prep school teacher had spoken to him. 'Christ Church's a cathedral. You wouldn't stand a chance.'

Agnes raised her chin. 'What?'

'Don't worry, Agnes. Richard saved my bacon. And he used to give me cigarettes in lessons.'

She smiled. 'The silly boy was always doing things like that. But I do know exactly who you are. He said you were interested in proportion. He tried to make some Latin pun that I can't remember about you having a sense of proportion, the joke being that in real life you…' She stopped as if realising what she would say was rude.

'…that in real life I didn't?' finished Matthew. He was enjoying speaking his mind.

'But anyway,' she chirped. 'I must go. A love of proportion will last a lifetime.'

It wasn't long before another face spun into view. It had Hannon's features. Hannon's mother. Mrs Hannon as she probably should be to him. Jane as she always would be. How would she appreciate the musical journey of life? Teachers and pupils' mothers shouldn't get together. She seemed to be looking at him across the room with disapproval. No. Scorn. No. Outright hostility. No, she was just joshing him. She was laughing.

'Well, Mr Marcan, I didn't know you were a drinker.'

'Yes, by the organ pipe.'

Chloë spun into view. What was he supposed to do, with both her and Jane standing with him?

'I'm Jane,' he heard.

'I'm Chloë.'

'What are you doing here?'

'Listening to music.'

'You sound like my thirteen-year-old. Are you a chorister mum?'

'No. Do I look like one?'

'No. That's why I'm curious. I'm not used to meeting young people. The school gate is like a waxworks. New mummies older than me with big arses pushing new-borns in prams. It's grotesque. People with good jobs leave procreation till they become death warmed up.'

'I don't have a good job.'

'Yes you do,' said Matthew, but they didn't hear him.
'What do you do?' asked Jane.
'I play in a band.'
'A local band? Do you like The Wild Bunch? The Seers? I love all this stuff. Am I going to know one of your songs?'
'No. I'm in a blues band.'
'Blues?' asked Jane. 'Why? What's it got to do with you?'

Chloë looked as if Jane had pressed her off-switch. Her energy sapped and her face dropped. Then her eyes deepened.

'Because I'm dead,' she said.

Jane double-took. 'Death? Like metal? What about Onslaught?'

'I like them. You should check out Muckspreading Holocaust.'

Jane didn't laugh. Talking about bands was too important. 'But why blues?' she pushed. 'No one wants to listen to it.'

'Exactly. No one wants to be reminded of truth. What do you do?'

'Nothing. I need to reinvent myself, now my marriage is over.'

'What happened?'

'No sex. With hindsight, I think it was a mistake that I let my kids be more important to me than he was. That batted him away. I was okay with a sexless marriage but then he went off with someone else. Are you married?'

'No.'

Matthew was amazed how candid the two strangers were.

'If you do,' continued Jane, 'avoid open-ended commitment. Have demonstrable goals and deliverables. Five-year plans with pre-arranged severance deals. Maybe that way it'll work out.'

Chloë's eyes had fallen. Jane read her look and turned to Matthew. Her expression turned incredulous – the man who hadn't been up for her had somehow succeeded with a beautiful and younger woman – but she recovered herself. Should he smile at them like a caveman: 'I possess this woman!'?

Jane touched Chloë's arm. 'Don't worry, I'm not always so direct. But I just can't see the point of beating round the bush any more. Can Matthew handle you?'

This time Chloë held Jane's eyes. She took a long sip from her glass, then her eyes gleamed and she tapped her head with her other hand.

'Did you and you husband connect through fantasy?'

Jane looked uncomprehending. 'Are you joking?'

'No,' said Chloë.

'I don't have time for the intricacies of the mind,' stated Jane definitively. 'I wanted a man who's good at one thing and stays out of the way. It's over but I got my children out of him.'

But as she stared at Chloë, Jane's defensiveness ebbed: 'What do you mean about fantasy?'

'We all spend most of our time fantasising, so you should make it part of your relationship.'

Jane stared back, stumped. 'I don't want to know what's going on in his mind.'

What force within a woman made them point at a man and say: you are going to father my children? Having made their choice, why did they turn away later from father in favour of children?

Chloë was speaking to him.

'Earth calling Matty. Who's Jane?'

They were alone in the hubbub. 'She tried to seduce me.'

Her eyes widened. 'What, Jane?'

'Yeah, she took me to her house and said if I didn't stay there was no lift home.'

'But she's a real woman. She's got a house and a car and children and…let's not mention the husband. She told me a lot while you were zoned out. She must have measurable standards for her men. You know, they've got to earn such and such and file their tax returns on time. And somehow you passed those tests. What happened?'

'I didn't…' Matthew felt pompous, dressed up in his suit under the vaults, wyverns and green men, yet unable to find a way to talk directly about his non-tryst.

He heard a squeal of laughter from Chloë. 'What, you limp-noodled her?'

'No, we didn't get that far,' he said quickly.

She held up her finger suggestively. Her laughter was infectious. He felt a gale of laughter at his preposterousness and held his head back while he let it out. 'But you said you were a Christian. What do you know about limp-noodling?'

'Whatever.' She laughed again. 'Don't worry, I won't do the evo-girl thing and say I'll pray for you.'

'I don't know if I believe in God.'

'I know that I do. You spend your whole life playing here and yet you don't fear Him. Wouldn't Bach think you'd missed the point?'

'Does a fugue that can be turned upside down prove the existence of God?'

'Probably, but you have to turn that into love and apply it to the world. It's not easy, but it's the only thing holding back the flood.'

'Chloë, if I mess it up with you, I've messed up forever.'

Chloë considered him with depth.

'I thought you were superman once you started improvising. Superman, that's what you said about your Walcha guy. I was blinded at first, but not so much now. The you who improvises is such a whole man. So complete in his musical fantasies. That's who I want to find in you. But to get there I have to cut through all these layers.'

Layers. The moles on her back possessed their own cosmology.

'Matty,' she said, 'what are you thinking?'

'I was thinking of your back, and when we lay in your bed.'

'Don't think of those letters. I've forgotten them most of the time.'

'Not the letters. The moles. Am I cut off at the trunk?'

'It's why you're an artist. I remember an American guitarist explaining to me that every creative person had what he called shy bowels. Whatever form it takes, the body and vision are never at one with each other. I feel lucky that my ears are the problem.'

'But why?'

'The axeman cometh.'

'That sounds like a blues song.'

'It should be a blues song. "Ask not for whom the axeman cometh, he's cometh-ing for you".'

'He's done cometh-ing,' Matthew said, but the word reminded him of coming. Tears were forming. He looked through them at her, opening his soul, so that she would be able to read his despair. When had he started to cry?

'The axeman got you, didn't he?' she whispered. He could hear her perfectly despite the chatter of dozens of drinking organ fans. 'I can see that. But don't worry. You helped me. I'll help you. We'll sow a seed. You can get some little shoots of recovery, like mine. They're small. I'm doing my Kodály, teacher, and it's working. I'm your fledgling and you be mine. It's not like having been growing properly the whole time, but it is better than nothing.'

Matthew closed his eyes. 'Will you cut me out of my tree?'

'Yeah,' she whispered. 'I'm going home now, but Matty…' She was on her tiptoes to breathe in his ear, her hand was on his neck. '…I'll cut you out of your fucking tree.'

Matthew stood back, eyes widened.

'Oh,' she said, her own eyes wide open in mock astonishment. 'Did I just say that? Hang on, "fucking tree" rhymes with "marry me". What does that mean? Good night, Matty.'

Once she'd kissed and gone, the wine made Matthew more lachrymose. He heard Jane laughing across the room, and saw himself as part of a montage in her eyes: the lonely man who couldn't find his way to the school canteen, the stop at the motorway breakfast eatery, the organ loft. She probably imagined his roomy flat with its twelve-foot ceilings as a shabby bedsit. And now he saw himself, sloshed on red wine in the chapter house. Outré, but not in the dangerous, interesting sense. She must hate his influence on her son.

Geraint emerged from the crowd. After seeming to contemplate him, he loosened Matthew's tie. Matthew stared up at him and tried to remain still for what seemed a lengthy and delicate operation. Heinz-Günther appeared too.

'Matthew, you are unbuttoning.'

Geraint raised yet another wineglass. Matthew was shocked. 'Geraint, why are you drinking?'

'I've been not drinking for long enough.' Sweat stood out on Geraint's brow. 'Anyway, shhh…'

'But what about your daughter?'

'She fucked off to Australia.'

'What about your…?' Did Geraint have any other family now? A companion?

'What about who?' Geraint said. 'It's just me and Richard's books. Richard's sister seems pretty frisky, though.'

'But what about you, Geraint?'

'What about me?' He laughed with worrying shrillness. 'I'm enjoying my descent.'

'You said drinking's like repeatable suicide.'

Matthew's eyes overflowed. Then Hannon and Jane were approaching. Why had he stood so close to the doorway, where she would have to pass within inches of him? Her face passed without stopping or acknowledging him. Matthew couldn't quell his tears. He must look a right fool. Abashed, he turned round and moved closer to Geraint, who looked down at him kindly. He was a tall man. Then that sucking in of breath.

'Matthew,' said Heinz-Günther. The German was still there. Had he made up with Geraint? 'You should think about retiring.'

Retiring?

'Come on, let's get you up to your flat.' That was Geraint. Heinz-Günther was held back by his admirers.

Geraint took Matthew's arm and steadied him out of the chapter house and up the stairs from the cloister. He waited as Matthew fumbled with the key to his door. Inside he deposited Matthew on his side on his bed. He filled two glasses of water in the kitchen and put them on coasters on the bedside table.

'You don't need a seasoned dry-mouth to tell you about the importance of water. You'll be okay?'

'Yes.' Matthew felt as if he was adrift in a sea of unsaid inexpressibles.

'Then I'll leave you to it. I have to find my own way home. Good night, Matt.'

'No, don't go.'

'Why not? You need to sleep.'

'No.' Matthew didn't know how to express it, but he wanted to be close to Geraint. 'Tell me about yourself.'

'That's rather sudden.'

'Then it's rather sudden. Sit down, tell me about yourself.'

'Matthew, you need to sleep.'

'I don't want to sleep.'

Geraint chuckled. 'Okay, what do you want to know?' He sat down on the side of Matthew's bed.

'Tell me about your marriage.'

'Straight in at the deep end.'

'Where else?'

Geraint stared into the milkiness of the wall. His thumb caressed the counterpane. His hand was chubby, hairless, the veins didn't show. It looked ordinary, flaccid, yet could play a keyboard with such skill.

'Tell me about your wife.'

Geraint came back to reality and looked down at Matthew. 'Sorry, I forgot you wanted to know. I met Mariam on a blind date. Have you ever been on one?'

'No.'

'Get your friends to organise one for you.'

Matthew didn't want to say he didn't have any friends. 'Tell me more about Mariam.'

'Okay. She's from an old family in Mobile, Alabama. We had our date at Rules, in Covent Garden. She was wearing a silk cocktail dress. I found her accent intoxicating. Do you really want to hear this?'

'Yes.'

'Well, upstairs in the bar they had a pianist, and when he took a break she asked me to take over. I played a medley of all sorts of things – obvious pieces like the slow movement from Mahler 5, less obvious stuff like *Verklärte Nacht*, all jazzed up.

Everyone thought I was playing lost masterpieces from New Orleans. People are such…'

'I would have recognised what you played.'

Geraint looked down at Matthew. 'I know. So when you go on your blind date, you'll have to specify she knows all about those old *Deutschen Orgelmeisters*.'

'Did she recognise them?'

'No, but she got the vibe.'

'So why didn't it work?'

'We struck sparks off each other. She used to call me Gerry in her Alabama drawl. But she was depressive, and it's not a good idea to have two depressives in one marriage. The highs are extravagant. For you, that is. Once our daughter was a teenager she found them excruciating. But the lows, everyone hates those. And the drinking. Both of us. That's why Julia doesn't want anything to do with us.'

'Julia's your daughter?'

'Ours, yes. She's just qualified as a doctor in Melbourne. She's paid for it all herself, with loans. That's more than either me or Mariam ever did.'

'And where's Mariam now?'

'In Chipping Sodbury. Or Sodding Chipbury. Not the right place for a free spirit from Alabama. We're still married as it happens. Till death do us part.'

'What do you think of death, Geraint?'

'You're not still on about that?'

'Yes, I am.'

'You're too young to ask.'

'No I'm not,' said Matthew. 'My mother's dead. Walcha's dead. Richard's dead.'

'But you're not.'

After a pause Geraint added: 'My father saw enough people die that to him it was a cigarette paper that any of us could pass through at any time, and we should do so with a smile. Because it's there.'

He looked down at Matthew and continued: 'I'm not going

to tell you what I think of death, but I'll tell you what I think of life. It can be like a cavalry charge, but one where you might not necessarily want to accept the butcher's bill. What was it Wellington said after Waterloo? My father used to quote him. "Nothing except a battle lost can be half so melancholy as a battle won."'

'My life's not like a cavalry charge.'

Matthew reached forward and squeezed Geraint's hand. He felt a squeeze back.

'Can I give a concert on the new organ?'

Geraint snorted. 'That's up to you, but it's not going to solve any of your problems. You need to get out there and live. It'll be easier for you in the long run that way.'

'What do you mean?'

'Look, in any field, ten percent of people do all the doing. At Kohima my father must have killed a whole Japanese battalion. As the Bible says, Saul killed his thousands and Daddy killed his tens of thousands. It's the same with music. You have to ask yourself if you're really in the top ten percent. Can you imagine carrying a concert at the Albert Hall, or in New York, or in Berlin? If not, it's better to accept you belong in the ninety percent. There's so much else to life. You're young. My God, you've got a girlfriend. I wouldn't want to get into a debate with her about who does the washing up, but she's gorgeousness on legs. One day you'll know what to do with her. And then you'll perceive the happiness the ninety percent can have, but which eludes us ten percenters.'

'I thought you said you were just a parrot.'

'Yes, but what a parrot.' Geraint laughed and slapped Matthew genially. '*Mon vieux*, this evening you certainly did your best to do ninety percent of the drinking. I'm going to leave you to your dreams now.'

Geraint left. Matthew drifted to sleep.

XXII

The Lady Chapel bustled with an extraordinary crowd for an organ recital.

But he definitely wasn't awake. That must explain why he was seeing the Lady Chapel from just below the vault, as if he was hovering ten feet above the crowd.

Was he one of the corbels?

This was much too life-like to be a dream. Was vision a better word?

Matthew glanced around the bustling audience drawn from all walks of life, and then at the programme. He was amazed. Geraint's choice of Baroque works showed not just knowledge but flair.

Geraint strode on and genially accepted the applause. He played from memory throughout. He started with a *chacona* and *passacailes* from the Spanish school by Arañés and Cabanilles. His fingering was light, with no pianisms, and he managed a precise *cantabile* that perfectly suited the music. It was a different facet of the Geraint who had played Chopin with such mellifluousness and Reger with such power. He performed a Buxtehude *ciacona* next and it seemed like dance music. After twists and turns, the programme ended with the astonishing *Es ist das Heil* by Matthias Weckmann. Each variation was more abstruse than the last. This was the *ne plus ultra* of a foreign style submerged in the past, yet Geraint made the archaic music soar. In fact, Matthew knew, he played it better than Matthew, despite his years of submersion and devotion.

He heard a voice: 'It was so lucky he met Chloë. Such a nice woman. So lucky that they had children. And her musicianship is so inspiring. So natural, so artistic.'

The insistent voice continued.

'Really, family must be his main consolation. It's funny, all of them crammed into that flat above the cloister.'

The voice cut to a whisper: 'He was the one who had a breakdown at Oxford. That's why he buried himself in Bamberg. Middle of nowhere in Franconia. That's why he's never got a top job. They can't have someone who crumples under pressure, especially if he can't play that well in the first place.'

He woke up a second later. He must have been asleep for more than a second. How many seconds in an hour? Then he heard it again. A creak. Something was alive in the flat. In a panic, he sat up. He was hot, damp and sweaty. He pushed off what seemed like insulation blankets. He was still in his clothes. Another creak. That must have been what woke him up. His tongue and mouth and throat were dry and sticking.

What was alive down the corridor? He fumbled for his watch but couldn't find it on the bedside table. What time was it? He was still wearing his watch. He couldn't see it. He reached for the light switch, knocking over a glass of water that was half drunk from yesterday. Why didn't he have a new one? Now he would have to get up to get more water. He stumbled out of bed and almost fell, swaying into the wall, managed to control his descent to the carpet. He could never get to sleep with his throat clamped up.

Another creak. Something was alive down there. He couldn't get back into bed because he needed water, but something was alive out there. The carpet was at an odd angle. It was comfortable though. But his mouth felt awful. His brain was expanding and contracting.

The corridor was longer than it had been. Whatever was alive was in the kitchen. That was where the water was too.

The kitchen door swung open in front of him. The overhead light was blinding but through mostly closed eyelids he could see someone sitting at the table. It was Geraint. He wasn't sitting, he was collapsed over the table. At least it would be easy to get to the sink. He wouldn't have to talk.

Matthew drew himself a long glass of water. The tap was powerful and spray bounced up to the ceiling from the bottom of the glass. It was too cold but he forced it down. He started a second glass but felt bloated. He turned back to the table. He was now behind Geraint. He could see what was in front of the man. An empty bottle labelled Rip van Winkle. That was Chloë's.

She was the love of his life.

Matthew stepped forward in anger and grabbed Geraint under the armpits. He couldn't move him. He was made of concrete, fifteen stone of it. All that fat had absorbed Chloë's fine bourbon, the whiskey that she favoured and had chosen to share with her beloved, no one else. It was wasted on Geraint. It wasn't as if she could go to the off-licence and get him another bottle. When was she next going to be in Tennessee? Why didn't Geraint just drink lighter fluid?

The back of Geraint's head rose and cracked Matthew on the temple. Even though he saw it coming it hit him like a cricket bat. He recoiled and almost fell. How could a block travelling so slowly cause so much pain?

'Julia,' mumbled Geraint. 'Julia, are you warm enough?'
'I'm not Julia,' snapped Matthew.
'How long are you staying? Are you back for good now?'
'Geraint, you have to go home.'
'What are you talking about?'
'You have to go home.'
'I'm not leaving, Julia. Can't you see?'

'You have to get up. Now.'

Matthew tried again to heave Geraint upwards. His flammable scent seeped from every pore. The motion triggered in Geraint an attempt to stand up, so the fifteen stone stood easily. Then it was fifteen stone swaying on the vintage linoleum, and it took all Matthew's strength to stop the tree-trunk from toppling down. They eased unsteadily out of the bright kitchen and down the corridor. The front door flapped towards them, Matthew finding his balance to keep Geraint upright without the door banging into him. The sturdily hewn staircase descended ahead of them, each step cut from a rock hacked out of the Redcliffe caves, constructed for a thousand years. Geraint stopped like a recalcitrant donkey. Matthew's mouth was starting to water queasily.

'You've got to go home,' he ordered through clenched teeth.

'You call that furnished coffin a home?'

Yes, the marble-papered hall was home. Then in an instant he recalled every detail of his vision of Geraint giving his concert in the Lady Chapel: the maestro, lording it over the musical life of the cathedral, lording it over him and relegating him to musical unimportance. But his stomach was gearing up to reject all this.

Geraint's leather-shod heel clopped on to the next step down. Matthew emerged from his fantasy and found his musical domineer now slightly shorter than him. The drink-worn, loosening skin could not deny the handsome and strong features. What a head! This swaying man had been fitted for greatness, even if he hadn't accepted it.

'I don't want to turn sixty alone there.'

Geraint took a second clop. Matthew's mouth was filling with saliva. He was going to be sick.

'Geraint, you have to sit down.'

'Why?'

Matthew felt bile rising. He had to be quick.

'I'll throw up all over you.' Every word was wasting time. He needed to rush to the bathroom.

Matthew clenched his jaw and pushed Geraint downwards

into a sitting position, sliding him down the wall while Geraint surveyed him with wide-eyed amusement. He rushed back to the bathroom and threw up into the toilet. Several spasms. Foul taste stuck up the back of his nose.

Now his head was clearer – not clear enough for any decision or plan, but clear enough to demand more water and sleep. Could he leave Geraint on the stairs till morning? There wasn't much he could do. He washed his mouth out and went to the kitchen for water. If he went back out, he would have to spend ages moving Geraint, and to where? The man might as well be a megalith.

If he did nothing, well, Geraint had stayed and drunk the whiskey and had then left. If he broke his neck or caught a chill that was his problem. Matthew could say he had been asleep all along. Sleep was where he belonged. He had to stretch his legs fully and repeatedly to remain standing.

'Matthew, what are you doing?'

That was Geraint's voice from the staircase. Why did he think Matthew was doing anything?

'Matthew, I want to stay here. Leave me alone.'

The man must be hallucinating. He would happily leave him alone. Matthew splashed more water over his face and looked for his toothbrush.

'Matthew, I am telling you to leave me alone.'

Then a second voice, soft, gentle, southern-inflected: 'You just be a good sir, Mr Geraint, and stand yourself up. Hoopla!'

Matthew trembled. He stared at the enamel of the sink and its network of grey micro-cracks. Reminiscent of Geraint's skin.

Troy was at the top of the stairs outside his front door. The Nothing Man was on the landing, alone with Geraint. Matthew forced himself upright, his vision dimming for a moment. He grabbed the doorpost and rounded the corner, then tore down the corridor. The front door was half-closed. He pulled it open. First he saw Geraint, standing, but he wasn't standing of his own volition. The tall man in his shapeless sweatsuit stood holding Geraint upright.

Troy turned and stared into Matthew's eyes with his weird blend of malice and mildness: 'It's lucky I'm here, otherwise he might fall.'

Matthew fumbled for words as best he could: 'Leave him alone or I'll call the police.'

'Chlo doesn't want that.'

'Leave him alone or I'll call the police.'

'I'm not here for him,' said Troy. 'I'm here for you.'

Matthew started to shake, and felt a chill pass through his innards. Geraint took a last clop on to the next stair down and swayed dangerously. He seemed to be balancing himself.

Troy's eyes hardened: 'But if you insist…'

Without taking his eyes off Matthew, Troy removed his supporting hand from Geraint and raised his arm theatrically. The fifteen-stone patrician rocked slowly forwards and back, each time further than the last. He passed the point at which he could return. He pitched forward. He fell for ages. Hitting level ground would have been far enough, but he fell like the hand of a clock. Six feet ahead was several steps down. Luckily, he turned slightly as he fell and his face missed the lowest of these steps, but the side of his chest audibly cracked against the Redcliffe stone. His legs swept upwards and then the fifteen stone was rolling down, coming to land on the flagstones broadside on. Geraint rolled once more, convulsed then relaxed, ending up limp and spreadeagled.

Matthew stared. Could he wake up? Could this dream or vision come to an end? Could he remove himself from space and time?

Troy had not averted his eyes from Matthew's face. Matthew stepped back into his lobby and slammed the front door. The latch clicked into place. He turned the key for good measure. Once upon a time he had wanted to push Geraint down the stairs. Now Troy had done that.

He shook himself awake. He needed to do something. What, he didn't know. He should help Geraint, but if he opened his door would he be attacked? He needed to step in and take action.

He set off down the hall, tripped, and slid down the wall. Back on his feet, he made it back to the front door. He couldn't open it. He couldn't risk being attacked. He moved back to his sitting room. The lights were off. He went to the window and looked out into the graveyard.

Hannon! Hannon was out there, pretending to be a gravestone.

'Hannon!' he shouted. 'Hannon.'

A figure broke away from the shadows and stood, looking up.

'Hannon, run, don't let him catch you.'

The figure remained still. It was too tall for Hannon, who didn't wear a hood. Then the figure turned back into the darkness.

Matthew ran for the hall, banging into furniture on the way. He swung open the front door and clattered down the stairs. Geraint lay as before, silent and quivering. Why was he not shrieking in pain? He would come back for him. Deal with the enemy first, then the wounded.

'Matt, why are you leaving me?' cried out Geraint. 'Help me.'

He ran past him. The door from the cloister to the graveyard was wide open. Probably had been all night. He ran out into the graveyard. He stood blinking, catching his breath, looking round the shapes of black on blackness, turgidly lightening as he got used to the orange sky. It was empty except for the dead. Orlick Strange, Richard *et al.*

Hannon wasn't there. He'd never been there. Hannon had gone home hours ago, with his disapproving mother. But a black-clad arm was, and the fist at the end of it slammed into his jaw. Matthew spreadeagled backwards, his left leg pointing vertically and straining tendons and muscles all the way to his back while his scalp smashed into and scraped down one of the gravestones. The mass bludgeoned him while the roughness cut through his skin and hair, raking out a burst of hot blood. He was swept up like a boneless dummy by the hand, joined by another one. They grasped him by the collar. Then they were round his neck. It was gentle but tightening and unbreakable. The hands massaged tighter and tighter.

What about everything he wanted to say or do?

He jerked upright as much as he could but he was trapped, leaning up against the gravestone.

He felt the hands contract. They were pulling him up by his soft and defenceless neck. The only things holding him up were the hands, and they were strangling him. Was this it? He was going to die. What about everything he contained and everything he hoped to do? What about his deepest visions? Everything would vanish. He was about to never know that he had ever existed.

He had to squeeze out the words: 'Chlo, Chlo, Chlo…'

Did he feel the hands relax a touch? He ventured everything, because he had only one card to play.

'Three thousand…'

He was gambling for his life. His feet were leaving the ground.

'…two hundred…'

Did he, could he, would he feel the hands relax? His sight was turning black.

'…and eighty-…'

The graveyard had vanished. He had space in his throat for one last word.

'…-five.'

The hands let go. His head fell back. He hung in the air weightless for a long millisecond. Then the expert hands caught him by the trunk before he could fall and hoisted him into a diagonal position, arms dangling. Only his heels touched the springy life-full turf. He could do nothing but hang. Other than the hammer blows of his pulse within his head, Troy's focused breaths were the only sound. They were joined in a weird communion. His heart throbbed. Hot blood flowed out through his scalp. He hung there, dripping. His body was entirely under the control of another person. His being was at their mercy.

Pain stabbed through his neck and head and face and through the spiderweb of his nerves to the extremities of his limbs. He surged with it to the frontier of feeling. Pain was feeling at its purest; amplified. Now he had felt, to the boundaries. He had experienced, to the boundaries. He had lived, to the boundaries, to the moment of death. It didn't matter what happened next. He was happy if the rest would be nothing but darkness.

'Troy,' he gasped, 'I'm the only other person in the whole wide world…'

His breath burned, but he had to say his sentence. He hacked it out as best he could …

'…who'd write three thousand two hundred and eighty-five times to Chloë.'

He was dropped. He collapsed limply through space into the inches of grass and moss till he was struck by the underbed of hard earth.

'Who's Hannon?' breathed Troy.

Matthew's arms were burrowing, as if he was a small rodent. He couldn't stop them.

'I know,' said Troy. 'He's your student. I saw you together after the concert, smoking your cigar together.'

'You were there?'

'I'm always there. He's your little you, isn't he? Your little way of making it seem like it's not just you and the big universe. You don't want anything to happen to him, do you?'

'No, no, no,' stammered Matthew.

'And if you're like me, then you understand.'

'I don't understand,' stuttered Matthew. 'I want to live.'

'Me too,' said Troy. 'Bigger than you. I want to feast my eyes on her, and her on me, and then fill myself with the biggest feeling there'll ever be.'

'I just had that feeling,' said Matthew, 'and even it's not enough.'

'Be that as it may, you send her to me, otherwise Hannon'll be next.'

Matthew felt he could lie contemplating the glowing clouds for eternity. He did, until a cry from the cloister recalled the man who lay there but hadn't accepted pain. His head cleared. He must phone an ambulance. This was far beyond anything he could help with himself. He got himself to his feet. He struggled through the cloister and up the stairs.

'Don't leave me again,' gargled Geraint as he passed. 'Forget about what you did to me, and help me!'

Did to him? What had he done? Back in the flat he called 999. The operator gave him instructions. When he was off the phone he went into the bathroom and turned the light on. His face didn't look too bad, but his head was fringed in matted blood. He drank some more water. Then he took a blanket, pillow and water down to Geraint.

He did what he could to make Geraint comfortable. He felt the sandpaper of his stubble and the sweat of his scalp as he positioned the pillow under his head, and the fattening flesh that sagged away from the bone like a geriatric's as he arranged him into what the operator had said was a better pose. The man was like a sack of gravel. Love and friendship developed out of the intimacy of physical contact. It might not be pleasant but that's what intimacy was. It was impossible not to like Geraint and feel sympathy.

He opened the door at the far end of the cloister that led out to the car park, so the ambulance crew would be able to enter. He wanted to smoke a cigarette outside but he should wait with Geraint. Part of his boss was still aware. He pressed his hands and said his name to stop him descending further into unconsciousness. The minutes passed interminably and finally the ambulance crew rolled in a stretcher. He tried to offer a full breakdown of events but they didn't pay attention to him. They worked efficiently and wheeled Geraint away.

The stonework was warping in his vision. His eyelids were flickering more closed than open. He clambered back up the cliff-like steps and slunk to his bed. He tore off his socks and trousers and jacket and slept in his shirt and pants, the darkness and warmth offering him a much easier route than the impossibilities afforded by consciousness.

He remembered the first time he had met Geraint: his cut

about the *trompe l'oeil* at the end of the enfilade of life and death. That cockiness had masked his superior's death wish, but Geraint hadn't banked on meeting the Nothing Man. But he, the assistant, alone, in darkness and with his humanity torn open, was stranded in the farther reaches of the enfilade. He had stepped through the illusory door. He wanted nothing but oblivion. Gradually relinquishing control and slipping into darkness was like controlling an orgasm. No wonder repeatable suicide was Geraint's goal. *Suonalo ancora*! Darkness might be recuperative, but he wanted it so that he could wake up anew.

XXIII

The piano was playing down below and he had taken Geraint's keys. Keyboard keys or door keys? Was Geraint's head bashed in by the octagonal door handle? Where was Geraint's father's cigarette paper? Did not life bring one further and further from perpetual rest? Was not rest, eternal or otherwise, to be desired? What if there was pain in that moment of transition? It was the breaking of that bitter wave that was fearful, not the sea of ease beyond it. Why were they rehearsing jolly music downstairs?

Someone was knocking on his front door.

All the happy chords downstairs made him hear Bach:

> *My heart ever faithful*
> *sing praises, be joyful!*

D major, Bach's brightest and most joyous key. An anthem Bach tossed out for a dreary Sunday, as he did every week. But balm.

He felt her breath, felt her touching his face with her soft hands. He basked in the fleeting moment of physical intimacy. He mustn't lose her.

'You'll never penetrate my skin like the Nothing Man did.'

Someone was pounding on the door.

'Matthew, come and answer.'

It was the dean's voice. He had to get up. He managed to

get to the hall and unlatched his heavy front door. Bryce was standing there with arms crossed like the photo on his desk, but he lost his composure when Matthew opened the door and revealed himself.

'Matthew, what happened?'

Matthew wasn't alert enough to be interrogated and stood blankly.

'What happened to your face?' asked Bryce.

'What do you mean, what happened?'

'Geraint's in hospital and you've been in a fight. What happened?'

'A fight? What's happened?'

Bryce stared in confusion, then his face set and he changed tack.

'When did you last see Geraint?'

Matthew heard the clop of leather. 'Here. I said good night to him. Did I?'

He peered down the stairs. Nothing marked the walls to suggest a heavy man scuffing downwards. Troy had left no more evidence than a ghost. Had any of it happened?

Bryce searched his eyes. The dean's stare drew the memories of last night into his vision as if by a magnet. He told Bryce some of what had happened, but not mentioning Troy. He had left Geraint to be sick, then opened the door and found Geraint at the point of falling. He had called an ambulance. He found himself embellishing details that put him in a good light. The dutiful assistant helps his drunk and transgressing boss. He also presented Geraint in an exaggeratedly good light. It was his balance, not the alcohol, and the stairs are treacherous.

All the while a voice said: 'You're going to get the job.'

Where was the voice coming from? He pushed it down.

'And what happened to you?' asked Bryce.

'What do you mean?'

'You're covered in blood.'

'Oh… I went into the graveyard and tripped over.'

Bryce eyed him as if he was a dunce, then told him to come to his office at eleven.

Immediately Bryce had gone, Matthew phoned Chloë. It took her some moments to work out what he was saying and why, but she said she would be right over. He forced himself through the annoying prerequisites of his body, bathroom, dressing, eating. His head thumped and his throat was dessicated, but he kept going. The kitchen worktop was awash, dried vomit encrusted the toilet and broken glass strewed the floor. He cleaned and tidied. Soon his flat was as evidence-free of the night's events as the spookily unmarked stairs and cloister. But the morning had stripped the sheen of worth from his flat, the cloister, and what he could see from his window: the garden of rest and the cliff-like south wall of the cathedral. He had used this complex of buildings as a set of moral scales for more than a decade but they now seemed not just indifferent, but hazardous.

It was time to see Bryce again. In the cloister, all was quiet except Derek's depressive typing. In the office the secretary bore a theatrically sombre visage.

'Saint Matthew,' he said with what seemed like grim enjoyment, 'the organist and master of the choristers has been located in hospital. He's more comfortable there I hope…' Derek leant forward and dropped his cigarette into the travel-sweet tin that served as his ashtray, and closed the lid to asphyxiate it. '…than on the slabs of the cloister.'

The melodramatic streak so loveable to a chorister or teenager now seemed puerile.

'Matthew.' Bryce stood in the doorway to his inner office, gesturing him in.

Once he was seated, Bryce said: 'My concern for Geraint's welfare goes without saying, but I must say that this behaviour, following on from previous examples of drunkenness and taking place within both the house of God and your – our – workplace, is grossly unprofessional and inexcusable. But I also have to admit that if you hadn't acted, Geraint could have been more seriously injured.'

Bryce looked at Matthew significantly.

'As a starting point, you now have to organise and execute all the music within this cathedral by yourself, as if a full team was present. I'm guessing, but I think we can assume he'll be off work for four weeks. He's broken at least one rib and hurt his legs. Sprains, not breaks. The rib will heal relatively quickly and he can be at home, but he might be on crutches when he returns. I'm not going to waste money adding more organists to the payroll, so don't dream of asking me to hire you an assistant or deputy.'

Bryce was effectively placing Matthew in charge. Matthew saw rôle, house and life within what, if he squinted, was still the setting of his dreams. If he did well, would that not advance him towards his ultimate goal? But as was now usual, opposing thoughts immediately filled his mind. Was it what he wanted? How would he flourish there with Chloë? With what he had now experienced, how would his more worldly self be contained within the dysfunctional department?

'In the meantime,' Bryce concluded, 'I will work out what kind of rôle that hospitalised drunk will return to.'

'Don't fire him.' The words came out, from where he didn't know. Wasn't he supposed to be glad Geraint's position was at risk?

'Then why do you chafe against him so much?' asked Bryce. 'What about those evensongs where he was spouting nonsense about all your mistakes?'

'I need to be a bigger person.'

'Doesn't he need to be a bigger person? And what about the wider team? I had a legitimate complaint from the mother of one of the choristers about how her son's singing had been affected by his behaviour.'

'Bryce, don't fire him.'

'That's not in your gift. This is not your cathedral. This is not about you or him. It's about our congregation, their souls, and the effect our ministry has on them.'

'Bryce, where is Geraint? I'll go and see him.'

'He's at the Infirmary, but don't visit him today. They'll be bandaging him up, assuming they can do that when he's still full of alcohol. You can probably understand that. You look the worse for wear yourself.'

Matthew sighed. He was indeed still steeped in alcohol and even he could tell that he exuded Geraint's lab-like smell.

Bryce carried on: 'When I was made a canon in the Episcopal Church – this was in Tupelo, Mississippi, as I've told you – I went home to Nebraska to celebrate with my family. We had quite a revel. Red Cloud only has a handful of junctions, but as luck would have it when I drove through one of those four-way stops without stopping, a police cruiser was behind me and pulled me over. He asked who I was and what I was doing. When I told him, he said "So they don't have stop signs in Mississippi?" and let me off without breathalysing me. That saved me, and my church, from much embarrassment. Did I deserve it? Did they deserve it? If I was someone else, would he have charged me? What are the answers? And what are the answers for you?'

Matthew spoke genuinely: 'I don't know.'

Bryce responded: 'We all get things right and wrong. I'm man enough to say that perhaps I was wrong. You have the potential to be the director of music of this cathedral, and in doing so I think you have the potential to gain some spiritual depth and come to the Lord. Geraint might be able to do the first, but I'd be surprised if he can do the second. I need someone who can do both. I'm prepared to overlook last night's incident. I'll set things in motion about the job.'

'Thank you.' Then Matthew felt a surge of vindication. A path had opened. He was going to be director of music of the cathedral. He shut up the nagging inner voice. 'I will do my best.'

'Good. You'll need to be focused. You'll need to do some

homework. You'll need to redo the music list to reflect the fact that there's only one of you. I don't want a single mistake, let alone any more train-wrecks.'

Matthew let Chloë in at her knock. She was pale and looked as though she didn't know what to do next. He put his arms around her so as to enfold her in the headiness he had experienced, and still felt an echo of.

She could tell he was feeling odd. 'What happened?'

He told her. When he reached Geraint's fall she interupted. 'Did he see Troy?'

'He must have done,' he answered, 'but he kept talking to me as if I'd pushed him. He was delirious with booze.'

Matthew carried on with the narrative, and told her about what happened in the graveyard, though he didn't include the intense feelings he had experienced.

'Hannon's Jane's son?' she interrupted.

He told her more about Nick.

'And you call him by his surname? I thought that went out with *Journey's End*.'

'Not here.' He carried on and finished his tale.

'What if I said: fine, let's let Hannon's head roll?'

The trapdoor couldn't open any further. Matthew gazed around the room with its sturdy woodwork and redoubtable mullions. Hannon. Orlick Strange, 1714, cut down like a flower. Did it matter?

'By which I mean,' continued Chloë, 'is anyone worth saving? Is my will to live so strong and selfish that I'll just chuck everyone under the bus and carry on with my little gigs? What's the point of any of it?'

'Are you sure you're not in danger?' he asked. 'We should call the police.'

Chloë groaned. 'There are some subtleties of the case that I'm not sure they'll appreciate.'

'We're covering for Troy.'

'I know.'

They sat in silence. Chloë was thinking; Matthew's mind was blank.

She said, 'They'll ask why I didn't tell them about Pete.'

This was the first time she had verbalised Pete's likely fate. Matthew looked her full in the face. 'Pete? We don't know where he is. He wasn't home when we went to his house. He could be anywhere.'

Chloë kept his stare. Her mind was working. 'So last night, could you say with certainty that Troy was on the stairs?'

Matthew kept eye-contact. 'I don't know. I was drunk. I banged my head.'

'Then whatever we do, we do by ourselves.'

'And you're sure you're not in danger?'

'Yes,' she said. 'My job, as far as Troy's concerned, is to watch and be impressed. It matters to him if someone is watching. All suicides jump off the townward side of the bridge.'

She sat up.

'My God,' she said, 'if I'm not here to watch him, nothing's going to happen. If I'm not here, Troy can't put on his show. You're safe. Hannon's safe.'

She looked at Matthew as if he fully comprehended her, but he was still a few steps behind.

'Darling,' she said, 'all I have to do is leave. Troy doesn't know where I live or how to find me. I don't think he'll buy one of my tapes and get my phone number. He has to come to my next gig, which is next week. He'll know that because the posters are up. But I'm going to cancel, and I'll let him know. I'll stick a 'Cancelled' sheet across a couple of the posters, saying "Chloë's gone". Once I've gone, and he knows it, you're all safe.'

'How are we safe? He could come here at any moment.'

'He wants my attention. If I'm not around he won't get it, regardless of what he does.'

'But if you're not around, won't he just hurt people to make you come back?'

'He can do what he likes. I'm not coming back.'

'How will he know that you're serious?'

'Because "Chloë's Gone" means "Chloë's Gone".' She gave him a despairing glance: 'And if that's not clear enough, once he does something and I don't come back, he'll know.'

'Where will you go?'

'Anywhere. I've got to go to Germany anyway. Darling,' she added, 'you come too. Let's leave now.'

Germany. The tour that they had discussed. He was going to accompany her. Hotel rooms, meals, drinks, blues gigs, new cities to discover. But it was just a dream.

'I've got to stay. I can't take time off now. I've got to run the whole music department by myself.' The love-filled German fantasy cut dead in his mind. The projector had stopped. No birds sang.

She said: 'If you want to make a new start, if you want to resign and leave, I'll do everything I can to support you. You can have half of whatever I have.'

The film of life started moving again. Brightness, happiness, love. But he was on the cusp of becoming director of music.

'I can't,' he said.

'Why not?'

'I came back to England for this. I've waited for years. It's within my grasp.'

'What if Troy comes to see you again?'

'What can he do?' he asked. 'I've won your red badge of courage.' He told her about how he had felt in the garden of peace.

'Do you want to go through that again?' she asked.

'No. But what else can I do?'

'Is it worth it?'

Was it? Every tangible asset of his success was within the cathedral: daily artistic work, the physical reality of the building and organs, the flat and possibly the house in which he could live. Was it all an insubstantial dream that he should leave behind? It couldn't be, because otherwise his whole life's direction had been wrong.

'Yes,' he said.

Her face showed admiration. 'It's a gamble, but if you've got to do it, you've got to do it.'

Gamble. She'd used the word. Was this the gamble he needed to take to justify his life?

She added: 'Leaving aside the music department you've got to run, you've got to finish *The Art Of Fugue*. You have to perform it.'

'Yes,' he said.

Yet he felt rebellion against his music, his artistry, his rôle and the cathedral. He was connected to Chloë by an umbilical, and that was being torn apart.

'Chloë, it's not much of a life.'

'My love, it's the only life we've got for the time being.'

'Will you come back?'

She came and sat with him and put her arms round him.

'If he comes, just tell him to go. You can do that because you don't want to see him. You're on fire now you've got the experience you've needed. But if he comes to me, he won't leave if I tell him to go. I told him to and he didn't, because he knows that deep down I still want him. That's why I have to go away.'

'Why do you still want him?'

'Darling,' she murmured, 'Imagine us living here, in a few years time. You've got your work, a purpose, a place to play music every day. You've got a future, consistent and fulfilling employment for decades until you retire. But me? My gigs have dried up. Our children, bless them, suck what's left out of me. And blues itself, where do you go with it? Five notes, three chords. It's brutal to get expression out of that. I'd be better off writing haiku.

'You've actually given me some hope. I can see a sideline in teaching coming out of this whole Kodály thing. Helping people not be like me. That's worthwhile. But it's still a sacrifice because it's not making original blues. That's what I was put into the world for, but I was put into the narrowest alleyway there is, and God forgot to put an audience there. I'm eternally driven and yet it's eternally pointless. And that's when Troy comes for me in my sleep. When I have to face the fact that I want to feel the point of that knife, that I want to offer myself up when he comes and gets me.'

XXIV

Chloë left. She would doctor some of her posters and then go to Germany immediately and wait there as best she could until her tour began in early July. And after that? They didn't know.

The purpose that had carried Matthew through the morning evaporated. His hangover reasserted itself. He had nothing to do till evensong. He slumped on his sofa and nodded off between forcing down glasses of water. His body hurt from cranium to nerve endings. His bowels were liquid. Later he was able to get up, and made himself some tea. He went out for lunch, or was it breakfast? It turned out to be half-past three in the afternoon. He bought a sausage roll, and forced himself to eat it.

He faltered back for the rehearsal and evensong. Somehow he got through it. Frank insisted on being the beater as they didn't have a conductor. What Matthew heard of the singing above the tone of the organ was acceptable. Hardly anyone came. Hannon, of course, was there. Did he need to keep an eye on the lad? Of course, but how?

Back in his flat he took up his station on the sofa. *Carnival of Souls* was on Moviedrome. The kind of film he could watch with Chloë. He imagined them watching it in Richard's sitting room, but the image didn't sit properly. How could his relationship with her be crammed into the cathedral purlieux? He fell asleep on the sofa, woke in the middle of the night feeling achy and grim, and took himself to bed.

Could he find out if Geraint had seen Troy? The next afternoon he trod his way to the Infirmary, having phoned to ascertain visiting hours. Chloë's mum worked there. Was she the voice on the phone? Geraint's bed was angled into a semi-upright position. He seemed half-asleep, but it was difficult to tell because he had bandages on his cheeks and nose. Through his open pyjama top, extensive bruising was visible. His left arm was bandaged. The skin around his eyes was pale and puffy. The eyes watched Matthew as if from behind a castle wall, but Geraint said nothing. He was probably drugged on painkillers. Matthew sat down beside the bed in an outsize and uncomfortable plastic-coated armchair. He reached for Geraint, who didn't respond. Perhaps it wasn't a good idea to grasp a hand or even touch his arm, if it caused pain.

'Would you like me to help you? I can run errands for you, do your shopping, help round the house. Do you need anything now?'

Geraint said nothing. Matthew didn't have the know-how to draw any conclusion about the man's condition, but the naked feet visible at the end of the bed had yellowing, uncared-for nails, and the physical injuries seemed an augmentation of a decline that was already underway.

'Do you remember what happened?' asked Matthew.

The eyes surveyed him. The minutes passed. Matthew positioned himself as comfortably in the armchair as he could. Heaviness descended. After a brief struggle he surrendered to the exhaustion. He was wakened by a nurse. Who knew what time it was, or had been when he was last awake? Geraint was asleep. Matthew left.

Though he wished he could lie down and do nothing, he had to turn his attention to the music department. He would now, for a rare moment in his career, have to lead himself without someone telling him what to do. Before he went to bed he forced himself to work through the music list, changing it so that till the end of term it consisted only of pieces that were unaccompanied, or that the choir would be able to sing without a conductor, and while taking leads essentially from the back of his head as he accompanied in the organ loft.

Nonetheless, he now had an opportunity to reset his relationship with the choir, many of whom he still didn't know well, even if they had witnessed the vicissitudes of the last few months. He planned the rehearsal carefully and started it on time, all to make a good impression with them. He led them through warm-ups and taught them the service music as thoroughly as he could. The evensong, and subsequent services, went surprisingly well.

Being responsible for all the organisation meant Matthew was much busier than he had been, including more meetings with the dean and other clergy. In comparison, his earlier period at the cathedral seemed like a charmed time when all he had to worry about was practising and performing.

But the musician in him resurfaced and he found the process of running the cathedral's music by himself stimulating. As he planned for the upcoming weeks, selecting works by appropriate composers to elucidate the themes of the various services, he began to feel pleased. This was his métier. He replaced Geraint's rather haphazard choices and enjoyed giving aesthetic shape to each service, even with simple settings. Hopefully the dean would feel the musical results and approve.

He remembered Bryce's exhortation, from seemingly a lifetime ago, to use his imagination. He forced himself to perform some modern worshippy pieces, and found much to enjoy. He saw Bryce listening with approval in the services. As for Geraint, he heard nothing from him directly, nor through the dean or the more unauthorised channel of the secretary, Derek.

Because time was short, he needed to maximise the hours he had for *The Art of Fugue*. He could practise during the day, but because the cathedral was open he could use only quiet stops and was often interrupted. He therefore set aside the time after the cathedral was locked as practice time. If he started at six he could get in four hours before turning in. There were occasional events to navigate around, but luckily the cathedral diary was largely blank.

Yet *The Art of Fugue* was long – twenty pieces taking up more than an hour, and filled from start to finish with contrapuntal entwinings. It took more time to memorise than he had. He tried to learn the lines of music from the end to the beginning, learning the final eight bars, then adding the eight bars previous. This would hopefully cement the counterpoint into his mind in more than one way, and make it less stressful playing the pieces, as he would move towards, rather than away from, material he knew better. But it was alarmingly slow. Each day he fell further and further short of his overall goal. He tried expanding his practice time at night so that he worked till about four in the morning, then slept till choir practice, then slept again till the afternoon rehearsal. He memorised more, and got just about enough rest to keep going, but he still fell short and was always tired.

He was in his ideal rôle, directing the music of Bristol Cathedral and preparing to perform on his ideal organ the set of pieces he loved more than any other, yet it was not enough. Music was not enough. Chloë was not there. She was what he wanted, and he wanted a life in which she could live.

Depending on where she was, she phoned occasionally, but the calls were expensive and her phonecards didn't last long. Worse, their conversations became strained. There was nothing to talk about, because they had no way into the future. He noticed that she called less often. His domestic life was functional at best. He had not made any close friends. He had not established friendships with any colleagues at the cathedral, but was stuck in a web of hierarchical and stressful professional relationships. It turned out that art did not fill the many gaps. Art needed to be part of life.

Two weeks passed. On a Tuesday at six o'clock he entered the Lady Chapel after the cathedral was locked up. His head was full of getting the choir to sing as well as possible at evensong, but Bach would shake that out within a few minutes.

Except that Geraint was sitting on the organ bench. Crutches leant neatly against the casework. A pile of volumes sat on each end of the bench. A backpack on the floor showed how he'd carried it all in. Matthew had seen him in this thoughtful pose before. Who was this man, whose existence he had forgotten? What was going to happen to his practice regime?

Geraint looked up and stared back at him. He was slimmer, fitter and more alert. Even his skin seemed to fit better. His hair was neatly trimmed. The white patches under his eyes had faded and looked more natural.

'I'd forgotten about you,' said Geraint, as if mirroring Matthew's thoughts.

'How are you?' said Matthew, feeling weak.

Geraint exhaled too energetically for it to be a sigh. 'I'm well. I'm moving fast.' He tapped the sheet music. 'I'm a new man. Maybe this way I won't drink myself to death in Sodding Chipbury.' Geraint leant forward. 'On which note, I'm doing my practice.'

Geraint inclined his head towards the way out.

'When will you be finished?' Matthew felt worry in his voice.

'I don't know.'

'I was hoping to practise too.'

'You're welcome to practise when I don't need the organ.'

'I'm preparing for my recital.'

'So am I.'

'But you're on sick leave.'

'So?' Geraint's voice grew quieter, so Matthew had to lean in to hear. 'You're here to do the work, not be the boss. Let's meet in the office so I can tell you what to do. Tomorrow at eleven?'

'Okay.' Matthew acquiesced. This new Geraint was painfully sharp. The accusatory stare must stem from a belief that Matthew had pushed him down the stairs. But if he and Chloë were committed to their course, he would have to put up with Geraint's imputation.

'Good,' said Geraint. 'Now, leave me. I've been given a chance to blow the audience out of their socks, and I'm going to take it.'

Matthew assumed he could practise after Geraint had finished. He waited for two interminable hours before checking the cathedral, but the organ was still playing. He tried to practise on the clavichord in his flat but the tiny sound could not satisfy him. He dutifully toiled till 10pm and then stalked down to the cathedral, but Geraint was still playing. By midnight the exhaustion which he had ignored through his new routine caught him.

He slept till ten the next morning, missing choir practice and dead to any sounds of the piano that might have risen up through the floor. By eleven he was downstairs. A few minutes after that, the clack of crutches announced Geraint swinging himself along the cloister. The sounds and movements were filled with energy, and prepared Matthew for the same Geraint as yesterday.

'You've been busy, I trust.' Geraint swung across the room to one of the two carved corner chairs Matthew had brought from the adjoining office.

'Kind of you to fetch the chair for me, but the crutches are psychological. I just twisted an ankle.'

After a pause Matthew asked: 'Would you like tea?'

'Is there any herb tea?'

'I don't think so but let me make sure.'

Matthew, realising with instant hindsight that he should have bought herbal teabags or even some fresh ginger root, fussed around the drawer. He heard Geraint lowering himself into the corner chair.

'How about Lapsang?'

'Fine. My father used to drink that.'

When Matthew brought through the tea, Geraint was looking through the new music list and crossing settings out with a pencil.

'No, that's too boring. No, I don't think we can pull that off. No, I just don't like that one.'

Geraint looked up and around the room, then at Matthew, who handed him his tea. For an instant they were joined by the cup. The eyes were sharp.

'How can I help you with your work?' asked Matthew again, hoping to avoid a combative answer.

'You can't. I've got plans.' Geraint handed him the music list. 'Ignore my scribblings. Do what you like. I don't want the music list to impinge on me. I'm going to give my recital, I'll be brilliant, and it's going to be my ticket back in here. I need this job till my pension kicks in. But in the meantime, over to you. I hear that you've done a superlative job in my absence, and pray continue. Apparently Bryce has given me some kind of stool to perch on by my music stand, but I shan't use it much. You run everything, and you've my blessing to rest your buttocks on it.'

Because Geraint was now practising in the evenings, Matthew fully upturned his schedule. He slept during the day and worked through the whole of the night. The upside-down schedule seemed more efficient. Once he was awake, he was alert all night long. He never felt mid-afternoon drowsiness transposed to early morning. At three-thirty in the afternoon he got up, showered and dressed hurriedly and stumbled to the quire for the rehearsal before the evensong.

Now he didn't have to worry about following Geraint's beat, the rehearsals and services whizzed by. The choir seemed to sing well. He worked his way through a stack of sight-reading for the pre-service voluntaries, to test his ability in public under pressure. As the choir filed out, he played a *contrapunctus* from *The Art of Fugue*. As Mr Quantock locked up, he went back to his flat for a cooked breakfast. He exercised his memory on his clavichord while Geraint used the organ, and at ten, which was when Geraint generally seemed to finish, he went to the Lady Chapel to work through the night, his music echoing back from the chill, empty darkness of the nave. The morning choir practice at eight was the end of his day. After the forty-minute rehearsal he climbed the stairs to his flat and went to bed.

But as the days went by and became a week and then two, his progress wasn't fast enough. To attain the mastery he sought, he needed yet more time.

Geraint occasionally passed wordlessly, as he traversed the cloister on his way to or from playing the new organ. In the third week he ditched one crutch and then the other, forcing himself along, first with a stick and then with no help other than a steadying hand on the wall. He was a *tour de force*. Every day powerful music swept through the precinct. Masterpieces of the Baroque were dusted off and thrown through the fire. When he heard Weckmann's *Es ist das Heil*, Matthew could not resist the lure and went to talk to his boss. That day Geraint was beaming.

'I still think of that prat Heinz-Günther. My teacher, obviously a pianist primarily, sight-read this for his final exam and won a prize. Anyway, I've done enough of it for now.'

Geraint closed the score and leafed through the rest of the pile. While the man's talent had reached its splendid apogee, his lack of methodical practice was dizzying. Despite the undeniable power and near-perfect sight-reading with which he ploughed through the Baroque, he rarely played a piece more than once, and didn't attend to the many slips and deficiencies. While filled with momentum, it was the overweening playing of a man who had not accurately assessed himself.

He was heading for a musical reckoning when what he thought he was capable of collided with a piece that was beyond him. Would that piece be the Weckmann at his concert? If so, Bryce would witness it, and that would be the moment he fired Geraint and offered Matthew his job. Geraint didn't seem to discern this. How could he tell Geraint to watch out, given the man's arrogance?

'It would be nice to hear you play the Weckmann again,' he ventured.

'No.' Geraint nodded at his cast. 'So what if it's full of canons? I'll keep it in my programme because the pedalling's not too difficult. My feet are still a bit gammy.'

Geraint obviously hadn't sight-read the later variations where the hazardous pedal part had two melodic lines to play at all times, one with each foot. This would be a dizzying surprise if he decided to sight-read the piece in concert.

'What about the double pedal sections?'

Geraint snorted. 'Double pedal, double pedal, double pedal.' Then his voice turned humane. 'Matthew, it's not good to be a creature of the night. I can feel myself relapsing, and I'm just doing some gentle playing in the evenings. You've gone full tilt. If you want to practise every day, come in at dawn. Two or three hours is enough. Be all done by choir practice. Then go for a run, and spend the day outside with your girlfriend. That would be healthy. Where is she?'

Matthew blinked at his superior. 'Oh, she'll be back soon.'

The sound of the Weckmann never filled the cathedral again. The potential meeting of minds with Geraint, finding common joy in fabulous masterpieces by wonderful composers, was not to be realised.

The phone rang. The proprietor of the Pension Kogel in Wuppertal wanted to connect him to Chloë. Hearing her voice made him see spider plants and a newspaper open on a pine table, all warmed by the afternoon sun.

'Where are you?'

'I'm knocking around in my big room.' Her voice was animated. Something had happened.

'How's it going?'

'The waiting's over. The band arrived. We're on tour now. It started slow but now we're cutting them down. It's hard. Lots of driving. Sound checks, which are the most boring thing since paint drying. We can only afford bad food, but we pass a thousand of your *Kaffee-und-Kuchen* joints a day. When I go to sleep I see great towers of *Schlagsahne*. And then I come down to breakfast and it's rye bread with salami.'

'I'm glad the gigs are going well.'

'They are, but I haven't got to the point. That big old train, the Express Chloë, is leaving the station. We were in Bremen at the weekend. After our gig I stayed to see the headliner. I'd heard the name, but not his music. Ronnie Earl. His band is the Broadcasters. That's an old Fender guitar, I guess that's where the name comes from. Four people, guitar, Hammond, bass, drums, all instrumental. No singing, no wailing. They were the best band I've ever seen. Each one of them is a genius. It was the best set I've ever seen – ever. It was the best everything I've ever seen. Ever. Every key, every technique, every pattern of song, every mood, every nuance – the whole history of blues and all the previous stuff that went into the blues – and the whole lot redone in their own style with complete originality. Everything was at its peak.

'The slow blues were the best – each one different and no time-wasting – and the solos stared into the abyss. None of that covers-band "let's fall back on this tune by such and such", and no allowing old men to ramble just because of who they are. They did it. Three chords, five notes, and a universe of passing chords. Parts of it were atonal. You'd've liked that. They blew the haiku out of the sky. I can see a future now. I want to play like that. I can, and I'm going for it like a greased gila monster.'

He felt admiration and gratitude welling up in him. She would overcome the challenges of her form. She was back as the leader he desired. 'Well, that's the blues,' he whispered.

'Yeah, the sky's fallen in, but I'm stuck in Germany.'

'I'm stuck here.'

'There's a cathedral in Bremen. They've probably got one here in Wuppertal.'

What if it wasn't Geraint who left the cathedral, but Matthew? Would he survive in the outside world? He had managed in Bamberg, even if he thought he had only been there while waiting to return to Bristol. His job at the Domkirche had gone to someone else, but there were other churches. And for the first time when considering this, his soul lifted.

'Chloë, putting our lives on hold won't work any more.'

'I know. Matty, I'm coming back.'

'When?'

'Friday.'

'That's the day of Geraint's concert. He's invited me plus one, which means you, to drinks beforehand. Would you like to come?'

'Sure, we can play "Guess which Geraint'll come out of the cupboard". But there's someone else in the cupboard.'

'I know. What about him?'

Chloë thought for a while. 'So if Geraint's giving a concert, then you, me, Hannon and him will all be in the same room?

'Yes.'

'Well, if Troy's got on a plane and gone, great. But if he hasn't, we can't live our lives like this. We need to have a showdown with him. If Troy wants a set piece, this is it. If he wants me, or if he wants to do in Hannon, he'll have to come to the concert. I'll meet him, and if necessary I'll…'

She broke off. Matthew's nerves prickled. Was a showdown with Troy safe?

She took a few deep breaths. 'There'll even be an audience,' she continued. 'That gives us a bit of protection and gives him even more of an occasion. And on this occasion, I need to tell him that it's between him and me. None of this bullshit with other people. No Geraint, no you, no Hannon. If he wants to harm anyone it'll be me, and if he wants to do himself in, then that's up to him. I'll walk him to the door but I won't go through it with him. And if he doesn't accept that, we'll call the police and send them to Pete's Capri. And then we get on with our lives.'

'How will he know about it?'

'The posters worked last time. Can you put a few posters up? You can make them say something significant. "Wanted: Nothing Man, Dead or Alive"?'

Many times over the years, Matthew had watched Derek create posters and programmes for the concerts and events in the cathedral. Derek had already put up various notices, and Geraint's concert was included in the cathedral's leaflets and newsletters and, as acting director of music, Matthew had already sent out more than a hundred personal invitations. But Derek was happy for him to help create a final poster that could be cut and pasted at the same time as the programme collage.

One of the bookcases in the office contained stacks of musical scores that, even for the cathedral, were outdated. While the music itself had been judged to be of no further interest, the title pages were filled with imaginative fonts and scrolled illustrations of muses, lyres, pillars and fronds. Derek loved them and used them as the basis for his designs, cutting out letters and words, sticking them to a fresh sheet of paper and using the photocopier to reduce or enlarge the size. The swirling results could then be printed on coloured paper. The poster that would serve as the Nothing Man's invitation made full use of these artistic resources.

The title of the concert, 'Journey of Life', and 'End of Term Concert', both used dramatic lettering. They rifled the cupboard and found sentimental illustrations of angels and cherubs, even a Stygian river with a Charon-like rower. It masqueraded as a piece of homespun art promoting a wholesome musical event, but Troy's macabre mindset would surely pick up a darker, subliminal implication, and realise that the poster had been designed with him in mind.

Derek was resistant when Matthew offered to do the poster run alone. This part of the secretary's rôle allowed him to escape the cathedral confines on a regular basis. So they went together, Matthew insisting that dozens more posters than usual were placed where he imagined Troy would see them; around the cathedral, the libraries, the docks, the quainter parts of the centre, places with aesthetic heft that seemed beyond the banalities of time.

When placed beside the eternal wheel of the countless lives and deaths of the city and its past, Matthew found that the musical life of the cathedral's services compared well. They had gone on day after day for the best part of a thousand years and were part of the movement of the city. His daily playing was part of that. The concert they were promoting fared less well. An individual's on-stage artistry felt too temporal. Geraint, who had no way of realising that his concert had been co-opted by Chloë to become a showdown with the Nothing Man, was placing hope and value in the event, but he was offering nothing more than self-expression, and the audience were seeking nothing more than a filler for their leisure time. This all now seemed thin.

Matthew grasped a feeling that had been growing within him as he prepared *The Art of Fugue*. He loved playing for services, and by himself or for Chloë, but that was the limit of his musical ambitions. He had no desire to face an audience and offer them a performance for its own sake in a concert setting. He was a musician and music dominated his life, but he wasn't a performer and didn't want to be. He could walk away from his *Art of Fugue* concert.

XXV

Chloë duly returned on the day of Geraint's recital. The same morning a postcard from Bremen arrived, sent before their conversation, outlining the peak of blues performance that she had seen, and determined to climb.

When she came to the cathedral to pick Matthew up for drinks, he held her in his arms. He felt relief and joy, but also exhilaration and adventure. He had forged a relationship that took him beyond rules, institutions and discipline. The foundations of his life were shifting into the unknown, but for one night at least his current rôle as cathedral organist made sense: he would be at the cathedral with her at his side.

They kissed. It wasn't like their first embrace. A recessive quality she had displayed then, as if she felt she had to live up to him, as if somehow he was musically dominant –that trait had vanished. He wasn't going to get that ravished look from her now. She was launched on a powerful and independent musical trajectory that was reflected in her poise. It was up to him to trail her. But holding her life force in his arms confirmed that was what he wanted. He was a loner, not a leader, and in a relationship he was happy to follow.

Under a deep blue, cocktail-hour sky, they headed straight for the organist's house at Dowry Square. On the way to this enclave of delicacy nestled among the main roads, they passed several of the posters for the concert. She approved. The organ recital was already going to be consequential, but Geraint's invitation perturbed Matthew. An alcoholic on job-probation arranging drinks before his performance seemed a wanton flirtation with danger. But that meant destiny was afoot.

He shuddered as they passed Clare's House of Mercy, 1784. While he could tell rationally that the square were innocuous, his perception had altered. The darts on the end of every railing lowered into his vision with a newly hazardous three-dimensionality. The iron muck-scrapers inclined out of the ground like axe heads. The gloss paint on the front door of Richard's – now Geraint's – house looked as fresh as ever, and Matthew caught his own distorted reflection. He was holding his head higher, not from pride, but from some instinct to look for danger that had shorn him of his downcast posture.

'It should be unlocked,' he said. 'He said just to come in. He doesn't want to go up and down the stairs.'

The front door opened to his touch, as light as stage-scenery. He held it open for Chloë, whose glow of purpose showed no waning. They entered the marble-papered hall. But had the paper faded? Was there a smell of must? The hallway seemed diminished, the stairs steeper. Had he and Chloë grown in stature?

'So this is where we'll park the pushchair,' she said. 'You can have your grand piano in there. Will I get a little practice cubicle under the stairs maybe?'

In his imagination, children rushed forward to meet them. He swept them out of his mind and motioned to Chloë to go first. He enjoyed the movement of her limbs ahead of him on the stairs.

'I thought they'd creak more,' she added.

'Shhh,' he said. 'You'll annoy him.'

'I know.'

They heard Agnes Westmoreland talking as they climbed the dogleg stairs. As she ascended Chloë looked around at the sage-green wainscoting and out of the arched back window to the real world of parked cars and many classes of house ascending the hill, all of which made the interior more special.

'Sarcasm aside, it's actually pretty nice,' she said. 'If Troy doesn't have another go at him, we should at least get him fired.'

He didn't know how many layers of irony were in her comment.

The sitting room door was ajar.

'Come in, Matthew,' Agnes called from inside. 'Does this room have the same proportions as the Bach *Passacaglia*?'

He motioned for Chloë to go first, and they entered.

Agnes was studying him intently from the box sofa. Hannon, perfectly turned out in his tie and blazer, sat on the footstool. Geraint was in the armchair; fit, handsome, robust. There was no trace of the injuries from his fall. He twinkled and raised his eyes to heaven as Agnes continued.

'I think they both relate to the golden mean.'

'I think the room's a bit off,' Matthew forced himself to say. Normally he would have enjoyed such a discussion but now it felt thrust upon him from a past life.

He moved forward into the room to catch up with Chloë.

'Agnes, this is Chloë.'

Chloë smiled. Agnes stood and offered her hand.

'Agnes Westmoreland.'

'Chloë Balducci.'

'And Nick Hannon,' said Matthew.

Nick stood up and he and Chloë greeted, but he seemed bashful, more teenager than musicologist. Was it because she was a young woman? The lad went back to his footstool.

Standing there with Chloë, Matthew pondered: had the gentle undulations of the plaster, the variations of the leather of the many books, the warp of the furniture – had they all lost their life force? He felt suspended in the flood of time. The house was a trap. As a nice old building it might be more desirable than a modern block of flats, office or hotel, but in actuality those were the places where the city's pulse was beating. Did his sense of aesthetics have any consequence in that contemporary world?

Geraint gave his most buccaneering smile yet and said to Chloë: 'You're still with him?'

Chloë blanched. 'Why wouldn't I be?'

'No offence meant,' said Geraint. 'I'm glad you're together. You can save him from himself. Anyway, we'll have champagne in a moment. Please, sit down.'

There wasn't room on the sofa for both of them. Chloë sat down next to Agnes and Matthew sat in the straight-backed wooden chair.

Geraint gazed at Matthew. 'Talking about the golden mean reminds me of our first conversation.' He turned to Chloë. 'When I first met Matthew, he was talking about his vision of the afterlife. I don't know if he's ever mentioned it to you.'

Why did that conversation have to be dredged up yet again? Matthew concentrated on the bookshelves.

'His idea was that the moment of death was a moment to savour and look forward to, because it put the whole of your life into proportion.'

'What, like your life flits past and you can make sense of it?' said Chloë with *faux* naïveté. 'My God, why didn't anyone tell me?'

She was ready to joust with Geraint.

'Yes,' said Geraint, 'but I think the idea has problems. Richard sat in here for years, imbibing the golden mean, but if you don't know when the end of your life is going to be, how can you make the events of your life fit in proportion to the whole thing?'

'But that's where destiny comes in,' said Chloë. 'There's not much you can do about the proportions of your life, but I wouldn't want to be the person who meets their destiny but doesn't accept it.'

'Maybe it's mutable.' Geraint spoke more cordially. 'I was destined to be a drunk. Falling down Matthew's stairs made me reassess. Now my destiny is to be a performer. A serious one; not somebody who just goes through the motions.'

Yet there was an emptiness in his tone. Did he believe himself?

'That sounds good,' said Chloë.

Geraint inhaled and studied the floorboards, as if a wasted lifetime could be read in their grain. 'Not that it's going to be easy. You can't be an artist unless you channel the abyss, but the abyss leaves its mark on you.'

Agnes, well-bred, rescued them from the resulting pause. 'Geraint, I would love to try Richard's harpsichord again.'

'Of course.' Geraint gave her a seemingly genuine twinkle.

Agnes turned to Chloë. 'You must see the interior of the harpsichord.'

Chloë followed her to the instrument. Matthew watched from his chair.

Agnes glanced at him. 'I'm sure Richard showed you the inside when you were a boy.'

'Yes,' Matthew said.

She opened the lid and read the epigram to Chloë.

'In life I was silent; in death I sweetly sing. Almost certainly written by a man. They think life's about death.' She gestured to where Matthew could visualise the marquetry with its arabesques and spirals. 'It's the only eighteenth-century English harpsichord with an epigram. Isn't it funny that Richard, who was so normative, ended up with the oddest of all English harpsichords?'

'I never met Richard,' said Chloë, 'but Matthew has talked about him.'

'I'm Richard's sister,' said Agnes.

'And you're a harpsichordist?'

'Yes.'

'Okay then, play,' laughed Chloë.

Agnes played Chloë some brief extracts to demonstrate the instrument.

'I know the notes are all the same volume,' said Chloë, 'but you make it so expressive.'

'Expression is the secret,' said Agnes. '*Rubato*, spreading chords, where you place the note in time. You can hold notes, too, to create a halo.'

She demonstrated, and made the harpsichord sound as if it had a sustain pedal like a piano.

'Do you play?' said Agnes.

'Guitar and a bit of piano.'

'Why not sit down? Try it?'

'Okay.' Chloë moved to the keyboard, though she didn't sit down. She picked out a melody like an old folk song. Then she caught Matthew's eye and played one of the Kodály ditties.

Agnes said: 'As a guitarist, you might like to know there was another instrument at the time, the *lautenwerk*. It had gut strings and was essentially a lute with a keyboard.'

'They should make one out of metal,' said Chloë. Agnes looked intrigued, so Chloë described her guitar.

Nick had been watching avidly: 'Yeah, they should amplify it, make an electric harpsichord.'

He came across the room to the keyboard. Even with his youth, years had fallen off him. He played the riff of *Sweet Child of Mine* on the antique keys. Geraint laughed sharply from where he sat. Agnes watched politely. Chloë couldn't hide being impressed; she would have found it difficult to play a melody out of thin air.

Nick spoke as he played: 'And I'd turn the volume right up, and then tell my mum, and my dad, and my brother and my sister, and my neighbours, and everyone aside from the people in this room, that they should just get off my back.'

Nick added his left hand and played the riff in octaves.

'Keep playing like that and I'll press-gang you into my band,' laughed Chloë.

Nick smiled at her. Matthew saw that even in a pupil he saw almost every day and whose progress he directed closely, there were shades of character that he had never seen, and surely more that he would never know about.

'Now,' said Chloë to Agnes with her band leader's decisive tact, 'you can show me how to play Scarlatti.'

Agnes beamed and took her place at the instrument. 'Of all the Baroque masters, he's the one who cuts through the artifice and speaks to us most directly.'

She played one of the Scarlatti sonatas with its compulsive repetitions and circular movement but also immediately apparent depth and breadth. The chords resonated through the instrument and the wood-panelled room, which seemed like an additional soundbox. Chloë was transported by the music. Nick, still smiling, stood watching Agnes's hands closely.

Geraint called across the room without waiting for Agnes to finish: 'Nick, go down to the kitchen and get the champagne.'

Nick trotted out. Geraint aimed his next remark at Matthew and spoke loudly enough to stop Agnes playing:

'The epigram always reminds me of *The Art of Fugue*.'

'Why?' Matthew felt defensive. He wanted Agnes to carry on.

'It's about being unfinished. Have I told you my idea about *The Art of Fugue*? When you give your concert, will you play a completed version of the final fugue?'

Many composers, including Walcha, had carried on from the haunting moment in the unfinished final fugue where the music breaks off, as if Bach, in mid-flow, went to answer the door and never returned.

'Sometimes I play Walcha's completion,' Matthew said quickly. Agnes was waiting to resume her Scarlatti.

'Well,' Geraint expounded, 'my theory is it's not unfinished. It's too neat. It's deliberately unfinished. There's a whole tradition of deliberately unfinished works. *The Canterbury Tales*, *The House of Fame*, *The Fairie Queene*.'

Matthew had never read the *The Canterbury Tales*, let alone the other two. How could Geraint draw upon this cultivation when he chose? Where was it most of the time, and where did it come from?

'A lot of Rembrandt's engravings seem unfinished, though I don't think they are.' Geraint sat back genially. 'Well, I haven't thought about this for twenty years, and I haven't worked it into a theory, but all these coincidences suggest a psychic link to me.

I don't want to sound too New Agey, but the clincher is this: have you ever considered how perfect the unfinished conclusion is? All the parts run out in such a wonderful way. It doesn't seem unfinished if you listen to it.'

That certainly seemed right to Matthew. 'But what's the point of leaving it unfinished?'

Light footsteps sounded on the stairs.

'Because how could he finish it?' Geraint went on. 'It could go on forever. It had to be unfinished, in recognition of its own power.'

The door was pushed open by Hannon. He balanced a tray set with nibbles and five of Richard's engraved, baluster-stemmed, saucer-shaped champagne glasses.

'Good timing, Nick. So you found everything?' said Geraint.

Matthew looked over at Agnes, still being kept from playing. Chloë stood beside her calmly, and gave Matthew a quick smile.

Geraint got up and placed the bowl of Bombay mix on the misshapen lunette table. He then turned the champagne bottle in his hands and read the label. Hannon offered him one of the hefty but as yet empty glasses.

'Agnes and Chloë first, Nick.'

'Sorry.' Hannon smiled and walked to the harpsichord and offered Agnes and Chloë each a glass. Chloë took both as Agnes had her hands poised at the keys.

'Thank you.'

Nick smiled and then offered Matthew his. Geraint was readying the champagne bottle. It was dusty from its long spell in Richard's cellar.

'Can I open it, Geraint?' asked Hannon.

'Of course you can.' He passed him the bottle.

Geraint showed Hannon his method, which was to drape a tea-towel over the mouth of the bottle. With a pop, the cork shot out, and was caught by the towel.

'Now, quick, get the glasses.'

'I've given them out.'

'Okay – hurry – pour it.'

In a delighted fizz, Hannon rushed over to Matthew with the overflowing bottle and filled his glass with bubbles.

'Hannon, ladies first.' Geraint put comic stress on the word 'Hannon'. 'And remember to pour one for yourself.'

Hannon filled the glasses. Cheery, he stood back and toasted: 'To Geraint: good luck.'

They raised their glasses and drank. Hannon looked proud as he took a big sip of his.

'What nonsense,' Geraint was saying, 'luck doesn't come into it. But anyway…' He turned to Agnes. 'You're itching to carry on playing. Please, go for it.'

Agnes looked at him quizzically. A moment earlier he had talked over her playing, and now he was politeness itself. She turned to the keyboards and began a fluid rendition of Bach's *Chromatic Fantasie*. Her body rocked forwards and backwards as she played it. Geraint chuckled at one point, but not loudly enough to interrupt. She reached the final resonant chord, after which everyone clapped.

'But not a subtle sound; no Dutch in it at all,' Agnes said, as if halfway through a sentence she had started before playing. 'Would you like to listen to the fugue?'

'I would,' said Chloë.

Agnes smiled at her. 'You can adjust the sound with these levers. I can make the sound mellower for the fugue, like this, with two choirs of strings at the same pitch.'

Agnes started playing. Matthew wanted to listen but Geraint started to recapitulate his *Art of Fugue* theory for Hannon, who asked pertinent questions. This time Agnes played on. When she finished, Chloë absorbed her attention with questions.

Matthew turned to Hannon: 'Do you want to play the harpsichord?'

'Not till I've learnt everything Bach wrote for the organ.'

'You'll be ninety by then, Nick.'

The 'Nick' came out as a 'Nchk'. Matthew was far better off addressing Hannon by his surname. Would the evening prove fateful for the lad? If Troy turned up, had it been right to risk him as bait?

Agnes was talking to Chloë. 'It's the combination of *cantabile* and fantasie I find most involving. But we'd better not detain you, Geraint.' She finished her champagne, then stood and put her glass on the tray. 'We must let you prepare.'

'I am prepared.' Geraint smiled with intimidating combativeness. 'Let's finish the champagne.'

He poured everyone more, finishing the bottle, then sat back down and drank half of his glass in one.

'I see my little offering is billed as an "end of term concert". I don't like the holidays. Everyone goes. So stay; let's drink.'

No one replied. Matthew met Geraint's eye for an instant before looking away. Geraint raised his chin. 'Come on, you never know where this might end. Think of Heinz-Günther's concert.'

'Yes, it was lovely,' said Agnes.

'You weren't there at the end,' said Chloë.

'What happened?' asked Agnes.

'Whatever happened wouldn't have happened,' said Geraint, 'if there had been enough champagne.' His voice faltered. 'We need more. Nick, there's more in the kitchen.'

Hannon left for another bottle. Matthew thought of his father, whom he had neglected to call for weeks. He remembered how he had felt when visiting him; conflicted, but at least partially good. He remembered the familiarities and scents, the little world in which his mother and father had created and moulded him. If the evening proved fateful, when would he see him again? He excused himself and went out on to the landing and down to the marble-papered hall where the Richard-era phone sat on the console table.

Impulsively, he dialled his father's number. Jiří picked up. Matthew didn't know what to say. He hadn't spoken to his father since his visit. How do you broach important and personal topics?

'Dad, it's me. You've got to help me. I'm in love. The job at the cathedral's a minefield. You have to tell me what to do.'

What he really meant was what to do about the possible assignation with Troy, but how could he explain that?

After a surprised silence Jiří said: 'Your mother and I invested everything in you. How old are you?'

'Twenty-seven.'

'And your job's a minefield?'

'Yes.'

'When your grandfather was less than your age he had already lived in three empires and fought the Reds for two years. When they couldn't escape to the west they went east and fought their way out via Vladivostok. They went round the world to return home. Fat and oatmeal; that's what you need to survive.'

Matthew's head spun. 'Then get me some fat and oatmeal.'

Jiří went quiet.

He couldn't remember if he had ever said anything personal to his father. 'Jiří, I've met a girl.'

'Not a girl, Matty, a woman. You're adult.'

There was a thick pause, but Matthew felt connected to his father.

'Dad, what should I do?' Again he hoped for an answer to the evening's conundrums.

Jiří remained silent.

What could his father say? He knew nothing about the relationship. But he would wait to see what he would advise. Then he heard a chuckle.

'Matty, you must marry her.'

'But Dad, I haven't told you anything about her.'

'You will need to earn some money, though. Which is not to say I wouldn't pay for the wedding. The garden here is big enough. Mrs Starver can chop cucumbers for the *okurkovy*. I will make *knedlíky* and garlic spinach. If you're lucky we will find you some pork.'

Jiří laughed whole-heartedly. After a moment Matthew joined in.

'Now,' said Jiří, 'I must go and bring the washing in. Then *Panorama* on BBC. We will speak soon.'

As he came up the stairs Matthew heard Chloë needling: 'Do you have to go to the basement every time you need a sugar lump?'

Geraint grunted, then looked up at Matthew as he entered. 'She's trying to make me feel lucky having a free house, but I think this house has strings attached.'

Matthew tried to produce an answer that didn't suggest he harboured plans to move in. 'I like the kitchen in the basement.'

'I agree,' said Agnes. 'I helped Richard make it cosy. I'm not sure what else you could use the space for.'

'A rehearsal room for my band, perhaps?' said Chloë.

'But all the original fittings are still there,' said Agnes.

'This is my house,' retorted Geraint. 'You all seem to think it belongs to you.'

'I just feel it's fate that before long I'll be hanging curtains in here,' said Chloë.

Agnes looked up sharply. 'I made these swagged silk blinds. Please leave them.'

'Yes,' said Chloë, 'but couldn't you knock through and put the kitchen into whatever's through that wall?'

'But what would you do with the basement?' asked Agnes.

'Look, this is my house,' snapped Geraint, 'and I'll do what I like with the swagged curtains.'

The door opened and Hannon brought in the second bottle of champagne. He had already opened it. Geraint's eyes followed him as he smilingly refilled everyone's glasses. Geraint drank his and motioned to Hannon to refill it.

'But if the kitchen's in the basement,' said Agnes, 'and the dining room and coffee room are on the ground floor, there's only one floor between them and it minimises the need to go up and down the stairs.'

'Coffee room?' said Chloë.

Geraint's eyes swung round and alighted on her. 'I don't like stairs.'

Chloë said nothing, but her posture stiffened at his tone.

Geraint swivelled his gaze to Matthew. 'I don't like men who hang around near staircases.'

Then he stared back at Chloë.

'I was at the top of a staircase recently, and only one other person was there. Has he told you what happened?'

'Matthew didn't push you,' blurted Chloë. 'The Nothing Man let you fall down the stairs. You don't realise how lucky you are to be alive.'

'The Nothing Man?'

As soon as she had spoken Chloë blushed. She was grasping for words but couldn't formulate anything.

'Oh, I understand,' said Geraint. 'You mean Mr Nobody?' Then malice crept into Geraint's smile. 'Yesterday upon the stair, I met a man who wasn't there.'

In her relief at him misconstruing her, Chloë smiled weakly.

Geraint seemed pleased with his joke and chuckled. 'Let's leave it at that. Anyway, it's time for you to go on ahead. I've got a concert to give. I just need a minute to myself.'

He looked at Hannon, still holding the mostly full bottle.

'Nick, pop that on the table. You go ahead with the scores.'

XXVI

They trooped to the cathedral in silence. When they reached the Lady Chapel Hannon moved to the front. He would be turning pages and pulling stops for Geraint. Agnes said she would sit close to him. Chloë and Matthew found seats towards the back, from where Matthew regarded the room. It was just like the vision he had dreamt before Geraint's fall, and it was eerie to see the vision come true.

The chapel indeed hosted an extraordinary crowd for an organ recital. As well as experts, enthusiasts and connoisseurs, there were people who Matthew guessed had never been to an organ recital before and knew Geraint from some other area of his life. There was also a smattering of the goth element from the Reger concerts. Everyone seemed appreciative, smiling as they eyed their programmes topped by *'Pasar una calle'* in grand lettering from Derek's archive. Several of the composers and pieces listed were obscure, but their inclusion showed not just knowledge but flair. At the end, fore-ordained, was Weckmann's *Es ist das Heil*. He'd only heard Geraint play it through once. The road of life was to be set to music; oversights, mistakes and career-ends included.

Clapping spread. Geraint strode on. While he accepted the applause with a genial hand gesture, a pained look suggested he didn't want to be there. Had he drunk the whole second bottle? Hannon approached with the score but Geraint waved him aside. The maestro settled on the bench and played the first piece, a *passacailes* by the Spanish composer Cabanilles, perfectly from memory. He followed this with a *chacona* by Arañés. His fingering was light, and he managed a singing *cantabile,* yet another facet of his musicianship that he could add to his mellifluous Chopin and powerful Reger. Despite the antagonism between her and Geraint, even Chloë seemed transported.

Applause. The piece must have ended. Geraint didn't take a bow, but put his head in his hands at the console. The audience stopped clapping and waited expectantly. Geraint sat back and looked at Hannon.

'Nick, where's the score?' he asked.

'On the music desk.'

There it was, right in front of him. Hannon moved closer and smoothed the pages.

Geraint managed to identify it: a *ciacona* by Buxtehude, a piece most professional organists would know well. Geraint's performance was adequate, but didn't disguise a worsening temper. His aggression was transported through the tips of his fingers into the wooden tracker-action of the organ, and to the palettes opening into each pipe, giving each and every note a crude start and finish. Geraint perhaps imagined that this conveyed passion, but it only curtailed finesse.

Luckily Rüdiger, who had crafted the instrument to be sensitive to the most exquisite touch, wasn't there to see his precision abused. Others could see it, including Hannon, whose loyalty was being eroded in three-time.

At the conclusion of the Buxtehude, Geraint slumped forward rather than taking a bow. Hannon cautiously set up the next score on the music stand. Geraint brushed it aside.

'Let's cut to the chase. Bring the Weckmann.'

'But it's not next,' said Hannon.

'I don't care.'

Geraint stood up as if to address the audience, but once he had found Matthew, he talked only to him.

'I'm going to play a piece now to show you don't have to be a purblind, pygmoid, mister no-life to derive meaning from Baroque music.'

There was a collective intake of breath. Hannon looked up open-mouthed at his director of music. Bryce, whom Matthew hadn't previously noticed, stood up.

Chloë turned to Matthew, then looked at Geraint, Bryce, Hannon and back to Matthew. 'He's getting himself fired,' she whispered.

'Why don't we have a competition, Matt?' said Geraint. 'Would you like to play the Weckmann? How about if we play alternate movements? Then Nick, or Chloë perhaps, can judge whether you have any heart.'

'Can you play it?' whispered Chloë.

Matthew could never sight-read the Weckmann, with its manifold complexities. 'No.'

'Well just say yes.'

Matthew looked at Geraint. It took everything he had to speak. 'If you want me to, I'm happy to have a go.'

'No,' responded Geraint. 'Sight-reading's not really your thing. Here's what we'll do. You spend the next year seeing if you can learn it, but I'll just play it for everyone now.'

Geraint raised his arm and swatted at him with the back of his hand. He scanned the rest of the shocked audience, who followed the argument by twisting round in their seats.

'Anyway,' he said, 'I'm going to dedicate this performance to my duplicitous assistant. He's a neophyte who's done everything he can to undermine me, because he's not happy being a second-rate hack.' Then he looked back at Matthew. 'You pushed me down the stairs. You wanted me to be hurt or even worse, didn't you? Then you left me there.'

Bryce said: 'Geraint, sit down and play.'

Geraint didn't seem to hear. 'You left me on that floor. You wanted me to break my neck!'

'No, I didn't,' responded Matthew. Why couldn't he sound convincing? He was telling the truth. He stared at his shaking programme.

'You wanted to disable me, or even kill me,' jabbered Geraint.

Bryce spoke with gentleness: 'Geraint, we all want to hear the Weckmann.'

'My assistant pushed me down the stairs. He tried to kill me.'

Someone in the audience gasped.

Geraint continued: 'He stood me up, said "hoopla", then pushed me. And when he realised he hadn't killed me, he left me. I lay there for hours. He knew it and did nothing. I could hear him stumping around ignoring me. I had visions that you will never be capable of. I was invaded by little beings who pricked me with needles and told me cold hard truths. One of them was you, about three inches tall, like one of the Cottingley Fairies, looking at me jealously and asking me why I play so well. You didn't seem to be able to understand what music is.'

'You can tell me everything in my office later.' Bryce spoke as if comforting an upset toddler.

Geraint had run out of words but stood stabbing repeatedly at Matthew with his index finger. Some in the audience were captivated.

'And I want him to know that even if he turns up with his gorgeous girlfriend, who he met because of me, what he tried to do to me failed, and whatever he tries to do to her won't work either. He doesn't even know what to do with her.'

The audience stirred and muttered.

Chloë's eyes widened. 'He'll be gone by morning.'

'Geraint, you're drunk,' said Bryce.

'That may be true,' began Geraint. Then a movement to his left caught his attention. His eyes focused, he took a step back, turned white and went silent.

'Geraint, either come with me or sit back down and play,' said Bryce. 'Playing's better. That's what we all want.'

Geraint was still mesmerised. Matthew followed his eyes. At the side of the chapel, just beyond the edge of the stone screen, Troy had appeared. He was looking at Geraint with the concerned manner of a doctor or therapist.

'Chloë,' gestured Matthew.

She turned and gasped. She started to twist up out of her seat.

Geraint was now looking from Matthew to Troy without understanding. 'Which one of you pushed me down the stairs? Which one of you was three inches tall?'

Troy had probably imagined he could sneak a look in at the back of the chapel, but hadn't realised that because of the position of the new organ against the altar screen, he would find himself in full view of the audience. He backed away, melting into the shadowy stonework. Chloë was already up, curving round the other listeners into the aisle. She reached him and touched his arm, speaking openly as if she were the host of a party:

'Troy, I hoped you'd come. Let's sit together.'

He looked embarrassed. His UTK shirt stood out among the suits and dresses. But he couldn't demur. She led him toward vacant seats. As he passed Matthew his pale eyes latched onto him.

'I thought you wouldn't send her.'

'But I sent for *you*. She asked me to.' Matthew gestured around, but as he did so he felt anything he said or did was futile.

Then the two of them were past and sat down. With graceful consideration, Chloë inclined her programme so that he could see it and pointed to what was coming next. Her gestures involved him in her beauty and mystery, and wove him into a sheen of normality: they were a man and woman at a public concert. Matthew couldn't hear what she said to him from then on, but at one point her lips seemed to mouth the word 'Weckmann'. He turned away. They had gone into the world that would only ever be theirs, and it would be gauche to intrude.

Geraint was staring at the two of them. How much of this could he understand? He flagged and looked senile. Then he spoke without conviction: 'If you think I'm drunk then listen to this.'

A dozen or so audience-members were now standing up to leave. Before they could move, Geraint sat back down at the organ and launched into the Weckmann. From the first note he played beautifully. The listeners sat back down. After all, they were there to listen, and surely they had been looking forward to the rare piece. Matthew too. The extraordinary and almost-never-performed variations glued him to his seat. If there was a piece Geraint should never play, this was it – the arcane, buried style Matthew had devoted the long, hard days of his still-young life to. Yet for all his inebriation, physical diminishment and stylistic ignorance, Geraint made the archaic music ring.

But he couldn't keep it up. The initial plenum verse and first four variations were sublime, but halfway through the complex sixth verse with its seven independent parts, including double pedal, he stopped dead. It sounded pretty good, as if the composition was deliberately unfinished. The parts ran out and the echo died. There was a hopeful ambience. The audience didn't give up. Matthew willed him onwards and Hannon leant in from his vantage point. Agnes raised her chin in support. Bryce's mouth hung open. Geraint, taking his time, began methodically pushing all the stopknobs in. As he worked his way through them Hannon pulled each of them out again until Geraint turned to him.

'Don't worry Nick. I won't be playing any more.'

Geraint raised himself up, sorted his scores, passed them to Hannon, and turned to the audience. A few people clapped, and then everybody. He blushed and gave a sheepish bow. Matthew felt his old liking for him. Why should a man with such positive qualities have such a public collapse?

Geraint stared at the audience in defiant confusion until his eyes found Chloë and took in the sight of her assiduously courting the attention of the Nothing Man.

'My God, why have I been I alive?' he said.

Geraint turned unsteadily and walked carefully and with dignity out of the Lady Chapel and towards the cloister.

The audience remained expectant as if he was going to return and finish the piece. Chloë had glued Troy to his seat with her charm and attention. He would need to use main force to break free. Matthew kept his eyes on Hannon, who stood sentry by the organ, holding Geraint's music scores. He would not let the lad out of his sight while Troy was around.

Jane appeared and scooped her son up, roughly taking his pile of scores and throwing them on the bench. She shot a glare at Matthew and hauled Nick away. No doubt she was angry at yet another display of irresponsibility from Nick's teachers, but if her anger took Nick home to safety then that was a blessing. There might still be a finale with Troy, but it wouldn't involve her child.

At a distance, Matthew followed Jane and Nick through the chattering crowd to the north aisle, so that he could see the two of them walk the whole length of the cathedral and turn out of the main northwest porch, to safety. After standing for a while to make sure they didn't come back in, he checked back to see that Troy was still pinned down by Chloë in the Lady Chapel. They were still sitting. She had grown more forceful and was saying no; it's over; never; enough; go. Troy sat resolutely, but surely even he would crumble soon and do as she directed.

Matthew felt redundant. He drifted out of the Lady Chapel and around the cathedral for a few minutes. People were making their way from the cathedral to the cloister and into the chapter house for drinks. Matthew was borne with them into the cloister. He found himself being drawn further. He knew where his feet were leading him. He passed the chapter house and the sturdily hewn stairs and reached the song school at the end of the cloister. Light shone from the open doorway and picked out the viney and animalistic abstractions of the mediaeval carvings. Geraint was leaning against one of the Bob

Cratchit desks, staring into space. After standing in the doorway unnoticed, Matthew knocked and entered the room, catching Geraint's woozy attention.

'Geraint, I'm sorry. I've undermined you. I've gone behind your back. I even wanted to kill you, not that anyone noticed.'

'Grow up, Matthew. Anyway, who the hell is Chloë sitting with?'

'Mr Nobody.'

Geraint stood straighter. 'Chloë said that he let me fall. Did you put him up to this? What's going on?'

Matthew felt cowed by the confrontation, as so often in the past. But what did he have to fear?

'I wanted your job,' he said. 'It's come close to derailing both of us. I'm sorry, I'm really sorry. But Geraint, I didn't push you down the stairs and neither did he. You fell because you were drunk.'

'Then what was he doing there?'

'I don't know. You fell, he left and I phoned the ambulance.'

Geraint studied him.

'Nice of you to clear up the semantics now you're evicting me and taking my livelihood. Big two-hearted river, as Mariam would say.'

'How am I evicting you?'

In answer Geraint exhaled and held up his hands.

'This isn't what I wanted to happen,' said Matthew.

'I've got bigger fish to fry,' responded Geraint. 'One of them is myself. There's hundreds of pounds worth of champagne in the chapter house. We've got to drink it.'

Matthew took a step forward. 'Geraint, if me being here has made you drink, I'm sorry.'

Geraint laughed. 'You're so green. I might have started drinking years ago because I had issues, but after a while the alcohol becomes a need in itself. I just want to drink. End of story.'

'Geraint, don't do this to yourself. Why not just phone up Julia? It'll be daytime in Australia.'

Geraint gazed at him with surprising gentleness. 'Do you know how sick I am of Julia, going on and on and on about how bad a father I was, and then getting Mariam all worked up so she threatens to slit her wrists? This isn't about Julia. It's about me, and everything being over.'

Matthew's anger flared up. 'My God, man, can't you see how lucky you are? Just do your job. Because your job isn't over.'

'The reason I don't give a toss about my job is that I don't like growing old in that damn house.'

'Get over it. We're all stuck with you.'

Geraint chuckled. 'I'm stuck with me, too. Do you really want to know why I drink?'

Matthew feared the truths that Geraint was about to utter, but couldn't think of a way to avoid them: 'Okay, tell me.'

'When I was your age, I had a future. When I was first married and when Julia was young, I still thought I had a future. But once the relationships went south, and the big career never materialised, I realised I didn't have a future. I was just about able to accept the lack of a musical future because, let's face it, who cares whether a concert hall full of idiots lauds you?

'But it was sex that undid me. When my marriage failed, Julia was still young. If I'd stayed in the marriage, as I had to, as her father, by the time I would be free of them all I'd be old; my age. As in, now. Who'd want me, and who does want me? That is, who, of the people I find desirable. No one. Take Chloë. I've fancied her from the moment I saw her. But would she entertain me? Yet I'm still saddled with my sex drive. I want it, but will never have it. It's torture. Years of waiting for nothing while I grew older and older.'

Matthew had expected a discourse that touched on aesthetics and idealism, not this fleshy explanation. He found his view of Geraint was diminished, but was this not because of his own preconceptions? He also found his eyes were filling with tears.

Geraint watched him, as much interested in his reaction as his own story.

'Anyway,' he added offhandedly. 'Drink makes all that go away.'

Matthew stepped forward. Geraint was still leaning against the chorister's desk. Matthew edged towards him. He didn't move. Matthew took a bolder step forward and opened his arms.

'Geraint, it'll be okay.'

Geraint gave a gentle snort, and Matthew felt the surge of affection for him that he had felt before. Geraint might not be able to hug him, but his snort was not dismissive.

'Take my arm.' Geraint manoeuvred himself out of the putative hug. 'My post-concert reception is roaring away. Let's go and meet my public. We'll blitz them.'

Matthew guided Geraint towards the door, where, because of the turn and through their own diffidence their arms detached.

Matthew said: 'They can see that you played really well. I wish I could play the Weckmann like that, let alone sight-read it.'

They ambled down the cloister and into the chapter house. As they entered, Roy and Frank spotted Geraint. Frank dived for the upright piano and banged into 'For he's a jolly good fellow.' A wave of applause rustled through the throng. Matthew felt Geraint's muscles enliven. He'd been flat and lonely in the song school, but the ovation was enough to fuel his extrovert's fire. He stood taller and set off on a victorious circulation. Matthew watched him embark on his lap of the chapter house. The audience had memory only for Geraint's splendid gifts.

XXVII

'You two should be fired.' Jane spat the words at Matthew, waking him from his trance. He was still standing among the music-loving drinkers. The party was starting to rage. Jane had planted herself in front of him. She continued her tirade:

'All this arguing about bar lines and note values and authentic fingering when neither of you can see the big human drama around you. You took my son, and put him through yet another evening of broken promises, wasted time and broken ideals. When we left he was obsessed with whether Geraint was alright. But what about Nick? If you want a thirteen-year-old page-turner, then play the music on the pages. Don't make him privy to your weird drama. This is the last time. I'm taking him out of the choir, and he'll never have another lesson with either of you.'

Why was she here, haranguing him? She should be with Hannon, taking him to safety. 'Jane,' said Matthew.

'What?' She slung the word at Matthew. 'You think my son's a young you, but he isn't. In a relationship, you sort out your problems first, and you don't expect the other person to bring you completion. You could learn that.' She widened her eyes, but despite her anger she was discreet, as she always had been, and no one else would have inferred her deeper meaning. 'But with a child, if you're a parent, you're raising them so they ultimately have the power to leave you, not so they spend the rest of their life obsessing about their line of descent. It's about them, not you. Nick is not your wide-eyed lackey. He's got a life to lead. You've got one too, and you won't have it for ever.'

'Where's Hannon?' asked Matthew.

'Shut up with your Hannon, Hannon, Hannon. I hate the name. It's not even mine, it's my husband's. My maiden name's Flynn.'

'Where is Nick?'

'I knew Chloë wouldn't take you on.' She stared viciously over her wine glass. 'Though she does like charity cases. Who was the tall remedial fellow she dumped you for?'

'Is he still here?'

'No, he sloped off ages ago.'

'Where's Chloë?'

'She ran when she saw me. Clawed her way past. What have you done to her?'

'She clawed her way past?' Matthew felt the flagstones shifting beneath him.

'Yes. She saw me and asked where Nick was. I told her Nick was walking home because I wanted to come back to have words with you two. She looked like she was going to be sick and ran.'

'When was this?'

'Ten minutes ago.'

Matthew's mind was finally focusing.

'How will Nick walk home?'

'On his legs. What's wrong with you both?'

'Which route'll he take?'

Jane looked at him blankly.

Matthew asked in as neutral a way as possible: 'He'll go over the suspension bridge?'

'Of course. How else?'

Matthew wanted to shout in panic. Troy wasn't going to take no for an answer from Chloë, he would follow Hannon and throw him off the bridge. Matthew wanted to call down the heavens. He wanted to run. But he forced himself to remain outwardly calm. Nick, Troy and Chloë were all heading for the suspension bridge. He had to get there as quickly as possible.

'Whatever you do,' said Jane, 'leave my son out of it.'

'Do you have your car?' he asked.

'No, I left it at home so I could enjoy a drink. When I thought it was going to be a nice evening. Not having to berate you and Geraint yet again. More fool me.'

Matthew smiled brusquely at her, turned and pushed his way through the crowd. He ran up the empty cloister and through the cathedral towards the porch, past the organ with its enormous open wood pipes and little door up to the loft and his old life.

Outside on College Green, the July evening was ominously marvellous. Sunset was an hour away. Golden light honeyed the stonework and gilded the rose window. The azure sky was livid, unspecked and deep as fate.

There were no taxis at the taxi rank and already a line of people waiting. Could he get a bus? He looked up and down the street but there was no bus, little traffic and no taxis. Could he find one in the centre? But that was the wrong way. Could he make it on foot? He was realising he would have to run, and he had rarely if ever run so far.

Beyond the crescent wall of the Council House, Park Street ascended at an angle that would both exhaust him and take him away from the bridge. He'd then have to fight his way past the Triangle and then across to the left along Queen's Road and through the squares of Clifton. Even if he could keep running it would be impossible. Because if he was too late... Beyond the council building, the streets lining the contours of the hill were each an impassable barrier. The whole was a concentric fortress that would stop him reaching Hannon in time. He had to intercept them. He stood baffled, but his body was telling him what to do; his view was being drawn to the left.

Of course. Along the valley that went under the bridge. Head for the water. But then...how to get up to the level of the bridge? The maps of the city he had pored over spun in his mind: Georgian ones; Victorian ones; modern ones; the A to Z. The vistas that had given meaning to his life swept across his vision. In his past years he had loved imbibing the sudden glimpses of the wider city below; now was the time to redeem those visions. He searched them for the gaps between terraced houses that revealed falling streets. Because if the street fell down the hill, it would lead him up the hill, to the level of the bridge.

Then he saw it. Simply keep going after Dowry Square, up Hope Chapel Hill, past the chapel, then Granby Hill, then wiggle round the crescents and cut along the terraces until he reached the footpath to the bridge. Easy in every way aside from the punishment of running it. Overall it was a mile and a half, and would involve scaling the height of the gorge. It would be the run of his life.

He stood for another few seconds to collect himself, then kicked off into a run. First it was fine. Level ground. He sprinted along Deanery Road, then slowed to sustain his pace. He breathed as deeply and evenly as he could. How did a runner control their breathing? He had no idea. If only he'd tried harder in PE. He could have learned something from the discipline of sports. His shoes were hard and percussed the pavement with each step. What a waste of energy. He could feel sweat breaking out on his back.

Then he segued on to Hotwell Road and the desolation of what had once been a prime Georgian spa replete with treatments of medicinal water and Laughing Gas. Traffic was light and pedestrians few. He couldn't yet see the craggy acreage of the gorge up ahead, but the prospect of climbing it seemed monstrous. His shirt was sticking to him with sweat. He scrambled out of his jacket and threw it into a mean bush overhanging the pavement.

His breath was metallic now. He tried to breathe in for four strides, then out for the same. It seemed to work. His heart was beating painfully fast. A lifetime of sedentariness. Surely fate wouldn't knock him down with a heart attack at a moment like this. He forced himself on. Stabs of pain in his stomach. Weightlessness in his legs. Would they support him?

Four strides per breath. He shot past Dowry Square. Would it be his home? It had been relatively flat running till now, and he started up the hill already winded. A hundred and fifty metres or so, and then a turn to the right. Aren't you supposed to be able to run that in about twenty seconds? Whatever the real incline, it seemed like 45 degrees. His lungs were burning. The air sawed them when he breathed. The chapel crept past. He rounded the corner in the roadway, grimly aware of vehicles in his peripheral vision. They'd avoid him. They'd have to. Someone honked. It was like being in one of the films he liked.

Where would Chloë be? Which route was she going to take? How fast could she run? Had she caught a bus or taxi, or purloined a vehicle? Would she beat them to it somehow, or would she follow and catch them up?

He was about halfway up to where he needed to be. This seemed to be the steepest bit, the steepest hill in Creation. He was stumbling. Each stride was a babystep. Four strides per breath, but he was hobbling. His trunk was a river. His trousers were starting to soak. His vision had expanded into Vistavision, and the backdrop bent past as if through a fish-eye lens.

The end of Royal York Crescent intruded into his vision like the bow of an ancient galleon, replete with multi-level pavements joined by curved staircases overlooking sunken areas like mad decks. At the level below the raised pavement, dozens of garage doors stretched into the distance. He forced himself onwards. Rows of houses. Wiggles of crescents. God, those Georgians went in for curvy lines.

Then he was on to Wellington Terrace. He felt like an out-of-control steam engine but he was only moving ever so slowly round the long curve that bounded the regular grid of the streets of Clifton. Blinding Bath stone terrace after terrace opened up on his right. A feverish realisation of the fakeness of Georgian architecture. How could it look on so calmly at the calamitous world that produced it?

His breath was aching and hacking. Finally, he was out of the streetscape on to the open grassy common ground that ascended to the bridge. Above, to the left, Brunel's colossal tower, and the sweep of its iron chains, were his reward. He'd figured it out – every turn – but had he arrived in time? He must have taken twenty minutes. Families were out pointing at squirrels and perambulating. He zigzagged through them. They looked as frightened of him as the pigeons that flapped desperately away from him.

Where was Hannon? Nowhere. Where was the Nothing Man? Nowhere. He staggered in a straight line up the grass. No more right angles. He was plodding, not running. He was sinking into the soil.

His breath was rasps. Surely not that loud. Another rasp. What was it?

A hot air balloon filled up his vision. Nothing but ultramarine sky and taut nylon in every bright permutation of the colour wheel. The jet of fire was gasping. It wasn't him, it was the fire. The balloon was enormous. There were more. The whole sky was rasping. A fleet of balloons. It must be balloon day. What a perfect evening up in the air but what a disaster on the ground. Where were Nick, Troy and Chloë?

As he strove up to the roadway, craning left, he at last had a view along the bridge. Close to his end, padding slowly but purposefully, was the dark figure he dreaded.

This was the man, the force, who was more than him, who had obsessed Chloë. So sexually intriguing it didn't matter that he was an impotent virgin. Philosophically so deadly it didn't matter that he was ignorant of all culture beyond some potted Nietzsche.

Sex and death, eh?

Would he have to push this man over the edge to claim Chloë? How could he possibly have the strength to do that if he could barely raise his feet? Was he about to find this vaunted rock bottom, letting someone else kill you, when the Nothing Man swept him up like a lamb and with a forbearing smile slid him over the smooth brass of Brunel's barrier?

There, at the mid-point of the bridge, about fifty feet on from the hoodman, on the same townward side, Nick Hannon strolled along, without any idea of the death force gaining on him. There were a few other people crossing the bridge, but they had no idea, and they'd be no match for Troy. Maybe they'd get thrown over too.

Matthew struggled forward.

There was no chance that he would catch up. The Nothing Man was now only twenty feet behind Hannon and still there were two hundred feet of bridge for the lad to traverse.

The boy was as good as dead.

'Stop!' he shouted, but he was not as loud as the balloons rasping above.

'Maniac,' commented some flaneur with a picnic hamper.

'Stop! You can't do this!' Matthew gasped. Was he making any noise? His head was thumping.

His footsteps rang hollow. He was on the bridge now.

Hannon still had a hundred feet to go.

'Hannon, run!'

Why couldn't they hear him?

'Hannon,' he screamed. 'Run.'

He fell against the barrier. It was as hard as a meteorite.

He pushed himself up and on.

'Hannon,' he screamed again, but no sound was coming out.

Sweat was pouring over his eyes. Out of the blur a figure appeared at the far end of the bridge, walking towards them on their townward side. It was her petite form. Chloë had got there first! She'd crossed to the Somerset side, to wait. Her laid-back slouchy walk was unmistakeable. Where did they build people like her, who could go into battle with such élan?

Matthew held on to the lattice barrier to keep himself upright. Brown water rolled far below; tiny cars on the Portway. He couldn't move forward any more. He held on and gulped in air and tried to keep his eyes ahead.

The Nothing Man saw her and stopped. She continued towards the two of them, growing in stature. She smiled at Hannon and greeted him as he went past, but she kept walking. He might have wanted to stay for a chat but her poise didn't permit it. So he just bobbed on, unaware of the ultimate nihilist a few stalks behind him. Once the lad was past, she stopped.

She gestured at Matthew to stay where he was, but he could scarcely move anyway.

What was the Nothing Man to do? He took some steps forward and stopped and faced her. He had to. Where and why would he possibly go? He had everything he wanted. The woman of his sighs, his tears and his darkness, alone on a white-cabled bridge canopied by a firmament fretted with balloons, the hoarse fire-jets exhaling the cacophony of life, the city of cities spread out below them.

He would have to pronounce himself: to be or not to be?

They argued. What were they saying? He could judge only by the way they moved. She laid it out. He considered. She remonstrated. He reiterated. Her posture became gentler and she offered. He agreed. Then he stood. He turned halfway to look over the harbour, the city.

She detached herself from Troy and paced the length of the bridge to Matthew.

'Chloë, let's run.'

'No, my darling. I've got to be here for the end.'

'Are you going with him?'

Her body stiffened. 'To where he's going?' she said incredulously.

'If you want to live with him it's fine,' Matthew enjoined. 'Or have him on the side. I'll never match his weird power. If you want him, have him. Have me too. Do anything you like.'

'I want to live,' she almost shouted with exasperation. 'That's why I left him in the first place. Matty, you've got to leave now.'

'I can't. He'll pull you over the edge with him.'

'If you want me to get back to real life, you have to go. Go, and don't look back.'

Matthew wanted to ask why and why not, but he sensed the terminal force between her and Troy. He needed to do what she said. But that would be to leave her hundreds of feet above a chasm with Troy. Leaving was the last resort, but he had no other hand to play.

She was holding back tears.

She reached forward and touched him. 'You did brilliantly. You mapped your way here. You passed whatever test that was. But you have to do what I say. Go now, my love, and absolutely don't look back. He wants me to be here, to watch and see. That's how he wants it, so that's how he'll get it.'

Her eyes flowed over, but she nodded back her head and wiped the tears away.

Matthew nodded. He touched her hand. He wanted to hold it forever. But he couldn't. He had to leave, and if she wanted him she could come and get him. End of. If she preferred to hold hands into the abyss with the Nothing Man, there was nothing he could do.

Could he express this to her? He squeezed her hand. Whether it was tears or sweat pouring into his eyes, she was undulating in his vision. Holding her hand was more powerful even than kissing her. He could hold her hand even with her Other on the bridge watching, and it didn't disrespect the connection between her and Troy. It was the handhold of two adults at the end of the world, and he savoured it. He had deeply touched another person. He had held the cigarette paper between life and death, but the gift of his life was not to be thrown away.

He stood straight, let go her hand, turned, and walked away. He was soaked, out of breath and in pain. But she could see him so he kept his back straight and placed his feet as carefully as could back across the tarmac then the grass. Going downhill was easier. He passed among the blithe strollers and sightseers who hadn't noticed the drama in front of them, towards and into the absurd gentility of the stage-set city built by slave-owners. Now its physical beauty could only be a sham. Part of the real world might abide within it, and such a beautiful stage-set could make life more agreeable, but the physical world was not the real world and neither could stand still. He would never find the eternal instant, at least not in this life. But if he could be born again, this life would be eternal. He slogged downwards towards the cathedral as the gasping parti-coloured balloons overtook him aloft.

XXVIII

Inside the chapter house the lay clerks were still partying. About half the audience remained. The psychedelic glass sparkled in the lamplight, and the green men and even a monkey chortled from the corbels. Even here, behind the bulk of the cathedral, the sound of a siren echoed as a police car or ambulance roared past outside. It didn't disturb the kitchen staff who stood stiffly in their starch. The guests were attacking the offerings. The champagne flowed.

Matthew, jacketless and drenched, hair plastered to his scalp, fought his way through the trays of oysters and plates of steak tartare on delicate circles of thin toast. Geraint must have arranged this all himself. He must be mortified that his planned fiesta was not relaunching his career, but at least the lay clerks and the remaining audience were working through the wineglasses lined up as thickly as at Richard's funeral.

Bryce stood in the centre of the mêlée with Geraint, and made no secret of berating him: 'You've let us all down. Service after service where you've given second, third or even fourth best. Deliberately. You're the director of music of an ancient cathedral, yet you feel this place is beneath you.'

Geraint stared back without speaking, a half-drunk glass of champagne lolling in his hand. Bryce went on and on. He had ceased to be the reasonable manager of God's house. God's fire was showing:

'Damn right you've wasted your talent. Think of the parable of the talents. Most people think it's about money. I guess a talent was like a dollar or something. But it's not about money. It's about talent, as in, talent. Your talent isn't your own. It's God-given. You still don't see that. And when He comes back, there's going to be an accounting. Yes, you've squandered yours, but it wasn't yours to start with, it was His. One day, sooner than we think, God is going to ask you why the hell you did that. And in case of collateral damage, I want you firmly out of the cathedral long before that happens.'

Geraint knocked back his champagne and looked over at the nearby fleet of bottles and glasses.

'I should put brandy in it.'

'Bryce,' said Matthew.

The dean was so intent on Geraint that he didn't hear. Aside from Agnes and Vanessa, both of whom hung on every word for different reasons, the crowd happily chugged through the drink and ground through the exquisite raw flesh.

'Bryce.'

'I've never had surf and turf like this,' said a happy boozer.

'Bryce,' shouted Matthew.

Bryce turned and, to Matthew's amazement, smiled gently at him.

'Matthew, you're sweating.' It wasn't Bryce who spoke, but the prim voice of Vanessa. Beside her was an elderly man who wore the purple shirt of a bishop.

'Matthew,' she said, 'meet Bishop Bill. He's come up for the evening.'

Matthew shook his hand.

'Where's your diocese?' he asked.

'This is my diocese.'

Vanessa twinkled. 'Matthew, this is my husband, our bishop. Bill, this is Matthew Marcan, our new director of music. Or as we used to call it, organist and master of the choristers. He's going to be our new Richard.' She looked at him and smiled kindly. 'Sorry, I meant our new Geraint.'

Matthew was flooded with conflicting emotions: astonishment; blasé acceptance; fear; joy; triumph; instant hindsight that it was too late. 'Organist and master of the choristers'. The phrase rang through his head in peals.

Vanessa lightly pinched his arm. 'Did I let the cat out of the bag?'

'Vanessa,' was all he could say.

'Matthew, come forward.' This time it was Bryce speaking. The dean shot Geraint a lethal glance then turned back to Matthew. 'Vanessa's husband and I are in full agreement. And so, should I say, is Vanessa. We would like to offer you the rôle of organist and master of the choristers. Starting immediately. The house will be available…' Bryce glanced at Geraint '…in thirty days' time.'

Matthew was still effectively stunned by his inner turmoil. He'd got the job. Organist and Master of the Choristers.

'Don't say yes too loudly,' said Bryce. 'Otherwise I'll offer the job to someone who hasn't waited their whole life for it.'

Life, rôle, house.

One of the choristers was singing. His bright, reedy voice was supported by Frank on the piano and soared over the mêlée. But it wasn't Hannon. The lad wouldn't be returning.

My heart ever faithful
sing praises, be joyful!

Chattering, wine, crowded ferment. The house, filled with Richard's antiquities would be his, from which he would bestow his musicianship on the charmed city. The treble voice echoed around them:

Sing praises!
Be joyful!

Bryce said: 'First thing tomorrow, I want you to start the search for your assistant.'

'Bryce,' Matthew said, 'the last thing in the world I want is that job.'

'Funny joke,' said Vanessa. 'I know you've wanted it since you were a chorister.'

'No, listen. I resign as organist.'

'Of course,' said Vanessa, 'you have to resign from your current job to take up the new one, but that's taken for granted.'

'No, I resign.'

Bryce said: 'We'll sort all that out tomorrow. Just stay for a few more minutes and hold the fort. Enjoy the food; don't get drunk.' Bryce rolled his eyes at Geraint.

Geraint responded with a look of disdain. He drained another glass. 'This time I'm not coming back.'

'Bryce,' said Matthew, 'I resign, from tomorrow, from everything. I'll be gone by morning.'

Bryce barely registered: 'Finish your glass and have a good sleep. I want the Michaelmas service to go well.'

Matthew stared around the room. The throng quaffed and chomped, and still there was more to eat and drink. Ranks of glasses stood ready like organ pipes, and a deep Georgian wine tray was stuffed with champagne on ice.

Geraint was also looking around at so much that must be eaten and drunk. He spoke past Bryce to Matthew: 'Help yourself. All hand-reared. The beef, that is. I don't know if you can hand-rear an oyster. And have some champagne. Drink it while you can. It's from Richard's cellar so I suppose I stole it from your future. Good luck in the house. Hope Chloë joins you. It's big enough for both of you.'

Matthew spoke: 'Geraint, I don't want to spend the rest of my life being three inches tall.'

Geraint laughed. 'Bryce has read you right. You'll have changed your mind by morning. But I forgive you. I underestimated you. I should never have intruded into your psychodrama. You've got the job. Enjoy it. You've won.'

Matthew thought of Chloë. If she survived whatever was happening on the bridge, would she be reconciled to live out her days in Richard's house? It was a cage for both of them.

'Come on Matt,' Geraint continued, 'accept it. Talent isn't enough. You've got the killer instinct. It's your job. Bryce is right.'

'You were pretty keen on the job back at the auditions,' replied Matthew, but he was no longer interested in parlaying. 'It's yours. Always has been. Keep it.'

Matthew turned away from the man once and for all. Their struggle was over, and they'd both won. He saw his world from a high vantage point. The house, the cathedral, its fine organs, the dramatis personae who surrounded it – Geraint, Bryce, Hannon, Jane, Agnes, Vanessa, Derek, even Frank and Roy, even the host of happy sots who'd entered the asylum for the concert. This crucible had allowed him an early life of aesthetic devotion, but it was time to leave. Richard was absent. He was not a guiding aesthetic or spiritual presence. He had departed entirely and could not be recalled. His spirit must be laid to rest with the finality of his lowered coffin, and the spool of life must play on. Matthew, left behind, was not a Hannon-esque pupil. He had woken up anew.

With a jagged peal a hundred wineglasses disintegrated. The flagstones must have floated out from under Geraint and he'd keeled over, taking a tablecloth and its squadrons with him. Bryce, hammering on about it being the most dysfunctional music department in the entire Anglican Communion, hauled Vanessa back. The smashing glass momentarily dimmed the din, but all those conversations about pipe scaling and counterpoint were too interesting to be interrupted and the crowd resumed their babble. The kitchen staff did nothing, but the resignation in their faces spoke of another mess to clear up.

Through the night Matthew packed his two suitcases and overnight bag. It took several trips to and from the organ loft to sort his scores and get them into his trunk. He manhandled this albatross down the stairs and left it outside the office. Derek would have to arrange its passage to wherever he was going, but after his years at the cathedral asking this favour was fair. Matthew didn't want to go to bed and then wake up exhausted and have to go through the whole process of getting ready for the day, so he washed, showered and dressed and then lay on his sofa for an extended nap till morning. When his alarm woke him, it only took a few minutes to get ready. The sun was bright and the light fresh when he stiffly rolled his suitcases through the cloister car park, around the west end of the cathedral and on to College Green. At some point a taxi would go past to convey him to the station. And thence…?

A figure sat alone on one of the benches. Chloë. His heart jumped. She was his best hope for new life. Without her, life looked meaningless, grinding, drab and a thousand times empty. But she was sitting there, and could be there only for him. He rolled his cases over and sat beside her. Her face spoke of tribulation, but it made her more lustrous.

'Have you been here all night?' he asked.

'I actually went home but I couldn't sleep. I've never had a sleepless night before. I walked down here at dawn.'

'What happened with Troy?'

'I told him to jump or leave, and that I'd watch. Whatever he did, I would give him my full and ardent attention. And then that would be that.'

'What did he do?'

'I can't tell you. Whatever happened is between him and God.'

They sat. His nervousness decreased. A pathway led to the future.

'What about you?' she asked.

'They offered me the job. Rôle, house, music, everything. But I gave my notice last night. I'm going back to Germany.'

She smiled at him. 'You've already been the organist of Bristol

Cathedral.' She put on her southern accent: 'You've already *done done* it.'

Their silence was comfortable. He didn't want to leave the pleasant aura that now encompassed the two of them.

'If you'd made it back before the party ended,' he said, 'I'd have proposed to you in front of everyone. I would have hoisted you on to one of those tables filled with glasses and champagne and canapés, and I'd have looked up at you like you were on stage, dancing on your knife-edge, and I wouldn't have let you go until you said "yes".'

She looked at him with a perk of happiness: 'It would have been quite an evening.'

'Yeah. It's now or never. I love you, Chloë. Will you marry me?'

She had already run out of tears but there was still plenty of depth left in her eyes. Troy must have felt equal to the whole world when her gaze transfixed him and sent him on his way.

'Germany?' she asked.

'Yes. Come with me. We'll get married there. It's either that or in my dad's garden.

A single bell chimed, once, twice, then another started, then all the cathedral bells swung into motion, chiming to announce morning prayer. Bell after bell, full peal after full peal.

She smiled her horse smuggler's smile. 'Yes, Matty, I'll marry you. Let's go to Germany.'

EKO

New Year's Eve. Bamberg lay under snow that reflected the Christmas lights in through the misty glass of the Stephanskirche, illuminating its creamy interior, even picking out the fancifully rendered Biblical episodes edging the vaulting. In the organ loft, Matthew could now play the whole eighty minutes of *The Art of Fugue* by heart. His old job at the Domkirche had gone to someone else, and good luck to them, but he had moved back to Bamberg to work at the Stephanskirche. Chloë liked her new double life, and the possibilities of having a foot in both Bristol and Bamberg. She worked like a fanatic and had clawed her way into the triangle of ear, composition and instrument.

She would shortly be walking down to the church for the private recital he had prepared for her: *The Art of Fugue* from memory and with his own completion. He could play it all with his eyes closed. Having the music inside him was its own reward. He would share it with her alone. He could already feel the warmth that emanated from her as she would sit beside him. He reached the final chord exultant, then lifted his hands from the keys and enjoyed the echo that took so long to die. He waited until all the sound was gone before opening his eyes. He could see her where she would be, speaking, laughing, singing, dancing.

ACKNOWLEDGEMENTS

Publishing Consultant: Scott Pack
Publisher: Tom Chalmers
Editor: Roland Clare
Copy Editor: Clio Mitchell
Cover Design: Ifan Bates
Author Photograph: Natasja Fourie

Readers: Joanna Briffa, Martin Cottam, Charles Jandreau, Stephen Jasper, Tilly Johnston, Lindsay Weaver

Cloister is a work of fiction. While Bristol and its cathedral are real places, they have been fictionalised. The sharp-eyed reader will notice that in reality they are not always as described herein; for instance, Dowry Square is not owned by the cathedral, there are no green men on the chapter house ceiling and such places as the widely hewn staircase up to the assistant organist's flat do not really exist.

The great organist Helmut Walcha (1907 – 1991) was a real person, though all scenes involving him are fictional. However, all the dialogue and ideas attributed to him are from the historical record.

Ronnie Earl and the Broadcasters did indeed give the performance of their lives at the Breminale in 1993 (recorded and released as *Blues and Forgiveness*).

Most of the song lyrics in the book were written by Chloë Balducci, but she also sang a number of old or traditional songs:

When I Wake up in Glory (traditional)
Oh, Dem Golden Slippers (traditional / James A. Bland)
Alabama Gal (traditional)

Thank you to:
David Galef, Janisse Ray, Greg Schirmer, Gregory Heyworth, Warren Steel, (the late) Barry Hannah, Tom Franklin, Mary Jenkins, Emily Holloway-Costa, (the late) Richard Luckett, George Ritchie, Dinah Ceely, John Havergal, and of course Clare, Henry, Beatrice and Edwin.

Thank you to those who supported this publication:

Patrons
Mike Bienenfeld, Glenda Fraser, Margarete Harvey, David Johnston

Holly Comiskey, Nick Flynn, Ralph Richards

Sam Balden, April Monoceros, Andrew Santacroce, Eric Talbot, William T. Van Pelt, David Wakefield, Takuya Yorita

Recognised Subscribers
Nicolas Bell, Amy Black, Philip D. Booth, William Farrell, Brendan Grimley, Pastor de Lasala, John Lester, Roy Levin, Denis Littleton, Findlay Muir, Pat Osborne, Sarah Plumley, Richard Powell, Donald Russell, Kitty Sage, Peter Stockwell, Paul Warren, Rebecca White

Subscribers
Sam Bartlett, Dan Beaman, Rob Blythe, Jason Bowles, Grant Brockhouse, Andrew Carter, Caroline Doig, Matthew Fisher, Maya Graffy, Paul Hale, Lisa Hatch, Jonathan Hellyer-Jones, Ivan Henshell, Bryan Jones, Nicola Joyner, Graeme Kay, Andrew Leach, Jon Liinason, John McFadden, David Menzies, Daniel Moult, Christopher Nickol, Ian Shaw, Eric Shepherd, Warren Steel, Carl Thomas, Henny N.M. Verhaar, Jonathan Wainwright